For Sarah Davies, my fearless Handler,
who always sees the way and always has my back

CONTENT WARNINGS:

This book contains references to suicide and self-harm.

SEASONS
of the
STORM

PROLOGUE

Wintergreen, Virginia

December 21, 1988

JACK

There's something inherently wrong with any home that's easy to get into and hard to break out of. The Winter Ridge Academy for Boys is both. I've cleared four of the five pins in the lock already, and I can practically taste the air outside, cold and sweet, seeping through the crack under the door.

My hallmates roughhouse behind me, their blood buzzing on cheap contraband rum, all of us high on the promise of one night outside these walls and the risk of getting caught.

We won't. I've been planning this for a month—timing the shift changes of the security guards, mapping their patrol routes every night after lights out, figuring out how to get us all back inside before morning head count. If anyone deserves a few hours of freedom, it's us.

We're the ones left behind—the worst of the screwups, whose parents didn't want us home for the holidays. The last bed check of the night was an hour ago. The teachers have all taken off for Christmas, and security's been whittled down to a skeleton crew. If I can get us out past the reach of the security lights, no one should come looking for us.

"Hurry up, Sullivan. What's taking so long?"

"Keep it down. I'm almost done."

They're like puppies, all quiet barks and rough whispers and stifled laughs as they scuffle in their puffy coats behind me. One of them knocks into me and I swear. But as I pitch forward into the door, the last pin slides home.

The lock opens.

The boys untangle themselves and huddle over my shoulder, their breath ripe with booze as the door creaks open, carving an angel's wing in the snow. I hold them back, craning my neck out. The hushed woods absorb every sound.

The exits in this place are equipped with cameras and alarms, except this one. Half hidden in the back of an old boiler room layered in dust, the dimpled door and rusted padlock hardly put up a fight. Tucked close to the woods, this corner of the dormitory isn't visible from the rest of campus. During the summers, it's overgrown with weeds, the patchy, neglected grass shaded by the dense, low limbs of the towering oaks and chestnut trees that surround the school, as if the staff's forgotten this door exists. The security guards don't even bother patrolling it. In the mornings, when we're released for outside recreation, it's the only pristine stretch of snow on the grounds.

"Go," I whisper, holding the door open for the others. I drag on my ski jacket and cap. The snow's thick, making it easy to follow their moonlit tracks. I run after them, the cold stinging my cheeks, a grin splitting my face so wide it's almost painful, as the lights of the school fade behind me.

My lungs burn and my heart's on fire. It feels like the first full breath I've tasted in years, since I first got dumped here. I'm tempted to turn away from the rest of the group and just keep running, but I've only got six months left in this place to satisfy the terms of my probation.

And then what? After graduation, where the hell will I go?

I dig in my pocket for the smuggled whiskey I brought, but it's gone. Ahead, the empty bottle catches the moonlight, dangling from someone's glove.

My roommate tosses me a can of cheap beer and I catch it against the front of my coat. It's still warm from whoever's dorm room it was hidden in, and now it's completely shaken up.

"Happy birthday, Jack," I mutter.

I crack it open and pound it before the froth spills out. It's been hours since dinner. The beer goes straight to my head, and my stomach still feels hollow, even after I knock back a second one.

We walk until my face is numb. Until we reach the high chain-link perimeter fence separating us from the ski resort on the other side.

"This is it," I tell them. A month ago, I sketched a map to this spot. My roommate's older brother works at the ski rental counter during his college breaks, and someone said he'd been saving money to buy a car. I convinced the boys in my hall to chip in for a bribe, wrote all our boot sizes on a slip of paper, and passed it to the guy's brother along with the money and the map when he was here during Sunday visitation two weeks ago. The opportunity to ski these slopes—slopes some of us can see from our dorm room windows but never get the chance to touch—was too good to pass up.

The boulder's tucked tightly against a copse of pine, its nose poking out of the snow, exactly where I marked it on the map.

We drop to our knees around it, groping under the snow. Whoops and *hell yeah*s rise up as I pull out six sets of skis and poles. We fish out a pile of buried trash bags and tear them open, counting out a set of boots for each of us.

"Jack, you're a motherfucking genius!" One of my hallmates gives me a drunken kiss on the forehead and shoves me backward into the snow. The metal fence rattles as we feed our gear through the opening, the sharp edges of the chain link snapping back over and over until the last of us clears the "No Trespassing" sign.

We lug our gear through a swath of trees and pause on the other side, an awed silence falling over us.

The slopes are dusted with windswept powder. It glitters like stars against the dark, disappearing into a night that feels suddenly infinite and ours.

I step into my skis. They hover over the crest where the slope meets the trail and I watch as, one by one, the others take off down the mountain with wild howls, their skis cutting left and right, polishing the edges of the roughest black diamond on the mountain.

The slope falls away when I try to look at it straight on. But out of the corner of my eye, I catch movement. A shadow, like a swirl of dark fog, weaving around the base of the trees.

"You okay, Jack?" my roommate asks.

"Yeah, I'm great," I say, hoarse from the cold and the laughter. I tear my gaze from the trees, kicking myself for slugging those two beers on an empty stomach. "Never felt so alive."

"Too bad we only get one run," he says.

One run. That's all we get. The slopes are closed. The lifts are down. By the time we make the trek back up the mountain to school, it will be nearly morning, and I'll be a prisoner in that place for the next six months. All I want is one perfect run, a few fleeting moments when nothing's holding me back.

"Hit it hard, Jack. No second chances." There's a reckless shine in his eyes as he shoves off. "Meet you at the bottom." His skis make a soft *swish* as they fade from sight. My eyes drift to the woods and I drag them back, ignoring the doubt creeping through my mind.

This is the one night you're not leashed to that place. The one night you don't have to answer to anyone. Don't lose your nerve.

I tug my hat low over my ears and follow him. The wind sears my face, stealing my breath. The night rushes by faster than I can see ahead of me. I take the first few turns cautiously—too cautiously—avoiding the first two moguls altogether.

We only get one run . . . no second chances.

I loosen my knees and lean into the turns, catching wind as I hit the next mogul straight on. Suddenly, I'm flying. My heart soars in my chest. My skis touch down, skimming a crust of ice. I dig in, but the momentum pulls me like a tow rope through the dark.

The slope disappears. Exhilaration turns to panic as the trees rush at me.

With a snap, my insides shatter, wood pummeling bone. The impact tears me from my skis and throws me backward into the snow.

I lie there, eyes closed, a deafening ring in my ears. The stars shimmer as I blink myself conscious, my warm breath curling like smoke from the wreckage.

There's no pain. Not at first. Just a low groan. The unsettling sense that something is broken. My hat's gone, and the back of my head is drenched and cold. The last of my friends' shouts fade downhill.

I have to catch up to them. I have to get up.

I move my . . .

My legs don't respond. No pain, no cold, nothing. . . . I feel nothing below my waist. Nothing but fear as it seizes me.

Shit, Jack. What the hell have you done?

I open my mouth to shout for help but the words won't come. I can't get enough air. Pain sharpens against my ribs. It swells until there's no room for breath or thought or anything else.

Please, no! Don't leave me here!

The night slips in and out of focus, the pain gripping me in waves. Snow seeps into the neck of my coat. Into my gloves. My heart slows, my hands shake, and my teeth . . . God, my teeth won't stop chattering.

You screwed up, Jack. You're going to die.

"Only if you choose to."

My breath stills. My eyes peel open at the sound of a woman's voice. They roll toward the forest, searching, barely able to focus.

Please . . . help me! Please, I can't . . .

The roots of the trees seem to snake up from the ground, writhing above the snow as if they're alive. My eyes drift closed again. I'm seeing things. Hallucinating. Must have hit my head. But when I force them open, the roots are still moving, braiding themselves together, forming a raised path above the snow.

A woman appears at the end of it.

Mom? Her name catches painfully in my throat.

"You may call me Gaia," she says.

No. Not my mother. My mother would never come. Has never come.

The woman's long white dress glows against the dark, her shape becoming clearer as she approaches. The walkway under her feet grows, extending toward me with each of her steps. The woven roots twist and fold into a set of stairs a moment before she descends them, then unravel behind her, disappearing into the snow.

She kneels beside me, her silver hair falling around her face as it comes slowly into focus. Everything but her eyes. They glimmer like diamonds. Or maybe I'm crying. My breath sputters. I taste blood. Suffocating on the smell of copper and iron, I reach for her in a blind panic.

Am I dead?

Her hand's warm against my cheek. She smells like flowers. Like the mountains in springtime.

"Not yet. But soon," she says. "Your spleen is ruptured. A rib has punctured your lung. You will succumb to your injuries before your body can be recovered."

But my friends—

"They will not come back for you."

No. I'm imagining this. She can't possibly know these things. But deep inside, I know this is real. And I know that she's right. Every word cuts. Every breath tears through me.

"I offer you a choice, Jacob Matthew Sullivan," she says. "Come home with me and live forever, according to my rules. Or die tonight."

Home. A wave of pain crests inside me. I grab her wrist as the crushing weight of my last breath pulls me under.

Please, I beg her. *Please, don't let me die.*

PART
ONE

1

OUT LIKE A LAMB

March 12, 2020

JACK

"Hold still!" Fleur barks. "I might cut you."

"I thought that was the point." At least, that's how we agreed to do it. Fleur wanted a less vicious method than last year. I wanted something quick and clean. After a lengthy debate about the multitude of ways she could kill me, we finally settled on the knife.

My head swims. I stare at the horizon over her shoulder just to keep myself from falling. I'm burning up just standing this close to her, and it's too hard to look in her eyes. Her pink hair lifts on a breeze, all tangled up in the red light of the transmitter in her ear and the blood-orange glow over the Virginia foothills behind her. Beautiful. Like something out of a fever dream.

"What the hell are you doing, Jack?"

I shake off the voice in my head, so woozy with fever I almost mistake it for my own. Chill knows exactly what I'm doing. I'll catch hell for it in three months when I wake up, but for now, I don't have the energy for the lecture he's spouting in my ear. I *let* Fleur catch up to me. Let her corner me here, because I was tired of running, and I just wanted more time. Just a few more minutes face-to-face with her before I go. To choose how we say goodbye this time.

Fleur gnaws her lip, the tip of her knife pressing into the skin just below my ribs, jarring me back to the moment. Spring's here, and my season's over. Our time's up, and now it's her job to send me home.

I feel a little lost just thinking about it. The Observatory won't ever be home. The second I die, I'll be completely cut off from her, yanked across the world through the ley lines like a deflated balloon and locked underground, sequestered in hibernation until next winter. I waver, the sharp edge of her blade making me feel a little untethered.

Deep worry lines crease her brow as she adjusts her grip.

I can't stop staring at her frown, the way she licks her lip when she concentrates.

There's an arm's length between us. She's too far away.

My voice goes gravelly. "My liver's a little higher." Chill swears at me. "It's deep. Between the third and fourth rib. You should probably come closer." Through my transmitter, I can hear Chill's head thunk against his desk.

The air thins as Fleur steps forward. Close enough for me to smell the lilies on her breath. To feel the heat of her shaky sigh against my face. I thought this elevation would buy me more time—the ice, the terrain, the trees shading the winding trails of the national forest—but she's so warm, I can't—

"Better?" she asks. I wince, light-headed as the point of the knife digs in, and her dark eyes flick to mine.

I nod, unable to form words when she's standing this close. I study the contours of her mouth, wondering what it would taste like. I can't imagine any way I'd rather die. "If you're squeamish, we could try something else."

She freezes. "Like what?"

"Jack?" Chill's voice rises. "I don't like where this is going."

She doesn't pull away. Doesn't say no. In a second, it'll all be over. Just a flash of pain and light and I'll be gone. But just once, I want to know what it's like to kiss her before I go. I tip my head closer. Close enough to let her close the gap if she wants to.

Her breath comes out on a tremble. My pulse ratchets up as her mouth slants toward mine. Just before our lips brush, she jerks sharply back. Across the short gap between us, I can hear Poppy screaming in her ear. Fleur's cheeks flush to match the redwood blooms on the tree behind her—blooms I swear weren't there a minute ago. "We can't do that," she tells me. "That's a terrible idea."

"Why?" I snap. "Because Poppy says so?"

"Because we'll get in trouble. You know the rules."

Yeah, I know them. A kiss is painful for the weaker Season, a fast-track ticket back to the Observatory, complete with probations and penalties I'd rather not think about. But I would have kissed her anyway. "I guess following the rules has been working for you," I say with a heavy dose of sarcasm.

She flinches, and I hate myself for it. Chill's mentioned how Fleur and Poppy have been slipping in the rankings. Probably because she's far too easy on me.

Idiot. If she only cared about the rules, she would have killed me a week ago.

"Never mind," I grumble. "You're right. It's a stupid way to die."

"Fine," she says through her teeth. She tightens her grip on the knife with a precision that says she knew all along exactly where it should go. "On the count of three, then."

"Don't be an idiot," Chill warns me.

Too late.

I brace myself. My breath comes fast. In a second, my season will be over. I'll be locked away, asleep in a plastic cage thirty stories underground for the rest of Fleur's season. . . .

"Step away from the girl, Jack."

It'll be another six months after that before my next breath of fresh air in the fall, when I'll be stuck chasing down Amber, and Amber can't stand me. . . .

"I am your Handler and I am telling you to get out of there, Jack!"

It'll be another three months after that before Fleur comes to find me. A whole year until I see her again. . . .

"Wait . . . ," I say. I can't get any air.

Chill bellows at me to run.

"No, no, wait! I'm not—" Fleur and I lurch away from each other at the same time, her blade scraping my rib as she's thrown off balance. Her eyes go wide. She drops the knife on the ground, shaking out her hand as if it's possessed.

"For Chronos's sake, Fleur! You cut me!" I cry out, my voice breaking.

"You told me to!"

"And then I changed my mind!" The pain's blinding. I twist, the wound screaming as I peel up my shirt and contort myself to see it.

"Don't panic," Chill says. "Stay calm. It's shallow. Your vitals are good." He's lying. My side looks like a bad take from a 1980s slasher film. "Get out of there while she's distracted. Keep moving."

Fleur cringes as blood seeps through the gaps between my fingers. "I swear to Gaia, I didn't mean to." She reaches for me. "Here, let me see it."

"No, no, no. Don't—" I back into a tree, too late to stop her. Her hand grazes the exposed skin of my side, and suddenly I'm a living conduit. Every muscle in my body spasms and the hot surge of magic rattles my teeth. I cry out again and she leaps back from me.

"I'm sorry!" she says. "I was only trying to help."

I drop to my knees, the world reeling as if I've stuck my finger in an electrical socket.

"You know what I said about your vitals before?" Chill asks. "I take it back."

"I know!" I holler at him, wishing he would shut up and leave us alone.

Fleur startles.

"I wasn't yelling at you. I'm sorry." I push to my feet, feeling like an asshole. Of all the hundreds of Springs Gaia could have chosen to stick in my tiny corner of the globe to kill me, why did she have to choose one who's managed to wedge herself into every corner of my mind? One who's interesting and beautiful and impossible not to think about? Why'd she have to pick one who might feel the same way about me? It just makes everything worse.

"Touching sucked," I tell her, holding the tree for support. "And we should definitely, definitely not do it again." I'll take the knife over slow death by electrocution any day.

Fleur hugs her arms to her chest. "I didn't mean to cut you. If I'd known you were going to chicken out—"

"I didn't chicken out!"

"Why are you so afraid of dying, anyway?" She bends to pick up her knife, and I stumble away from it as she gesticulates wildly. "I mean, how many times have we been through this? I've killed you, like, twenty times."

"Twenty-seven." Her eyebrows rise. She lowers the blade. "And I'm not scared of dying," I lie. "I just wasn't ready to go back yet." I sound pathetic and overtired, like a kindergartner fighting naptime. She's right. If I had any balls, I'd get it over with. She probably doesn't run from Julio when he comes for her every summer. According to Chill, she doesn't even seem to mind. And I'm not sure which is worse: that she's not afraid of dying, or that she actually *likes* Julio. "You know what? I just . . ." I press the heels of my hands into my eyes. It's too hot. Everything hurts. "I can't be this close to you right now."

I turn and climb the rough trail up the slope behind me.

Chill cheers me on. I hear his hand smack the desk through my transmitter, followed by frantic keystrokes in the background as he monitors my progress from our dorm room, probably recording every humiliating second of this. "That's it, Jack! Go!"

Fleur calls my name and I push myself faster. The wound in my side feels like it's tearing wider with every step. My boots slip on the soft, wet ground, and Chill curses me for leaving such obvious tracks for her to follow.

Higher. I just need to get higher. If I can get someplace colder, I can buy myself more time. My side pulls painfully as I slip off my jacket and drape it over a tree limb for Fleur. The cold is hard on her. It drains her magic and slows her down.

I keep climbing, wheezing and dizzy when I finally collapse into a patch of snow lingering at the foot of an evergreen. I listen for Fleur's footsteps as the last drops of winter slip from the tree's needles. The steady patter smells all wrong, and I look down, surprised to find a puddle of crimson slush. A crippling cough takes hold of me. I press back against the trunk, holding the skin around the wound together, but it's no use. I'm only putting off the inevitable.

There's no point in hiding from her. Her magic is drawn to mine like a magnet. She'll know exactly where to find me.

"I know you're there, Jack," she says through a weary sigh. "I can smell you."

I reek like fever sweat and blood. I'm long past my expiration date.

"Stay calm," Chill whispers in my ear. "I'll find a way to get you out of there. You've got enough juice left in you to make it another day, easy."

I shake my head. My power's almost gone, draining like a dying battery. I'm on stolen time and we both know it. I could keep running, but what's the point? The only thing worse than being killed by Fleur is suffering a slow death alone.

I peer around the trunk of the tree as she slides her arms into the sleeves of my jacket and draws it around herself, hugging it close. She slumps down in a clearing a few yards away, stirring an explosion of butterflies from the wildflowers that have sprung up around her. I dig my hands into my shrinking island of snow, willing it to stay. To freeze. To keep me here.

"It's the end of March, Jack. Winter's over," she says sullenly. She wipes my blood from her knife and falls back on the grass, her boots thumping the ground and making the long, loose fabric of her skirt pool around her knees. A bright orange butterfly alights in her hair and she huffs an irritated breath at it. A long, pink strand flips back from her eyes, but the butterfly only stirs and lands there again.

"Quit staring," Chill badgers me. "You should be looking for a way out."

With a flurry of irritation, I turn my transmitter off.

I lick my dry lips and blow an icy breath across the clearing, rustling the fabric of her skirt and making her hunch deeper into my coat. The butterfly beats its wings once . . . twice . . . before falling, frozen, onto her cheek. I press back against the trunk, dizzy from the effort, kicking myself for my own stupidity. I don't know why I did that. Maybe just to prove that I can.

She sits up and nudges the butterfly with a finger. Her cheeks pale as if touched by something cold, and she turns to glare in my direction. Cupping the butterfly in her hand, she blows into it. The space between her fingers glows, so faintly I wonder if it's just my raging fever, if I'm imagining it, when she opens her hands and the butterfly bobs away on a breeze.

"You can't keep running. You already know how this ends." Her voice echoes, high and clear and annoyed, from every direction. "You've dragged it out long enough. If I don't send you back soon, someone's going to notice."

"Notice what?"

She falls back in the grass, one arm thrown over her face. "That I don't want you to go."

It hurts to breathe. She's never come out and said it before. "What *do* you want?"

"Does it matter?" she asks hopelessly. "Nothing's going to change."

"It matters to me." I'm surprised by how much I mean it this time. I asked her this same question once, years ago, in a desperate attempt to stall her as she was trying to kill me. She'd just stood there, slack-jawed and blinking, as if she'd never stopped to consider the answer.

She flings her arm from her face and frowns up at the sky. "You don't even know me."

If she could see the size of the surveillance file Chill keeps on her, she probably wouldn't think that. "Then tell me something about you." Another cough takes hold. I press my palm into my side to slow the bleeding, but my fingers are numb and the ground is soaked red.

She doesn't answer right away, as if she's weighing how much of herself she's willing to share. "What do you want to know?"

Everything. I squeeze my eyes shut, struggling to stay focused. There are so many things I want to ask her. Like why she carves my initials into a tree at the end of every spring. But I've already pissed off Poppy enough for one day.

"What's your favorite food?" I ask, though I already know the answer.

She hesitates. "Pizza," she finally says, swatting the red light in her ear.

"What kind?" I rasp.

"Mushrooms, peppers, onions, and sausage." I wait. ". . . And extra cheese."

"Favorite band?"

"U2."

"Favorite movie?"

"Thelma and Louise."

"Please tell me you're kidding." My laugh becomes a cough. Seasons aside, sometimes I think Fleur and I couldn't be more different. I slump against the tree, too weak to hold myself together anymore. "Why do you read all those books, anyway?"

"What books?"

"All the ones with tragic endings?" Her library hold list is just depressing. I used to check them all out after she returned them each year, but I ended up throwing most of them against the walls.

"You read them?"

"Maybe," I say, angry with myself for talking too much. I feel reckless—punch-drunk and a little delirious. "I might have read some of them," I confess. "But I draw the line at poetry." The poetry books she checks out of the library are old—like, seventeenth century old. And no matter how many times I've tried to understand what she sees in them, I just don't. My head feels heavy. I lean it back against the tree and the world goes wobbly. "I guess *1984* wasn't so bad, but *Orpheus and Eurydice*, *Anna Karenina*, and *Wuthering Heights* were horrible. And Romeo and Juliet were just idiots. I mean, who drinks poison and just gives up like that?"

"There was no hope for them," she says, snapping the head off a weed. "It's called a tragedy for a reason."

"Of course there was hope! They just had a shitty plan."

"And yours would be any better?" She sits up, ripping a fistful of grass from the ground. "No, seriously, Jack! What would you have done?"

Her tone's sharp. Cutting. It brings the world back into focus. "I would have taken her and run!"

"There is nowhere to run!"

"But would you . . . if there was?" *Shut up, Jack.* I bury my head in my hands. Fleur's quiet for a long time. Too long.

"Maybe," she says, "but it doesn't matter. It's just a story. A dream. It could never actually happen."

I hate how resigned she is to all this, that this is her life. *Our* life. But more than that, I hate that she's right. We're leashed to the Observatory by our transmitters. If we were to take them off and try to escape, we'd never survive off the ley lines. But that doesn't mean I haven't spent the last thirty years thinking about it, searching for a way out. I've done it before.

And look where it got you, I remind myself. "Romeo and Juliet just trusted the wrong people to help them. That's all."

"It's a tragedy," she says stubbornly. "They're not supposed to have a happy ending."

Something hot boils up inside me. I don't know if I'm angrier at her for giving up, or at myself for dying. "Yeah? Well, if they were both just going to die anyway, maybe they should have gone down fighting!"

It's only when she roars to her feet that I realize exactly what I've done.

FLEUR

"Is that what you think? That we should go down fighting!" I scrape up my knife and stalk toward the trees. The flash of crimson on snow gives him away as he scrambles deeper into the woods away from me. "Fine, then let's give Chronos and Gaia exactly what they want!"

Poppy urges me on. "You've got him, Fleur. Do it now!"

"No," he gasps, his black hair plastered to his pale forehead and his chest heaving. "No, no, no, that's not what I—"

I lash out with my mind, my consciousness digging through the soft soil into the roots of a narrow sapling. My thoughts slide into it, the tree conforming to my intentions like a glove, the roots stretching out in the direction of Jack's voice until they're curled around his ankle.

His fingers struggle for purchase, his T-shirt riding up as I haul him viciously over the ground. He kicks at my snare. The force of it knocks me back a step. His body smears the grass red as he reaches frantically for the patch of blood-soaked slush behind him. I yank him toward me, but he manages to snag a handful, freezing it into a shiv as he jerks to a stop at my feet.

He points the makeshift blade at me. It trembles in his hands, the pink ice melting from its jagged tip and dripping down his knuckles. He could slash my roots to free himself, leaving me with a nasty scar. I wouldn't stop him—Gaia knows, I deserve that and more—but he doesn't. He won't.

"Is this what you meant when you said we should go down fighting?" Tears well hot behind my eyelids, blurring his face. "Because that's what they want, Jack." That's what Poppy and Chill want. That's what Chronos and Gaia want. But Jack's the only one who's ever cared what *I* want. And I don't want to fight anymore.

I don't want to kill the boy who cares that hurting him makes me squeamish, who leaves me his jacket on cold nights, who'd rather die than lay a hand on me.

I release my roots.

Jack's head drops softly to the ground and his fist falls open, his

December-gray eyes glassy and slow to focus as the shiv rolls off his palm into a smear of blood on the grass. He turns away from me, curling in on himself with a violent shiver as a cough takes hold.

"Do it, Fleur!"

"Shut up, Poppy!" My voice quakes as I stand over him, fists clenched around the knife, searching for the right hold. The right angle. The right moment. He's sweating, shaking like a wounded animal, and my throat closes. He chose the knife because it seemed quicker, less painful somehow. Maybe it would have been, if I hadn't hesitated before.

"Quit dragging it out! If you take him down now, we might be able to salvage some ground."

"I said *shut up*, Poppy!"

"It's time, Fleur—"

I swat at my transmitter, cutting her off, even though I know she's right. There's nothing I can do for him. The stronger I am, the weaker he becomes. If I touch him, I'll only make it worse. Just standing this close, my body temperature alone is probably a slow form of torture for him. And if I kiss him—Gaia, if only kissing him could fix this—we'd all be in so much trouble. I'm already under a microscope, and I don't think Poppy and I can survive much more. Our rankings are low, dangerously close to the Purge line. Because my seasons are too short and the mid-Atlantic winters drag on. Because I wait too long, stall too often before sending him home. Because I let Jack run sometimes, just so I can spend a few more days chasing him, and Chronos doesn't grant points for compassion. His rules don't condone love. The entire system is rooted in opposition. In fear and animosity. The only way I survive is by killing Jack, but I don't want to do it anymore.

I never wanted to.

His eyes are fading behind heavy lids. Blood slicks his ribs where his shirt's ridden up, and I can't stand the thought of causing him any more pain.

I fall to my knees beside him. His eyes flutter closed, his cool breath held and waiting, his blue lips so, so close as I lean over him, my blade pressed against his side. For a moment, it looks as if he's sleeping. Like my job is already done.

"What are you waiting for?" he whispers. "We both know how this ends."

2

FIFTY-FIVE DAYS LATER

JACK

The cloying scent of wildflowers sticks in the back of my throat. I blink myself awake, the glare through the window of my stasis chamber nearly blinding me. I stare up at the white drop-tile ceiling and the posters on the wall, struggling to remember how I got here.

"Welcome back, Jack." Chill's voice grates through the speakers beside my head. I wince, everything too bright, too loud, and too soon all around me. My fingers and arms tingle. There's an ache in my chest, and I reach for the place under my ribs where Fleur stabbed me.

A cluster of flowers—tiny white lilies—falls from my hand. Across the room, Chill sits at his desk, logging data into his tablet: the date, time, and "conditions of my arousal." While his back is turned, I raise the sagging stem to my nose. The flowers smell faintly like Fleur, a tenacious sweetness lingering in the pale, crushed petals.

Something Professor Lyon once told me springs suddenly to mind. The first time he caught me picking a lock to the catacombs under the

Winter wings, searching for a way out of the Observatory, I told him I didn't want to exist here, trapped in this stupid cycle, anymore. He quoted physics at me, insisting it simply wasn't possible. *The total amount of energy in a closed system cannot be created nor destroyed*, he'd said. *Like water that moves from sea to sky, we are merely changed from one form to another and back again.*

Fleur must have put the lilies in my hand before I died. And somehow the flowers made it all the way here, their matter and energy tucked inside my own, becoming part of that same hopeless loop.

Chill's chair swings around and I close my fingers around the petals.

. "How long have I been out?" My throat's dry, my voice hoarse from disuse.

"Just a cat nap." I follow his movements through the lid of the plexiglass cylinder that surrounds me like a cocoon. He dims the artificial window, then lowers the thermostat, shrugging on an extra sweater to keep himself warm. "Fifty-five days. Your stasis times are getting shorter. Your off-campus times are getting longer. You're getting stronger every year, Jack. Kicking ass and climbing the ranks."

Only because Fleur's been increasingly reluctant to kill me, and I've been increasingly reluctant to die. I lift my head as far as the confined space will allow, swearing when I smack it on the lid. I grope for the release bar, but the chamber's still locked from the outside.

"Take it easy, Sleeping Beauty," Chill says. "It's only been fifty-five days. Give your brain a minute to engage before you come tumbling out of there." He sets a bottle of pills and a glass of water on the steel cart by my feet.

I drop my head back against the platform, claustrophobic and sleep addled, impatient for the sound of the lock's release.

"Don't be so hard on yourself. You kept Fleur on her toes those last few days, and we climbed a few percentage points in the rankings. If we keep this up, we'll be eligible for relocation." The wall behind Chill is papered in maps of our assigned region, blue pins marking every place I've killed Amber, and red pins marking every GPS point in the mid-Atlantic US where Fleur's ever killed me. He leans back in his chair with a gloating smile, but I don't feel much like celebrating.

Chill frees the lock with a tap of his tablet screen. The lid of my chamber slides open around me, the cold air circulating inside rushing out and the familiar smell of our dormitory rushing in. I breathe shallowly against the pungent bite of the pine-scented cleansers the custodians use on the industrial tile floors and the peppermint air freshener they pump through the ventilation ducts in the ceiling. The artifical fragrance left behind by the detergent in the starched sheets on our bunk bed in the other room makes my tongue thick, and a sharp, cheesy smell spills from the open bag of smuggled Doritos hidden somewhere in Chill's desk. It all makes me want to puke.

I sit up and swing my legs over the side of the chamber, careful not to tangle myself in the cluster of wires dangling from the adhesive pads on my chest. Head bent over my knees, the details of my most recent death come back to me like a bad dream.

The last thing I remember is Fleur's knife between my ribs and the look on her face when she sent me back. I toss the lilies into the plastic bed before Chill can see them. Rubbing Fleur's face from my eyes, I ease my feet to the floor. I'm hungry. Empty. Everything hurts. That's the price of immortality, as Gaia likes to remind us.

When I open my eyes, Chill's standing in front of me. "Missed you, man." He holds up a fist. We bump knuckles, but my heart's not in it. "I was about to lose my mind from the boredom. This place isn't the same when you're out cold."

I try to smile for his sake. It's the least I can do, since it's more or less my fault he's stuck here, thirty stories below the Royal Observatory in Greenwich and the Prime Meridian. As long as he's my Handler, Chill will never leave this place. His sole purpose in this world is to drag out the length of my season—to keep my body alive out there as long as he can, then haul my matter back here through an underground network of electromagnetic energy lines so he can babysit me through my recovery.

It sounds complicated, but it's really just a circuit. My remote transmitter is the antenna that connects me to Chill. Chill's the wireless router connecting me to the ley lines. When my season is over, my physical body breaks down into a glowing ball of particulates, and Chill conducts all my matter, magic, and energy home. The circuit ends in my stasis chamber—a capacitor that stores my energy while it changes back to my physical form, exactly the way it remembers me. For the next few months, my plastic coffin acts like a giant battery charger. And I pop out good as new—my magic fully charged and my body immortally young, with an eternally adolescent neural system that's uniquely responsive to risks and rewards, exactly the way Gaia and Chronos expect us to be.

Chill claps me on the shoulder. He's my GPS, my cleanup crew, my roadie, and my pallbearer—the only person in this world I trust, which (by default) makes him my only friend. In 1988, I chose Ari "Chill" Berkowicz. And when it comes to choices, Gaia gives us only three.

Choice number one: live or die. But that's not really a choice when you're dangling by your nuts over the precipice. When we're nose to nose with death, we all want to live. So when Gaia holds out her slippery hand with the promise of a second chance, we don't stop to think of the consequences. We just take it.

Choice number two: our Handler. Save another young person from the brink of death, putting their life in eternal debt to us. Someone we don't mind spending the rest of time with, because once the choice is made, we're stuck with them. Forever. Ironically, there wasn't much time to think about how long *forever* really was.

And choice number three: a new identity, any name we want, to prevent our old lives from finding us. But as far as most Seasons are concerned, our names are the only choices that are truly ours.

I chose Jack.

I'm not entirely sure I chose Chill.

He frowns through his glasses as he checks my vitals. There's no prescription in them—they're just empty black frames. He doesn't need the lenses anymore. His perfect health is guaranteed by Gaia as long as we stay in the program. But thirty years ago, Chill made me fish them from the bottom of the frozen pond I pulled him from, insisting he felt naked without them. *Even gods wear loincloths. This is mine*, he said, dripping wet and shivering as he pushed them back on his face. *I'm Ari.* He reached to shake my hand, and I told him, *Not anymore.*

Chill's never seemed to mind his life here the way I do. Never seemed bothered being stuck with me. I'm probably the best friend Chill's ever had, which is sad, because I'm pretty sure I don't deserve him. Most days, I don't feel much better than the assholes from our school who made him walk that pond on a dare and abandoned him when he fell in. Sometimes, I wonder if he would have been better off if I'd never found him at all. In thirty years, he's the only thing I've ever saved, and when he looks at me through those missing lenses as if I'm his own personal hero, it's hard to look back. Saving Chill's life never felt like a conscious choice. And yet for reasons I'll never understand, he keeps choosing to save me, over and over, anyway.

Chill tosses me a pair of boxer shorts. "Now that you're back, maybe Poppy will quit bugging me. She's been hounding me every day, waiting for you to wake up, pestering me with questions. Speaking of which, are you going to tell me what that was all about?" Chill pushes his glasses up his nose, staring me down through the empty frames.

"What?" I wince, careful not to catch my IV cannula on the fabric as I drag on the boxers. I disconnect the catheter and roll out my shoulders, shaking fifty-five days of sleep from my bones.

"You. Tuning me out on that mountain pass." He tosses me a bottle of vitamins and I catch them against my chest, nearly dropping them.

"What are you talking about?" I take the cup of water he offers, shake out a couple of pills, and slowly swallow them down.

"Do you have any idea how long it took me to find you and bring you back? That shit isn't easy to pull off in the mountains, even *with* a transmitter." My throat closes around the last sip. I nearly choke on it.

My transmitter was *off*.

My memories of that day are still hazy, shrouded in the fog of the fever. I remember arguing with Fleur . . . feeling desperate for a moment alone with her. I *remember* turning off my transmitter because I was angry at Chill, and I don't remember turning it on again.

I sink down on the edge of the stasis bed. How the hell am I even here right now? Chill must have used Fleur's signal to find me and route me home.

"You could have died out there," he says sharply. "For good. *Forever*. Your magical ass would have been lost in the wind if Fleur hadn't been holding—" Chill falls abruptly silent. I perch on the edge of the bed, waiting for him to finish. He fumbles for his tablet and pretends to study the screen.

"What?" My heart rate climbs on the monitor. Chill doesn't answer, so I lean in closer. "What was she holding?"

"Back off." He swats the air, wrinkling his nose. "Stasis breath."

I fight the urge to punch the rest out of him.

"You." Chill sighs, tossing his tablet aside. "She held *you*. For the three freaking minutes it took me to find you and get you back online."

I touch the place where her knife pierced me.

I'd nearly bled out. As weak as I was, my death—my *permanent* death—should have been quick. Without a connection to Chill—without a leash to the ley lines—there would have been no way to bring me back. Chill's right. My particles should have dissolved into the ether, lost in the wind, adrift somewhere high over the mountains of Appalachia long before three minutes were up.

"Why . . . ?" I rub at the soft spray of pollen inside my palm. Fleur must have realized my mistake. She must have turned my transmitter back on for me. Even so, it shouldn't have taken three minutes to locate my signal, if Chill already had a lock on hers. "Why'd it take so long to find us?" But I know. Somehow, I already know the answer.

"Because Fleur turned off her transmitter, too."

I'm still rooted to the spot beside the stasis chamber, processing Chill's last words, when the monitor over his desk lights up.

"Turn on your camera, Chill. I know you're in there." Poppy Withers's face fills the screen. She taps the lens of her video cam and drums her desk impatiently.

Chill heaves a sigh. "Every. Damn. Day," he whispers.

"I heard that," Poppy answers. "You do realize your microphone's on."

Chill mumbles to himself. I scrape the lilies off the stasis bed, hiding them in my fist as he switches on the camera.

Poppy leans closer to her monitor, her nosy blue eyes scanning the contents of our dorm room. They open wide at the sight of my open chamber.

"Thank Gaia!" she says through an impatient huff. "You're finally awake." Poppy's prone to theatrics. Probably because her childhood was spent confined to a hospital bed and she missed all the drama in high school. She's the most annoying sixteen-year-old I've ever met. And down here, that's really saying something. "Is anyone going to tell me what in Chronos's name happened up there? Why was Fleur's transmitter off?"

"You're her Handler," I mutter. "Why don't you ask Fleur?"

"I did! She won't tell me." She points a finger at the camera. "If you hurt her—"

"Ha!" I tear the adhesive pads from my chest, shoving the tangled pile of wires to the floor. "If I hurt *her*? This is earth science, not rocket science! She's a Spring. I'm a Winter, Poppy! I couldn't hurt her if I tried!"

She bites her lip, probably because I'm right. A rising Season is nearly impossible to kill. By the time they find the waning Season, we're far too weak, and they're far too powerful. Even if it was as simple as luck or circumstance, the punishment for breaking the cycle is enough of a deterrent to keep us from trying. We run, we hide, and eventually we die. Exactly as natural law commands us to.

"Back off," Chill barks. "He just woke up, and you're jacking up his vitals."

Poppy's eyebrows disappear under her white-blond bangs. "Or what? You'll break down my door and make me?" Chill grumbles something unintelligible. Poppy knows this is as close as they'll ever come to being in the same room together. "Exactly what I thought," she says, leaning back from the camera. Behind Poppy, Fleur's stasis chamber is dark, still empty, and my thoughts leap to the last moments I spent with her. To the things she confessed to me.

"Don't you have someplace you need to be?" Chill snaps.

Poppy drums her chewed-up nails on her desk. Checks her tablet. She pushes her chair back from the camera with a sigh. "I have to go keep an eye on Fleur," she says with a hint of aggravation. "Julio was scheduled for release this morning. She'll be ready for transport soon."

Meaning Fleur will be dead soon.

Something doesn't add up. "Wait," I say, my stasis-addled brain struggling through the math. "You said it's been fifty-five days. It's only the beginning of May. Why would Fleur be ready for transport?" Chill blinks at me, clearly as confused as I am. Fleur was strong on that mountain. As strong as I've ever seen her. There's no way Julio could take her down so fast. She should have at least two, maybe even three more weeks out there before Poppy should have to bring her in.

"It's Julio," Poppy says, rolling her eyes. "She makes it far too easy for him."

"What's that supposed to mean?"

"Don't look at me," Poppy says defensively. "I don't like Julio any more than you do. How do I know what she sees in him?"

Something green rears up inside me. Julio Verano (né Jaime Velasquez), that sweaty asshole of summer. I try not to imagine it—him riding in half naked on his surfboard, smelling like Coppertone and Sex

Wax, or the infinite ways he might kill her. I hope she keeps her transmitter on. And he keeps his big, dumb lips to himself.

Poppy taps her pen on her desk. "What am I supposed to tell Gaia in my report?"

"How am I supposed to know?" I grumble. "I'm not the one with a soft spot for the Heat Miser."

"I'm not talking about Julio! I'm talking about what happened on that mountain. With *you*."

I rake my hands through two months of bedhead. Poppy's right. Going offline is no small breach of the rules. If two opposing Seasons go offline together, that just looks suspicious. We're supposed to hunt each other, kill each other, and send each other home. Any contact beyond that is expressly forbidden. The entire system is rigged to keep us apart. To keep us in line. "To maintain the balance of nature," Chronos says. But sometimes I wonder if there isn't more to it.

Poppy's still waiting for an answer. Our stories will have to corroborate. And once Fleur's in stasis, it'll be months before she wakes up again.

"Did you get any footage you can use?" I ask.

She picks at a nail. Raises an eyebrow. "You mean that excellent ten seconds when she dragged you kicking and screaming from the woods? Yeah, I got it."

I bite back a hostile retort. "So submit that. After she caught me, it was a normal takedown. We had technical difficulties, and I lost my signal."

"And Fleur's?" she asks, sucking a tooth like she's not buying a word of it.

"Her transmitter dislodged when I kicked her. She stabbed me.

34

Foggy conditions slowed the recovery. Chill brought me home. The end." I reach around Chill and switch off our camera.

Chill rubs his eyes through the empty frames of his glasses. He blinks at the blank screen. "I hate her."

"Keep an eye on her anyway." I scrape off the last of the adhesive pads before heading for the shower. "Let me know when Fleur's back."

I pad into our adjoining bunk room and open my closet, accidentally crushing the lilies in my fist as I catch the rolled-up maps of the Observatory that come spilling out around my feet. I shove the dusty maps back into the corner. I haven't bothered unrolling them in ages. I drew them all years ago, meticulously recording every elevator and ventilation duct and closet door. I mapped every exit from every wing to the city above and every passage into the catacombs I could find, sketching out what I could see through the plexiglass barriers at the end of our wing, re-creating what little I could remember of the administration levels below. It was pointless. Lyon told me as much every time he caught me picking a lock or crawling out of a tunnel I had no business finding. "Think hard, Jack," he'd say with a provocative smile. "If you *could* find a way out of the Observatory, how would you survive?"

Fleur was right. There's only one way out of this place. And only one way back in. Maybe there's no use fighting it.

Using the closet door as a screen, I slip my lock picks from their hiding place inside an old pair of sneakers and pop the tumblers in a small metal footlocker on the floor. The lid creaks open and I lay the lilies on top of the collection of Christmas ornaments stacked inside—all twenty-seven of them, one for every year Fleur's killed me. I find one every fall, hanging on a tree near the site of my last death beside a set of carved initials—*J.S.* I've never confessed to finding them, not even to

Chill. Never told anyone it's the first thing I hunt for every winter, or that I arrange to have each ornament shipped here, addressed to myself, every spring. The first year, when I found a fragile glass snowflake hanging by a red thread and I saw my initials and death date carved in the tree beside it, I assumed Fleur was mocking me. But with each passing year, the ornaments became more personal—a pink-haired girl made of frosted glass; a golden retriever made of clay with a name written on his collar; a silver angel stamped with the logo of a local children's hospital; a stack of tiny porcelain books, the spines all painstakingly, tragically labeled . . . Each ornament revealed a new secret about her, little glimpses into her present or her past. Her hobbies, where she grew up, her favorite colors and flowers and subjects in school. But this past year's ornament—a cherry tree in a snow globe of swirling pink blooms—had made my throat swell. It felt like a wish for the future.

Now, with the wilted lilies draped over the mounded contents of the box, the slate-gray footlocker looks more like a headstone. A place where wishes come to die.

I slam the lid closed and grab a towel from the closet.

"Are you at least going to tell *me*?" Chill asks. I stop, unable to turn my back on him as much as I want to. "I'm your Handler, Jack. It's my job to know where you are. And I can't do that if you're shutting me out. What really happened up there?"

I don't want to lie to him. I just don't know what to tell him. I don't understand what's happening between me and Fleur. Or why. Or what any of it means. I throw the towel over my shoulder and head for the shower.

"Give me a few years to figure it out."

3

HOUNDS OF WINTER

FLEUR

There's no sign of summer anywhere. The night's too cool, too dismal. It smells too much like the city in spring. I jaywalk across all three lanes of Woodmont Avenue, my running shoes slapping against the shallow puddles that reflect the bright lights of the marquee where Julio and I usually meet. I press my back against the wall of the theater, taking shelter from the rain under the red awning out front. The faces rushing by are all half hidden under hoods and umbrellas.

"Do you see him anywhere?" I hunch into Jack's coat, my collar raised against the windblown mist. My transmitter'ssilent in my ear.

"Come on, Poppy. You can't possibly still be angry with me." The incident on the mountain with Jack was almost two months ago. I didn't tell her everything that happened after I turned my transmitter off so she wouldn't have to lie for me. But I shouldn't have to tell her everything just because she's my Handler. There should be moments in my own life I'm allowed to keep for myself.

Poppy begs to differ.

Poppy was eighteen months younger than I was in 1991 when we died, back when eighteen months felt like an eternity, when just the number eighteen still felt like an attainable goal. Poppy must have seen Gaia that night in our room. Gaia sat in a beam of light from the parking lot outside our window, in a chair at the foot of my bed, nosing through my poetry books, waiting for me to die while the rest of the hospital slept. Poppy only pretended to sleep. She turned off her respirator the minute I flatlined, determined to come with us, as if she had nothing left to hold on to but me.

Sometimes, she just holds on too tightly.

"Don't be like this." I lean back against the brick under the shadow of the awning. "It's one night—one stinking movie, for crying out loud. If I didn't know better, I'd think you were jealous."

"I'm not jealous," she says begrudgingly.

A young couple rushes past, heads bowed, laughing as they jog to beat the rain. They're so wrapped up in the moment, they fail to notice the low-hanging branch of the tree ahead of them. I slide my mind inside its roots, then up through its trunk, lifting the heavy limb just high enough for the couple to clear it. They don't notice the small movement in the dark, and I feel a pang of loneliness when their lips meet as they dash beneath it.

"I bet he proposes over dessert," I say, just loud enough for Poppy to hear, certain she noticed them, too.

Her sigh's heavy. "Peanut butter cheesecake."

"They'll move in together. A condo in Georgetown."

"No. A house in the suburbs."

"She'll get him a puppy for Christmas."

"A shelter dog," Poppy insists.

"They'll have two kids." This time, the sigh is mine.

It's a game we've played for years, since before we were what we are. I remember our reflection in the window of our hospital room, Poppy's oxygen lines and my IVs tangled around us, the light fog of our breath where we pressed our faces to the glass to watch the people in the parking lot below. There was something hopeful about predicting the futures of strangers, like throwing coins into a fountain, even if neither of us had a future of our own to wish on. But now, the game only leaves me aching, wanting . . .

"Any sign of him yet?" I ask, kicking off the brick. The crowd in front of the theater has thinned. The sidewalk's nearly empty. Poppy doesn't answer. I check the time on the clock above the ticket counter, my last hope of the evening slipping away on another sigh. The ten-o'clock shows are already starting.

"If you're listening, you'll be happy to know I'm heading back to my room now. I'll try again tomorrow." And she'll still be mad at me then. Poppy hates that Julio and I get along. It worries her. We're falling in the rankings. But the truth is, I've been gradually falling for years, since March 1997, when I cornered Jack in the men's room of a bus station in Baltimore. He was cowering in a stall, using the metal door to shield himself from me.

"What do you want?" he shouted.

"From you?" I asked, surprised that the answer wasn't obvious.

"From any of this!"

It was the first time anyone had ever asked me that. I listened to him panting on the other side of the door. After all those years, he was still afraid of dying. Terrified of it. Willing to fight to the last breath, even though the outcome was completely inevitable. No one had ever bothered to ask me what I wanted from my life. It had always been assumed I wouldn't live long enough to know the answer. Life had been taken from me the day I got my terminal diagnosis, then given back the minute I died. And then there had been Poppy, clinging to my side and choosing our names, and Gaia explaining the rules. And no one ever bothered to ask me what *I* wanted, what I was willing to fight for.

No one but Jack.

I was thrown so off-balance by the question, I let him walk out that door. Because up until that moment, I didn't have an answer.

I duck out from under the awning to the slap of windshield wipers and the glare of headlights, darting between gaps in traffic as the sky begins to pour. My hotel is twelve blocks north, and I'm drenched before I make it halfway there. All I want to do is curl up in a warm bed and sleep. I slip into a convenience store, sneakers squeaking on the floor tiles as I scavenge for something to take back to my room to eat. My hand hovers over a bag of M&M's when I'm struck by the feeling of someone watching me. A soft popping sound is coming from the next aisle over, the slow cracking of someone's knuckles, one by one.

I glance over the top of the divider. The blond-haired boy on the other side lowers his eyes. I carry the M&M's to the register, darting a quick look over my shoulder as the cashier counts out my change, but I don't see his spiky blond crown anywhere as I turn to go.

The bells on the door jangle as it sweeps shut behind me. Too soon, they clang again, as someone else leaves the store. I pick up my pace, the hair on my neck prickling the way it used to years ago, back when Julio used to hunt me. I draw in a breath, but all I smell is the chocolate in my pocket and the dumpster in the alley up ahead. I risk a backward glance as I turn the corner. Through the wet strands of my hair, I can just make out the boy's shadow, his quick gait stretching toward me.

"Poppy?" I whisper. "I think I'm being followed."

Something moves up ahead, to my left. Another dark figure crosses the street toward me. A third matches my pace on the opposite side of the street. I know, in the bone-deep way that only someone who's been hunted can know, that they're herding me.

"Poppy, I need an exit." I may be a Spring, but there are three of them and one of me. And every weapon I could summon to defend myself in this city—every root, every branch, the trunk of every tree—is anchored in concrete. I'm too far from my hotel. I'll never make it. "In half a block, I'm cutting east. Get me out of here."

The deafening silence that follows is broken by the boy's footfalls behind me. Where the hell is she? Poppy's been quiet too long. She would never leave me alone in a situation like this, even if she's pissed at me.

The stench of trash grows stronger. I hook a sharp right, following the smell into an alley. As soon as I clear the corner, I break into a run. The doors I fly past are bolted, the windows all boarded or spray-painted black. The dark path ahead of me grows clearer as I near the end of the passageway, and I jerk to a stop in front of a high brick wall.

Dead end.

"Poppy, where are you?" I turn, fists clenched. Three shadowy figures block my only exit. The one in the middle steps closer, until his blond crown becomes visible in the pale light ghosting over the wall. A spark ignites in his hand, the flame growing brighter as it hovers over his palm, illuminating the silver scythes embroidered on their sleeves. My blood runs cold.

Chronos's Guards.

"Your Handler has been dismissed for the night," says the Guard holding the flame. A heavy metal door swings open beside me. A fourth figure looms inside, bracing it wide.

The blond Guard juts his chin toward the condemned building. "Step inside, Fleur Attwell. We'd like a few words with you alone."

My mind gropes for a root. For anything I can control. But it's like searching for a match in the dark. The Guard's eyes dip to my twitching fingers, and his fire sparks. "I'll only ask once."

There's no point in running or trying to escape. I can't smell them. Can't overpower them with any elemental magic they can't already tap. It would be far too easy for them to hunt me down, and my punishment for fighting them or trying to evade them would be far worse than whatever's waiting for me on the other side of that door.

The Guard holds his flame aside as I pass. My shoulder jostles the female Guard in the doorway as I push my way around her into a pitch-black room. Water drips, the leaking pipe's rhythmic spatter broken by the echoes of the Guards' boots behind me. The air smells like piss and something putrid and rotten, and I plant my feet to avoid tripping over something gross in the dark. One of them shoves me deeper into the building, guiding me around debris, through narrow passages, and up two winding flights of stairs.

Ahead, a dim light grows steadily brighter until I'm standing in the doorway of an empty room. The walls are devoid of windows and covered in graffiti. A kerosene lamp burns on the floor in the far corner, casting ominously long shadows against the water-stained ceiling above me. A chair sits empty in the middle of the room.

The blond Guard gives me a final shove through the door. I avoid the chair, keeping my back to the wall. The light gleams off their patches as, one by one, the Guards filter in. The tall blond with the tousled spikes—the leader, I assume—is first, followed by the Guard who opened the door, a dark-haired girl with a spill of loose curls, holding a coiled length of rope. A chestnut-haired boy leans against the far wall, one leg propped behind him, cleaning his nails with a pocketknife. He glances up at me, one eye surveying me with clinical disinterest before returning to his nails. His other eye is nearly swollen shut, the skin around it darkened by deep purple bruises.

A wiry Asian girl with close-cropped hair is last to enter. She drops a backpack on the floor and checks a remote tracker around her wrist. I draw in a subtle breath, hoping for some clue to who they were before they were promoted to the Guard. But any traces of their former Seasons are long gone now. Now they're Chronos's lapdogs, gifted with all four elemental powers, their magic perfectly balanced to mask their scent—his perfect hunters.

"Sit down," the leader says, dragging the rickety chair around to face me. I take a small step away from it.

"I don't think we've been properly introduced." I make my voice loud, as steady as I can manage. But it's an obvious and pathetic stall. The leader raises an eyebrow.

"I'm Captain Douglas *Lausks*," he says with a sardonic degree of emphasis. "And this is Noelle, Lixue, and Denver. We'll be handling your Reconditioning." The knuckles of the captain's left hand pop softly at his side as I back farther into the corner.

"Reconditioning?"

43

That's what Chronos calls it. The rest of us call it what it is—behavior modification through corporal punishment, a slow form of torture to remind us who we are. We've all heard stories of what happens to opposing Seasons who've grown too close. We've all been lectured on the risks—climate confusion, hurricanes and floods, failed crops that lead to famine. There is a natural order, Chronos tells us, a balance that must be preserved, boundaries that must be honored, but Julio and I have always been so careful not to disturb that order or hurt anyone. We've always been careful not to draw attention to ourselves. Is that why Julio's late? Is that why he's not here? My gaze leaps to the chestnut-haired Guard and his swollen eye, and my heart stutters. They must have found Julio before Julio found me.

"Don't act so surprised," the captain says, shoving the chair closer with the toe of his boot. "You can't turn off your transmitter and expect no one will ever know."

I shake my head, my heel connecting with the wall behind me. Julio and I have bent our fair share of rules, but I've only ever turned my transmitter off once . . . with Jack.

I drag the sleeves of Jack's coat down over my hands, wishing I could disappear into it as I turn to look into each of their faces. Douglas Lausks, Noelle, Denver, Lixue . . . The captain emphasized each of their names. They all have cold names. Northern names. *Winter* names. And like all Seasons, their names give them away. These Guards were all Winters once, just like Jack; who else would be better suited to punish me? To make me fear the cold? To make me hate Winters enough to kill Jack and send him home with the detached, calculated efficiency that's expected of me?

I steel myself and sit down hard in the chair. When I don't proffer my hands, the captain inclines his head to the Guard with the rope— Noelle. She steps in front of me, refusing to meet my eyes as she pries my stubborn hands out herself. Her fingers are cold enough to burn, and I clench my teeth to keep from crying out as she wrestles my arms behind me. The rope chafes as she cinches it in place. Suddenly, she pauses.

The captain's eyes darken as he studies her face. "What is it?"

Behind me, the scrape of Denver's knife against his nails falls quiet.

"It's nothing," she says, trying and failing to harden her voice as she drags down my sleeves. Fear grips me as the captain steps closer. "I said it's nothing," Noelle insists through her teeth.

The captain nudges her out of the way. My shoulder wrenches painfully as he pushes up my coat sleeve, twisting my left arm toward the light to see the scar. An entire conversation seems to pass in the silence between them as he comes around the chair to face me.

"It seems someone on my team has been keeping a very close eye on Jack Sommers, and you by default." The captain sniffs. His eyes dip to my coat as if he can smell Jack all over it. "I found the tree, the oak you carved with his initials and the date of his death." I force myself not to flinch. Not to give away a single reaction as he paces in front of my chair. "It must be painful, memorializing him that way." He circles back to face Noelle. "Imagine . . . being so fiercely loyal. So devoted to someone." His cold, blue eyes land squarely on hers and she withers under his stare.

"It has nothing to do with loyalty," I bite out. I've carved Jack's initials into a tree near the site of every place I've ever killed him to assuage my own guilt. Because it seems wrong that Jack should be the only one to bleed. "Only a monster could inflict pain on someone else and feel good about it."

The captain stops pacing. He chuckles darkly. "Are you suggesting I'm enjoying this?" he asks through a grimace. "Because I can assure you, I find nothing about this situation amusing."

I gasp as he jerks my transmitter from my ear.

Poppy! I can't be sure I didn't cry her name out loud. Frostbite blooms where the captain's fingers brushed me. "Give it back!"

He tosses it over my head to Denver. "I was under the impression you like to live dangerously."

I swallow sour panic, twisting in my chair as Denver tucks my transmitter into his pocket. The captain leans close and says through a cold breath, "Tell me what happened on the mountain between you and Jack Sommers and this will all be over quickly."

Anger bursts from me like a white-hot fire. I throw my head forward. Feel his nose crack against my skull. The captain swears, the thick, warm smell of blood rolling over his lip. I've spent my whole life preparing to die, but I'll be damned if I go quietly for Douglas Lausks.

The room stills, silent except for the sound of the captain's pride spattering against the floor. I feel the others tense, the room practically crackling with magic. Thunder rumbles outside. My mind reaches out, groping blindly for signs of life—a tree, a root, anything growing under the building I can call to me.

The captain snatches my face in his hand, his breath tinged with the smell of iron. I recoil as his eyes glaze over with frost. "I have a deeply personal dislike of your kind. Be very, *very* careful how you treat me."

He releases me with a shove, his icy fingers leaving stinging welts on my cheeks. "I came here with every intention of letting you leave alive. Don't make me change my mind. It would be easy to call it an accident." He wipes his bloody nose on his sleeve, his voice thick. "Someone on my team recorded an interesting phenomenon—an interruption in two transmitter signals, fifty-five days ago—the same day you killed Jack Sommers and sent him home. The same date I found carved into the tree, and into your skin. There's a three-minute gap in your surveillance feeds that coincides a little too neatly with the interruption in those signals. Now," he says, the honed edge to his voice sharp enough to sever any argument, "tell me what happened on the mountain with Jack Sommers."

I bite down hard on my cheek.

"How *exactly* did you kill him?"

"It's all in my Handler's report."

"That report is a lie, and we both know it." He shifts into my line of sight, the knuckles of his left hand popping softly at his side, same as they did a few moments ago when I asked for their names. Not a threat. More like a tell, hinting at his impatience. "Did you kiss him?" Noelle's head snaps up, drawing the captain's attention. His eyes linger on her, a hint of pain stirring in them when he asks, "Do you love him? Are you foolish enough to think he loves you?"

"Knock it off, Doug," Denver says quietly. Lixue blanches, looking between them as if she's expecting the captain to lash out, but the captain doesn't punish Denver for it. Instead, he turns away, pacing the tight space as if he's trying to pull himself together.

Lixue reaches into her backpack and offers him a water bottle. My heart stills as he pours some into his hand and washes the blood from his

47

chin. All it would take is a handful of that water to kill me. If he's strong enough to master fire, he could just as easily drown me where I sit. He must read the fear in my eyes—must sense compliance in my sudden quiet.

"Fine," he says, slowly screwing the cap back on the bottle. "Let's play it your way and assume you don't have feelings for Sommers. Why turn off your transmitter in the presence of an enemy when you're so close to falling below the red line?"

I search his face for signs of a lie. My stomach clenches when he smiles, at the glimmer of pity in it. I knew Poppy and I were close to the Purge line, that I was at risk of being cycled out for my performance. I'd let Jack's seasons go on too long. Had let my emotions go unchecked, the spring rains running out of control. I had let Julio kill me too quickly, too easily. My downhill slide in the ranks has been building momentum for years, but time is strange here, hard to grasp, both fleeting and endless with the perennial promise of immortality hanging over our heads. When I turned off my transmitter, I hadn't stopped to consider how much a moment alone with Jack might cost me.

That my next death might be my last.

I lift my chin. Erase the fear from my face. No matter what these Guards have planned for me, I'll face it alone. I refuse to drag Jack down with me. "If I'm so close to the red line, maybe I deserve what's coming to me."

Something shimmers beneath the hard frost of Doug's eyes. "I suppose we'll find out, won't we?"

I suck in a breath as he tosses the water bottle to Noelle. She catches it against her jacket. Their eyes hold, his voice rough with emotion when he says, "If you won't confess to your feelings for Jack Sommers, I'm left with no choice but to test where your loyalties lie."

Denver swears under his breath. "Let it go, Doug. So she made a mistake. It was a long time ago."

"It didn't mean anything," Noelle says softly.

"If it meant so little to you, why are you still watching his feeds?"

Noelle's throat bobs with her hard swallow.

"Let's just do what we came to do and go home," Denver says. I jump at the snap of his blade flipping shut. The rope doesn't budge, no matter how hard I twist.

"Doug—" Noelle starts.

"Captain!" he corrects her. Her cheeks flash red.

"Captain," she says sharply. "I don't think—"

"Who exactly is it you're afraid of hurting, Lieutenant?" There's a challenge in his eyes. Whatever she did wounded him badly, and I'm going to be the one to suffer for it.

The chair creaks under me as I struggle to get free.

Noelle adjusts her grip on the bottle, and all the color drains from her cheeks. The temperature in the room plummets. I start at the telltale crackle of water freezing, at the groan of plastic as the ice expands and the lid breaks. Noelle's eyes glaze over, swirling with white fog, the same way Jack's do when we argue. Rime splinters over the walls, sizzling over the surface of the lantern. My teeth begin to chatter, my magic retreating deep to keep warm as Lixue and Denver close the circle around me.

Breath steams from my lips. Every gasp of chilled air burns, the Guards' magic filling the tight space too thickly with smells: peppermint, winterberry, pine, chimney smoke . . .

Winter smells. Jack's smells. The smells I cling to at night when I'm curled around his coat.

I stare the Guards in the eyes. So when it's over, I'll remember. So when it's over, I'll recognize their faces and remember they're not him. I picture Jack's night-black hair and storm-gray eyes. The shadow of his lashes against his cheeks and the way they fluttered closed as he lay in my arms. I remember every delicate detail, every soft and vulnerable piece of him, clinging tightly to the memory of that moment when I held him, the rush of magic—the pulse of electricity that jolted through me, leaving me weak when our skin touched.

It felt right, felt different at the end, when our transmitters were off. When it was only the two of us.

Not like this.

Anything but this.

It isn't until my eyes swell closed with frostbite that I forget who I am. That I forget what I want. That I'm certain I'm going to die.

4
MAY FLOWERS

FLEUR

Julio doesn't even try to conceal his arrival. The sun peeks through the clouds and the Potomac River Basin grows unseasonably warm a moment before he finds me. He sinks down beside me on the damp riverbank and scoots close until our knees are almost brushing, careful not to make contact with my skin. Shivering in jeans and a windbreaker, he blows into his cupped hands. His breath smells strongly of chewing gum. Under that, faintly of cocoa butter and the sea. Smells I loved a lifetime ago, but that only manage to set me on edge now. No matter how attractive the package, Julio's here to kill me. If he ever gets around to it.

"Took you long enough to get here," I say without looking up. The long ends of my hair have escaped my hood, the damp wind blowing the strands across my face enough to hide my bruises. I left Jack's coat at a secondhand store where I traded it for the hoodie, unable to tolerate the smell of it anymore.

"I went to your hotel as soon as I got here, but they said you checked out."

I pluck a blade of grass from the ground between my feet and toss it away. "I had to move. The front desk staff started asking questions." Wondering where my parents were, why I wasn't in school, how I got the bruises. Decent hotels pay attention. For the last three days, I've been relegated to the kinds of cheap roadside motels that turn a blind eye to these kinds of things.

Julio reclines on his elbows, stretching out in the brightening sun. The lapels of his windbreaker fall open, the T-shirt underneath snug against the swell of his chest and the tight lines of his stomach. It may be early in his season, but he's already strong, radiating heat. "Didn't take long to track you here. You could at least *pretend* to hide from me. If you give up too quickly, it takes all the fun out of it."

Poppy doesn't say a word, content to let Julio do her job for her.

"I was expecting you a week ago."

"Admit it, you missed me," he says with a lazy grin. He tips his bronzed face to the sun, the soft waves of his dark hair just visible in my peripheral vision.

"I want to go home."

"Ouch!" he says, rubbing his chest. "I'll try not to take it personally."

I bite my cheek. Truth? I did miss him. I miss our lighthearted banter and his harmless flirting. He makes me laugh, and he never takes himself or anyone else too seriously. Normally, I look forward to his company. He makes me feel human. But this year, faced with the most painful parts of my inhumanity, I'd honestly rather sleep.

His face falls. "Sorry, I didn't realize you were in such a hurry to get back. I scored us tickets to a Nats game on Thursday. You know,

World Series champions? 'Stay in the fight'?" The sun dims when I don't answer. Poppy remains mercifully quiet in my ear.

"I waited for you at the theater," I grumble. "Where were you, anyway?"

"I got held up. In-room suspension."

"For what?"

"One of Chronos's lackeys caught me coming back to my room after curfew."

A reluctant smile pulls at my split lip. "Heartbreaker," I mutter, peeking through my veil of hair. I shake my head at his rakish grin. Julio's reputation at the Observatory transcends the barriers separating our wings. The Summer girls are the only ones who can have him. Still, I've heard the whispers in the Spring rec room. Read the confessions written in small, dreamy letters on the walls of the locker room stalls. After a handful of his surveillance pics started floating around the dorms, more than a few Springs swore they'd take a voluntary hit to their rankings for one dying night alone with Julio Verano.

"I was in my own damn wing. And this arrogant washed-up snowflake in a scythe patch threatened to strip my rec privileges just because I left some girl's room after hours. I told him he'd need a better reason than that."

"And then what?"

"I hit him."

I stare at him, dumbfounded. "For Chronos's sake, Julio! You hit a Guard? You're lucky you only got suspended." A week ago, I might have laughed. But now the prospect of never seeing him again feels too real, too imminently painful to think about. "If you're not careful, you'll be Terminated from the program."

He sits up slowly, his face sobering as his eyes skip over my face. "I could say the same about you."

I suck in a sharp breath as he reaches for my hood. It's been years since Julio's raised anything more than a kind hand to me, but Reconditioning has left me raw, defensive. A faint purple bruise colors the skin around his knuckles, and I fight off a flashback of that freezing cold room, my mind seizing stubbornly on a memory of the chestnut-haired Guard with the swollen eye—Denver, they called him. I let myself hope he was on the receiving end of the punch that landed Julio in suspension.

Julio slides my hood back from my face, his mouth a tight line as he takes in the worst of it. The sky darkens. A hot wind whips over us, conjured by the rush of his anger, scattering cherry blossoms over the river's edge. A bright flicker of lightning clears the basin of tourists, making them run in search of shelter. A middle-aged woman with a camera around her neck slows as she passes us, her face a snapshot of motherly concern as she registers our bruises, probably assuming the worst. Julio kicks up a misty wind, and she retreats under her jacket. His voice is a low rumble once she's gone. "Who did this to you?"

"Chronos's Guards," I say quietly. "Four of them cornered me in an alley last week."

"For Reconditioning."

I look up, not bothering to mask my surprise. The bitter look on his face suggests he's had a taste of Reconditioning before.

"Was it because of me?" he asks.

I know what he's thinking. I assumed the same thing, too, at first. There's never a sign of struggle in our death reports. Never any blood. But no one in the Control Room has ever seemed to notice.

"No," I tell him. "Not because of you."

I prod my sore cheek, hiding the humiliating rush of blood to it.

"What did you do?" he asks in a strangled voice.

I don't know how to answer that without making it sound even worse than it was.

"Jesus, Fleur. Did you—?"

"No! And it's none of your business if I did!" I rip a dandelion from the ground. It's no one's business who I kiss, or who I want to be alone with. And it's definitely no one's business who I fall in love with, if that's even what it is.

"I was going to ask if you stopped to think about how close you are to the red line!"

"Thank you!" Poppy exclaims in my ear. "I'm glad at least one of you is being sensible."

"Calm down," I whisper as the last of the tourists give in to the shifting weather. "You're making a scene."

"Only because I care about you."

A faint string of profanities streams from Julio's transmitter. His Handler, Marie, has zero patience for our annual chats. She hates me, and I can't say I blame her. She and Poppy are the ones stuck covering for us after conversations like this—destroying feeds, editing surveillance photos, fudging reports . . .

I try to wipe away a tear before Julio sees it, but my reflexes are slow.

He pulls me to his side, careful not to touch my skin. I want to take comfort in it—to bask in a touch that doesn't hurt for a change—but this close, I hear every muffled reprimand Marie shouts in his ear, echoing all of Doug's warnings.

Julio ignores her. "What do you say?" He squeezes my shoulder gingerly, as if he knows where all my bruises are. "You've got at least a month left in you, and your rankings are probably in the toilet. Let's drag out the hunt like old times. We'll make it long and bloody! I'll even give you a head start."

"Fighting is stupid," I mutter into his jacket.

"So is slipping below the red line," he whispers against my hair. "You're better than that."

I sniffle and exhale a shaky sigh. The thunder's gone quiet and the hostile winds have calmed. The last of the fallen blossoms drift limply to the shore. The river basin is full of them. Peak was a few weeks ago, when people came from all over the world to admire them, but now the pale pink petals are brown at the edges, clumped on the ground in exhausted wet piles. I don't have the heart to tell Julio I've already slipped below the Purge line. If Marie's aware, she's smart enough to keep it to herself. If Julio knew, he'd disappear and drag out my death for weeks, making me work like hell to find him. He'd sacrifice his own rankings in some futile attempt to save mine, but I don't have the strength to hang on long enough to fight with him.

A bumblebee alights on a clover blossom beside us, and I tear my head from Julio's shoulder. I watch it, wary of how long it's been hovering around our conversation.

"Damned snitches," Julio mutters. With a casual wave of his hand, he gathers a swirl of mist from the air. It coalesces into a floating bullet of water and hovers in front of his pointed index finger. With one eye closed, he takes aim at Gaia's spy, pulling an imaginary trigger and squirting the bee off its perch. Julio's grin is smug as the bee zips away. But I worry about how much the bee saw and if Julio will be the one to pay for it.

"What's wrong?" Poppy asks. She's been paranoid and clingy since Doug reconnected my transmitter and she got a glimpse of my face in my hotel room mirror.

"Nothing. Just a bee," I tell her. "It's gone."

"You should get out of there, Fleur. A commuter bus just stopped at the corner behind you. If you're fast, you can make it before the doors close." Julio glances over his shoulder at the bus, too. Marie's probably suggesting he push me in front of it.

Poppy's right. Gaia's spies are close, and I should at least make a good show of it for Julio's sake. But I don't want to.

I rest my cheek in my hand. "What do you want?" I ask, looking sideways at Julio.

"I want you to buy me a box of Jujyfruits and take me to the new Tarantino movie."

"Not now. I mean, what do you want to do with your life, more than anything in the world?"

"More than anything?" He scrunches up his nose, as if I'm asking a trick question. He stares out across the water, thinking. Nostalgia touches the sun-kissed creases around his eyes when he finally answers. "I just want to catch one big wave, one more time. East Coast swells in the summer are nothing compared to the winters back home."

"So what are you doing hanging out here with me?"

His knee knocks gently into mine, and the sun peeks through a cloud to warm me. "Saving your life, one double feature at a time."

I laugh, my first time in months. It feels good, even if it stretches the split in my lip and makes my bruised ribs ache. "I'm serious."

"I am, too. Someone has to keep you above the red line. You're doing a lousy job of it."

"So put me out of my misery and send me home now. It'll be good for your ranking. You could earn a relocation to California." The answer to Julio's longing seems so obvious. I'm an easy target.

He looks at me like I'm nuts. "I blew any shot of that a long time ago."

"How?" I rest my chin on my knee, my curiosity piqued by his reluctance to tell me. After a moment, he shrugs.

"Ditched my transmitter inside the territory boundary and started walking. It was June of ninety-one." I do the math in my head. That was the year before I met him. "Figured if I hitchhiked, I could make it to the West Coast in three days and have a couple of months to surf before . . ." His voice trails off, his sea-foam eyes becoming glassy and distant. "Doesn't matter," he says with a shake of his head. "I made it less than ten miles into West Virginia before Gaia found me. There's no way she'll let me go home."

Julio was lucky. Stepping one foot outside our assigned regions is grounds for Termination. And my heart hurts knowing that was probably the outcome he'd been hoping for. He pulls me closer to his side and rubs some warmth into my shoulder. "It's not so terrible here. I like hanging out with you."

Julio swears as another string of profanities screeches into his transmitter. He stifles Marie with a finger. "One thing's for sure," he says, fishing a piece of gum from his pocket and popping it into his mouth. He chews it hard. "If I ever do make it home, it'll be on my own terms. And I'm not wearing a goddamn transmitter when I go." He pulls the pink wad from his mouth and mashes half of it around the microphone in his ear. The other half, he mashes around mine. The resulting silence sets off warning bells in my head.

"Relax," he says at the flash of fear he must read on my face. "Your transmitter's still on. We're not technically breaking any rules."

I prod my sore cheekbone, searching for Gaia's bumblebee spies in the grass. Our disparate magic, our conditioning, our segregated campus with its mantraps and cameras and Guards, and Chronos's rules . . . It's all working to keep us apart. And yet here we are, sitting close enough to touch through our clothes, muting our transmitters and confessing our secrets anyway.

"Why us?" I ask, letting myself huddle into the warmth of his side.

"What do you mean?"

"Why do we get along?"

"Weren't you the one who just said fighting is stupid?"

"Yes, but it feels like more than that."

Julio bites the wistful smile tugging on his lip. "Do you remember the night I caught you puking your guts out in the bathroom of that bar in Fells Point?"

I cringe. That was 1997, the year I realized I was falling for Jack. Numbing myself with frozen daiquiris had seemed like a good idea at the time. "It was nice of you to hold my hair back instead of drowning me in the toilet."

"As far as I could tell, you were doing a fine job of killing yourself."

My memory of that night is hazy at best. It felt like I sat on that cold tile floor, talking to Julio, for hours. When I was finally empty, he picked me up and carried me out of the bar. I was sure he'd kill me in the alley out back and I'd wake up in stasis three months later. Instead, I woke up the next morning, tucked into bed in my hotel room, hungover and still wearing my clothes.

"It's hard to want to kill someone once they've saved your life," he says solemnly.

"I never saved yours."

"You'd be surprised."

My thoughts rush back to the mountaintop with Jack. How we each foolishly turned off our transmitters without realizing the other had too, both of us hungry for a moment of privacy—a safe place to be vulnerable. Something happened in those moments when he lay dying in my arms. When we touched. When it was only the two of us.

I muster the courage to ask Julio the question that's been eating at me for weeks. "At the end of your season, do you ever . . . feel something strange?"

"Like what?"

"I don't know," I say, struggling to find the words to describe it. "Like a weird surge that kind of leaves you weak when Amber touches you?"

"All the time." He wags his eyebrows suggestively. Then wrinkles his nose at the absurdity of the question. It's normal for him. He's the waning Season in September when Amber finds him. She's *supposed* to drain his strength when they touch, same as I drained Jack's in the moments after I stabbed him. His power passed into me, then through me like an electric current. That first touch hurt him, weakened him, the same as Julio's would weaken me now if we weren't being so careful.

"When I touch Jack, *I* shouldn't feel weak, but that's sort of what happened when I held him," I confess, careful to leave out the part about our transmitters being off. If he knew I'd been so careless, I'd never hear the end of it.

Julio heaves a sigh. It feels like he's passing judgment. "You've got it bad for him, don't you?"

"You would know." I shrug out from under his arm as he gapes at me.

"What's that supposed to mean?"

"Don't look at me like that. I'm not an idiot." His face gives him away. His confident facade crumbles every time he hears Amber Chase's name. "Does Amber know you're in love with her?"

The tips of his ears turn red, and he jams his hands into his pockets. I recognize evasive maneuvers when I see them. "Does it matter? I'm pretty sure she hates me."

"Maybe she just feels guilty and doesn't know how to say it."

"Or maybe she just *likes* stabbing me in the back."

I pick at the grass, slipping just enough of my consciousness into each blade to feel the tear inside my chest. Is that how Jack feels about me? Does he wonder if I hate him? *Will* I hate him next time I see him? Will I ever be able to look at him without picturing a Guard's face?

I have one spring left to save myself. I'll have to be brutal when I wake. I'll have to fight Jack while he's still strong and kill him without hesitation. If I show him any mercy, it's the end for me. If I ever want to see him again, I'll have to push him away. I'll have to do things that will make him hate me.

"You've been through it before, haven't you?" I ask. "Reconditioning?" The clenched muscle in Julio's jaw tells me everything I need to know. Julio's got almost ten years on me. Amber has nearly twenty on him. They've been hurting each other since 1989, when Amber was reassigned here. "Does it ever get easier?"

A shadow passes behind his eyes. His forehead creases. "No. It never gets easier."

The bus behind us pulls away, leaving a cloud of exhaust.

I sit up, my broken ribs protesting, wishing I could savor one last deep breath of fresh air, but it's time. I hold out my hand, ready to go.

Julio swears quietly, withdrawing a vial from his pocket. He takes out the cork, reluctant to give it to me.

I lean in to take it from him. The clear liquid inside smells sweet and deadly. At the last moment, he holds it just out of reach.

"It'd be more fun just to kiss you," he says, his face close as he pries the gum off his transmitter. Then mine. He raises one eyebrow, dragging a weary smile out of me.

"Not on your life." I reach for the vial again, but something in his eyes makes me stop.

"Promise me," he says with an earnestness that dissolves my smile. "Promise me you'll save yourself, no matter how you feel about him. Promise me you'll fight." Julio ransoms my death, as if I have any choice. As if anything I do matters.

"I promise." I take the vial, checking to make sure Poppy's tuned in and no one's watching before raising the poison to my lips. I feel Julio's arm reach around me to catch me as I drop. And then, blissfully, I feel nothing at all.

5

LIONS AND SMAZES

JACK

I'm eight days out of the chamber, a full week shy of Gaia's guidelines for safe post-stasis reentry into the training program. No trips to the gym, no solid foods. I'm supposed to be recovering in my room, sucking my lunch through a straw like a post-op patient, but my growling stomach's ready to tear through the walls and eat Gaia's damn rule book.

Chill left for the cafeteria twenty minutes ago. As the door swung shut, food smells wafted in from the Winter mess hall, and I haven't been able to think straight since. The faux window behind the sofa is illuminated to an obnoxiously bright midday setting, and I mindlessly flip the channels on the remote, searching for a landscape that doesn't remind me of Fleur. The screen on the other side of the window frame flashes between snow-capped pines and frost-covered creeks. A phantom pain aches beneath my left rib and I flip past them, settling on a recorded loop of children sledding in Greenwich Park.

I adjust the thermostat on the remote, dropping the temperature in the room until rime builds on the vents and the metal starts to crackle. Then I bury myself under a comforter on our sagging, worn-out sofa, and stare a hole through the drop-tile ceiling. Greenwich Park feels like a world away, not an elevator ride above me through thirty stories of tightly packed earth and stone. Below me is a dead-end labyrinth of tunnels and catacombs. Even if I could find a way out, where the hell would I go? My life outside these walls was designed to last exactly one season. Maybe I could survive long enough to make it someplace perpetually cold. But what's the point? I'd be stuck somewhere in outer Siberia, alone, hiding from Chronos and his goons, waiting for them to sniff me out. Without a transmitter, without some leash to a stasis chamber where I could recharge my magical batteries, I'd be doomed. Fleur's right. We can look for a way out of this place all we want, but every exit leads to the same end.

I throw an arm over my face, the hunger headache gnawing at my mind and making me irritable. When I can't take it anymore, I shove off the comforter and drag myself up, rubbing the stasis hangover from my eyes and waiting for the room to steady.

I need air. And food.

I slip on a pair of shoes and poke my head outside our dorm room. I don't make it two steps into the hall before the first smaze finds me. The dark gray mist trickles like smoke through the vent in the wall. Gathering itself into a churning cloud, it tumbles to the floor and ghosts along behind me. I kick it, muttering at it to get lost, momentarily scattering it. But the persistent little shit only reforms, hanging back a cautious distance this time.

I hate smazes, almost as much as I hate the bees and flies and crows that seem to lurk around every corner down here. We've all heard the stories of what happens when Seasons are Purged, how Gaia reclaims our magic—magic that's bonded to our human souls. She sucks it out of our empty husks. Breathes it into some other pathetic creature, doomed to become her pet. Our magic, memories, and souls belong to her, even in permanent death. Terminated Springs become the bees that spy on us from hives in the dormitory walls. Autumns get stuffed into the bodies of crows. The fate of the Summers is enough to make me shudder. Possessing the fat black flies that haunt the kitchens, they're like maggots clinging to a corpse. But the smazes—the cold, restless ghosts of purged Winters—are creepiest of all.

I glance over my shoulder, unsurprised to see the little gray cloud still following me. Probably the same relentless shadow that's always on my heels, as if it's waiting for me to do something stupid. And why shouldn't it? If it is the same one, it's caught me plenty of times before.

When I push open the cafeteria doors, the smaze tumbles off and disappears into an air duct. I can't say I blame it. A barrage of conversations in dozens of languages echoes off the metal benches and cinder-block walls. The fluorescent bulbs chafe against my stasis-sick eyes and I wince, struggling to take it all in. My reflexes are slow, and I duck a second too late. A snowball hurtles into my shoulder, ice spraying my face.

"Jack! You're awake!" Gabriel drawls. The Louisiana Winter dusts snow from his hands. As if one snowball wasn't enough to get my attention, he begins conjuring another, freezing the humidified air as it falls from the vents in the ceiling. A cafeteria attendant in a hairnet hollers at him, threatening to make him mop up his own mess. A rowdy knot of Southern Winters at the back of the room laughs her off, until a Guard stops chewing and looks over at their table. The group falls suddenly quiet, the snow forgotten.

The Guards are no better than the smazes. The only reason they eat in our cafeteria and sleep in our dorms is to keep an eye on the rest of us. The Winters settle, waiting for the Guard to lose interest. When he finally returns his attention to his meal, Yukio waves me over to their table.

I acknowledge them with a half-hearted wave and keep walking. I wouldn't call them friends. Not really. They're just the people I hang out with while our time here overlaps—Winters from similar climate zones in the same part of the world. Gabriel, Yukio, and the others . . . they're all okay on the surface. Not much different from the boys I knew back in juvie boarding school. As much as we pretend to be on the same team, almost anyone in this room would kill the Winter sitting across from him if a Relocation—or Termination—came down to "him or me."

The tables on both sides of the aisle are full of Handlers, but Chill's easy to spot, surrounded by a clique of high-ranking Handlers, too busy regaling his friends with a new, improved story of my most recent death to notice me as I walk by. The story's bloodier than I remember it, smoothly molding itself to fit the story he and Poppy put in their reports. I fight down a wave of nausea as I grab a tray and head for the lunch line.

The usual gossip swirls around me, and I do my best to tune it out.

Rankings . . . Days up top . . . Top ten . . . Relocation . . .

I slide my tray over the counter in front of the steam table, scrutinizing my options through the condensing fog. Grilled summer vegetables, sautéed winter vegetables, baked root vegetables . . . Gaia's vegan menus are a carnivore's nightmare. I'd stab someone for a bacon double cheese-burger right now, and I regret not hitting a Burger King one last time before Fleur found me.

"Welcome home, Jack," Holly says through the steam. The word *home* grates, but I force myself to smile back anyway. It's hard watching Holly age down here. The more powerful the Season, the slower we're supposed to age when we retire, but it feels like a pretty shitty reward. Holly must not have been a Season for very long. Every year she spends in retirement, there are a few more wrinkles around her eyes and wiry gray hairs on her head. She smells like menthol. I can't tell if it's her arthritis cream or the scent of old Winter magic clinging to her long-retired bones. There's an old black-and-white photo of Holly in a trophy case in the Winter training center down the hall. She was a knock-out back then—seventeen, with full lips, a sparkle in her eyes, and glossy blond hair styled in switchback waves so tight you could almost ski down them. The photo was taken in 1969, the year Holly retired from her region in Michigan to work here—the same year Amber arrived—a fact that's hard to reconcile as Holly's age-spotted hands set a bowl of clear broth on my tray.

I frown at it. "Seriously, Holly?"

The loose folds of skin under her neck wobble as she shakes her head at me. "You know the rules. Hospital diet restrictions for two weeks after waking."

I look past Holly to the other attendants, hoping one of them won't know me. But I've been in this place too fucking long.

I lean over the steam table and lower my voice to a whisper. "Come on, Holly. You're killing me."

The tight wrinkles around her lips soften. "It'll be our secret," she says, sliding a handful of saltine packets onto my tray before shooing me along. "Now go on. You're holding up the line."

As I lift my tray, a set of doors swings open behind her. Boreas, the Winter food services manager, pushes his way through, his dolly loaded down with empty vegetable crates that mask all the contraband he sells to students on the sly. He acknowledges me with a nod. "Good to see you, Jack. Need anything?"

Besides a shovel to dig my way out of this place? "Nothing I can think of," I tell him.

"Let Chill know his stuff came in. I'll drop it by sometime tomorrow." Boreas backs through another set of double doors, dragging his dolly behind him.

This. This is what Chill and I have to look forward to after a few decades of promotions—a glamorous retirement from our lives of magic and violence. Our golden mortal years will be spent in mundane service to Gaia and Chronos, smuggling beef jerky and weed down the service elevators for petty cash, like Boreas and his kitchen crew.

Appetite gone, I carry my tray into the dining room, right into Doug Lausks and his damn patch. It's embroidered with his rank, and I can't help but wonder how many Seasons he must have shit on to get promoted so fast. His cold blue eyes lock on mine, old vendettas shimmering like steel inside them.

Noelle was right. He's never going to let me live this down.

Noelle Eastman and I were just sparring partners. That's all. I never should have agreed to take her back to her room after her argument with Doug. But she was upset, and it seemed like the right thing to do. I could blame what happened next on the bottle of smuggled peppermint schnapps we shared, but that would be a lie. I was depressed and lonely, and when she leaned in to kiss me, I let her. And I've felt shitty about it since.

Head down, I veer around him. His best friend, Denver, steps right in my path, knocking into my tray. The contents go flying, glass and silverware skittering brilliantly over the tiled floor. Every Handler and Winter in the room cranes their necks to see what's happened. Chill turns lazily toward the commotion and his smile dissolves.

"Look who's back." Doug kicks a pack of crackers off the toe of his boot. "Barely out of the chamber and you're already starting trouble."

I throw a pointed look at the healing break in his nose. "Apparently I'm not the only one."

Doug massages the knot in the cartilage. The yellow-green bruise that straddles it matches the one circling Denver's left eye. Glass crackles under Doug's boots as he encroaches into my personal space. "It's a great story, Sommers. You should hear it."

I take a step back. "I don't want any trouble."

"Too late." The knuckles of his left hand pop softly at his side. I watch it warily, half expecting him to throw a punch at me. "Gaia wants to see you in her office. Now. Your Handler, too." His lip twitches at my shocked silence. Denver hauls Chill up by the back of his shirt and ushers him roughly toward the hall. The fear in Chill's eyes as he and Denver march past is enough to gut me.

Doug gives them a head start toward the Crux before shoving me through the double doors after them. As soon as the doors swing closed behind us, he starts into me.

"I had an enlightening conversation with your girlfriend, Sommers."

"I've told you a hundred times, Noelle and I—"

He turns on his heel and grabs me by the collar. "Don't you even utter her name."

"For Chronos's sake, Doug! We're just friends."

"I was talking about Fleur." He lets me go with a shove.

Fleur's name is a punch to the throat. I have to force myself to keep walking. To keep my voice steady as we resume our slow march to the Crux. "Somebody gave you bad information, Lausks. Last time I saw Fleur, she dragged me over a mountain and put a knife in my spleen."

"You sure about that? Because I'm betting the only bad information the Control Room's getting is coming from your Handlers' reports."

I rein in my temper, acutely aware of the smaze weaving in and out between my ankles. "There's nothing going on between me and Fleur."

"Funny, she said the same thing at first. But Reconditioning has a way of dragging the truth out of a Season." His bruised knuckles crack quietly in the space between us as that single word ricochets through my head. They put Fleur through Reconditioning. They let Doug torture her because of me. And when she wakes up, she'll hate me for it. She'll hate everything about me.

Doug shakes his head. "I wasn't sure at first. She was hell-bent on protecting you. Elusive when we asked about her transmitter. Evasive when we asked about yours." He watches me, hungry for a reaction, but I refuse to give him one more reason to be suspicious of her. "What the hell is it about you that inspires such loyalty, Sommers? I mean, the memorials she carves in those trees . . ." His forehead wrinkles with disgust. "You'd think she was actually in love with you."

The words cut clean through me, so deep I can barely breathe. "Doesn't mean anything," I say through clenched teeth. "They're just hash marks. Trophies." But his smug smile says he knows exactly what they are. It feels like he's intruded on a secret, something sacred between me and Fleur. Like he's intercepted a private letter and read it out loud, and suddenly I want to kill him for it.

"Maybe. I can't tell if she's crazy about you or just punishing herself. Either way, she has an impressive tolerance for pain." He leans close as if he's about to confess a secret. "She's tougher than she looks. It took me hours to break her."

My vision glazes with frost. I land a single punch to the side of Doug's jaw before he grabs me by my collar and returns it threefold. Denver takes me in a chokehold from behind. With a rush of heat, Doug conjures a flame. It writhes in his palm and I wrench away from it, straining against Denver's grip as the fire inches closer.

"Mr. Lausks." We all go still at the familiar stern voice behind Doug. Professor Lyon.

Doug's flame gutters. He cusses under his breath, but I've never been so relieved to see anyone in all my lives.

"You and your colleague are dismissed," the professor says. "I'll escort Mr. Sommers and his Handler from here." Chill shrinks behind Professor Lyon's back.

Doug's breath is hot on my face. He clenches a fist, his body wound tight. "Back off, old man. This doesn't concern you."

Chill stiffens, his eyes wide in the empty frames of his glasses. Daniel Lyon may be retired, but the legendary Lion of Winter held the coldest region in the world for three hundred years, and his name commands respect here.

"'Old man'?" Professor Lyon parrots back, a hint of disdain in his smile. "You assume I'm frail? That I keep my teeth in a jar beside my bed?" The professor's arctic blue eyes darken as he leans close to Doug's ear. "I've far sharper weapons than teeth in my head, Mr. Lausks. Be careful how you bait me."

Denver releases my neck. I sag, struggling to catch my breath.

Doug's nostrils flare, his mouth twitching as he utters a warning. "Next time Fleur sees you, you'd better hope she buries you." He gives me a last shove, the palm of his hand still searing hot from the fire. "Stay in your lane, Sommers. And stay away from my girl."

Doug backs away, reluctant to tear his gaze from mine as Denver takes him by the shoulder and steers him back to the cafeteria. When he's gone, I lean over my knees, rubbing the burn where he pushed me. Professor Lyon's dress shoes appear close beside me.

"Thanks," I manage, still starved for air.

Lyon adjusts his cuffs without looking at me. "Follow me, both of you. You're wanted in the Control Room."

No sympathy. No lectures or his usual reassurances. Lyon sets off toward the Crux without another word.

They know. They know what happened on the mountain. They think we're in love. That we're hiding something. They've already punished Fleur for it.

A cold dread settles deep in my bones at the thought of what awaits us.

6

ASH TO ASH

JACK

The smaze hugs Professor Lyon's heels as they click briskly down the hallway to the Crux. The campus is divided into four cardinal wings: Winter to the north, Summer to the south, Spring to the east, and Autumn to the west, the segregated living spaces radiating from the center of campus like the spokes of a wheel. The Crux lies at its heart. The circular corridor is divided by a series of controlled checkpoints, designed to restrict access between the wings and regulate passage to the administration floors below.

"What do you think they want?" Chill whispers as we pass the Guards stationed at the end of the wing.

"I don't know." The lie comes far easier than the truth.

Professor Lyon waves a key card over the scanner. The light beside the plexiglass divider blinks green, and the pneumatic door to the Crux slides open for him. The rush of temperate air that greets us fogs the professor's glasses. He peels them off, wiping the thick lenses with a handkerchief he draws from the breast pocket of his blazer as we wait for the elevator. The Crux is dense with the discordant smells of the other wings. Through the clear barrier to my left, I can just make out the entrance to the Spring wing, the view inside obscured by tendrils of creeping ivy that grow from giant pots beside the gates. Fleur sleeps somewhere on the other side of them. I rub my swollen lip, my jaw already sore where Doug clocked me. Our entire scuffle lasted no more than a few seconds. But Fleur . . .

Hours, Doug said. It took him hours to break her.

"Clean yourself up, Mr. Sommers." I tear my attention from Fleur's wing. The professor holds out his handkerchief without meeting my eyes as we file into the elevator. I take the cloth, pressing it to my split lip, unsettled by Lyon's tone. By the simple fact that he won't look at me.

He calls me Mr. Sommers whenever I'm teetering on the edge of doing something I shouldn't be. He's always been amused by my choice of surname. We're expected to take a name reflective of our season, entrenching us in our new identity like some crappy cell-block tattoo. The fact that I chose a name that flies in the face of Gaia's expectations of me is a constant source of curiosity for him. "A rebel," he called me during my first year here, when he'd caught me picking the old iron padlocks to the catacombs under the school. He's always looked me in the eyes, smiled even, when he's caught me doing something stupid. And he's never once submitted me for disciplinary review.

At least, until now.

I tuck the stained handkerchief into my pocket as the mirrored elevator doors open. The high-ceilinged corridor on the other side is awash

74

in artificial light. Chill's head tips back, wonder parting his lips as he takes in the domed sapphire ceiling swirling with iridescent stars. He pauses at every sculpture, every mosaic. Chill's worked decades for the chance to walk these polished marble halls, eager to be Culled for a promotion. The walls of his room are still plastered in the same posters he hung up in the late 1980s when we first got here, glossy romanticized landscapes of the most coveted winter regions—the Canadian Rockies, the skyline of Toronto, the northern lights over Fairbanks, Alaska— places he'll never see. As long as I've known him, he's been moved by some intrinsic desire to be the best at something. To be respected by his peers. And then I turn my damn transmitter off to be alone with a girl and manage to screw up everything.

Lyon gently nudges me along, just like he did thirty years ago on the day I first arrived here. The gallery to the Control Room is warm, just as I remember it, but it still manages to make me shudder. The same portraits line the walls. Father Time, wielding a scythe, dragging his child into the air by an ankle. Then Time, clipping Cupid's wings. I drop my gaze and stare at the floor until we've passed the worst of them—a Baroque of the Titan Cronos, similar only in name (and probably temperament), tearing into his own child's heart with his teeth.

There are no portraits of Chronos's late wife, Ananke. No sculptures of his daughter, Gaia. It's as if Chronos only shows off the mythology that suits him. Here, Time rules everything.

The only exception is the fresco that trails over the arched ceiling high above our heads. The painted story of our history spans the entire length of the gallery. Chronos and the Staff of Time loom above us as we walk, Ananke's slitted diamond eyes following our procession to the

Control Room. As the legend goes, in the beginning, there were Chronos and Ananke—Time and Inevitability. Their arms encircled and controlled Chaos, an empty expanse containing only matter and energy, and from it Gaia was born. Her image materializes at the end of the corridor, with silver hair and glittering eyes, carrying air, water, wind, and fire from the blackness. And from those four elements, she made us, the Seasons.

Chronos likes to tell us our magic comes from a place of chaos. That, just like our mother, we're dangerous and unpredictable. He's convinced we'll find balance only under his thumb . . . or, more accurately, his scythe. Given Gaia's silence on the matter, I'm guessing she doesn't have a problem either way.

An arbor of ancient figs frames the end of the gallery. A fountain gurgles on the other side, the water trickling down a rough stone wall, through a winding runnel of river rock embedded in the marble floor. Chill tiptoes over it, his head tipped toward the conjured smells of holly berries and evergreens wafting through the vents.

Our reflections move like ghosts past Gaia's menageries, past bees, flies, and birds in ornate cages and fancy terrariums, their artificial habitats enclosed behind thick walls of glass. A crow tips its head, tracking us from its perch. Chill's too enchanted by the gleaming quartz winking at him from the walls and the elaborate bronze torchères to notice.

I walked this corridor once before with that same wide-eyed wonder, just as naive and eager. Entranced by the magic, high on Gaia's attention, drunk on my power to control wind, to make snow, to escape my own death . . . Until the Control Room doors closed behind me, and I realized how powerless I was.

I fight the urge to pull Chill back by his collar as he approaches the Control Room, unable to shake the feeling that I'm marching headlong into something I can never come back from.

Professor Lyon whispers to the waiting attendant. She holds her tablet against her high-necked blouse and presses a finger to her lips, warning us to remain silent before escorting us through the arched iron-wood doors and directing us to wait at the back of the room.

Gaia's office is laid out exactly as I remember it, disturbingly reminiscent of a courtroom, with high-beamed ceilings and mahogany pews. The walls behind the smooth plaster and polished wood paneling are the same sandstone and clay of the catacombs below us, and under the tangled smells of the handful of Seasons already seated in the wooden benches, I can almost smell the fetor of death seeping up through the cold stone floor.

The only sounds in the room are soft whispers from a handful of girls seated in the front row and the clack of computer keys from a line of workstations behind Gaia's desk. Chronos's Control Room stands out starkly against the rich woods and antique bronze torchères of Gaia's chamber, as if he built it in the narrow space behind her head to remind her just how easy it is to look over her shoulder. Flickering light emanates from a wall of sleek flat-screen TVs behind her. News tickers roll over them in a dozen languages, below satellite images and weather maps. Digital clocks mark the time zones around the world to the millisecond, and our rankings scroll like the arrivals and departures boards in an airport terminal on the final screen. Below them, a dozen Guards sit before a row of computers, monitoring feeds from all ends of the globe and every corner of the Observatory, their hard drives and fans creating a white-noise hum.

"What's happening?" Chill whispers. "What are we doing here?"

"I don't know."

"What do you think they're doing here?" he asks, jerking his chin toward the girls in the front pew. I draw a shallow breath. One Spring, one Summer, and their Handlers, judging by the smell of them. The pairs sit slightly apart, exchanging harsh whispers with each other.

"I don't know."

Gaia leans against her desk, her back to the screens, watching a tar-gray smaze thrash inside a decorative glass orb at the center of it. It reminds me of the fighting fish I've seen lined up in tiny bowls in pet store windows, their heads beating against the glass, fighting to get out. Fighting to get to each other.

I try not to stare at it. Or at her. Gaia's platinum hair falls in iridescent waves over her shoulders. The same shimmering color as her eyes, it doesn't give a clue to her age, a number none of us know and wouldn't have the balls to ask.

I start at the rap of Chronos's staff against the floor. The pointed heel of its slender handle stabs at the stone and its crystal eye seems to watch us from its mounting at the top. The curved blade of the scythe swings with his purposeful strides. Every whisper quiets as he slices down the aisle with two of his Guards. Noelle Eastman is one of them. Her eyes flick to mine and my stomach drops as she assumes a sentry's position beside him. He dismisses the Guards seated at the computers in the Control Room. I glance over my shoulder as they file out, searching for Professor Lyon. But when the doors close, the room is empty of everyone but me and Chill and the girls in the front pew.

Chronos flicks dust from the lapel of his suit. His silver beard is perfectly trimmed, his wavy hair impeccably styled over one cold blue eye. A simple black patch covers what is rumored to be an empty socket—the eye supposedly clawed out by Ananke, the patch not entirely concealing the scars she left behind.

Chronos summons the girls in the front pew to the dais. His scythe catches the light, the crystal eye above it casting rainbows over the floor. The girls go rigid as the colors turn to images. Chronos's frown deepens as he studies them. "Your choices of late have been questionable," he tells Gaia, pulling her attention from the orb on her desk. "Chaos has no place here. Nor do willful children. Am I understood?"

She nods tightly, her jaw clenched as he takes the remote control from her desk and switches off the screens behind her. All but one.

Prerecorded footage of a storm plays in a muted loop. The cyclone is a monster, uprooting trees and ripping off roofs, washing away cars and submerging towns along the coast of northern Australia. A death toll of more than one hundred thirty-seven people . . . I turn away, the images hard to watch.

"I'll have an answer for this," Chronos demands.

When the silence drags on too long, he catches the Spring around her neck by his scythe, pulling her gently toward him. "Well?"

She swallows hard, careful not to make any sudden movements. "The sea . . . it was too warm. I didn't know—"

Chronos casts her away from him with a careless jerk. "You are a Season. It is your job to know."

"I'm new!" The Spring touches the paper-thin cut along her neck, surprised when her fingers come away red. She gestures roughly to the Summer beside her. "Kai's strong! She's been here longer."

The Summer remains silent. She stands at attention, pale and shaking with stasis tremors, her hair damp with sweat where it brushes her collar. She's from the southern hemisphere, probably just waking up, so fresh out of the chamber, I'm surprised she hasn't puked on Chronos's shoes. He surveys her high chin and her fierce stance.

"What is your name, child?" he asks her.

"Kai Sampson, Father."

Chronos angles his staff to the light, his brow wrinkling over the images projected on the floor.

"A curious choice in placement." He smooths the edges of his beard, his eye casting suspicious glances at Gaia as he rotates the crystal counterclockwise. "Why hasn't the Summer earned a region better suited to her talents?"

"It was a short-term placement. We had a void," Gaia says quietly.

Chronos tips his head, changing the direction of the staff's turn a few degrees clockwise. He pauses, his gaze skipping first to Kai Sampson, then to the back of the room. To me.

His blue eye pierces me, holding me helpless in its stare. His cheek twitches below his patch, and I let out a held breath when he finally tears his gaze away from me. He covers that side of his face, concealing the spasm under his hand. "See that Kai is enrolled for training with my personal Guard," he orders Gaia. "She will report directly to Captain Lausks. Ms. Sampson and her Handler are free to go."

Kai and her Handler rush from the room, the sweet smell of desert flowers swirling in their wake. The Spring turns to watch her opponent go. Chronos makes a dismissive gesture toward her as he returns the remote control to Gaia's desk. "The Spring will be Terminated for her recklessness."

The Spring's head whips around. Her Handler gasps. Chill stops breathing beside me, and all the relief I felt a moment ago is suddenly ripped away.

Gaia's lips part. She takes a tentative step toward him. "Father," she pleads, "the storm was unavoidable. She's young, and Springs are uniquely sensitive by nature. It was a poor impulse, but I'm sure she meant no—"

"Don't." His snarl echoes off the walls of the Control Room—a room designed to hear and punish every whispered secret. The muscle ticks below his eye patch, and he reaches to still it. "You sound just like your mother. Ananke used to spew the same rubbish."

Gaia's nostrils flare. "Still, I do not think her offense merits Termina—"

In a flash of crystal and silver, the scythe is at Gaia's throat. The room crackles. Noelle's mouth turns down at the corners, as if she knows what's coming. As if she's seen it before.

Chronos tips Gaia's chin up with the point of the blade, forcing her eyes to his. "Have you learned nothing from her?" Gaia's upturned throat bobs as she stares into that cold blue eye, the patch, the scars . . . "Allow one child to overstep the rules, and the rest will overrun you. If you will not maintain control in my house, then you will find yourself replaced as easily as your pets." He forces her chin to the side, toward the smaze in the glass on her desk. "Your fondness for them makes you weak, has made you weak before. If you will not do what must be done, then I shall do it for you." Gaia swallows, barely breathing as he lowers the scythe. Her eyes close, not in relief, but in surrender.

The Spring stumbles backward, her fists clenched stubbornly at her sides. "But it's not fair! I followed Gaia's rules!"

Chronos turns on her, the outrage in that single eye sucking all the air from the room. Chill's hand slides closer to mine. "'Fair' would have been to let you rot in your coffin after you fell to your death, a death brought about by impulsive choices. Gaia may have granted you your wasted life, but you remain alive at my behest and are subject to *my* rules!"

Noelle stares straight ahead at the wall across the room. Gaia averts her eyes. I brace for what's coming, too slow to turn away from the flash of the scythe. The Spring screams. A red stain spreads through her pale yellow shirt. Chill's hand grabs mine as the girl's Handler cries out, falling beside her. The air around them begins to crackle and hiss, throwing sparks toward the ceiling. Their bodies shrivel, bending over double before slumping to the floor. The wind whistles through the room as if being sucked through a crack.

Then everything goes still.

Chill and I hardly breathe, paralyzed by the two small piles of ash on the floor. Chronos paces before them, as if he's impatient to be someplace else. The gray pile of dust that was the Spring's Handler doesn't move. But the ash that was a Spring a moment ago—a girl strong enough to set off a cyclone—begins to sparkle. Small glowing needles of light lift from her remains like fireflies from a field.

Gaia's hair lifts, static sparking between the strands. Her eyes shimmer with tears as she opens her mouth, drawing the girl's magic back into her with a long, shuddering breath.

The light fades in her throat. The girl's magic, gone.

Chill shivers, pungent sweat breaking out on his skin. I feel like I might be sick. Purges are always conducted behind closed doors. Few Seasons have ever witnessed Terminations, but there are stories . . . rumors . . .

My eyes dart back to the writhing smaze in the orb. I start at the sound of Chronos's timepiece snapping closed.

"I expect her replacement to be assigned within the hour." He slips the silver watch back into his pocket and turns to go, his staff swinging at his side like the arm of a metronome. Light catches the crystal, scattering beams over the floor as he cuts smoothly down the aisle with his Guards in tow.

He pauses beside my pew. His eye rakes over my face. "I've seen you before." My throat catches, unable to form words. "You are the same Winter who turned down an offer to join my Guard not long ago. The one with the ill-fitting name."

Noelle breaks protocol to look at me.

"*Sommers*, was it?" His mouth twitches at the corners. "I should have known. Should have seen it in the irreverence. The brazen audacity of that choice." His reluctant smile stretches the scars on his cheek. "But yours is a difficult future to read. Your rankings seem at odds with every possible outcome," he muses, stroking his beard. "Proceed carefully, Mr. Sommers. For a Winter, you demonstrate a rather foolish tendency to tread upon thin ice."

"Sir?" I stammer.

Chronos rotates his staff. The crystal catches the light. The beam it casts on the floor at my feet sears an image into my mind. There is no sound. No smell or pain or context. Just a glimpse of my future, flickering like a scene from a silent movie. In it, I see the Summer who was dismissed just moments ago—Kai Sampson. Her teeth are clenched, her face framed by the jagged, dark ends of her hair, one eye narrowed above the shaft of the arrow in her bow as she aims it at me.

The image flickers again, flashing to the cracked surface of a frozen lake. The ice breaks under me, plunging me under the water. Blood swirls in the bubbles around me as I sink.

Chronos's breath is cold against my ear. "Pity you have to die."

In the chill of his whisper, I hear the unspoken words. The implication. This future, this vision he's chosen to show me, reflects my final death—my Termination.

I blink, unable to move or speak as Chronos and his Guards march from the room.

Gaia bows her head over her desk. I jump when her hands smack the wood. She leans over the orb, her lips pressed thin as she watches the smaze struggle to free itself. Her shoulders rise and fall with her deep, quivering sigh, and her white gown hugs the floor, reluctant to turn with her.

"Come forward, Winter. Bring your Handler with you." Chill and I approach the dais on weak legs. Her eyes are unsettling, hard as diamonds, their clear facets blinding in their intensity as we come nearer.

My heart stops when I feel them staring at my bruises.

Chill kneels deeply. When I don't follow, he shoves an elbow into my hip.

"There's no need for formality." Gaia's voice is raspy and deep. Her hair, sparking with rage a moment ago, is limp against her shoulders. "I suppose you know why you're here."

Chill shakes his head. She levels me with a pragmatic stare. I shake my head, too.

She reaches for the intercom button on her desk. "Send Professor Lyon in."

The doors behind us open. I can't make myself look at him as

Professor Lyon crosses into my field of vision, carrying a hinged glass dome. A bumblebee hovers inside, its legs struggling for traction against the glass. Gaia steps close, her eyes catching Lyon's. He watches her with a quiet reverence as she opens the lid.

The bee buzzes feverishly, its stinger poised as Gaia reaches in. With coos and whispers she traps it, bringing her cupped hands to her lips and blowing into the space between her fingers. Her hands glow with magic—magic she took from the Spring Chronos killed.

Gaia releases the bee, but it clings to her. Docile and quiet, it bows under her touch as she strokes its furry back. With a wave of her hand, she dismisses it. The bee takes flight, but doesn't fly far, settling on the arm of Gaia's desk chair.

Lyon closes the lid. He glances down at the two piles of ash, then at me, over the cage he holds solemnly to his chest.

Pity you have to die.

Chill's eyes squeeze shut. His lips move in silent prayer.

I can't just stand here. Can't let Chill die for my mistake. My pulse quickens as I step forward. "I can explain."

"That won't be necessary. The numbers speak for themselves." Chill's eyes lift to the monitors as my rankings appear on a screen. The days I've spent eluding my own death are weighted against weather reports, human deaths from exposure and traffic fatalities, combined with my training records and behavior reports . . . all of it culminating in a final score. On the screen beside it, a red name scrolls by so fast I almost miss it—Fleur Attwell.

She's below the red line.

"Your performance over the last few years has been . . . impressive, Mr. Sommers."

Fleur. Next year, she'll be up for the Purge. My knees threaten to buckle. "I don't understand."

Did I do this? Am I responsible?

I barely register Gaia's next words as I watch Fleur's name disappear from the screen. "I realize we're still two years from the next Culling for promotions. However, one of our North American Winters has not returned from her hunt. She is, as we say, in the wind."

I turn my attention to Gaia, my racing thoughts scrambling for traction in the conversation. A Season in the wind isn't just gone. She's dead, lost forever, her matter irrevocably scattered.

Gaia smiles tightly. "I'm offering you her position." A map of Anchorage, Alaska, fills the screen.

My mouth goes dry.

"Oh hell yes," Chill whispers, all his fear from a moment ago swept away by the swell of his pride.

How? How is this possible? Doug knew about my transmitter. They know I broke the rules. It doesn't make sense that Fleur's being Purged and I'm being promoted for it.

"I've requisitioned a member of Chronos's Guard to manage the vacancy in the interim, so you'll have plenty of time to make arrangements for your Relocation. Over the next year, our Resources Team will assist your Handler with the transfer of any financial accounts you wish to move and the shipment of any personal belongings to a storage facility in Anchorage, where it will await your arrival next November. Meanwhile, you'll be working directly with Professor Lyon over the next eighteen months to prepare." The professor nods. "He knows the region well. And he knows the physical demands. You'll have longer stasis and recovery periods, longer hunting seasons, and less time to train." She darts a pointed glance at the bruises Doug gave me. "Though I see you've already been stretching the rules when it comes to training during your mandatory recovery period. I hope it's safe to assume you're up for the challenge?"

I touch the bruise on my cheek. One more year. Fleur has one more year before the Purge. I have one more year before I'm sent to Anchorage. A knot tightens in my throat. Lyon raises an eyebrow.

"Yes, Gaia," I manage in a low voice.

"Good, then it's settled. Professor Lyon will see to everything you need." Their eyes meet as she sweeps past him, close enough for their hands to brush. From the corner of his eye, Lyon watches her go. He lingers, waiting for me.

My feet are rooted to the spot, the walls closing in around me as I watch the smaze throw itself against the orb.

Gaia's assistant enters the room, carrying a broom and a dustpan. She bends to sweep the remains from the floor, then dumps them into a waste bin without ceremony.

In the cloud of dust that billows from the bin, all I see is Fleur.

Lyon touches my shoulder. I turn to find his blue eyes creased with compassion, his lips pursed, as if holding on tightly to something he desperately wants to say. "Fear not, young lion," he whispers. "Winter's crown may be heavy on your head. But you hold eternal spring in your heart."

And with a reassuring pat, he's gone.

7

LEGENDS AND FABLES

JACK

A rope of beef jerky dangles from Chill's mouth as he pulls a smuggled box of assorted contraband into his lap. "Check it out! Your new thermal scope came in."

I peer out from my blankets at the shiny new gadget Chill's unpacking. He's been like a kid at Christmas ever since our meeting with Gaia. The crate Boreas delivered to our room this morning hasn't helped.

"It's light," Chill says, weighing it in his palm. "I'll be able to mount this one on a drone. We'll see Fleur coming a mile away next spring. And Amber won't stand a chance."

The drones, the sensors, the stupid night vision goggles Chill stuffed in my luggage last year . . . none of it matters. Fleur's sleeping just in the next wing and I still can't see her, and I'll find and kill Amber with or without the crazy devices Chill buys for me. Seasons have been killing each other for eons, since before transmitters and stasis chambers even existed. Time is fixed. Death is inevitable. Everything else—the operating accounts and allowances Gaia pays, the technology Chronos commissions, the contraband Boreas smuggles in—is all just an illusion to make us feel in control.

"Where does Boreas get all this stuff, anyway?" I grumble.

Chill shrugs. "Electronics dealers, mostly. Military surplus. He charges me extra for the Twizzlers and Doritos and stuff. He has to order them from back home."

Back home. After thirty years, this place still isn't home for Chill, either. I don't have the heart to tell him that "back home" doesn't feel much like home anymore anyway. The best we can hope for is eternity here, smuggling nostalgia in cardboard boxes and coming up with slower ways to die.

"Don't let anybody catch you taking out the trash," I tell him, sucking down the vitamins he's left for me on the table beside my head.

"I won't. Boreas'll get rid of it, the same way he brought it all down." Chill spins the propellers of a new drone with the tip of his finger. "It's vegetable day. The kitchen will be chaos for the next few hours while they bring all the crates down the service elevators. No one will notice a few extra boxes coming or going."

"Lucky for you." I stare begrudgingly at the faux window. Chill reprogrammed the menu of images the same day we got our new assignment. They rotate by the hour: a cityscape of Anchorage, the railroad through Grandview Valley, the northern lights over the Chugach Mountains, and the occasional moose. I bury my head in the sofa so I won't have to look at them anymore. But every time I close my eyes, all I see is a mountain of ash. And all I hear is Doug's warning.

. . . you'd better hope she buries you.

Fleur has one season left. One chance to scramble over the red line and save herself. To do it, she'll have to outperform every other name below that line. She'll have to come at me hard and fast and end my season early—but will she? Would I stand still long enough to let her, knowing this is the last time I'll see her?

I owe her that much. More.

She stayed with me on that mountain. She held me and kept me from permanently burning out. She risked her own neck for me, and now she's going to die and I'm going to Alaska, and I'll probably never understand why. I wish there were a way out of here for both of us. I wish I could stuff her in a vegetable crate and wheel her out of this place without anybody noticing. Without killing us both.

"Did you unplug my battery charger?" There's an exasperated edge to Chill's voice. It's the one he reserves for me when I've done something wrong, or when he's assembling toys with too many parts.

I draw the blanket back from my face to find Chill frowning at the drone's remote. He pops open the battery compartment. Even from here, I can see the connections are backward. "Try turning them around, Einstein."

Chill shakes them onto the floor. One by one, he loads the four batteries back into the compartment, careful to line up the connectors this time—positive to negative, negative to positive. When the last battery slides into place, the drone lights up.

Chill sets the drone down on the lid of my stasis chamber and fires up the propellers, turning my human-sized battery charger into a launching pad for his new toy. I guess things could be worse. Before the invention of the stasis chamber, Seasons were disposable, designed for one-time use. They fought until they expired or died in battle. But thanks (or no thanks) to modern technology, I get to come back and screw things up with Fleur over and over again.

Over and over again.

Like Chill's batteries . . .

Chill drags his attention from his instruction manual as I cast off my blankets and slowly pull myself upright. "You feeling okay, Jack? You look pale."

Seasons have been killing each other for eons . . .

I barely hear Chill's question over the nagging hum of my own thoughts. If Seasons have always been disposable, how is it possible that we can be recharged? You can't stick a disposable battery in a charger; they're not designed to work that way. I tried once. It leaked chemicals everywhere and nearly started a fire. So how is it that dead Seasons can be stuffed inside a stasis chamber and come out alive?

Biology hasn't changed since before the chambers were invented. Neither has physics, or even magic. Only the technology is different. So if we really were disposable before, how is it possible that our deaths are reversible now?

I scrub a hand over my face, wrestling with the logic. What if I've been thinking about this all wrong? What if Seasons were never disposable in the first place? Nature is cyclical. Patterns repeat themselves. Shouldn't it be inherent in our basic design for our life cycle to end and then start over again?

My thoughts race as I stumble past Chill into our bunk room to change. "I'm going to the gym."

"The gym?" he calls after me. "You just came out of stasis a week ago."

"Ten days," I say through my sweatshirt as I drag it over my head. "You're supposed to wait another four!"

Until we're strong enough to train without risking a setback.

Until we're fully recharged . . .

I pull on a pair of bright white sneakers. "Low impact. Back soon. I promise," I tell him as I rush out the door.

I lied. I'm not going to the gym. But if I had told Chill where I'm really going, he'd have had a total meltdown. There's only one way down to the Hall of Records, and that's the elevator in the Crux.

Hood drawn low, I cut through a hall of darkened faculty offices, avoiding the recreation room and training center where most of the Winters congregate on weekends. It's Sunday. The Winter lecture halls are locked, the corridors empty. Motion sensors activate the overhead lights. They flicker to life in rapid succession, turning off again behind me as I move through the halls. Still, I have the niggling sense I'm not alone.

I peek over my shoulder. A smaze hovers behind. I swat at it but it slips like smoke through my fingers. Dropping low, it weaves in and out around my legs.

"Get lost!" I hiss, giving it a sharp but useless kick. It slips into an air duct, and I wait to make sure it's completely gone before I move any closer to the end of the wing. The punishment for being caught on the wrong side of the glass at the end of this hall isn't something I really want to think about.

I pause at a covered electrical panel in the wall, searching inside it for the switch that controls the motion sensors in the lights. I press a fingertip to the breaker. Metal crackles as frost spreads through the wires. One by one, the lights around me flicker and go dark. I shut the panel with a quiet snap and tiptoe through the shadowy hallway toward the Crux.

Crouched low, I creep to the clear barrier, using a finger to wipe a layer of frost from the glass. The Crux on the other side is still brightly lit. Like all the other access points to the segregated wings, the Winter port is a mantrap—a narrow plexiglass tunnel with key-protected doors on each end, making it harder to sneak through. If I freeze the wires to the pneumatic gates, I wonder how long I'll have to make it through before anyone realizes I'm inside.

Condensation trickles down the glass, obscuring the Spring port to my left. To my right, the view into the Autumn wing is dry and clear. No sign of the Guards. The only port I can't see is the one opposite from me—the Summer wing—directly behind the cylindrical elevator shaft at the center of the circular hallway.

I draw back from the barrier as the gate between the Summer and Autumn wings glides open. The fast fall of approaching boots presses me farther into the shadows, and I hold my breath as the gate to the Winter wing hisses open, less than fifteen feet from the recess in the wall where I'm hiding.

I hold perfectly still as the Guard walks briskly by, her dark curls bouncing with her determined stride. Noelle Eastman slows, stops, and backs up a step, her eyes lifting to the ceiling when the lights don't come on. She sniffs the air, her head tipped curiously.

"Who's there?" A spark ignites in her palm. The silver scythe on her shoulder catches the light as she turns, and I take an instinctive step away from her. "Jack?" Her eyes narrow as she brings the flame closer. "What are you doing here?"

I raise an arm against the glare. Nod at her patch. "You never told me you were promoted."

"Maybe I would have if you'd returned my calls." Her cupped fire grows brighter and I flinch back from the heat. She was a Winter last time we talked. Her magic was the same as mine—comfortable, familiar. The sight of her wielding another Season's power is as jarring as that patch on her sleeve.

"Your boyfriend made it pretty clear he didn't want me talking to you." Every bruise hidden under my hood is a testament to that.

Noelle's flame wavers a little. "He was upset," she says weakly. "He had every reason to be."

She closes her fist and shakes the heat from her fingers. I incline my head toward them, my eyes readjusting to the dark lighting. "I'm impressed."

"Don't be." She massages the warmth from her palm, as if it makes her uncomfortable. "This is the only other element I've managed to figure out yet. Water's too unwieldy. And plants are impossible to master. Even Doug hasn't figured them out." She glances back to the Crux and lowers her voice. "Doug's not so bad. He's just . . . complicated."

I lick the scab on my fat lip. "I'll take your word for it."

"I'm serious. He's just jealous." She raises a hand before I can utter an objection. "Not just because of what happened between us," she explains. "Doug's wanted a position on the Guard for years. It's all he talked about. And when Chronos chose you for it first, I couldn't tell if Doug was grateful you turned it down or pissed at you for not taking it."

"Why would he be pissed?" I ask bitterly. "He got exactly what he wanted."

"Because now he'll never know if he truly earned it or if he only got picked for the job because you thought you were too good for it." Noelle's gaze falls to her feet. Her voice is barely more than a whisper. I'm not sure we're talking about Doug's promotion anymore.

"Noelle," I say gently, "I'm not too good for anything. That had nothing to do with it."

"What was it, then?" she asks, meeting my eyes, as if she's daring me to answer.

"It just didn't feel right. That's all." It would have been easier if I had felt something—anything—when we kissed. Being with Noelle was a safe option. We were alike. It was allowed. But kissing her made me feel powerless, as if I'd given up on the idea of wanting anything else. Same as I would have felt if I had joined Chronos's Guard. Any dorm that has a need for guards is really just a prison. And after the Termination I witnessed yesterday, I'd rather eat Chronos's patch than swear fealty to it. "I'm happy for you and Doug. Seriously. But I'm not cut out for the Guard. After what I saw in Gaia's office . . ." The memory of those girls turns my mouth to ash. "I could never do it."

Her head snaps up. "I wasn't the one who took a scythe to those girls."

"No, you stood by and watched."

The light dims in her eyes, as if some bit of magic just died in her.

"Sorry. I was out of line. Forget I said anything." I jam my hands into the pocket of my hoodie and veer around her, back toward my room. The longer I stay here, the worse this conversation goes. And I'm not any closer to figuring out how to get through the Crux.

"Jack, wait." She makes a clumsy grab for my sweatshirt and

accidentally yanks back my hood. I turn slowly to face her. Her mouth falls open, and I rake my hair from my eyes as she gets a good look at my bruises. "I'm sorry." She swallows hard. My face must look even worse in the dark, and I feel more like a jerk for making her feel guilty about it. It's not her fault Doug's an asshole. She reaches for me. "I swear, Jack, if I had known they'd put you through Reconditioning, too, I never would have reported what I saw on those surveillance feeds."

The words are slow to sink in. Suddenly, it feels like I'm staring at a stranger.

"It was you?" Her hand's still hot from the flame and I shake it off. "You were the one who reported us to Doug?" Had she been at his side as he dealt out Fleur's punishment? Had she stood by and watched that too?

I wait for her to rattle off some lame excuse. To insist it was her job. That she wasn't spying on us. That she found the feeds by accident.

"I'm sorry," she says.

"Don't be." My voice is so cold, I hardly recognize it. "You weren't the one who threw the punches, right?"

She reels as if I've struck her. "Don't you dare put this back on me. You're the one who broke the rules! If you were summoned to Gaia's office for falling for a Spring, it's your own damn fault!"

"I wasn't punished in Gaia's office! And I didn't get these bruises because of Fleur." I turn my back on her before I say something I'll regret. I should go back to my room. Take a shower and clear my head. It was stupid to come here anyway.

"Jack! Don't leave," she calls after me. "Why are you sneaking around in the dark?"

"I'm not sneaking around."

"Then show me your pass."

"Don't have one," I snap. She sounds too much like a Guard. Nothing like my friend.

"Then tell me who you were going to see."

"Why? So you can report me?"

"So I can take you!"

My feet still.

"Jack, please," she says. "I'm sorry. How many times are you going to make me say it?"

Her guilt cuts through my thoughts like a pick through a lock. I turn, taking a few cautious steps toward her. She's given me an opening. All I have to do is bend the truth and push a little.

"I was going to see Professor Lyon," I school the urgency from my face. "He's helping me with a research project. I was supposed to meet him in the Hall of Records ten minutes ago, but I lost my pass."

Noelle bites her lip. She glances behind her into the Crux. "Fine. But after this, we're even." She waves her security pass in front of the scanner. I run back through the corridor in time to dart through the gate behind her. The Crux is at least ten degrees warmer than the Winter wing, and a layer of rime forms on my skin before we reach the elevator. I drag my hood over my head as a security camera swings slowly toward us.

From the far side of the circular hall comes the tread of boots. Frost blooms under my hood as I recognize Doug's gruff baritone and Denver's laugh. Noelle swears under her breath. The elevator doors slide open just as they round the corner, and she shoves me inside.

"Noelle, wait up!" I keep my head down when Doug calls her name.

"Don't do anything stupid," she whispers, slipping something into my hand. She slams the button for the administrative floor, and the doors slide closed before I realize what she's done.

I stare down at Noelle's key card as the elevator descends. I'm in the Crux without an escort, holding a key to every secure wing in this place. If I'm caught in possession of this card, I'm as good as dead.

So don't get caught. The little voice inside my head sounds a lot like Chill's, and I fight the urge to talk back to it as the elevator lurches to a stop.

The doors open, and I tuck the key card in my front pocket, my shoes squeaking on the polished marble as I cross quickly under the high domed ceiling of the atrium. I listen for the whine of a camera or the click of a teacher's shoes as I wave Noelle's key card over the scanner beside the solid steel door to the old wings.

A buzzer sounds and I haul the heavy door open. The air that greets me on the other side is dank and musty, the ceilings lower, the lights softer. The corridor stretches ahead of me, forked with mysterious doors leading to the endless maze of caverns and catacombs below the Observatory. I follow the route by memory, envisioning the dusty maps I drew decades ago, after my last trip down here, only taking my first full breath when the crisp white tiles give way to stone slabs and packed earthen walls.

The hall grows blessedly cold. The drop-tile ceiling ends abruptly, the flickering fluorescent tubes overhead yielding to gas torchères mounted on the rough-cut walls. The shadows they cast move like smazes over the floors. I tell myself that I'm alone. That no one knows

I'm here. There are no cameras in the ancient passageways. No power in these oldest sections of the campus, with the exception of the library, where generators preserve the temperature and humidity and keep the entrance to the Hall of Records secure.

I listen for the buzz of wings or the caw of a crow as I scent the passage ahead, relieved to find it empty. The growl of a generator grows louder. A white light glows in the distance, the arched door to the library flanked by ornate electric sconces illuminating the carving in its facade. I pause in front of the tangled and twisted Tree of Knowledge, fishing Noelle's key card from my pocket. The red eye of the card scanner blinks at me. I pass the card over it with shaking hands, my held breath slipping out of me when the light turns green on the first try.

The iron locks snap open. The doors groan in protest as I lean into them. Motion sensors trigger the lights inside one by one, like falling dominoes, through the adjoining rooms. I pause, listening through the echoing silence. The air inside the Hall of Records is as cold as the catacombs, dense with medieval smells—damp stone, worn leather, old parchment—lightly masked by the scent of the lemon wood polish coating the rows upon rows of hardwood shelves.

"Hello?" My voice bounces off high stone walls and tall bookcases with sliding ladders. I jump at my own reflection gazing back at me from a glass display case containing scrolls and stone tablets, its contents too old to be trusted to the elements.

My first summer at the Observatory, I was forced to take an orientation class, a crash course in relevant subjects that would keep me above the Purge line: self-defense, light weaponry and combat tactics, meteorological and political science, the natural laws that govern us, and the modern history of the Seasons . . . The history portion was limited, covering a period from the late eighteenth century onward. Every trip to the Hall of Records was supervised, our reading selections scrutinized, our time in the stacks strictly limited to the minutes we needed to complete our assignments.

I navigate the shelves by memory, my fingertips grazing the cracked spines and deckle edges of yellowing pages, until I find the specific set of volumes for the time period I'm searching for.

We've been taught that the first stasis chambers were modeled after the Leyden jar, a simple glass container that could store an electric charge, which was invented in 1745. It didn't take long for the Observatory to latch onto the idea, developing a life-size version and using the ley lines as conductors. But what if the inspiration for both of these inventions originated long before that? From *us*. What if the entire notion of a rechargeable battery came from the potential chemical energy stored in every Season's magic, because we were capable of recharging *ourselves*?

Think hard, Jack. If you could *find a way out of the Observatory, how would you survive?*

Professor Lyon had never said it couldn't be done. He'd only challenged me to consider how. What if surviving away from the ley lines—without our transmitters and stasis chambers—isn't a dream at all? What if it's actually possible?

My hands comb over the spines of the books. All I need to do is work backward from 1745, to find some small detail in our history that reveals how we might have charged ourselves before.

I pause.

The History of Natural Order Volume 121: The Age of Enlightenment Part II, AD 1745—1815 is in its proper place, leaning against volume 122. But the previous volume is gone. And every volume before it. Where the hell would they—

"Mr. Sommers." The quiet voice behind me nearly stops my heart.

Slowly, I turn around. Professor Lyon leans against the end of the stack, a worn copy of *Aesop's Fables* tucked under his arm, as if he's been here all along, casually watching me. Suddenly, I'm eight years old again, caught sneaking into my grandfather's tool shed, messing with grown-up things I don't have permission to touch. I don't remember much about my grandfather, only that he and Lyon have the same sharp glimmer in their eyes. And the same uncanny ability to stand right behind me, without being seen, the minute I manage to get myself into trouble.

"Professor . . . ," I stammer.

Professor Lyon saunters closer, a small gray smaze peeking out from behind his leg. "I ran into Noelle Eastman in the corridor upstairs," he says, mocking my surprise. "She informed me I was late to meet with you, so I thought it best to come straightaway."

I glare at the smaze as Lyon studies the shelf behind me, turning his head to read the spines. "Tell me, Mr. Sommers. What exactly is the focus of our joint research today?"

I clear my throat, hoping a shred of truth might save me. "Rechargeable batteries."

"I see." His blue eyes slide to the empty space on the shelf. "It would seem you are searching for the previous volume."

"How'd you know?" The question slips out before I can take it back.

"Because you've snuck in here like a thief, and the volume you seek, like all those prior to it, is stored in a vault in the restricted archives, accessible only to administration and staff." He leans in conspiratorially and whispers, "If you were here to read a book intended for you, Mr. Sommers, you'd have asked permission."

I don't know what I resent more: the school for treating us like criminals, or Lyon for mocking me for it. "Why would the school lock up a book?"

"For the same reasons parents today insist on childproofing doors," he says placidly. "Because there are things on the other side—be they dangerous or delicate—they don't want their children to touch."

His condescension rubs me the wrong way. Just because he looks old enough to be my dad doesn't mean he knows a thing about parenting. "We're not children."

"All the more reason to strengthen the locks." His stare is heavy on me before he turns to go. At the last moment, he tosses me the book of fables tucked under his arm. "Consider it homework. We'll start tomorrow. Come to my office at nine. I trust you'll have sufficient time to read it before then. Don't be late, Mr. Sommers."

The thin storybook with its illustrated cover and oversize print is hot in my hands as I watch him go. I want to dump it on the nearest shelf. Drop it in a damn waste bin. Instead, I tuck it into the front pocket of my sweatshirt along with Noelle's key card as the heavy doors to the Hall of Records slam closed.

I turn the card over in my hand, thinking about all the doors it could open. About what Lyon said about locks and their purpose.

. . . *there are things on the other side* . . . *they don't want their children to touch.*

My body goes rigid.

Touch.

Could that be it? They don't want us to *touch*.

I flinch at the memory of Fleur's hand on my skin, the electric shock that pulsed through me and stole my strength while our transmitters were on. Yet that same touch had preserved my life when our transmitters were *off.*

My thoughts race backward, to the batteries in Chill's drone. One positive end, one negative. Positive and negative charges attract each other, the same way lightning is attracted to the ground, the same way a rising Season's magic is drawn to a waning one's—it's how we find each other, as if we're pulled together by some natural force.

What if we only have to be different to work?

It explains so much . . . why two Winters can touch without hurting each other. Why Noelle and I could kiss and not *feel* anything. But me and Fleur . . . Together, we react.

Suddenly, it makes sense why Gaia and Chronos keep us apart. Why we're punished for getting close to other Seasons. For not following the rules. Why they segregate our dorms. So we won't figure out what we're capable of together. So we won't figure out what will happen if we touch.

8
PROOFS AND THEORIES

<u>JACK</u>

Fleur had held me while our transmitters were off. I was untethered, off the grid, unable to connect to the circuit of ley lines. Yet somehow, I had survived long enough for Chill to find me, loop me in, and route me home. I'm not sure exactly how, but I have a theory. And it's killing me that I'll have to wait another nine months before I'm in a position to test it out.

I press against the wall of the elevator, offering up a silent prayer that the Crux is empty when it opens on my floor. I peer into it, taking a few cautious steps into the circular hall. The port to the Spring wing is shrouded in green leaves and dripping condensation. Fleur sleeps some-where on the other side, and Noelle's key card is burning a hole in my pocket. I'd give anything to see Fleur. To touch her just to see if I'm right. But even if I could get into her room without Poppy catching me, it's too soon to open her stasis chamber and try.

Don't do anything stupid.

I should find Noelle. Return the card before I'm caught.

Hunched under my hood, I circle the Crux toward the Winter port. A quick glance through the barrier into the Autumn wing reveals a layout identical to my own—a familiar long wide central hall, branching off into intersecting corridors at the same regular intervals. I shouldn't be surprised. Gaia designed this place. Nature leans toward symmetry. Tilts toward balance. The Observatory is laid out beneath Greenwich Park like a giant compass rose, each of the four wings pointing in a different cardinal direction, the exits from the tip of each wing to the surrounding neighborhoods above forming a perfect diamond on a map.

The realization that it wouldn't be hard to find my way around—to find Amber Chase somewhere in those halls and test my theory—feels too much like a sign. It's ten o'clock. Peak training time. And if I know Amber, the training center is exactly where she'll be.

I wait for the camera to rotate the opposite direction before waving Noelle's access card over the scanner. My pulse quickens when the Autumn port glides open and the warm, dry air inside rushes into the Crux. It smells dangerous, like tinder and hot coals, but before the gate slides shut, I dash through it, and then it's too late to change my mind.

All I'd have to do is find Amber and convince her not to kill me or report me. And the only way to convince Amber to do anything is to appeal to her sense of pride. She's smart, lethal, and capable, and she knows it. In all the years I've hunted her, she's never backed down from a challenge.

I move quickly, my hood pulled low, to keep the cameras from capturing a clear shot of my face. Muscle memory guides my turns. Left, then right, then left again, the sharp smell of pool chemicals and the metallic tang of iron telling me I've landed exactly where I hoped I would.

I snag a wet pool towel from a bin inside the locker room and drape it over my head, masking myself in the scent of bleach and chlorine. As soon as I'm beyond range of the cameras, I lean against the wall to catch my breath, the stasis sickness slowly catching up to me. The hall to the training area smells foul, like moldy leaves and sweat. In the windows of the sparring rooms, every training mat is full of Autumns coming into their Season, prepping for the hunt.

A twinge of panic grips me.

I'm here alone, without Chill, completely outnumbered. Frost melts down my back, soaking through my sweatshirt. I reek of Winter and nervous sweat. My scent might as well be a flashing beacon, as glaring as Christmas lights on Halloween, but the voice that nudged me through that gate is screaming at me to keep going.

Drawing the towel tighter around me, I cast a quick glance into the window of each sparring room for a glimpse of auburn hair. A few of the fighters pause, their spines stiffening when I pass. I move quickly to the next. This was a stupid idea. I'm about ready to give up my search when I catch a flash of red in the last room.

I hug the wall, peering around the window frame as Amber delivers a roundhouse kick to her opponent's head. Physically, he doesn't look much older than she does—maybe nineteen. He's lean and muscled, with the posture and buzzed haircut of a soldier. Still, I'm hardly surprised when he stumbles, slow to recover. Even less surprised when she slams her fist into his jaw before he gets a chance. He hits the mat and taps out.

She eases off him, adjusting the black belt cinched around her waist. Sweat trails down her temple. She swipes her brow with the back of her hand, the wraps protecting her knuckles absorbing the perspiration that clings to the wisps of her hair. The rest is pulled back in two tight French braids that sharpen her cheekbones, making her angular jaw and crooked grin look all the more severe.

Her opponent peels off his hand wraps. He throws them into his faded green duffel, too busy glaring at Amber to notice me as he snatches it up. I slip behind the door as it flies open, careful to stay downwind and out of view.

"See you around, Hunter," she calls after him. He flips her off as he goes, and I can't help sympathizing with him. Her triumphant smile crumbles when she sees me staring back at her through the glass.

As I enter the room, she takes a step back, clutching the bright yellow sun embroidered on the collar of her gi as if it's a talisman against the cold. The training room is uncomfortably warm, the air thick with the smell of aggression. Instinct makes my fingers itch, and I resist the urge to summon a frost.

"How did you get in here?" Her eyes dart to the door, calculating the distance as it closes behind me.

"Wasn't hard." I pull the key card from my pocket just enough for her to see the flash of its silver edge. There are no security cameras inside the sparring rooms. No panic buttons. And I know, maybe better than anyone, Amber's far too proud to scream. Her gaze leaps back to the door, then the window. If she wants out of this room as badly as I think she does, she has no choice but to go through me.

She flexes her fingers to conjure a flame, but the wraps around her knuckles stifle the flow of oxygen to her hands.

"What are you doing here?" She scowls at me as I kick off my shoes and slide the towel back from my head. I should be asking myself the same thing. I haven't eaten anything solid in months and I'm only ten days out of the box. If I'm lucky, she'll let me live long enough to crawl quietly back to my dorm room. If I'm not, she'll report me to Gaia. Either way, I'm probably screwed.

"Came to pick a fight."

"Looks like you already found one." She juts her chin at my fading bruises.

"I had a disagreement with a Guard."

One touch. That's all I need.

I step out onto the mat, praying Amber doesn't take off her hand wraps and cook me. "What's wrong? Afraid of being alone with me?"

She drags her eyes from the door. "Not even a little." She adjusts her stance, rolling her shoulders as I inch within striking distance. She throws a quick test swing. "What are you really doing here?" she asks as I dodge it. I'm slower than I should be.

"Just came to talk."

"We have nothing to say to each other." She throws a punch to my ribs that doubles me over. I suck in a sharp breath. I was hoping she'd go for the face. "Whatever it is you're up to, you're going to get us both in trouble."

"Only if you kill me," I say through a wheeze.

"Don't tempt me." Her catlike eyes narrow as if she's actually considering it. "You think I don't know you're only a few seasons away from a promotion? Well, guess what. So am I. And I'm not giving up my shot at Arizona for you." Her wrapped knuckles fly at my face. My head snaps back, my eyes watering at the explosion of pain in my teeth.

Woozy, I watch her hands, braced for the next hit. Her knuckle wraps . . . they're getting in the way.

I wince, prodding my bloody lip. "What's in Arizona?"

"None of your business."

My focus slips to the sun on the collar of her gi. "Can't be that important, or you would've won it already." She's strong. Fast. The most skilled fighter in our region. If she'd wanted to be in Arizona that badly, she would have fought for a relocation years ago. Yet here she is, hovering just below the leaders on the board, stuck in the mid-Atlantic with Fleur, Julio, and me. "If I didn't know better, I'd say you were holding back."

Amber drops, sweeping my legs out from under me. In half a heartbeat, I'm ass-side down on the mat. She kneels over me, two fingers pressed to the groove of my throat, applying a steady pressure that steals my breath and sets my pulse racing. "I'll show you holding back, you arrogant son of a—"

Amber gasps. A current surges through me, electric and disorienting. She leaps to her feet, wobbling a little as she backs into the wall. The stray hair that's come loose from her braids sticks up around her face, charged with static. "What did you do?"

I get up fast, flooded with adrenaline, the wooziness gone. Amber stares wide-eyed at my lip where she hit me.

I run my tongue over the spot where her fist connected, over the scab that's already closed the wound.

Our eyes catch.

We made contact, skin to skin. It should have sucked away my strength. Instead, it made me stronger. I was right. The stasis chamber isn't the battery. It's only a receptacle, a holding station for our energy. *We* are the batteries. And every battery has two sides: a positive and a negative, an anode and a cathode, a charged end and one that receives that charge.

Amber and I formed our own circuit—a closed loop.

She leans against the wall. Presses her fingers to her temple. "What the hell just happened?"

I touch my rib where she hit me. It's not even tender.

This. This is why they reward us for violence, why they condition us to hate each other. This is why I'm not supposed to be here. Why we're punished for a kiss. Why we're Terminated if we're caught breaching the Crux. Not because we'll hurt each other. Because we'll heal each other. Suddenly, every far-flung fantasy I've ever had about me and Fleur—taking her hand and running from this place—seems within reach. She said running was just a dream. That it could never happen. But that was before either of us knew it was possible. That was before she fell below the red line.

If she knew . . . if I could find a way to tell her . . . would she run with me? Could we get her out of here, away from the Observatory and off the ley lines, before the next Purge?

My hand slides to my pocket, the key card inside it suddenly heavy, as if it's made of more than plastic. As if it's made of gold.

Amber's shout is tinged with panic. "You have thirty seconds to explain what's going on!"

"I've got to go," I mutter. It's a risk, telling Amber anything. She would just as soon slit my throat as let me get away with anything. Not unless there was something in it for her. I keep an arm's length between us as I drag on my shoes and head for the door. My mind's on fire with questions. Countless possibilities. I don't even notice when Amber kicks out my ankles, using my own momentum against me. My face slams into the mat.

"If you walk out of here without explaining what the hell just happened, I swear to Gaia, I'll tell her everything I know!"

I haul myself up, right in her face, forcing her to look up at me. "Which is what, exactly?"

"That you snuck in here with a stolen key card. That you picked a fight with me, and . . ."

"And what?" Her mouth falls open, then closes again. "Who's going to believe you?" She can't prove it. Not without leaving the Autumn wing and breaking all the same rules. Not without risking her own Termination. Chronos would cut her down before he'd let those rumors spread like wildfire through the dorms. My lip throbs and my nose is bleeding. A tendon in my ankle is strained where she tripped me. "Do yourself a favor and forget I was here. Forget what you saw."

I got what I came for. I don't owe her anything. I sling the pool towel over my head and limp out the door.

9

CLOSE AND SECRET

JACK

I slam the book of fables closed and throw it across our dorm room, narrowly missing the faux window. Chill stirs in his bunk in the next room. I rub my eyes, my nose still tender where the mat caught me. The purple and green northern lights on the window's screen are the same colors as the bruise. I should have been in bed hours ago, but sleep won't come. The dog-eared chapter of the professor's book—some story about a lion who fell in love with a girl and gave up his teeth to be with her—has nothing to do with anything, but it reminds me of Fleur. It's the same kind of tragic book she would probably check out of the library. For all their sacrifices, the lion and the girl don't even get to be together, and the fact that the story has a crappy ending makes me resent it even more.

I prod my swollen lip. Every inch of me is exhausted and sore. Just a few hours ago, I thought I had all the answers. I've figured out how to keep us alive out in the world, but I can't find a way to get us there. Noelle cut me off as I was sneaking back into the Winter wing. She took one look at my fat lip, snatched her key card from my hand, and stormed off without a word. And that card was my best hope for getting us out of the Observatory. Even if I could convince Fleur to run away with me next spring, I can't turn my back on Chill. Chronos would Terminate our Handlers as soon as he realized we were gone, and there's no way I'd ever leave this place without taking him with me.

I guess I could *try* talking to Poppy. Convincing her to save herself shouldn't be hard. But with the promise of Anchorage dangling in front of Chill, convincing *him* to run won't be easy.

He was quiet when I limped into our room a few hours ago. He never asked me what happened to my face or where I got the book. Never bothered to say "I told you so" when the stasis sickness came back with a vengeance this afternoon. It may be my name on that ranking board in Gaia's office, but my decisions reflect on both of us, and I guess I can't blame him for not wanting to know where I went, or what I was doing. He hid behind his computer most of the day, pretending to be busy. Never bothered to ask if I wanted to walk with him to the mess hall before ordering my dinner, delivered to our dorm room on a tray, like I was some kind of hospital patient. He went to bed without bothering to say good night.

Shivering and queasy, I stare at the cellophane-wrapped bowls of cold vegetable broth and applesauce. My head aches and my stomach grumbles, my insides hollow and hungry for things I can't have. Fleur's probably right. Running from this place is just a stupid dream. It'll be another nine months before I'll have an opportunity to even talk to her, and that's assuming she doesn't kill me first. Even if I could manage to convince her to listen—to show her it's possible—getting Chill and Poppy out of here would be a logistical nightmare. I've mapped out every viable scenario in my mind. There's no way we could pull it off on our own.

Chill's computer hums quietly, his desk neat except for a few telltale orange Dorito crumbs. My stomach rumbles again. Blanket draped over my shoulders, I reach for his bottom desk drawer, following my nose to a stash of smuggled junk food he keeps hidden under a stack of files. My fingers hover over the familiar fat accordion folders containing Chill's surveillance records. Of Amber, Julio, and Fleur. How they hunt, what they spend their money on, the places they avoid and the ones they're drawn to . . . all their weaknesses.

I pause over Amber's. As strong as she was today, she reached for that yellow sun embroidered on her collar whenever she got nervous. Arizona is a soft spot, a vulnerability she clings to. All I have to do is figure out why. And if she wants it badly enough to risk helping me.

I shed the blanket and gather up the heavy stack of folders, surprised to find a fourth thin file underneath the others, labeled with a name I've never seen before.

Philippa Elaine Wells.

Curious, I set the others aside, surprised to find this fourth file is full of pictures of Poppy. Chill must have hacked her records from the Control Room servers, but why? I skim the contents for any clue to what he might be up to.

Cause of original death: respiratory failure resulting from cystic fibrosis, on the same day, in the same hospital, as Fleur. It's all here—her surviving relatives, the websites she frequents, the music she downloads, the foods she eats . . . But Chill doesn't need to hunt Poppy or even hide from her. He doesn't need to know her weaknesses, so why bother keeping a file?

Unless it's not Poppy's weaknesses hidden in this folder, but Chill's.

I tuck it back inside his drawer, feeling guilty for invading his privacy. My sleeve catches the edge of the stack and the other three folders smack onto the floor.

Breath held, I listen as Chill stirs. When he falls quiet again, I ease down beside Fleur's scattered dossier. Under the dim circle of Chill's reading lamp, I gather the pages into a pile in my lap: reconnaissance photos, bank statements, her library hold list, classes she's taken, a list of the places she goes when she's released . . . I memorized most of it years ago.

Fleur Attwell, formerly Mackenzie Ray Evans, born September 26, 1973, in Frederick, Maryland, died May 26, 1991, in Washington, DC. Cause of death: lymphoma.

I pause at a photo Chill must have hacked from Fleur's personal files. A selfie of Fleur and Julio sitting side by side, their legs dangling over the edge of a boardwalk. She's laughing, her pink hair blowing across her soft-serve ice cream cone. I try not to read too much into their relationship, but it's hard not to. I can't imagine sitting in a dark theater beside Amber. Can't imagine either of us relinquishing our weapons long enough to share dessert.

I tuck the photo back into Fleur's file. I wonder if Julio knows she's up for the Purge. If he cares about her enough to risk his neck to save her.

Julio's file is thinner than the others, containing only tangential details I've never concerned myself with beyond the parts that pertain to Fleur. I collect the spilled contents, trying to see them from a different angle as I return them to the file, searching for facets of his life I may have missed before. Gaia picked him up in Southern California in 1983 after a surfing accident. As far as I can tell, he has no remaining family. His younger sister died of a brain injury shortly after Julio's accident, and his parents split three months later. Both have since passed on.

I thumb through a few reports, but there's nothing to suggest he has the same warm-fuzzy feelings for Amber that he has for Fleur. Their kill records are brutal and bloody. No ice cream receipts, no movie date surveillance. He has to have *some* weakness. Somewhere he aches to go. Something he desperately wants. Someone he yearns to be with, preferably who isn't Fleur.

I drag Amber's file out from under the others, collecting the last of the loose documents and pictures from the floor. A sheet of yellowing paper rustles under the coffee table and I slide it toward me.

A thin and brittle police report filed in Phoenix, Arizona, in May 1969. It's so old, I've never bothered reading it before.

"What's so important to you in Arizona?" I whisper, holding it closer to the light.

Missing: Claire Sanford, seventeen years old. The report was filed by Claire's mother, her sole guardian.

The photo's stained with ochre tints. Amber's hair was longer, wavy and parted down the center, hiding the sharp lines of her jaw. But her full lips and catlike eyes are unmistakable. It's definitely her. The report was filed by her mother, her sole guardian.

I flip back through Amber's bank records. A revolving charge appears on the first of every month, paid to a nursing home in Phoenix. If Amber was seventeen in 1969, her mother could still be living there.

But maybe not for long.

I stuff the records back into their files and return them all to Chill's drawer. This might not be a key to the surface, but it might help us make it that far.

10

CHOICE AND CONSEQUENCE

<u>JACK</u>

Professor Lyon studies me over the rims of his glasses as I enter his office and take my usual seat in the worn leather armchair in front of his desk. His blue eyes linger on the spectacular new bruises blooming on my face, which now overshadow the pale yellow ones Doug gave me less than a week ago.

Without a word, his attention returns to whatever task I've interrupted. I sink back in the chair, the book of fables he assigned me for homework resting in my lap as I stare at the posters on the wall to keep my eyes from closing. Last night was long. Fitful and full of nightmares when I finally slept. I woke to the sound of my fists against the wall. I dreamed I was trapped in a snow globe, a blizzard swirling around me. The pins and needles in my sleeping arm stung like angry bees.

A laminated poster of Cuernavaca, Mexico, hangs behind Lyon's desk. "City of Eternal Spring," it reads. The old city's nestled in a rolling green hillside, dripping with flowers, and all my thoughts run to Fleur . . . how quickly the lilies wilted after the stasis chamber was opened, the way the petals had inevitably shriveled and crumbled, like the Spring Chronos cut down in the Control Room.

"Why Cuernavaca?" I ask, interrupting the scratch of Lyon's pen. Why not hang a poster of Harbin, Murmansk, or Saskatoon? Some frigid city where a Winter could last indefinitely?

"Why not?"

"It's a weird choice for a Winter."

"Is it, Mr. Sommers?" His lip twitches with amusement. "I've seen enough snow to last a hundred lifetimes. And last I checked, there were no rules that prohibit the admiration of flowers." He throws me a brief but meaningful look. My face warms as Lyon returns his attention to the papers on his desk. A disciplinary report . . . I lean closer, surprised to find the name on the file isn't mine.

"Why didn't you turn me in?" I ask, when I can't stand the silence any longer.

"Is that what you were hoping? That I would report you?" His pen's still moving over the paper, as if he knew what I would ask and had already considered his answer. Which wasn't really an answer at all.

"No." Maybe. The guilt's gnawing away at me. I'm here for a promotion I don't deserve. One that will inevitably kill Fleur. "Are they always like that? The Terminations?"

Lyon sets down his pen. He removes his glasses and rubs his eyes. Then he looks at me as if this is a question he wasn't prepared for. As if this one deserves more of an answer than he's able to give. "Terminations are always difficult. Gaia and Chronos do not approach them

118

lightly. Balancing the universe is a tricky thing. It's heavier than you might imagine it to be." He pulls a handkerchief from his breast pocket and cleans his lenses. "But you're not here to talk about demotions today, are you?"

"I guess not." I pick at a loose thread in the arm of the chair. I'm here to learn the things I'll need to know to keep Chill and me safe in our new region. To keep him happy. But the last thing I want is a relocation to Alaska. It's a distraction. A deadline. Just one more clock ticking.

"Yesterday in the Hall of Records, you told me you aren't a child. And yet here you are, sulking like one. Tell me, are you a man, Mr. Sommers?"

It feels like a trick question. "I'm a Winter. A Season." It comes out sounding impetuous.

"That's not what I asked of you." I shrink back in my chair, too ashamed to admit I don't know the answer. I feel old and tired, yet somehow no more a man than I was the night I first died. "Seasons were not always so young," he explains. "Chronos has only recently come to prefer teenagers, children who are physically mature enough to rise up and fight, yet young enough to still be compliant. When I was made a Season, we were a bit older. There were no rules. No rankings," he says with a hint of bitterness. "There were no Purges or promotions."

"When was that?"

Lyon's eyes lift to mine, but I'm not making a dig about his age the way Doug did. His mouth turns up with a knowing smile. "Long before the book you went looking for was written. Our world was different then."

I sit up in my chair. "Different how?"

He glances at the closed door behind me, testing the point of a tooth with his tongue as he takes in my posture, my forward lean, as if deciding how much of the vault he's willing to risk unlocking for me. "We didn't have Handlers then. There was no need. Our magic was untethered. We weren't told where we were permitted to live or whom we were allowed to take into our beds. We sought our own rewards, carved out our own regions. We made our own alliances and chose our own lovers. When we wanted more land, more power, more strength, we took it." Lyon rises from his chair, the fire in his eyes growing brighter as he speaks. "If your heart beat for Alaska, then it was willing to kill and die for it. And if it ached for something else . . . some*one* else . . . then the risks, and the spoils, were yours to take."

The hair stands up on my arms. I was right. They could go anywhere. With anyone. "So you weren't *assigned* to Antarctica. You fought for it. You *chose* it."

"I suppose you could see it that way." He perches on the edge of his desk, rustling the contents of his pocket. "I was banished there by Chronos for three hundred years," he confesses quietly, "forbidden to return to his house until I agreed to give up the power Gaia granted me."

"But you just said there were no borders. No rules."

The light in his eyes dims. "We don't always win what we covet."

I sink back in my chair, picturing it. Being dumped and abandoned in a strange, cold place. Spending three hundred years alone. No Chill. No Fleur. Not even Amber. I imagine the suffocating silence, the loneliness and homesickness picking away at me, stealing bits and pieces until there's nothing left. Thinking about it feels a lot like dying. It's no wonder Lyon gave up his . . .

I look down at the book of fables in my lap, remembering the warning growled into Doug's ear.

You assume I'm frail? That I keep my teeth in a jar beside my bed?

"You're the lion," I say, putting the pieces together. "The lion who gave up his teeth."

The professor's smile is wistful. "Aesop's story was written long before mine, but I won't deny certain parallels."

"But you were the most powerful Winter in the world. Why would you give that up to be . . . ?" I catch myself. His eyebrows rise expectantly, his slight grin suggesting he knows exactly what I was about to say.

"An old man? A teacher?" He runs a hand over his salt-and-pepper mane. "Sacrificing for another takes courage. Chronos believed that by stripping me of my power, his daughter would see me as less of a man. I had to believe she would see me as more of one."

"You gave up your magic for *Gaia*?" I remember the quick catch of their eyes in the Control Room, the furtive way their hands brushed.

"Only for a place in her world," he corrects me. "Some choices have consequences. But that doesn't mean we shouldn't fight for them." He leans closer, fixing me with the eyes of a hunter. "Tell me, young lion, is it Alaska your heart desires? Is it Alaska that keeps you up at night? That you ache to possess, body and soul?"

Heat floods my cheeks as the professor pulls back the curtain on thoughts I'm afraid to admit to.

"I didn't think so," he says. "And yet here we are. You with your assignment, and me with mine—to prepare you for your journey." He studies me thoughtfully, as if he knows the answer to a puzzle I haven't figured out yet. "As your adviser, entrusted by Gaia to impart to you all the wisdom of my many years, I submit that you already possess all the knowledge you need to survive the path that lies ahead of you. What you lack is the courage to choose it."

He says it as if I have a choice at all. As if my path weren't just predetermined for me.

Pity you have to die.

I scrub a hand over my face. Wipe the vision Chronos shared with me from my head. But I can't shake the question that's stuck with me since. "Chronos said something to me in the Control Room. He said he saw my future in his staff."

Lyon tips his head. "What did he say, specifically? Do you recall?"

"He said that my rankings are at odds with every possible outcome." I leave out the vision and the part where I died. Saying it out loud would only give more weight to it. Make it feel inevitable. "What did he mean?"

Lyon slips his hands into his pockets. He stands with his back to me in front of a frosted artificial window, as if he's seeing through it. As if there's a whole landscape on the other side I can't see. "You know how the Staff of Time works, yes?"

"Not really." I mean, we all know Chronos has the power to see the future in his staff, that it's driven by magic. But none of us know exactly how it works.

"He who possesses the Staff of Time holds the power to maintain the natural order of our world. He controls the throne, and therefore everything and everyone in its domain—the Observatory, the Seasons, the revolution of the Earth, and Gaia. . . ." Lyon's brow pinches, his voice trailing on the last syllable of Gaia's name. He clears his throat softly and continues. "The scythe itself belongs to Michael, or as he is more commonly known by his title, Chronos: Father of Time, Keeper of Order, Ruler of the Throne of—"

"Michael?"

Lyon raises an eyebrow, amused by my disbelief. "As you are well aware, Mr. Sommers, few of us use our given names here." He pauses, as if giving me time to wrap my mind around that. It's not that I can't believe Chronos could have another name. It's just that *Michael* seems so . . . mundane. So ordinary. Lyon continues, pulling me out of my thoughts. "Chronos's staff controls time and immortality. But the eye— the ability to see the inevitable—that belonged to his bride, Ananke. He took possession of it when she died."

"You mean when he killed her."

Lyon nods gravely. "Chronos sought to control Ananke, but Ananke would not be controlled. Her magic and her mind were her own. One day, he struck her. Enraged, Ananke clawed out his eye, leaving the other intact. To punish him, she revealed to her husband a future he didn't wish to see. Terrified of the inevitability of it, he cut her down, not realizing that her absence would do little to change the ending." The professor's sigh is deep and unsettled. "Some say Chronos took Ananke's eye as a token, a reminder of his love for her. Others say he took it in recompense."

"What do you think?"

"I think love owes us nothing," he says quietly. He rubs at a small wrinkle on his hand. I wonder if he regrets his choice to give up his immortality and his magic. And for what? The professor and Gaia never got their happy ending.

The professor clears his throat and turns to an old blackboard on the opposite wall. I pivot in my seat, watching him over the back of his armchair as he draws the head of the staff with a single arrow feeding into its eye. "History is linear," he says, tapping the arrow with his chalk, "a series of unchangeable events. The past illuminates the crystal as a singular beam of light, but the crystal itself—our present," he explains, drawing a polygon at its center, "is a prism containing many facets. The choices we make in the present are informed by our past, and affect the way the light bends—our future." The professor draws several arrows exiting the other side of the eye. "The crystal projects every possible outcome based upon every decision we *could* make now, giving Chronos the power not only of hindsight, but of foresight as well. As long as he knows your location—the hour, minute, and second where you exist between degrees of longitude and latitude—he can see your pivotal memories, as well as every possible future that lies ahead of you. But he is blind to the present."

"Why?" I ask, puzzled. "Wouldn't the present be the easiest thing to see?"

Lyon sets down the chalk and claps the dust from his hands. "Because inevitability is inextricably tied to our choices, and you are the only person who knows your own heart as you make them."

"So basically, Chronos is saying every choice I'll make will lead me down a shitty road?"

Lyon laughs, his eyes crinkling at the edges. "That's one way to put it, I suppose. Jean de La Fontaine once said, 'A person often meets his destiny on the road he took to avoid it.' And perhaps that's true. But remember this, Mr. Sommers." He pauses in front of me, his face sobering. "Those who've seen a glimmer of your past may try to anticipate your choices, but unless they know your heart, they will always choose the future that suits their own ends."

"So Chronos could be wrong?"

Lyon eases into his chair. "Chronos's eye is only as clear as our own memories, and only as reliable as our willingness to look deeply enough into our own hearts. It is only our lack of vision that limits our choices."

"So there *is* another possible outcome?"

"Only inasmuch as you choose it," he says.

I think about the story of the lion and the girl. About the crappy way it ended. I wonder why things couldn't have ended differently for Lyon and Gaia. If there's any way it could end differently for me and Fleur.

"Follow your heart, Jack. Wherever it takes you, it will not steer you wrong." He gathers his mug and his briefcase. "If you'll excuse me, it seems I'm late for a meeting."

"Professor, wait. Your book." I hold out the dog-eared copy of *Aesop's Fables*, but Lyon doesn't take it.

"If you've finished reading, it can be returned." He scoops up a heavy, leather-bound volume from his desk and drops it in my arms as he heads for the door. "Would you mind returning this one to the library cart as well? There's a certain Spring who'll be very disappointed if it's not on the shelf when she wakes."

And with a wink, he's gone.

The book of poetry is heavy in my lap. Curious, I open the cover. There's a circulation card in the pocket in the back, and I spot Fleur's name immediately. It's listed over and over again, every September. She's checked out this same book of poems for years.

I thumb through the pages. A sprig of lilies, crushed and brittle, falls from a poem called "The Good-Morrow" by John Donne.

And now good-morrow to our waking souls,
Which watch not one another out of fear;
For love, all love of other sights controls,
And makes one little room an everywhere.
Let sea-discoverers to new worlds have gone,
Let maps to other, worlds on worlds have shown,
Let us possess one world, each hath one, and is one.

My face in thine eye, thine in mine appears,
And true plain hearts do in the faces rest;
Where can we find two better hemispheres,
Without sharp north, without declining west?
Whatever dies, was not mixed equally;
If our two loves be one, or, thou and I
Love so alike, that none do slacken, none can die.

My hands shake as I set down the book. It feels too much like a sign. Like we've been dreaming about the same things.

We both know how this ends. Those were the last words I spoke to her. And now . . . now I'd do anything to take them back.

I fumble for a pen on Lyon's desk. Turning the book sideways, I scribble a message in the margin:

We know how the story's supposed to end. But what if it doesn't have to?

11

THROUGH THE LEY LINES

FLEUR

The light pulls me, a sharp tug to the belly, like someone yanking a leash around my waist until I'm flying. I'm everywhere and nowhere. I'm energy, yet powerless, my body moving backward so fast I can't stop. Too fast to grab a root and hold on.

I pass over mountains and plains, through wind and water, under cities and towns. My life—people I've known, places I've lived, things I've done, lives I've lost—all of it flashes past like scenes through the window of a runaway train. The visions of my last life flicker and go dark again, the movement, the sheer speed of it, lulling me toward sleep.

Dreaming.

I must be dreaming.

Through the window of the train, I see Julio's face. The sun-kissed crinkles around his eyes when he smiles. The way it falls as he catches me in his arms and I'm gone.

Then Jack. Always Jack.

The way he looks over his shoulder when he runs. As if he's left something behind. Or he's afraid to get too far ahead of me.

What do you want?

It's a whisper in my ear, near enough to send a chill through me.

I turn from the window, expecting to see Jack sitting beside me.

Douglas Lausks smiles. There's blood on his teeth.

The lightness in his eyes is at odds with the darkness lurking behind them. His mouth moves around Jack's words, twisting them into something hopeless and hideous.

We both know how this ends, he croons.

A callous laugh rings out behind me. Denver sits in the next bench, his arm and the silver scythe on his sleeve swung casually over the seat back. Lixue leans on a stanchion, blocking the closest exit, her body swaying with the motion of the train. Across the aisle, Noelle watches Doug watching me. She turns away, heat flooding her cheeks.

I start at a loud thump. It vibrates the window at my back. I turn, confused. Jack clings to the side of the train, his face pressed to the glass. His fist beats against the window.

"This is the Red Line train to Shady Grove Station." The voice through the overhead speaker is garbled, clipped by static. "This is a terminating station. This train will no longer be in service. All passengers must deboard at this time."

Jack's eyes open wide, his face contorted with fear, his shouts growing urgent as he pounds on the side of the train. Lights flash around him as we hurtle through the tunnel.

He presses his palm to the window, his breath fogging the glass.

Our eyes meet through it. His mouth moves. One word. Over and over.

"*Run!*"

Frost splinters over the glass. Crackles over the walls, crystallizes over the metal handrails. The air in the cabin becomes thin. Frigid and dry. Ragged breaths billow from my lips. I'm cold. So cold.

Doug, Denver, Lixue, and Noelle watch me with Winter-white eyes. Smazes curl around their necks. Weave between their ankles.

The train jerks to a stop, pitching me to the floor, my body screaming with the pain of the impact.

I turn back to the window. Jack's gone.

The walls of the train car shrink around me, until I'm encased in a capsule of plastic and steel.

Through the speakers, a familiar voice.

"Welcome back, Fleur," Poppy says. "I'm so glad you're home."

12

ABOUT ALASKA

JACK

"What in Chronos's name is going on in here?" I jump, so engrossed I didn't even hear Chill come into our room. He nudges the door shut with his heel, his narrowed eyes roving over the sketches and scraps of notepaper spread over the floor, then jumping to the dozens of maps I've taped over the walls of the room.

Surveillance records drift from my lap in my rush to get up. "I'm glad you're here," I say, as calmly as possible. "There's something I need to talk to you about."

Chill sinks into his rolling chair. "Why do I get the feeling I'm not gonna like where this is going?"

I draw in a deep breath. I tell myself it's just like ripping off a bandage. I'll just come out and tell him. Chill's always had my back before. Once he understands what's at stake, he'll come around. "I met with Professor Lyon this morning—"

"About Alaska." His eyes climb back to the maps on the wall—pencil sketches of all four cardinal campus exits, the buildings they feed into on opposite ends of Greenwich Park, road maps of London, nautical charts, shipping schedules, flight plans, highway maps of the United States—and in them, I see his heart plummet.

"Yeah, about that . . ."

The rest comes out in an agonized rush. I tell him about my theory about what happened when Fleur held me, about the lion and the girl and the history books in the vault. He cringes as I tell him about my trip into the Crux with Noelle and my sparring match with Amber. His head's still buried in his hands when I finally rest a drawing in his lap.

The paper rustles, his grip tentative around the circuit I've drawn. Four batteries, one for each Season. Two negatively charged. Two positively charged. Opposites touching. No transmitters and no ley lines. A closed loop.

His eyes lift back to the maps. His head shakes back and forth as he puts it all together. "No way. Absolutely not."

"We can do it," I tell him. "We can live off the grid. We don't have to stay here."

"Says who?" he asks, shoving the paper at me and rolling back to his desk.

"Says Lyon! Says the books locked in the vault. Says all the history Chronos doesn't want us to know. Because he can't control us out there if we're not leashed by a transmitter to the ley lines. He can only control us in here."

Chill's voice rises to a fevered pitch he's never used with me before. "What are you asking me to do, Jack?"

131

"I'm asking you to *live*."

"I've got a life! Right here!"

"You spend all day watching TV, playing video games, and arguing with Poppy over a webcam."

"I finally get to go to Alaska, and you're going to make me walk away from that?" His face scrunches up like he'd really like to hit me. Maybe he should. Maybe then he'd understand. He's never had to draw someone else's blood in all the years we've been here.

"Don't you get it? *You're* not going to Alaska!" I throw an arm at the posters on his wall. "The pictures, the video feeds on your tablet, and that fake fucking window . . . None of it's real! You're not *going* anywhere. You'll be *here*, thirty stories below the goddamn ground, no matter what region they send me to!" I shut my eyes so I won't have to see the look on his face. I've just hung out the lie he's been telling himself and skinned it, bare and bloody. He can't pretend he doesn't see it. He can't keep looking away. "The rankings, the promotions . . . It's all a game. This"—I point to both of us—"this is real. The world outside this place," I say, pointing skyward. "That's real. You want to go places? Then let's cut the cord and go someplace real. Someplace *we* choose."

Chill's lip quivers, belying the defiance in his stare. "And what happens if I don't want to?"

"Then Poppy and Fleur die." Saying it cuts like a razor. My voice cracks on the words. "You can't pretend you didn't see their names on the rankings board. They're below the red line. They've only got one season left before they're up for the Purge. All we have to do is convince them to come with us."

Chill pales. He glances at the webcam on his desk, then quickly away.

"We both witnessed that Termination. We both saw what Chronos did. Could you live with yourself if that happened to Poppy?" Chill flinches, unwilling to look at me as I turn the knife. But maybe he needs to feel some pain to understand why we have to do this. I kneel in front of him. There's no way I can survive this without him. And I won't leave him here alone. "We can stop it. We can get them both out of here before anyone knows we're gone, but the only way this works is if we're all on board. All eight of us."

Chill swears quietly. He rubs his eyes beneath his frames, the resolve worn from his voice. "How the hell do you plan to manage that?"

"Fleur and Poppy have nothing to lose. If I can find a way to get through to Fleur, they shouldn't be hard to convince." Discarded sketches and plans crinkle under me as I rise to my feet. I rake my hair back, trying to see past all the obstacles, hoping some solid plan will form from the debris.

"What about Amber?" Chill crosses his arms and leans back in his chair, one dubious eyebrow cocked as if to say "Fat chance of that."

"I don't know," I admit, scrubbing a hand over my face. "Amber's mother's in Arizona, in some kind of nursing home. Amber wants to see her, but she hasn't let herself be Culled for a relocation out west. I can't figure out why."

"I'll give you two reasons," he says, counting them off on his fingers. "Julio. Verano."

I drag my face from my hands. "You can't seriously think she has feelings for Julio."

Chill snorts to himself. "Every girl here's got *feelings* for Julio. Just ask Fleur."

"They're not like that!"

"Whoa, Frosty!" He rolls his chair farther away from me as my body temperature free-falls. I turn away so he won't see the storm swirling in my eyes. The northern lights move like a green smaze through the faux window, and I rest my head against the glass, willing myself to calm. Frost blooms where my skin touches it. Chill sighs. "All I'm saying is that unless Julio's into Amber as much as Amber's into Julio, your plan isn't going to work. For all we know, that kiss back in 1990 didn't mean a damn thing. I mean, look at you and Noelle—"

I jerk my head from the window. "Back up. What kiss?"

Chill fishes Julio's file from the floor and flips through the pages. I snatch the fatality report from his hands, sinking onto the sofa as I read it. September 12, 1990. Worcester County Jail. Deceased: Julio Verano. Prevailing Season: Amber Chase. Cause of death: osculation.

"What's that mean? Osculation? Is it like suffocation? Asphyxiation?" Smuggling a weapon into a detention center is nearly impossible. She must have used her hands.

Chill laces his fingers behind his head. He raises a smug eyebrow, as if he's surprised I don't know. "It means prolonged contact of the lips."

They kissed.

I lurch off the sofa and grab the back of Chill's chair, spinning him around and rolling him to his computer. "Pull up the surveillance video."

Chill wrinkles his nose. "I don't keep that kind of stuff. What do you think I am? Some kind of voyeur?"

"They kissed in a jail. Jails have cameras."

"Marie and Woody would have confiscated the footage." He's right. Their Handlers would have buried it.

"Check the archives on the Control Room servers."

"Jack—"

"Just do it!"

With an aggrieved huff, Chill draws his keyboard into his lap. I pace the room, waiting as he hacks obscure back channels into the Observatory's main frame. "There. Are you happy?" He pushes away from his desk, rolling out of my way as I lean toward the screen.

The footage is old, black-and-white and snowy with static, but there's no mistaking who it is or what I'm seeing. Julio's locked in an empty cell. Amber tosses him a transmitter through the opening and Julio slips it around his ear. He stumbles to the bars, reaching through them to pull her face close. This wasn't a quick self-inflicted wound. The lead-up to their kiss is drawn out and slow, his hands tangled in her hair, hers digging into his shirt, struggling to hold on to each other as their lips meet and Julio disappears.

"It doesn't mean anything," Chill says.

"No, it means *everything*. He was trapped without a transmitter in a concrete cell, and she threw him a life rope. It was mid-September. His season was up." Chill doesn't argue. He knows exactly what that means. Julio had staggered to those bars like a dead man walking. If Amber hadn't tossed him that transmitter, he would have been *in the wind* before his jailers even realized he was gone. That bright yellow sun embroidered over her heart on her gi has nothing to do with me or Arizona. It's not a talisman against the cold or a token of where she wants to be. It's her reason for holding back. "She's in love with him," I say, certain that I'm right. "She saved his life. Same as Fleur did for me."

"Jack, that was decades ago. As far as I can tell, they've hardly spoken since. They spent months in disciplinary review for that stunt."

Chill hands me an infirmary report detailing the injuries Julio sustained in Reconditioning—contusions, burns, lacerations, fractured ribs . . . I feel sick when I imagine Fleur going through the same thing. "Julio put in for a transfer the very next year, but Gaia denied it."

"A transfer? To where?"

He tucks Julio's file back into his drawer and fishes out an open bag of smuggled Doritos. It crinkles as he grabs a chip and pops it into his mouth. "The West Coast," he says between crunches. "Presumably to get as far away from Amber as possible."

I pinch the bridge of my nose against the sharp smell of powdered cheese. The cartilage is still sore and I feel a headache coming on. I thought for sure I had it all figured out. And we're almost out of time. Amber leaves for her hunt next week. And if Fleur's Reconditioning was as bad as Doug says it was, I'll be lucky if she'll even listen to me. "I must be crazy to think I can save Fleur and Poppy. I can't even figure out how to get us out of the damn Observa . . ."

Chill pops another chip in his mouth and licks the powder off his fingers.

Don't let anybody catch you taking out the trash . . .

"Vegetable day," I say under my breath.

"'Scuse me?"

Boreas'll get rid of it, same way he brought it all down . . .

The crates I saw on Boreas's dolly in the mess hall were huge. Big enough to stow a person inside. "That's how we'll get out of here. Boreas will do anything for a price. You said it yourself—no one will notice a few extra boxes coming or going."

Chill stops crunching. His throat bobs as he swallows a mouthful of dry chips. "This is not a crate of beef jerky or Pop Rocks we're talking about smuggling, Jack."

"We have money. Lots of it. We've been investing our allowances and skimming from our operating accounts for thirty years. You've seen Fleur's and Amber's financial records. You know they have, too. How much do you want to bet Julio's been doing the same?"

He rolls up the bag of chips and drops it into his drawer. "Even if you *could* get everyone to agree, there's no way we'd get out of here without Chronos finding out. So what's your brilliant plan, assuming he doesn't already know what you're up to?"

"I don't know." I drag a hand through my hair, kicking at discarded plans and drawings. Chill's right. Chronos knew I was going to do something stupid even before I did. He'll see every possible move in his staff before I make it. I've got a dozen different plans taped to the wall, and every one of them is dangerous. They're all flawed. I don't know which one to choose. I rub my eyes, wishing the answer were obvious, remembering what Lyon said, about how the eye of the staff is only as clear as our own memories. Our own choices.

I lift my head to the maps. To all the schedules and routes and half-baked plans. And suddenly, the fact that there is no one right answer makes perfect sense. "I can't be the one to plan the escape."

Chill looks at me like I've completely lost my mind.

"If I come up with the plan, Chronos will know the whole thing before we get one foot out the door. So we break it up. Delegate responsibilities. Everyone has a job. You hack us off the Guard's monitors. Julio and Marie get us out of the Observatory. Amber and Woody arrange to get us out of London. I get us someplace Chronos won't find us, and we keep moving." I pace the room, talking faster as ideas shake loose and tumble from my mouth. "We'll plant bread crumbs everywhere. Map out dozens of routes. Book multiple flights to different destinations. We'll shift our plans as we go. Chronos will see too many possible outcomes. If my future isn't clear, he won't know where to look for us."

Chill whistles, long and low. "You know this is crazy, right? Like, two-beers-on-a-double-black-diamond-level crazy?" In other words, he's pretty sure we're all going to die.

"Yeah," I tell him. "I know."

13
THE PATH OF LOW RESISTANCE

<u>JACK</u>

I've spent the last week preparing for this, and I feel a little sick. Sweat slicks my palms as Boreas unlocks the cold-storage room off the hallway to the main service elevators and ushers Chill, Poppy, and me inside. Chill and I consolidated all our mattress cash—money skimmed from our operating accounts and left over from our annual stipends. We paid Boreas half to get us all here. The other half paid for his silence.

Poppy hugs herself and shivers. She lingers by the door, casting distrustful glances at me and Chill. Chill glances back with equal amounts of uncertainty. Poppy refused to meet with us at first, only agreeing once we told her that we'd come up with a way to save Fleur from the Purge. But the longer the anxious silence drags out between the three of us, the more I worry she's changed her mind.

We all jump when the door to the cold-storage room flies open. Amber stops dead, the heel of one boot still planted in the hall outside.

139

Her eyes dart over each of us—me, then Chill, then Poppy. A Spring Handler poses no threat to her, but a Winter—even one just out of stasis—shouldn't be underestimated in a tightly enclosed refrigerated space. My Handler's presence only heightens the risk.

"What's this about?" She waves the cryptic note I paid Boreas to deliver to her room, a single sheet of notebook paper folded around two hall passes, containing one hand-written word—*ARIZONA*.

Amber's knife hand is twitchy at her side, level with her hip. Weapons are forbidden outside the sparring rooms, but Amber would be a fool to show up unarmed to a mystery meeting with me.

"Thanks for coming." I keep my hands where she can see them. "This is Chill, and Poppy."

"What are they doing here?" she asks, foot lingering strategically in the hall.

"Maybe you should've brought Woody along, if you were worried about being alone with me."

"Real diplomatic, Jack," Chill mutters.

Amber saunters into the room, watching me around an auburn curtain of hair. It falls over one shoulder, covering her ear. She's wired. I expected no less. "Unlike you, I don't need a team of babysitters," she says irritably.

Chill grumbles to himself as he taps commands into his tablet, clearly stung by the babysitter comment. His glasses ride low on the bridge of his nose, and when he looks up, he glares at her over the empty frames. "Woody's on his way. I put a block on your signal right after you got here. By now, I'm betting he's freaking out because you're not answering. By my calculations, given the shortest distance between your room and the service hall, Woody ought to be joining us in . . ." He glances at his tablet. "Three . . . two . . . one."

There's a crash as the steel doors down the hall swing open into the walls, followed by the frenetic pounding of feet. Woody's ratty Converses skid to a stop in front of the open storage room, his long hair clinging to the sweat on his narrow face. He bends over his knees, breathing too hard to speak.

Amber reaches over the threshold and drags him inside. She kicks the door shut. "Spill it, Jack. What's this all about?"

Up until now, I've been intentionally vague about my reasons for wanting to bring the five of us together. And this—right here and now—is my moment of truth. If I've assessed them right, the dominoes I've lined up will fall in a perfect path out of here. But if I'm wrong, any one of them could bring the entire plan crashing down around me. I can't afford to screw this up.

"I found a way out."

Woody pants, mopping sweat from his brow. "What do you mean, 'out'? What is he talking ab—"

Amber holds up a hand. "Get to the point," she snaps.

"I've been meeting with Professor Lyon—"

"Wait. You mean *the* Professor Lyon?" Woody asks, finally catching his breath.

"He's supposed to be coaching me for our relocation to Anchorage next season."

The color drains from Poppy's face. "You're leaving the mid-Atlantic?" Her voice is thin, tinged with worry. A new Winter poses a threat, an unknown variable in an already impossible equation. Fleur's got one season left before the Purge. Even if she manages to get herself over the red line next spring, any change in her routine will only make it that much harder to stay above it.

"We all know Fleur doesn't have much time. And when a Season is Terminated . . ." I clear my throat, finding it harder than I'd thought to look her in the eyes and speak the words out loud. "When a Season is Terminated, her Handler is Terminated, too." Chill's gaze drops to the floor, no doubt picturing the same dustpan I am. "I don't want that to happen any more than you do—to you or Fleur—but maybe it doesn't have to."

"So you're going to help us?" she asks, cautiously optimistic. "You're going to help get Fleur out of the red? Because I've done the math," she says, her voice rising, the words coming faster. "If I can get her released from the Observatory by March first, and she kills you by March fourth, if she can hold on until June twelfth, there's a chance her scores could climb enough to get her over the red line. She just needs to keep her moods under control. You know, the rain . . . She's been depressed. The storms have been—"

"And then what?" I ask. "What if she can't? What happens the next year?" Poppy's face falls, because she already knows. It's the fear she won't face—not until it's too late. "Every Spring under that red line will be gunning for high scores, desperate to save themselves. Even if I let Fleur kill me early, there's no guarantee it would work. But there's another way to save you both."

Poppy shakes her head, looking from me to Amber to Chill. I see the moment the light switches on and she realizes where this conversation is going. She stumbles back against a vegetable crate. "Have you all lost your minds?"

"We're not stuck here, Poppy!" I fight the urge to reach out and shake her. "We have a choice. We just never realized it. If she knew, she could choose—"

"Fleur doesn't have a choice!" Her lip trembles. "She has to follow the rules. Whatever you're up to, it's going to get us all killed!"

"Only if they catch us."

"Jack," Amber says, her tone guarded. I can see the wheels turning as she stares at the healing cut on my lip. "I know what you're thinking. But what happened in the sparring room doesn't prove anything."

"I can get us out of here alive, Amber. I know I can."

"What do you mean, *'get us out of here'*?" Woody asks, stepping around Amber.

She puts a hand out in front of him, holding him back, as if to protect him from me. "Newsflash, snowflake. Handlers don't get to leave."

"They can't stay behind," I say. "They'll be safer with us. Off the grid."

"What do you mean, *'off the grid'*?" Woody asks over her head. "Is that even an option?"

"No one's ever done it and survived. You go off the lines, you're in the wind. It's suicide. Everyone knows that." Amber's eyes bore into me. She stands stubbornly between Woody and me, determined to keep the truth from him.

"We *don't* know that. None of us know," I say, the pressure building inside me like a storm. "Don't tell me you've never noticed the missing portraits of Ananke in the gallery. Don't tell me you've never noticed the books missing from the Hall of Records. Chronos only tells us the stories he wants us to believe!" And I have to believe my own future is one

143

of them. That Chronos chose the vision he did to frighten me, to keep me here, to discourage me from pursuing the truth. "Haven't you ever wondered why our lessons don't include any history before the invention of the stasis chambers?"

"Because it's simple! They all died, Jack!" Amber's voice rises, as if she knows she's losing ground. "One season, that's all they got!"

"If that's true, how do you explain Professor Lyon?"

Woody's brows knit. The fight slips from Amber's shoulders. No one's sure how old Professor Lyon actually is. The only time I dared to ask, the answer he gave me was vague. But there are whispers around campus. Rumors that drift from the faculty lounges and swirl in his wake through the halls. Some say before he was a Winter, he served in Queen Elizabeth I's court.

"He was in *Antarctica*," Amber reasons. "Winter never ends there. He could have lived there forever, if he wanted to."

"But he didn't! He only lived there for three hundred years. You really think he survived a hundred years before that alone?" None of them speak. "Seasons survived off the lines once. We coexisted. Professor Lyon told me as much. He was there. He lived it. There were no stasis chambers. No ranking systems or Purges," I tell Poppy. "There were no segregated dorms. Lyon made his own rules, and we can, too."

Amber's eyes lift to mine. The room smells earthy, like the contents of the crates piled high on every side of us, like root vegetables and potatoes. Autumn and winter. And maybe a little like hope.

Woody is first to break the silence. "But how would you survive away from the ley lines? You need the stasis chambers to regenerate."

"We wouldn't need them if we never burned out. Ever heard of a secondary cell?" I unfold my sketch. Woody steps forward and takes it from me before Amber can stop him.

"A rechargeable battery," Woody says, studying the drawing. "But how?"

"I think Seasons used to work together," I explain. "In pairs. Groups, even. I don't know exactly how, but I have a theory that the polarities between us and our connections to the ley lines form a circuit.

"When Amber and I fight, a chemical reaction between us causes a discharge of energy every time we touch. At the end of her season, she's weaker than I am—negatively charged. She takes the hit of my positive charge whenever we make contact. But that energy doesn't feed her. It flows *through* her to the next point along the circuit—into the ley lines—taking the last of her power with it until she burns out."

"A dead battery," Woody says, passing the drawing to Amber.

"Exactly." I let out a held breath. Poppy leans in, reluctantly looking over Amber's shoulder. "If we eliminate the ley line, we close the loop. Our bodies will redirect their charges back to one another, creating a circular flow. As one Season strengthens, it recharges the other, until we eventually balance out."

"How?" Woody asks.

"Sustained contact between the polarities." They all give me quizzical looks. "We hold each other."

Amber's jaw drops. She looks away, her face flaming.

"How do you even know it will work?" Poppy asks.

"Amber and I charged each other during a sparring match last week."

"For, like, two seconds!" she says, folding her arms over her chest.

"It worked for Jack and Fleur, too," Chill adds. "Their transmitters were off. She kept Jack alive just long enough for me to find him and channel him home. The only reason he isn't in the wind is because she wouldn't let go."

Poppy holds herself, paling as she sags against a crate. All her questions about what went wrong with our transmitters on the mountain are finally being answered, but her sickened expression tells me she wishes she didn't know.

"Then how do you explain the no-kissing thing?" Amber asks. She shrinks back from the question when we all turn to gape at her.

"I've been thinking about that, too." My cheeks warm when their raised eyebrows turn to me. "I think a kiss acts as a catalyst. It speeds up the chemical reaction—"

"Creating a path of low resistance, until the weaker of the Seasons shorts out," Chill adds.

Woody nods. "So as long as there's no kissing, everyone's cool."

"No!" Amber and I say in unison. Our eyes catch. I finish for the both of us.

"Once we close the loop, it should be possible to balance the load. As long as we're balanced, no one shorts out."

"So as long as you're paired with a different Season—one with different powers—you can balance each other," Woody says, catching on. "Then you can move freely without disrupting the weather or hurting each other."

"That's why the Guards can go anywhere without being detected," I explain. "They have the power of all four seasons. Their magic is inherently balanced."

"In case you've forgotten, they're designed that way for a reason," Amber says. "To make it easier for them to *hunt* us. There's no way they'll let us just disappear out there."

"It's only four of us," I point out. "There are hundreds of regions around the globe. We're small potatoes, blips on a radar map. Any impact we have would be limited to a radius of a few hundred miles from wherever we are. So we keep moving. We don't stay in one place long enough to cause any real damage, and after a while, they'll all give up and stop looking for us. We could hide anywhere."

"That's great for both of you, but what about us?" Poppy pushes herself off the crate, anger coloring her cheeks. "*Your* magic comes from Gaia. She *gave* it to you. It exists *inside* you, which makes it a whole lot easier to *steal*," she says, piling theft onto our list of crimes. "But what happens to *us* out there?"

"Poppy's right," Chill says. "Handlers don't have any magic of our own. Chronos controls our immortality, and as far as he's concerned, it's just a fringe benefit of the job we do. If we're lucky enough to make it out of here, we have to assume we'll age at a normal rate, same as Lyon. Same as all the retired staff and faculty do." The Handlers exchange sober looks.

Amber shakes her head. She backs toward the door, taking Woody by the arm. "No. Absolutely not. We're out."

Woody plants his feet. He holds my gaze, a fervor in his eyes. "I want to go with you."

Amber gapes at him. "You heard Chill! There's no guarantee how long you'll have out there. You could get hit by a bus or get mugged or die of the flu!" She holds up a hand, signaling the end of the conversation.

"No! *I* go out into the big dangerous world. *You* stay here where it's safe so you can take care of me."

Woody rounds on her. "Would you stop thinking about yourself for once!"

Amber's lips part. She inhales shallowly, as if it hurts to breathe.

Woody's voice falls soft, pleading. "When was the last time you saw the sun?"

Her eyes water. "One hundred and seventy-two days ago," she answers, as if every day's a hash mark etched in her heart.

"I miss it too," he says, touching his chest. He reaches for the piece of paper in her hand and holds it out in front of her. She blinks at the word *ARIZONA*, and a tear falls down her face. "I've known you almost fifty years, Amber. Longer than anyone. *Better* than anyone. You wouldn't have come here if you didn't want this, too."

She darts shamed looks around the storage room, as if she wishes it weren't so small and we weren't all here. "But you're all I have left," she whispers.

"I'm not *asking* to leave you. I'm asking to go *with* you." He rests a hand on her shoulder.

She swats away a tear, pretending it's something else.

"We'll stop in Arizona," I offer. "For whatever's there. However long you want. I promise."

Woody turns to the rest of us before Amber can muster the voice to argue. "If Jack's right, it will take all four of you to survive off the grid. Where's Marie?"

"She refused to come." I glance pointedly at Amber. "One of us will have to talk to Julio."

She shrinks away from me, her jaw hardening as the others look at her, too. "No. Are you kidding? I can't be the one to do it! There's no way Julio would let me get close enough to talk to him."

"He let you get close enough to kiss him," Chill mutters.

Amber's face glows hot enough to set us all on fire. I elbow Chill in the ribs.

"Tell them, Woody!" she barks at him. Woody just stares at her, holding my drawing as if it's something fragile, precious. "Fine!" she says with a roll of her eyes. "I'll talk to him. But I'm not making any promises."

The rush of adrenaline I feel is almost dizzying. We're one step closer to the ledge. "That just leaves Fleur."

Poppy's silent, her arms crossed tightly over her chest. She shakes her head, her voice trembling when she finally speaks. "We still have one spring left. I can get her above the red line. We don't have to do this." She shoulders past Woody and Amber.

"Poppy!" She stops just before the door, refusing look at me. "This is Fleur's life, too. She should have a say in it."

It takes all Poppy's weight to pull the release lever. She nearly trips on the threshold in her hurry to go. Chill starts to follow.

"Let her go," I tell him. Poppy isn't going to budge. She's in denial. She's too afraid. Somehow, I'll have to get through to Fleur alone.

14

AS THE CROW FLIES

JACK

"You're early, Jack." Amber pushes past me with a gentle shove. I rub the burning sensation she leaves on my solar plexus, wrinkling my nose against the sickly sweet fetor of death and the pumpkin spice Frap dangling in a Starbucks cup from her hand. She adjusts her backpack on her shoulder and smooths down her hair. "Too early. It isn't even Thanksgiving break yet."

She maneuvers through the crowded hall, through animated conversations about exams and parties and a soccer game that happened over the weekend, as I struggle to keep up. It's all so mundane, familiar in a far-off way that makes me irritable and nostalgic all at the same time. I don't know how Amber stands it. I can't imagine choosing to spend my only free three months each year pretending to be a high school student. A teacher walks by, shielding his full coffee mug from the throng of oncoming traffic. He slows, frowning as he passes, as if he's trying to place me. I slide in behind Amber, letting myself be carried along by the rush of students on their way to class.

I lean over her shoulder. "Did you talk to Julio?"

She takes a slow sip of her Frap. Shrugs. "I managed to get a few words in."

Someone jostles me from behind, knocking me into her back. "Can we go somewhere we can talk about it?"

"I'll be late for class. Come back in a week." My temperature plummets. Nobody's making Amber go to class. She won't even be here long enough to finish out her semester, and we have far more important things to worry about. Amber shivers. She glares at me over her shoulder. "Back off, Jack. You're freezing. And your eyes are doing that creepy Winter thing."

I grab Amber by the shirtsleeve and drag her into an open janitor's closet, kicking the door shut when we're both inside. She swears when I accidentally brush her skin as I grope blindly for a light switch in the dark.

A spark snaps to life in her hand, the wavering flame casting shadows over her scowling face. She aims a pointed glance at her knee between my legs.

"Come on, Amber. This is important." A pull string hangs close to the flame and I jerk it hard. The closet floods with harsh white light. "What did Verano say?"

She snuffs out the fire and sinks back against the wall, shoving a mop bucket out of her way with her foot. "I tried, okay? He was at some party when I found him. I chased him a mile down the boardwalk before he finally stopped to listen. He refused to mute his transmitter, and Marie wouldn't give us two seconds alone."

"Did you tell him about Fleur?"

She nods, jabbing her straw in and out of the lid of her cup. "He took it pretty hard. He just kept saying it was his fault. I've never seen him so upset before."

"So you waited, right? You tried again?"

"Not exactly." She looks up at me through her lashes, still stabbing her drink. "He didn't give me a chance. He just said, 'Thanks for coming, Red, but I'll find my own ride home.' Then he turned his back on me, like he didn't even care if I came after him. I didn't know what to think. He reached for his transmitter and I panicked. I was afraid he was going to turn it off and do something stupid. So I sent him home." She winces, as if that last bit hurt her as much as it hurt me.

I fall against the wall beside her. "Poppy still refuses to take my calls or return Chill's emails, so I paid Boreas to smuggle a letter to Fleur."

"Did she read it?"

I shake my head. "Poppy intercepted it, shredded it, and sent it back to me in about a hundred pieces." I scrub a hand over my face. "She's going to push Fleur to come at me hard. How the hell am I going to slow her down long enough to listen to me?" I only have three months to cash out my investments, tie up loose ends, and convince Fleur to come with us. I'll need every possible hour I can steal from what's left of Amber's season to pull this off.

She stares into the swirling remnants of her cup. "You'll find a way to get through to her," she says through a wistful sigh. "She'll listen to you. And Julio will listen to Fleur, I'm sure of it. If there's a way to save her, he will." I glance over at her. I've killed Amber dozens of times, but I've never seen her look so defeated.

"Were you able to handle the rest?" I hope she at least managed to secure a getaway vehicle.

"I found us a—" I hold up a hand before she can tell me anything more. The less I know, the safer we are. She presses her lips tight. Nods in understanding. "Boreas is handling the arrangements." Boreas is a necessary risk, an outside mind to insulate us from the details of our own plan until we're clear of the Observatory. "How about you? Did you find a safe house?"

"It's handled," I tell her.

I haven't been to my grandfather's cabin since the winter Gaia first found me. The property's been abandoned since he died. The cabin itself was simple and rustic, but it had been shrouded in trees off an unmarked road, making it the safest possible place for Fleur. There had been no house number or mailbox. No distinctive features that would make it easy to identify. No recent receipts or transactions Chronos might pick from my memories. My recollections of the place are fuzzy at best—me and Chill huddled by the fire after I pulled him from the pond, trying to make sense of what had happened to us. I shake off the memory, forcing all thoughts of the safe house from my head.

"I'll book us a few flights out of London," I say. To Zurich, Toronto, Amsterdam . . . From those cities, I'll buy train tickets, bus tickets, reserve a few rental cars. I'll line up a few apartments and hotels. The more possible escape routes Chronos sees in my memories, the harder it will be for him to find us. "That should keep him busy for a while. By the time we make landfall, he'll probably assume we're in the wind and stop looking."

"And if he doesn't?"

I shut my eyes against the vision in Chronos's staff. Of Kai Sampson sighting me down the length of her arrow. Of the ice cracking under me, drowning me. I will myself to change it. "Then we keep running."

Amber kicks off the wall with a firm shake of her head. She sticks a finger in my chest. "Let's get something straight, Jack. I'm not *running* from anyone."

I nod, careful not to say anything else that might piss her off. This truce between us feels shaky at best. Claire Sanford ran away from home. She froze to death on the streets of New York, and she's never kept her contempt for me a secret. I know what it's like to fear the cold. To die by its hand. It's costing her more than she's letting on to make this fragile peace with me.

"Then why are you doing it?" It feels like I should know. Like she deserves that much. She eases away from me.

"I'm doing this for Woody and my mom." She picks at her straw, her jaw set around whatever it is she's not saying. I haven't seen my own mother since the day she dumped me on the front steps of my boarding school, and I can't think of a single reason I'd go looking for her now.

Amber's throat is tight when she finally breaks the silence. "I left home when I was seventeen," she says. "I ran off with some boy because my mom told me not to. The last words she said to me were, 'You only ever think about yourself. You'll never change.'" There's a hint of irony in the hopelessness of her laugh. "If only she could see me now. I'm autumn incarnate—the very embodiment of *change*. For fifty years, I've tried to be the person she wanted me to be. I've gone to school even when I didn't have to, I've come home on time, I've followed the rules . . . So why the hell do I still feel like she's right?" She tosses her empty cup into a mop bucket. "I'll get you as far as Arizona," she says. "I'm not making any promises after that."

She draws a folding knife from her backpack and drops the backpack to the ground.

She holds the weapon out to me, bracing herself as I take it.

But the knife feels heavy and all wrong somehow.

With an impatient sigh, she flips open the blade and presses the grip into my palm. "They're counting on you. Don't fuck this up." Chin held high, she stares into the distance over my shoulder. For a flash of a second, I think I see the desert—the glimmer of heat waves like a mirage on its surface—or maybe it's her soul in her eyes.

15

ONE FINAL HUNT

March 11, 2021

FLEUR

"We can still do this. Be ruthless." Poppy thrusts a suitcase in my hand. Everything I need will fit inside a backpack, which means she's probably stowed a few weapons that would never make it onto an airplane in a carry-on bag. "Find Jack as soon as you land and get it over with. The sooner his season is over, the better. We need all the days we can get." I nod, for Poppy, even though my stomach turns at the thought of it. We both know what's at stake this time.

I take the Spring transport elevator at the end of our wing to the surface. It opens inside a small rowhouse just east of Greenwich Park. All the blinds are drawn, daylight seeping in around the edges of the windows. A Guard's stationed at the desk in the parlor. She checks my papers and my transmitter before signing me out.

The hazy gray sunlight outside is blinding, and my stasis-sensitive eyes water against the glare. Greenwich Park is a rolling carpet of green on the other side of the brick wall across the street, and my shoes suddenly feel too tight as I watch couples picnicking and children playing on the lawn. Every cell in my body yearns to walk barefoot through the grass, to coax an early blossom from the buds on the trees, but my directive is to get settled in my region as quickly as possible, with minimal disruption to the others I'm forced to pass through on my way. No conflicts or storms or unnecessary displays of magic. No engaging with other Seasons until I reach my destination. Then I can be as cruel and merciless as Doug and Poppy expect me to be.

Poppy's got me booked on the first flight into Washington, DC. But the fact that Jack is actually in DC seems odd. By the time I make it to the US coast, he's usually holed up someplace high and cold. His choice to stay in the city this late when he knows I'm coming has Poppy on edge.

I can't help but wonder if this reckless change in his pattern is indicative of some larger, more significant change between us. If his punishment was as brutal as mine, I'm not entirely sure I blame him for returning the note I asked Poppy to send through Chill—he hadn't even bothered to read it, she said.

Still, facing off in the city feels aggressive, as if he's stepping into a ring and he plans to go down fighting.

You can do this, I tell myself. *Apologize and get it over with. It'll be better for him this way, too.*

The second the plane touches down, I turn on my cell phone and find a message from Poppy. She's got a signal on Jack. He's boarding a Red Line metro train, heading downtown. I duck into a restroom and transfer my pocketknife, toothbrush, and a change of clothes into a backpack, leaving the suitcase in an empty stall before catching a cab into the city.

In less than an hour, I'm downtown.

I find an empty park bench near the Washington Monument and wait for Poppy's call. The sky is uncertain, sunny and blue one minute and obscured by chunky clouds the next. A cold north wind rustles the buds in the trees and snaps the ends of the flags. I don't know what to expect when I find him. Don't know who we'll be to each other. All I know is that the person I have to be today—the person Poppy needs me to be—isn't anyone I've let Jack see before. And I already hate myself for it.

My phone buzzes.

"He's on foot. Heading east on Independence."

I start toward the Smithsonian at a brisk jog, blending in with the other afternoon runners doing laps around the National Mall. I pick up speed as I catch Jack's scent—a combination of smells that makes the hair on my neck stand on end. Peppermint and evergreen and holly berry . . . These should be smells I miss. Instead, I grind my teeth against a phantom pain in my jaw, angry for reasons that shouldn't make sense.

Slowly, the smells give way to more familiar ones. The earthy scents of moss and mulch flood the air as I skid to a stop outside the Botanic Garden.

The Jack I know wouldn't be caught dead here.

And yet I feel him . . . close.

An abandoned jacket is slung over a bench by the door. I look around for signs of its owner, but the sidewalk is empty. I pick it up and press it to my face. The liner is cold. It smells like pine and winterberries, and just holding it makes my chest ache.

I can't bear to put it on. But I can't make myself leave it.

I tie it around my waist. Cautiously, I open the door to the gardens and step inside. The air's sticky, sweet with pollen and far too warm for a Winter to tolerate, yet there are hints of him everywhere. I'm drawn toward an invisible trail—a crisp, cold draft that leads me into the greenhouses. It grows stronger, radiating from a thawing circle of frost on the edge of a raised flower bed.

A single broken lily lies in the middle of it. My heart skips when I catch sight of the tiny slip of paper tucked inside its frozen bloom.

"What is that?" Poppy asks.

"Nothing." I pick it up, angling it out of range of the transmitter's view. "I lost his scent. See if you can find him on a heat map." While Poppy's busy getting a lead on Jack, I pry the paper loose.

We both know how this ends. But what if it doesn't have to? Our First life is passed. Our 2nd is at a crossroads. We're standing on the corner of our Independence. Read between the lines. It's all possible.

I fold it quickly before Poppy sees it in her feeds.

We know how the story's supposed *to end. But what if it doesn't have to?* Those were the words written in the margins of "The Good-Morrow." I had read the inscription. Had even let myself wonder. And now I'm certain the message was from Jack. But why? What does it mean?

It's all possible.

"I've got him!" Poppy's all fireworks and alarms in my ear. "Moving fast. A quarter mile. Almost due east of you."

I rush for the exit, breaking into a sprint when I reach the gravel

159

path. I pass the Capitol Building and First Street, dodging joggers and tourists. A taxi grazes my knees as I slam to a stop at a red light.

"Where is he, Poppy?" I crane my neck to see over the cars on the adjacent streets. The roads here are a grid, but the one I'm on splits, forking diagonally to the right.

"I don't know. There are too many buildings. Too many people. They're drowning you out." Because my blood is warm, like the rest of them. But Jack's runs cold. He should be easy to find. Which means we've lost him. "Where are you?" she asks.

I check the street sign overhead. "I'm at the corner of Independence and Pennsylvania . . . Just past . . ."

I look left. I'm just past 2nd.

Our 2nd is at a crossroads.

The light turns green and pedestrians flood the intersection, weaving around me, shoving me with their elbows as they rush past. I turn toward the huge gray building between First and 2nd Street. The Library of Congress.

Read between the lines. It's all possible.

I dart between oncoming cars toward it. Racing up the front stairs of the library, I throw open the door to the vestibule and jerk to a stop.

A line forms in front of a row of metal detectors. I watch as tourists and visitors empty their pockets and put their purses and backpacks on a table to be searched by security guards. Jack's scent is faint, but stronger the closer I get to the checkpoint. He's here. Unarmed.

I back out of the building, reach under my sweatshirt for my pocket-knife, and dump it into the nearest trash can before getting back in line.

"Seriously, Jack?" I mutter to myself once I'm cleared through. "You had to pick the biggest library in the world?"

Static crackles in my ear. "I'm having a hard time hearing you, Fleur. There's a terrible echo."

"Never mind," I say loudly, drawing a glare from a lady behind a reference desk. I keep moving. The place is enormous. I stand in the center of a cavernous room, surrounded by archways and balconies. If I were Jack—if someone were hunting me—where would I go? Where would I hide?

I follow signs to the elevators and check the directory. Ten years ago, I managed to shake Julio in a hotel in Atlantic City by taking the elevator to every floor. This building only has five levels and a basement.

The Basement: Geography and Maps Room.

It's harder for Poppy to pick up his signal below gound. He's burrowing. He's done it before.

I reach for my knife before I remember it's not there.

"I don't like this," Poppy says. "Not one bit. He's trying to get you alone. You can wait outside and nab him when he surfaces. Do not get in the—"

I step into the elevator alone.

When the elevator doors open, Jack's scent is everywhere and I fight back the urge to be sick.

I pause at a set of double doors. They drip with condensation. They're still cold where he touched them.

"Tunnel to Cannon House Office Building (Staff Only)," a sign reads.

A tunnel . . . That explains why Poppy lost his signal.

I kick the wall. "Where is he, Poppy?"

But all I get through my transmitter is static.

I follow Jack's trail backward to an empty table in the far corner of the Map Room. It's littered with open books and marked-up documents. A chair is pulled out, left at an angle, the wood still chilled where he sat.

I sift through the abandoned atlases Jack's left open. Meteorological maps of the Atlantic. Physical and climate maps of the United States. Highway maps with multiple routes highlighted from one coast to the other. And in the middle of them all, a volume of poems, opened to "The Good-Morrow."

My eyes skim the words I already know by heart.

Let maps to other, worlds on worlds have shown,
Let us possess one world, each hath one, and is one . . .

If our two loves be one, or, thou and I
Love so alike, that none do slacken, none can die.

None can die.

Beside the mountain of books, four rechargeable batteries pin down the curled corners of a DC subway map. A diagram's scribbled on the back, the closed looping circuit of a secondary cell.

And a note.

From Jack.

What if the Red Line isn't the end for us? What if it's only the beginning?

I sink into Jack's empty chair, struggling to make sense of it all. Slowly, the messages and the poem and the maps and the batteries all begin to overlap. Suddenly, I see his plan—the path he's laid out so clearly.

And if I'm right, I know exactly where to find him.

I sit alone in the subway car, my pockets empty of weapons and my earpiece blaringly silent, staring out into the blackness under the DC streets as the train hurtles down the tracks. There's no signal this deep underground. Poppy's probably livid. Or terrified. And I wonder if maybe I should be, too. How well do I really know Jack beyond the few weeks of cloak and dagger we play every year? Beyond our arguments over tragic love stories, my intentional misses, and his casual flirtations while he's still strong enough to laugh at me?

This is crazy.

Jack kills Amber. I kill Jack. Julio kills me. Amber kills Julio. That's how the game works. That's how the world works. Jack's crazy to run from Gaia or Chronos or any of this. Crazy to think the rules don't apply to all of us.

Isn't he?

I step onto the platform at Wheaton Station. The Red Line stop is the deepest station in DC, seventy meters below ground, the same station Jack fled through, desperate to lose me, the first time we met.

The air in the subway tunnel is close—musty and warm—but he's been here. I'm certain of it. The herd of people ascending the escalators to the ground level is stubborn and slow, the sky already dark when I finally push my way to the top.

I lift my nose to the wind. The street sign above my head reads Georgia Avenue, but none of these buildings or shops or restaurants look the same as they do in my memories. Across the street, the twinkling lights of a construction site catch my eye. It was a shopping center then. Soon, by the looks of it, another will spring up in its place. And it seems both tragically wrong and completely right that he's brought me here.

What if it's only the beginning?

Static crackles in my ear as Poppy's signal returns. But there's a reason Jack's been leaving messages in codes, deep underground where Poppy can't see them. As if he's trying to share a secret. Or he wants to be alone. Maybe it's not only Chronos's Guards he's hiding from.

I shut my eyes against a ripple of fear. A memory of Noelle's icy hands and Doug's sneer.

I sniff the air. Catch Jack's scent. And I turn my transmitter off.

16
OUR WAKING SOULS

FLEUR

Jack's scent bleeds out of the underground parking garage beneath the spines and crossbeams of what will soon be a new mall. I catch a glimpse of his shirtsleeve through the chain-link fence at the edge of the construction site. The rest of him lies hidden behind a concrete barrier and instinct makes me reach for the knife I dumped earlier, before I remember it's gone. I stoop to grab a broken bottle instead.

My shoe splashes in a shallow puddle. Jack starts. Doesn't rise from where he's sitting on the cold, damp ground. His hand shakes, barely strong enough to hold him upright.

Approaching the barrier with cautious footsteps, I slide down the concrete so we're sitting back to back, and I set my broken bottle down, just out of reach. We both know six inches of concrete and a wire fence between us is nothing more than an excuse not to kill him. And we both know how the night is supposed to end.

I tip my head back against the barrier, breathing his scent through my mouth, tamping down the bone-deep urge I feel to take up the broken bottle again. The wind shifts, cedar and pine washing over me, fight-or-flight adrenaline raging in my blood. I close my eyes and listen to his labored breathing. To the cough he tries to stifle. To the steady drip of water from a crossbeam overhead.

"Do you remember the first time we met?" His voice is gravelly, as if he's fighting sleep. "It was right here. On this spot. You had no idea what you were doing." I can almost hear the slow curl of his smile.

"Me?" I squeeze my eyes shut tight, forcing all the ghosts from my mind—Denver and Lixue, Noelle and Doug. I smile a little, too, as the memory of that night with Jack comes back to me. "You were the one who was confused."

"I wasn't expecting you. I was expecting Welby. He got reassigned right before you started. He was six foot three with bad breath and chronic gas, and he had a disturbing fondness for long swords."

A choked laugh slips out of me. "Were you disappointed?"

"No."

I open my eyes, blinking up at the night sky through the shadows of the support beams overhead. There was a roof back then. "Even after I pushed you?"

"I fell long before you pushed me," he says quietly.

A knot swells in my throat. "I'm sorry."

"I'm not." His hand slides close to the fence. I hate myself for not trusting myself to do the same. For recoiling from the cold. How is it so easy for him?

"Tell me something about you," I say, desperate to chase away the brutal images the Guards burned into my mind.

"Like what?" He sounds tired, but not weary. More like sleepy in a dreamy sort of way.

"I don't know," I say, trying not to sound as irritable and desperate as I feel. "I feel like you know everything about me. But you've never told me anything about you." All those ornaments I left him suddenly feel foolish. Jack was smart never to reveal too much to me. Every peek into our personal lives makes a Season vulnerable. Every insignificant detail—our habits, our dislikes, our history—is an angle that can be turned against us during a hunt.

He responds without a whiff of hesitation. "What do you want to know?"

"What's your favorite band?"

"The Ramones."

"Movie?"

"*The Empire Strikes Back*."

"Food?"

"Tacos."

"Not ice cream?"

"Stereotype."

A smile takes hold. This time, it's rooted someplace real and deep. Something relaxes inside me, the adrenaline slowly beginning to recede. "Coolest place you've ever been?"

"Vail," he rasps. "You?"

"Nowhere."

"Not a valid answer."

"I thought this was about you."

"This is about both of us."

My smile from a moment ago is gone. I hug my knees to my chest.

Dredge up a small piece of my soul I've never shared with him. "I was supposed to go to the Grand Canyon once."

"What happened?"

"It was supposed to be my Make-A-Wish trip, but my parents freaked out any time I wasn't hooked up to a monitor. At the last minute, they told my doctors I couldn't go. Most days, they wouldn't let me out of their sight to go to the bathroom. What about yours?"

I listen through a painful pause, trying to find a way to take back the question when he says, "Long story."

"Siblings?" I ask, hoping Jack's childhood wasn't as lonely as he sounds.

"One. An older brother."

"Have you seen him? You know, since?"

"Once," he confesses. "He's an investment banker in Cleveland. Divorced. A couple of kids in grad school. He was in town for a convention. He didn't see me."

"But you're so easy to find."

At this, he laughs out loud. Wheezes. "Touché," he says, his voice thin.

"Girlfriend?" I ask to keep him talking, even if I'm not sure I want to hear the answer.

I hear his grin turn up around the edges. "No one serious. What about you?"

"No girlfriends."

"Boyfriends?"

I consider lying. Fabricating a Spring boy from Niagara Falls or Myrtle Beach. It would be easy. But he's not hiding. And I'm not trying to hurt him. Not now.

"Not since seventh grade." My face flushes hot and I'm grateful he can't see it.

"You're kidding, right?" He sounds surprised. Or maybe doubtful.

"It's hard to meet eligible guys in a terminal ward with Poppy as a roommate."

"That was before. What about now?"

I shrug, thinking back on the handful of awkward kisses I've shared with other Spring boys over the years. Late-night games of truth or dare in someone's dorm room after a few too many smuggled beers. Or an unexpected lingering peck on the lips in an empty Spring stairwell. "I wouldn't exactly call them dates."

"So . . . you and Julio? You never . . . ?"

"What? Kissed?" I wrinkle my nose at the thought. I wish he could see it. Maybe then he'd believe me. "I have an aversion to coconut." He laughs again. Coughs. Takes a minute to catch his breath, and something inside me reaches for him. Reaches for him without wanting to hurt him.

I slide my hand closer to the fence.

"Julio will never admit it, but he's in love with Amber." I can see exactly what Jack was thinking when he set those four batteries on the table in the library. "Your plan. Do you really think it could work?" I listen for his answer through his labored breaths.

"It has to be soon," he says. "This summer, before the fall Purge. I know Poppy's afraid. I know she wants you to fight." I sink my teeth into my lip, remembering my promise to her. My promise to Julio. "But if we don't get you out soon, we won't get another chance."

"A chance at what?" I want to hear him say it. I need to know this is about something more than just me and the red line. "What is it you want, Jack?"

As I wait through a heavy silence, I worry that maybe he doesn't know. When he finally speaks, his voice is so weak, I have to listen with my whole heart to hear the answer.

"I want to ask you out without wondering when you'll have to kill me. I want you to look at me without feeling sorry for what you're about to do. I want . . ."

Jack falls silent again. For a moment, I don't hear him breathing. "Jack?" I scramble to my knees and grab the fence, but he's already there, pale and shaking, his fingers laced through the chain link. He presses his forehead to the mesh.

"You have to talk to Julio," he says, his face wrenched with pain. "You have to persuade him to help you. Amber and Woody are already on board. Tell Julio to find a way to contact Woody. Woody knows what to do."

Pale pinpricks of light glow beneath Jack's skin.

I reach for his hand, desperate to hold him here. It worked before, it could work again. But Jack shakes his head.

"I have to go." His whole body's trembling now. "Last time. I promise," he says with a weak smile.

Last time. A wave of panic grips me. Chronos or his Guards could kill me next week. I may never make it home or wake from stasis. I may never make it out of the Observatory alive to see Jack again. Our future feels like it's teetering on a fulcrum, and suddenly I know which side I want to be on. I've already crossed the line. We're already falling . . .

"I'm not sorry," I tell him.

Our noses brush as I reach through the fence, making sure his transmitter is on. Then mine. I feel his breath, soft and cold through the opening in the chain link. Before our lips meet, I feel him slip away.

17

SPECIAL DELIVERY

Five Months Later

JACK

The waiting is the hardest part. I pace behind Chill's desk chair, watching his tablet over his shoulder. The call from Boreas came hours ago and I'm praying nothing went wrong. Our heads snap up at the quick rap on our door. Chill scrambles to his feet and we nearly trip each other in our rush to open it.

A crate fills the opening. The words "FRAGILE" and "THIS SIDE UP" obscure the ventilation holes drilled into the wood. Red-faced and sweating, Boreas wheels the dolly across the threshold and deposits the box in the middle of the room.

We stand back as Boreas takes a crowbar to the top corner of the crate. The nails creak as he pries it open and slides back the lid. The figure folded tightly inside uncoils himself, stretching on stiff legs and blinking against the light. A rush of hot air escaping the box with him.

Sweat drips from Julio Verano's temples. His hair's matted and damp, and perspiration drenches his shirt. Still, he looks exactly like

I'd always imagined he would, same as his surveillance pictures. What catches me off guard is the way he smells. Like sea water on sun-warmed skin and fresh-cut grass. Like every forgotten summer of my youth. Even if he didn't look like he could carry Fleur out of here under one arm, I'd still want to punch him in the dimples.

"What took you so long?" I snap, impatient to make up for the hours we've lost. Julio grabs the shoulder strap of a long, black tactical case and thrusts it at me.

"Got held up in the airport." He uses the hem of his shirt to mop his face, revealing another six-pack of reasons to hate him. As he climbs out of the crate, he gives Chill a cursory once-over. He doesn't expend any more energy scrutinizing me. Julio's in peak season. Chill, on the other hand, hasn't taken a phys ed class since Reagan was in office, and I'm still green, only three weeks out of stasis. Julio could murder us in our dorm room and no one would ever know.

I shove the black bag at him. "Maybe if you hadn't brought a rifle with you, you wouldn't have held up security."

"It's not a rifle, you idiot. It's a guitar. I stopped by my dorm room to pick up my stuff." Julio eases the soft black case back into the crate.

Chill hands Boreas an envelope. Boreas fans through the contents before tossing me a set of keys. I catch them against my chest.

"South Dock Marina. Slip three," he says, throwing two sets of cafeteria smocks and hair caps to Julio. "You have six hours to make it through the lock before low tide. Don't be late."

I stare after his balding head as it disappears into the hall. I spent most of my season cashing out stocks and selling off investments I've accrued over the years, consolidating earnings and interest until I had

172

enough to pay for the boat Boreas bought for us under an assumed name. In that envelope, he carries the wire transfer instructions for an offshore account containing what's left of my entire life's savings, minus the few thousand dollars I held back for food, fuel, and supplies for the trip.

"We don't have much time," Julio says, pulling on a smock that barely closes around his chest. He tucks his hair into his white cap and hands the other set to me. "Let's get this over with before I change my mind. What's the plan?"

Chill slides his arms into the straps of one of two backpacks containing everything we can afford to bring with us, which isn't nearly enough. He grabs his tablet and swipes it on. "I wrote a dummy program that'll broadcast Fleur's vitals on a loop. From the Control Room, it'll look like Fleur is comfy and sleeping. It should buy us at least a few hours before they figure out she's gone. Once you make it to Fleur's chamber, I'll switch out the feeds. She should sleep like a baby through the whole thing. Woody's going to set the other three charges. The power surges will be strong enough to take the stasis chambers offline at carefully timed intervals. Once the charges are set, he'll meet us at the freight elevators. But . . ."

"But what? What's wrong?" We have zero margin for error, and I don't like the way he's gnawing his lip.

Chill pushes up his glasses. He darts an uncertain glance around the room. "Once the stasis chambers go down, there's no coming back. Our tablets, our transmitters . . . all of it has to stay down here. If we get separated, we'll have no way to regroup. If anything happens—"

"Nothing's going to happen." I slide into my cafeteria scrubs.

"What about Amber?" Julio asks.

"Woody set up a rendezvous. She's meeting us up top. Where's Marie? I thought she was coming with you."

Julio hooks a thumb over his shoulder. "She's in the box."

Chill and I rush to the edge of the crate. Marie's shaggy dark hair falls over her face, her head drooping against her chest. The guitar case is propped against the sleeve of her olive drab army jacket, and her wrists are bound around the backpack cradled in her lap. A wide strip of gray tape stretches across her mouth. The slight rise and fall of her silver dog tag necklace is the only clue she might be alive.

"What the hell did you do?" I sputter.

"I sedated her."

Chill gawks at him. "This was not part of the plan!"

"I didn't have any choice. She refused to come."

"Then leave her here!" I shout. She made a choice. We all made a choice. By the time she wakes up, we'll be long gone anyway.

"If we leave her here, she's as good as dead, and I'm not taking responsibility for that."

Chill looks like he might be sick. "Did you have to tie her up?"

Julio chuckles darkly. "You obviously don't know Marie. She's *not* going to be happy when she wakes up."

I press the heels of my hands into my eyes. Getting out of here with one unconscious body is going to be hard enough. But two? We'll be lucky if we're not arrested on kidnapping charges before we're out of London.

Something rustles in the box. I look up as gray ball of fluff pokes its head from the backpack in Marie's lap and taps her chin with his paw.

"What in Chronos's name is that?"

"It's a cat."

"No shit! What the hell is it doing here?"

The temperature in the room skyrockets as Julio gets up in my face. His bitter breath smells like coffee and grapefruit and his T-shirt reeks. "Fleur said we could each bring one bag of things we can't live without. This," he says, pointing to the cat, "is Slinky. He's the one thing Marie can't live without, and I'm not leaving him. Now are we doing this or not?"

"Great. I guess we're doing this." I sling my backpack to Chill, mentally preparing myself to break out of a magical bunker with two comatose girls and a guitar in a very large litter box. Julio hefts the lid back on the crate and levers the dolly off the floor, rolling it behind me.

I pause to stare down the cold, white hallway, slightly dizzy as my stomach falls away. It's like I'm standing on the precipice of a downhill slope with switchback turns I can't see around, ice looming everywhere. I take one last look at our room. Then at Chill, hoping it's not the last time I see him, too.

"You've got this," he says. It's the same thing he's said to me at the beginning of every winter, before every hunt, as long as we've known each other.

Julio rolls the dolly into my ankles, bumping me into the hall. And with that, I set off to do the second-most stupid thing I've ever done in all my lives.

18

SUMMERS

JACK

Julio stands sentry, shielding me from the camera's eye as I kneel in front of Fleur's door and slide a pick into the keyhole. The door flies open, and I fall over the threshold, landing on someone's feet. Poppy grabs me by the collar and drags me inside, swinging the door open for Julio and the dolly.

"Took you long enough." She shoves an envelope at me. "My participation is entirely compulsory, just so we're clear."

It's stamped from Washington, DC, two months ago—two months after I left Fleur on the construction site. The letter inside smells faintly of lilies.

Poppy,

My time is up. It may seem like we have no choices left, but maybe we do. When the Summers come for me in August, know that I want this. For both of us. If you won't trust anyone else, then trust me. Consider this my last dying wish of you.

    Your friend—always,

    Fleur

I don't say anything to Poppy. I'm afraid anything I try to say will ruin it. She's let us into their room, and two backpacks wait beside the door.

Julio drops to his knees beside Fleur's stasis chamber, searching for the emergency release latch. "Call Chill. Let him know we're ready to take her offline."

"Wait!" I grab Poppy's elbow. Through the glass, Fleur's face is peaceful. Her eyes move under their lids as if watching her dreams play out inside them. Her pulse is steady on the monitor, her skin warm. All that will change the minute we open the chamber.

"She'll be okay," Poppy says, gently prying my hand from her arm. "I'm sure of it. She's been incubating long enough. Julio sent her home early, which I'm guessing was part of the plan." She throws him a glare. "She'll be tired and cranky, but her vitals are good."

The locks slide open. Warm, humid air rushes from the broken seal, carrying Fleur's scent with it. Instinct pushes me a step back from her chamber. Julio inches closer as Poppy wedges open the lid and a flash of Fleur's skin—shoulder to hip, thigh to toe—reveals itself. Suddenly, an instinct I've never felt before grabs me by the throat. I seize Julio by the collar of his smock and spin him around so our backs face the chamber. He's no lightweight, and the effort makes me dizzy.

Poppy grunts, fabric rustling as she struggles to dress Fleur. Julio's knuckles crack. He checks his watch and peeks over his shoulder.

"We don't have much time. I could help her, you know."

"If you so much as lay a hand on her, I'll freeze your balls off in your sleep."

He raises an eyebrow. "Jealous much?"

"Just wary of your base instincts."

"A little help here?" Poppy groans as she hefts Fleur's torso from the bed. I reach her first, wrapping one arm around Fleur's waist. She flops against me, her head lolling against my chest, the curves of her body soft and warm in a pair of leggings and a fleece sweatshirt. For a moment I'm paralyzed by it. By the weight of her life in my arms. It's taking all my strength just to hold her upright. I don't have the energy to lift her.

"Let me do it." Julio reaches for her, waiting for me to pull away before looping an arm under her knees. He lowers her gently into the crate beside Marie, pressing a chaste kiss against Fleur's forehead and holding it there.

"Hey!" I bark at him.

Julio wobbles, a little unsteady as he straightens and secures the lid. "Relax, Sommers. I'm just testing your theory. You think I'm going to risk her life out there just because you and Amber say it works?"

My eyes frost over, that instinct rearing up again. The overwhelming need to grab him and keep him away from her. Not because he wants to hurt her. But because now I know he never would. Not if he didn't have to.

"Satisfied?" I growl.

"Yeah," he says, looking a little peaked as he shakes the cobwebs from his head. "Let's go."

"This was in her hand." Poppy presses a slip of paper into my palm. "It's for you."

I unfold the letter as Poppy gathers their things. Julio's voice seems distant as he calls Chill and Woody to let them know we're on our way with Fleur:

Jack,

If you're reading this, we've come this far at least. We may not know how this is all going to turn out, but I'm okay with not knowing the future. For the first time in my life, I know exactly what I want right now. And no matter what happens next, I'd make the same choice again. Take good care of Poppy and Julio for me.

Yours,

Fleur

Yours. I pocket the note, committing that one word to memory.

"Get a move on, Romeo," Julio says. "I don't know how much more time we have before the Control Room realizes my transmitter's hidden inside the shower rod in my hotel room." He empties the battery from his phone and drops it into the waste bin by the door. "The charges are set. Woody and Chill are on their way."

Poppy and I dump our phones into the can with Julio's. We can't take any devices with us. Nothing traceable or trackable. From here on out, we're on our own.

Poppy hefts both backpacks and gives their room one last look. I crack the door and check the hall. Two bees bob on the breeze from the ventilation ducts just outside Fleur's room. I blow a frosty breath into the corridor, and they retreat into the warmth of their hives.

I signal Julio through.

His muscles strain under the weight of the dolly, and a pungent sweat's already creeping through his smock. I nudge Poppy ahead of him as two Spring Handlers pass through the security gate toward us, certain they'll catch his scent. I lower my head as Poppy waves at them, greeting them by name, but the girls only walk faster, averting their eyes as if she isn't there.

Poppy doesn't spare them a second glance as she leads us through a back corridor to the Spring cafeteria. "What was that about?" I ask when they're out of earshot.

"We're below the red line," she says with a stoic lift of her chin. "It's easier for people to pretend you don't exist than to have to look death in the eyes."

For the first time, I feel a stab of sympathy for her. Chill's been basking in his popularity because of our rankings, but as far as everyone in this wing is concerned, Poppy's already dead. Which makes her reluctance to leave this place that much harder to understand.

"Excuse me."

The crate nearly slips off as we all skid to a stop. Poppy and I turn slowly toward the woman's voice as the door to the staff lounge swings closed a few yards behind us. Julio cuts his eyes at me. The teacher blinks at us, her head tipped as if she's trying to place a scent. Her chestnut hair is threaded with gray and smells faintly of old roses. I hope she's been retired long enough for her senses to dull.

"Poppy, where are you going? The cafeteria's closed until lunch." The teacher may be speaking to Poppy, but her gaze is fixed on Julio and me.

"I wasn't feeling well this morning, and I missed breakfast," Poppy says smoothly. "I was just going to grab a yogurt from the snack machine."

"So you're not with them?" the teacher asks.

Poppy looks back, as if surprised to find us behind her. "No, ma'am."

"Hurry along, then."

Poppy gives us a last look over her shoulder before rounding the corner at the end of the hall.

Marie's cat mews inside the crate. It's the only sound for miles.

The teacher's nostrils twitch. My heart hammers as she takes a step closer. "What's inside that box?" A bee alights on the lid of the crate. "You know we have a strict policy against pets in the dormitories. To whom is this to be delivered?"

I swallow hard. My mouth falls open as the bee discovers an air hole and crawls inside.

"Well?" she demands.

"The contents of that crate belong to me. I assume there isn't a problem." We all turn as Professor Lyon approaches from the hall down which Poppy just disappeared. My breath rushes out of me.

Julio throws me a panicked look, his arms shaking under the weight of the dolly.

"I . . . I didn't realize . . ." the teacher stammers. "My apologies, Professor. If you'll excuse me . . ."

Lyon smiles tightly as she retreats through the doors to the lounge.

The bee emerges from the air hole. With a frenetic buzz, it darts off toward the staff lounge. The professor's hand shoots out, catching it before it reaches the vent beside the door. In a movement too fast to anticipate or comprehend, he drops it and crushes it under his shoe.

The Spring's light flickers and dies.

"Go," Lyon whispers, darting anxious glances at the hallway cameras. "I'll do what I can, but you won't have much time."

I can't breathe. Can't tear my eyes from the circle of ash on the floor.

Julio shoves the dolly into the back of my knees, urging me on, watching the professor warily from the corner of his eye as we run.

19

SCRATCH THE SURFACE

JACK

Poppy's waiting with Woody and Chill in the hallway behind the Spring kitchen, wringing her hands in front of the service elevators, when Julio and I arrive, breathless.

"Thank Gaia! Did the professor find you?" she asks.

I nod. "How did you know?"

She slams the elevator button, bouncing on her heels as she watches the floor numbers descend. "I ran into him on my way here. He stopped me and asked where you were. It was weird, like he *knew* or something."

"Did you tell him?" There's an edge in Julio's tone.

"Of course not." Once our plan was firmly in place, I didn't tell a soul outside our group. And I'd paid Boreas a generous sum to keep quiet about it. If Lyon knew, it didn't come from me. I punch the elevator button over and over, but it's stuck on the floor below us. "Why isn't the elevator moving?"

"I have a bad feeling about this," Chill whispers.

An alarm sounds—three short blasts. A prerecorded message pours through the intercoms in the ceiling.

"This is a test of our campus security system. All Seasons and Handlers, please remain in your dormitories until notified."

Poppy stares at the ceiling. "What's happening?"

"I don't know," I tell her.

We listen, watching, waiting for the elevator to move. The heavy thunder of boots grows louder through the wing.

"The Guards. What do we do?" Chill asks.

A swarm of bees clouds the air through the open doors at the end of the service hall. I draw a deep breath, blowing a blast of icy wind, scattering them and tossing them backward. Woody scrambles to shut the doors, barring the handles with a fire ax from a cabinet in the wall.

He points to a sprinkler nozzle over our heads. "We need a distraction. If we can set those off, it'll trigger the sprinklers and drown out your scents."

Julio wrenches open the crate. Fleur's scent hits me square in the face and I tamp down a wave of panic as he rummages in Marie's jacket, pulls out a lighter, and closes the crate again.

He climbs on the the lid and waves the flame under the sprinkler nozzle's sensor. We cover our ears as an alarm rips through the hall. The sprinklers sputter on, drenching us in a cold spray. The ceiling lights die, plunging us into sudden darkness. The absence of light only makes the wail of the alarm feel louder. A generator vibrates somewhere deep within the walls, and the emergency lights flicker on. All but one.

I blink against the deluge. The elevator button isn't lit. The floor indicator is dark.

I call Chill's name. Rivulets of water trail down the frozen features of his face. "They've disabled power to the elevator," I shout over the alarm. "How do I get it running?"

He pushes his frames higher on his nose, his focus sharpening. "Open the emergency panel. Look for the wire that connects the lock key to the floor button," he shouts. "To jump-start it, you'll need a charge." He points at Julio. It takes me a second to figure out what he means. It'll take two of us to generate enough power. All we have to do is direct a charge into the wires.

I pry my wet fingers between the elevator doors. Julio helps me wrench them apart. Cool air rushes from the open shaft. I can just make out the top of the elevator, parked at the floor below us.

"Jump!" Julio braces the doors open.

"You need to jump with me."

He glances back at the crate.

"They'll be okay," I tell him.

"Are you sure about this?"

"Either we die in here or we die up there. There's no going back now."

I leap, my knees buckling as I drop down onto the elevator car. It's quieter inside the shaft, the shriek of the alarm muted by the thick stone walls. The elevator shakes when Julio lands beside me, and I grab the cables to steady myself. We both look up. Three sopping wet heads peer down at us. The walls above us are smooth—too smooth to climb.

"I hope he's right about this." Julio opens the emergency hatch and we lower ourselves into the elevator car. Our clothes drip, the water collecting into a puddle on the floor.

He shivers beside me as I drag a pick from the soaked back pocket of my jeans and pry open the control panel, exposing the wiring inside. Poppy's voice rains down from above, hollering at us to hurry. But I've done as much as I can do alone. I wipe my palms on my jeans.

"Ready?" I hold a hand out to Julio, clutching an exposed wire with the other.

He swears under his breath. Utters something in Spanish as he summons the puddle of water at our feet into a funnel and directs it out of the open hatch. "Whatever happens next, Sommers, I'm not fucking kissing you." He dries his hand. Slaps it into mine. A bolt of electricity charges through us, almost knocking me off my feet. The lights inside the cabin flicker. The emergency control board hums to life and the elevator begins to ascend.

Julio grits his teeth as we inch toward the floor above us. The second the elevator stops, he collapses against the wall.

I pry open the interior doors to the deafening ring of the alarm. Poppy, Woody, and Chill wait on the other side, wide-eyed and dripping, their hands pressed over their ears.

"Get in!" I maneuver the dolly through the doors, pinning the others into the corners of the elevator until we all fit. Pulling the exterior door closed behind us, I shut us in.

The air inside the car is stuffy, thick with the smells of sweat and wet Seasons. We rest against handrails, breathing hard, listening to the muffled scream of the alarm. Julio's still hugging the wall, but my mind's alert, my body humming with adrenaline. I'm pretty sure some of Julio's energy looped into me. If I'm right, if we rely on each other's strength long enough, our bodies will find a balance.

I hold out my hand. He hesitates to take it.

"It's the only way out," I tell him, grabbing a wire.

He clasps my hand, teeth clenched against the burst of energy that crackles through us. The panel sparks to life. The lights flicker on, the interior doors close, and we lift our eyes toward the sky as we rise to the surface.

20
A THIN RAY OF LIGHT

<u>FLEUR</u>

My alarm's ringing. The sound hurts my ears. It's cold. I'm tired, not ready to wake up yet.

Twenty more minutes, Poppy. I curl into myself tighter. Why won't she turn it off?

The alarm fades. Voices argue in another room. My bed shakes violently, and I hit my head on something hard. Cold water spatters my cheek. I try to move, but my backside is numb, my legs folded into a tight space, tingling with sleep.

Not my bed.

My eyes blink open. Thin shafts of light filter through dripping holes above me. A kaleidoscope of shapes and colors swirls outside. I'm jostled, my shoulder smashing against rough wood. The room spins. I need to vomit. I lay my head back, shut my eyes, and will the world to stop moving.

A car door slams as tires squeal.

Through the holes, I smell wet leaves and hot sea air, a burning forest of pine. Body odor, somewhere close. Something feral and feline. My stomach roils.

"What took you so long?" A girl. She's angry. Worried.

"We're busted." I know this voice. A boy. Breathy and panicked.

"Maybe when you're done complaining, you could get us out of here!" The stab of a memory. Lips pressed against my hair. The gagging sweetness of poison. *Julio?*

"Open the doors. Help me get them in the van." *Jack.*

I open my eyes. Try to lift my head.

The walls shake and I sink back against them.

"Be careful with that!" *Poppy?* "If she has so much as a bruise when we open that crate, I swear to Gaia, I'm going to—"

The room sways and drops hard. Doors slam. Light dims.

"What's he staring at? Is he high?" Julio. He's mad. "Come on, Abbey Road! Get in the van!"

"Lay off! He hasn't seen the sun in fifty years."

More doors slamming. Voices arguing. An engine turns over, another squeal of tires. The momentum throws my body into the side of the box.

A box . . . I'm in a box.

I swallow. Shut my eyes again.

Please don't be sick. Please don't be sick. Please don't be . . .

The van brakes hard. Accelerates. Swerves. Turns. Muffled voices filter through the holes in the crate. Through the holes in my consciousness.

"Barely got out . . . Professor Lyon . . . He said he'll hold them off . . ."

A horn blares. The box slides, wood scraping metal.

"Slow down! We're going to get pulled over."

"You want to drive?"

"Can we please ditch the crows! They've been circling us for a mile."

A burst of speed. A sharp turn to the right. "Relax, Jack. We're almost to the bridge."

"We need to get to the boat before low tide."

Tires scream. The box rocks to the side. Pain explodes behind my eyes.

"Best shot . . . open sea . . . lose them in the dark . . ."

PART TWO

21

ADRIFT

FLEUR

I rouse to the odors of mildew and salt. To the steady slap of waves against a hull and a rolling motion that pitches the acid in my stomach until it threatens to come up. My bones feel bruised, my skin raw and my muscles sore. Like I died fighting.

I wade through the fog for the last thing I can remember. Julio's face. A tiny vial.

"You're sure this is what you want?"

"I'm sure."

I swallow the sick feeling building at the back of my throat and curl in on myself, shivering under a thin blanket that smells strongly of spruce . . . and pine . . .

Winter.

My eyes fly open. I hold perfectly still, careful not to breathe. The room is semidark, barely flushed pink. The crumpled T-shirt in front of me gives way to a chest that rises and falls, deep in sleep, and a cold, pale arm draped heavily around me.

My hand lunges for my knife and comes up empty. The dark head silhouetted against the cabin's window snaps awake. I scrabble upright onto my knees, fists raised. My head smacks against the low ceiling, awakening a bruise.

A box. I was in a box.

I hold my head, listening for Poppy's voice, my eyes slow to focus, not entirely sure where I am. Or *when* I am. Unable to remember exactly how I got here.

"Hey, it's me," says a low, familiar voice. "It's okay. You're safe here."

It's Jack.

But it's not Jack. There are no shadows under his eyes. No sickly flush to his skin. He's sunlight on snow, like his portrait from his high school yearbook, the same one I secretly clipped and taped to my closet wall. His hands are up, like he's afraid I might strike him. Or maybe so I won't be afraid *he'll* strike me. I rub the bump on my head, confused. Everything feels flip-flopped. Turned upside down.

The horizon bobs in the small circular window behind Jack's head, blue on blue, nothing upon nothing but waves and sea. The boat rocks and I fall back on my heels as it all comes crashing back to me.

"What month is it?"

"First week of September."

"Where are we?" My throat's parched, my mouth nearly too dry to speak.

"Just past the Canary Islands." He keeps talking, slowly, softly, the words beginning to ground me. "You slept through the worst of it. The trade winds will carry us most of the way across the Atlantic from here. We can lie low for a while—no radios, no fuel stops. Stay off Chronos's radar."

Us, he said. Soft guitar notes filter through the walls. And smells . . . palm leaves and wild grass. The sharpness of cinnamon and the snap of sour apple. "Julio and Amber. They're here. Your plan . . . it worked."

I clutch the front of my sweatshirt. I'm not wearing a bra. My hair is tangled and snarled and smells faintly of vomit. My head throbs, the bruise on it swelling to the size of a walnut. I draw the blanket up to cover myself—no, not a blanket. An old flannel pullover that must belong to Jack.

The low sun washes the room with dusky light. His cheeks are pink in the glow of it. "We didn't . . . you know. I just . . . We held hands. That's all," he says, a little flustered. "I must have fallen asleep. How do you feel?"

How do I feel? I'm supposed to feel strong with him. Stronger *than* him. My skin's clammy and my hands shake with stasis tremors. I turn away, not wanting him to smell me. Wishing he didn't have to see me like this.

The boat rolls. My stomach pitches.

"Hey, sunshine! Welcome back." Julio reaches inside the small cabin and ruffles my hair, making the bruise on my head scream. He wrinkles his nose. "Don't take this the wrong way or anything, but you smell worse than usual. And you look like shit."

I lurch from the bed feet-first, sending him sprawling backward out of the berth.

"You're awake!" Poppy exclaims as I shove my way into the narrow hall, dive into a bathroom, and slam the door. Braced against it, I breathe shallowly in the tight space. The boat sways with the next wave and my stomach drops with it. I lurch for the tiny sink.

When the dry heaves pass, I cringe at my face in the mirror. Purple shadows ring my eyes, and there are dark hollows under my cheekbones. My roots have started to grow out, pale pink dye giving way to streaks of brown. I wash the sour taste from my mouth, grit my teeth through an icy shower, and rush to put on the warm clothes Poppy must have left on the shelf for me. Something jabs me through the pocket of my jeans. My hand closes around the reassuring weight of a small utility knife.

I crack the bathroom door. Voices argue upstairs. A pan clatters on a stove. I follow the scent of chicken broth into a long, narrow cabin with high portholes and sleek wooden walls. Julio, Jack, and Chill are seated around a table, talking. They cease their conversation and stare at me.

Chill shrinks into his padded orange life vest. For a moment, I wonder if I should be wearing one, too. But no one else seems to be as I look around the room. A long-haired boy I've never met before sits at the captain's wheel. Not a Season; he smells like patchouli. Poppy stirs a pot on a stove in a small galley kitchen. On a sofa across from her, a fierce-looking Autumn with auburn braids watches Julio over the pages of a book. This must be Amber, coming into her season, judging by the smell of her. The tension between her and Julio is palpable, the scent of them so strong, it's overpowering in the small room.

Jack clears his throat. "Everybody, this is Fleur. Fleur, this is . . . everybody."

The redhead turns. She blinks her cider-brown eyes at me, taking me in. She's pretty. Striking, even without bothering to smile. I glance down at the cover of the novel she's reading. Lips pursed, she cocks a brow, unimpressed.

Poppy shoves a steaming mug into my hands. The soup swirling inside smells like reconstituted bouillon cubes from a box, but my stomach growls like an animal for it. I start toward Julio's end of the table, but Poppy holds me back, sliding into the space between us.

"Glad you're here," she says brightly. "We were just discussing the plan."

"You mean the one we don't have?" I look for the source of the familiar raspy voice. Marie sits alone in a far corner, huddled into a faded army jacket, flipping the wheel of a cigarette lighter.

"It got us this far," Julio says.

Marie's harsh laugh startles the cat in her lap. "It's a miracle they haven't caught us yet."

"Do they know where we are?" I ask.

"We don't think so." Chill hugs his life vest. "We lost a few crows in the high winds once we left the Channel—"

"All but one," Marie mutters. Amber flips her off without taking her nose out of her book.

Chill ignores them. "If we don't mess with the weather patterns and we stay off the radio, we should be safe for a while." He squints at a nautical map spread open across the table, stripping off his glasses as if to wipe a smudge from the lens before remembering they don't have any. He frowns and rubs his eyes instead, and with a frustrated huff, he slides them back on.

"How are you feeling, Fleur?" I drag my gaze from Chill. The long-haired boy's soft voice and gentle eyes are disarming. This must be Woody, Amber's Handler.

I take a slow sip from my mug, wary of where this conversation is heading. Wondering why everyone's looking at me. "What do you mean?"

"You and Jack have been . . . you know . . . recharging for a few weeks." A few weeks? I've been a sick, sweaty, vomiting mess, passed out in his bed for *weeks*? "Do you feel any different?"

Aside from humiliated? Vulnerable? "No." I bury my blush behind my mug.

Woody treads lightly on his next question. "Fleur, I know this might be uncomfortable to talk about, but we're trying to figure out if prolonged contact leads to any transference of powers between Seasons."

"Do you feel cold at all?" Chill asks. "Can you freeze anything?"

I glare at him over my soup.

"How about you?" Woody asks Jack. "Have you noticed any changes since you and Julio hooked up in the elevator?"

I spit a mouthful of broth across the table.

"Yeah, Jack. Do you feel any different?" Julio asks with an impish grin. "Stronger? Hotter? Better looking, somehow?"

Jack throws him a disgusted look. "I'll be sure to let you know if I notice any itching or burning discharge."

Chill snorts.

Julio turns on him. "Shut it, Flotilla, or I'll grab you by that life jacket and throw you overboard!" Chill's laughter dies. He draws his vest tighter around himself, pushing those strange glasses higher on his nose.

"That's enough!" Poppy's hand slams down on the table, making everyone jump. "You've been at each other's throats since we left the Observatory. What's the problem?" Marie and Julio stare at opposite sides of the room, refusing to answer. Amber blinks lazily over the spine of her book. "While we're stuck on this boat for the next three weeks, I expect everyone to be civil."

"Three weeks?" I look toward the hall I just walked through, counting the tiny berths from memory. There can't be more than four of them. Two doubles, two sets of bunks, two tiny bathrooms.

"You know," Julio says with a teasing lilt, "Fleur wasn't here when we voted on the sleeping arrangements. But now that she's awake, I'm guessing she'd rather sleep with me. I make an excellent bed warmer." He winks at me before his eyes slide to Amber.

If he's trying to make her jealous, it's working. The temperature in the room plummets. I slam down my mug, sloshing broth onto the table. Just because I agreed to go along with this plan doesn't mean I agreed to sleep with anyone.

"The sleeping arrangements don't change!" Jack says before I can get a word out. A layer of ice creeps over his skin. "Fleur bunks with Poppy. I bunk with Chill. Amber bunks with Marie, and Julio bunks with Woody. Anyone who has a problem with that can swim home." His storm-gray eyes survey the faces around the table. All but mine. He gets up and leaves the room, retreating to the berth where I woke with him earlier.

Poppy leans in and whispers, "I'm sorry I left you alone with him. It was my fault. He's been coming to our room every day to recharge you, but it makes him so tired. I didn't see any sense in waking him." She rambles, her argument picking up speed the longer I don't respond. "It's been fine. Really. Just a few hours a day. He asked me to stay in the room with him. Usually, I just read or something. He's actually not as horrible as I—"

"Excuse me," I say, pushing out from the bench and following Jack down to the berth. The hall is dark and narrow, the boat's swaying, and we bump into each other as I'm coming and he's going. His pullover's tucked under his arm, but now that I look at the cabin more closely, I see Poppy everywhere. Her duffel, her clothes, her cross-stitch project strung over a pillow. My backpack beside the bed.

"I'm sorry," I tell him, our faces uncomfortably close in the small space. "I'm just feeling . . ." I don't even know what I'm feeling. Powerless, terrified of what we've done? Completely adrift? "It's just . . . This isn't how I pictured it. Or *us*." It's hard to stand this close to him. He's tall. Taller than I realized, because he's always been crouching or dying or lying at my feet. And he's strong. His shoulders take up the breadth of the narrow hall, and his hands were so steady when they held me. How do I explain that I feel small? That this version of me—the one he's never seen until now—feels so much less courageous than the one he asked to run away with? The last time I saw him, he looked at me through the fence as if I were the goddess come to save him. And now he's stuck being my nursemaid because I'm too weak to take care of myself. And it's wearing him out, but he's too kind to say so. And all I want to do is puke on his shoes.

"You don't have to explain. If you'd rather bunk with Julio, I understand." His brow crumples as if it pains him to say it.

"No." His eyes lift to mine. I can't read them. I can't be sure what they want me to say. "It's fine. I'll stay with Poppy."

He nods tightly. Careful not to touch me, he maneuvers past me down the narrow hall, taking his pullover with him.

22

NONE SHALL SLACKEN

JACK

"Dammit!" Marie's shout erupts through the bathroom wall into the cabin just before lunch. It's the most she's said in a week, and we all look up from our crossword puzzles, books, and maps, confused by her sudden outburst. Poppy rises slowly to her feet. She reaches into one of the storage cabinets and fishes through a box of camping supplies, withdrawing packages of tampons and pads.

Amber and Fleur exchange concerned looks as Poppy carries them down the stairs and raps gently on the bathroom door. Her shoulders are heavy when she returns to her seat at the table. She's been skipping meals, persistently queasy since we left the rough seas around the Canaries, and she clears her throat of the cold that's been bothering her for days. "Thanks for remembering, Woody," she says with a mournful smile.

"I'm glad you mentioned it," he says quietly. "I wouldn't have thought of them." Apparently, neither did anyone else. Not even Fleur and Amber. Seasons don't age. We don't experience normal human cycles. Neither do our Handlers. Not while they still have their magic . . .

Chill hugs his life jacket. The creases deepen around his eyes as he struggles to focus on a loose thread in the seam. With an exasperated sigh, he takes off his glasses, frowning at the empty frames.

Woody acknowledges my unspoken question with a slight nod. Poppy's sniffles. Chill's vision. Marie's menstrual cycle. Their magic is already fading, their bodies remembering what it is to be mortal, progressing through normal stages of life as if time never stopped for them.

I watch Chill huddle deeper into his life jacket, feeling a pang of guilt for every time I questioned my choice to spend the rest of my life bound to him. Suddenly, eternity doesn't seem long enough.

The cabin falls unusually quiet. No bickering. No low guitar notes from the berth downstairs. The only sound is the scratch of Slinky's paws against the dry rice we sacrificed to his makeshift litter box and the rain spattering the windows above our heads. Woody's got the helm, his brow pinched with worry over the low-pressure front that's blown us another day off course.

I come up behind him, checking our heading against the nautical chart spread across his lap.

"I can make up for a little lost time." I pitch my voice low so I won't worry the others. "A little wind. No big deal." We're about a week from the mid-Atlantic coast, and I'm as eager to get off the boat as the rest of us.

Woody shakes his head. "We shouldn't risk it. These fronts are all tracked by radar and satellite. Someone's sure to notice an anomaly. We'll be past the worst of it in a few hours, and we'll need your strength when we make landfall. Might as well save what you can." He glances toward the kitchen, where Fleur is standing over a pot of soup. Our eyes brush as she pours a mug for herself and retreats to the far corner of the cabin to eat alone. Things are still weird between us. There's no privacy. No space for any conversation that doesn't involve everyone. I know what Woody's thinking. Fleur and I haven't touched since the morning she woke up. And at some point, that's going to have to change.

A dry cough from the lower berths breaks the silence. Fleur holds her mug poised at her lips, listening as Julio's cough becomes persistent. Amber stares down into the pages of her book, her stillness the only clue that she's listening, too. It's a sound the three of us recognize. One we've learned to listen for. The last breaths of a dying Season start with a tight chest and a mild fatigue but progress quickly into symptoms of the flu.

A sniffle and a groan rise through the floor. I could go to him. I'm strong enough to hold off death for a while, but only just.

Fleur glares at Amber. Amber hasn't turned a page in the last five minutes, but she doesn't look up.

Julio's cough deepens, followed by a rattling wheeze. Fleur launches to her feet, drops her mug in the sink, and heads for the berths.

Amber slams her book shut. "What are you doing?"

"I'm going to help him."

Poppy's playing cards fall to the table. "Fleur, you can't!"

I stand in front of the stairs. To slow her down. To make her think before she hurts herself. "She's right. He'll drain you dry."

Marie shoves her way past us into the cabin. "The fever's already set in. Fleur's not strong enough." She drops a bowl of water and a damp towel on the table. Her dog tags rattle as she rakes her hair back from her eyes, making her look like a frazzled army nurse. She rolls up her sleeves, revealing tattoos that don't quite cover the scars on her wrists. "It's got to be her," she says, knocking Amber's feet off the couch. "Come on. Get down there and get this over with."

Amber sets down her book. She eases to her feet until she's standing toe to toe with Marie. The air goes cold, dry as tinder, when she says, "I don't take orders from Julio's lackey."

"So help me," Marie hisses, inching closer, "if you don't do this, I'll gut you in your sleep."

"And why should *that* scare me?"

"Because once Julio's in the wind, there'll be no one left to bring you back!"

The boat seems to hold its breath.

A low moan rises from Julio's bunk room, followed by another burst of hacking coughs.

"Fine," Amber mutters. "But I'm not going in there alone."

"I'll go with you." Woody slips down from his bench. "Somebody take the helm—"

"No," Amber says, turning to point at me. "You know how this works. You're coming with me."

As I turn for the berths, Fleur grabs my hand. We both jump at the static-like shock. "Thank you," she whispers. She presses her lips to my cheek.

I don't move. Can't speak. She's still holding my hand and her mouth is so close and the yearning I feel is enough to bring me to my knees. The raw nagging hunger to kiss her leaves me dizzy and a little weak. She pulls away slowly, as if maybe she's feeling it, too.

"Better get down there," Woody says, his lip twitching with a smile.

The lingering spot of warmth on my cheek spreads to the rest of me as I watch her walk away, lost in the color of her hair and the shape of her hips. The way her bare feet curl under her legs as she settles on the couch across the room. "Yeah. Right."

Head buzzing, I descend the stairs to Julio's berth. The tight space smells strongly of perspiration. He's hardly conscious, shivering through his sleeping bag, his skin sallow and his hair slicked with a layer of sweat and salt.

Amber backs into me as another cough overtakes him. "What do I do?" Her voice is small and uncertain. She looks ready to bolt from the room.

"It's not hard." I clear the lie from my throat, thinking back to the long hours I spent holding Fleur's hand, watching her sleep, waiting for her to wake, wondering if she would. Some nights it felt like the hardest thing I'd ever do. "All you have to do is touch him."

"Will you stay?" she asks, her eyes pleading. I don't recognize this Amber, the timid one who doesn't know what to do with her hands. The Amber I know could be bleeding out in the dirt and would just as soon spit on my shoes as ask me for anything. The air in here is too warm, the room nothing more than a small bunk bed and a narrow strip of floor, thick with the smell of dying summers. There's hardly room in here for two, much less three of us. And I don't relish the idea of being a fly on Julio's bedroom wall.

"Sure," I tell her.

Her breath shudders out of her. I ease to the floor at the foot of Julio's bed, my knees curled against my chest and my back against the bunk. It creaks as Amber settles into it beside him. Julio murmurs restlessly, as if stirred from a fever dream.

He coughs, gentler this time. Moans softly in his sleep.

I shut my eyes, feeling the ghost of Fleur's body against mine. The weariness of every sleepless night since. And I hope, maybe for the first time, for Amber's sake, that her heart survives the night.

23

ANYWHERE

<u>FLEUR</u>

Jack and Amber disappeared into Julio's berth hours ago. The rain has stopped, the sea calm after the storm, and I head out onto the deck for some air. A lighter scrapes over and over, throwing sparks as Marie struggles to light a cigarette in spite of the wind.

"Thank you for what you did back there." I lean on the wet railing beside her, watching thick clouds blow over the moon. She's been livid with Julio since she woke up in that crate beside me.

She throws me a side-eye as I sink down onto the deck next to her. "It's my job to watch out for him," she says around her unlit cigarette.

Abashed, I look away. I may not have been the one to drag her along, but I'm the reason she's stuck here. "I'm sorry."

"For what? You weren't the one who stuffed us in a box." She shakes her head. "For reasons I may never understand, Julio likes you. A lot. But Julio didn't do this for you. Julio did this for Julio. Trust me. He has his own reasons." The hard line of her mouth softens, and she takes the cigarette from her lips. It feels strange to sit beside her, just talking. I'm so used to hearing her through Julio's transmitter, her urgings to kill me tempered by thirty-seven hundred miles, thirty stories of earth, and Julio's reluctance to hurt me.

Her cat burrows out from inside her jacket, sniffs the wind, and then disappears back into it, rustling the dog tags around her neck. "How'd you meet Julio, anyway?" I ask.

Marie squints at me sideways. Some people, like Julio, never talk about how they died. But it feels like I should know this. Like I should know these people who've sacrificed, willingly or not, for Poppy and me.

"Fell off the Coronado Bridge."

"Fell?"

Her cold eyes pierce me, the line I've crossed drawn in the strands of dark hair blowing across her face. "Fell." She frowns out at the water. "Julio found me right before I slipped. The guy has a hero complex. It makes him do stupid things."

So he tried to save Marie, too. And he succeeded, or failed, depending on how you look at it.

It's hard to want to kill someone once they've saved your life.

No wonder Marie refused to come with us. Julio's life wasn't at risk back at the Observatory. She was probably determined to keep it that way.

"He cares about you," I say as she sticks the cigarette back in her mouth.

"He has a lousy way of showing it."

"Maybe." An image of my mom and dad flits through my mind. The torn-up plane ticket to the Grand Canyon. All the radiation treatments and the chemo and the machines. "Or maybe it's the people who love us most who'd do anything to keep us alive, even when we don't ask them to or want them to."

She gives up on the lighter and shoves it back into the pocket of her army jacket with a muttered curse.

"You know those things will kill you, right?"

"We're all going to die anyway," she says.

I resist the urge to ask for a drag, even though I've never smoked one. It feels like a conscious choice to pull death into your lungs, to blow it back out in spite of everyone around you. "Where did you get them, anyway?"

"From Julio," Marie says, heavy on the sarcasm, as if she's just proven a point. I catch the curl of her smile before she turns, letting the wind conceal it under her hair. "'Marisol,'" she says in her best imitation of Julio, "'you're rotting your lungs.' But every year, he buys them for me anyway."

"Marisol," I say, copying her accent. "That's pretty."

She grimaces. "My real name's Marie. That's the name my dad chose for me, and I wasn't about to let anybody change it. Julio picked Marisol so I wouldn't get in trouble." She levels a finger at me. "And he's the only one who ever gets to use it."

Even though she pretends to hate him, there's a glimmer of adoration in her eyes when she talks about him. It feels good to have this thin strand of common ground between us.

"You don't have to be by yourself all the time." I jerk my chin toward the cabin. "They're not all so bad, you know."

Marie shrugs. "Amber's okay, I guess."

"I wouldn't know," I say, hanging my arms over the rail. "I don't think she likes me very much."

Marie smirks. She doesn't deny it. I wonder if they talk about me behind my back as they're falling asleep. "Amber's tough. Crazy smart, and she's got wicked close-combat skills. She should have been promoted years ago," she says thoughtfully. "I always suspected she had it bad for Julio. Lucky for him, I guess. She's his best shot at surviving this mess." She scrapes her hair from her face and raises an eyebrow, as if she's letting me in on a secret. "She was a runaway before, you know. Phoenix to Woodstock in the summer of sixty-nine."

"Is that where she met Woody?" With his long hair and John Lennon eyes, I can picture him there, like a scene from an old, washed-out photo.

Marie nods. I can just make out her frown in the dark. "Amber froze on the streets of New York that winter. Woody was there around the same time, protesting the war. A couple of enlisted boys beat the shit out of him and left him to die in an alley. That's where Amber found him."

"That's horrible."

"Was it?" She tosses the hair back from her face, letting the wind whip it behind her. "I don't understand why everyone's so protective of him. Woody's a coward. A draft dodger. Is that really the kind of person you want watching your back in a war?"

"Is that what you think this is? A war?"

"I think that's exactly what we're sailing into."

"If that's the case, shouldn't we all be on the same side?"

Marie pushes to her feet, cradling the purring bulge under her jacket. "Just because we came here in the same box doesn't mean I want to be buried in one with you." And just like that, our conversation is over, and I'm left trying to figure out what I said wrong.

I feel Jack's presence in the cold snap of the wind before I notice him behind me. He rests his elbows against the rail, his dark hair blowing back from his moonlit face and his T-shirt billowing with the wind. I take a long breath of him that makes my chest ache.

"Are Julio and Amber okay?"

"They will be," he says.

"What have we started, Jack?"

His face looks pained in the moonlight. "I thought you wanted this."

"I do. But did they?"

Jack's quiet. His clothes hang loose and his face is drawn, as if he hasn't been eating or sleeping. "We needed their strength. Enough to get us out of the gates. You and I would have been too weak to do it on our own." He shakes his head. "We needed them, Fleur—all of them. We couldn't have done it alone."

He stares out over the water as if he can see what's on the horizon. "You heard Woody. So far, everything's working exactly the way we thought it would. All we have to do is make it to the safe house and lie low until things blow over." But I don't know who he's trying to convince, himself or me. Our plan relies entirely on evasive maneuvers. Run. Hide. All the things Jack's become good at. But what if Marie's right and it comes down to a fight?

"And after that?"

"After that, we head west. Amber wants to see her mom in Arizona. Julio's been talking about a trip to the coast. Chill, Woody, and Poppy have a whole list of places they want to go." He smiles to himself, as if that thought makes him happy. As if this is how he's made peace with what we've done. "And I thought maybe the two of us could go to the Grand Canyon. Alone," he adds, with an uncertain sideways glance at me.

"The Grand Canyon?" It comes out on a breath of laughter. My Make-A-Wish trip. The one cool place I never got to go. "Are you asking me out?"

There's a gleam in his eye. "I guess I am."

"I guess it's a date, then."

He grins. Bites his lip to keep the smile from spreading across his face until he can't hold it back anymore.

I pull myself up by the rail. "And what about you?" I ask, letting instinct and peppermint and pine draw me to him. I shut my eyes, blocking out the image of Doug's face, telling myself this will get easier over time. "Where do you want to go when the dust settles?"

His smile softens as I come closer. His lips part, as if they're holding back a secret. The air between us feels so thin.

"Can I try something?" I ask, a little breathless.

Jack nods, his expression both curious and cautious as I reach around his neck and rest my head against his chest. Hesitantly, he wraps his arms around me, too. There's no jolt this time, just a hum, a gentle vibration where our skin touches. He's cool. Solid and tender. All my fear and guilt and doubt slip away when he whispers against my ear, "Anywhere. We can go anywhere."

24

LANDFALL

JACK

There's a soft splash as Julio drops the anchor. The black water's indistinguishable from the dark smudge of charcoal sky, and I draw the brisk autumn air deep into my lungs, certain this is the first full breath I've taken since I came out of stasis.

Julio swings down from the upper deck. He surveys the shoreline, a little unsteady on his feet. Virginia Beach glows in the distance, hotels and boardwalk lights glittering to the north and the buoy lights of Rudee Inlet flashing just beneath.

"Those lights to the south," he says. "That's Dam Neck Naval Base. We'll need to stay north of it, out of sight. We'll come ashore there." He points to a darkened strand of shoreline. "That's Croatan Beach. There's a neighborhood behind it. Mostly vacation homes. This late in the season, it'll be a ghost town. We can grab what we need and hit the road while it's still dark."

He shivers. The cold's already wearing on him and daylight's only a few hours away. The sooner we move, the better. "I'll round up the others," I tell him.

The cabin is pitch dark, a bustle of activity and a barrage of smells. Woody folds his maps into his backpack by flashlight. Chill, Poppy, and Fleur load our camping gear and supplies into duffels. Slinky's iridescent eyes are visible where he weaves between the rolled sleeping bags and backpacks Amber and Marie have carried up from the berths.

"The lifeboat's ready," I tell them. "Load as much as you can. Anything that doesn't fit goes down with the sailboat. Everyone grab a life jacket and meet on deck in five. We're swimming in."

The whites of Chill's eyes find mine in the dark, the outline of his life jacket painting a false silhouette around him. The others shuffle past me toward the deck, their arms loaded down with duffels and supplies.

"I can't," he says when we're alone.

"You have to. In five minutes, we're jumping."

"I'll ride on the lifeboat."

"There's no room."

"But the water—"

"You have a life jacket."

"It's cold, Jack. Really cold, and I—"

I round on him, livid for reasons I can't put into words. "That's what you wanted, wasn't it? More snow, longer winters? You wanted to be the biggest, baddest Winter around. Or was that all a show for Gaia's benefit?"

"That was different! It wasn't real."

A layer of frost pushes its way to my surface. "Real for who?"

"I *died* out there!"

I shove his chest through the thick foam of the life vest. "That doesn't mean you died in here!"

Through the window, the others are waiting. The inflatable boat is packed to the brim. There's no room for any one of us to ride in it without sacrificing food or survival gear. There's nothing more I can do for Chill. This is something he has to face on his own. I touch his chest again, gentler this time. "The only person holding you under the ice is you."

I pull the door shut behind me. Water slaps the hull, and the wind whistles over the mast.

Fleur shivers as she hands me a life vest. "Where's Chill?"

"He'll come." I move quickly, casting off the extra lines to the lifeboat. All I can do is keep moving us forward and hope Chill finds the courage to keep up.

Poppy's long hair blows across her face. She scrapes it back, her eyes glued to the closed door. "Why isn't he coming?" She starts for the cabin and I take her gently by the arm.

"Don't," I whisper. "He'll come when he's ready."

Amber corners me as I move to secure the last remaining line to the lifeboat. "How the hell are we going to sink the boat if Chill's still on it?"

"We won't."

"If we don't sink the boat, the Coast Guard will *find* it."

"And Chill can get a ride to shore with them."

"Are you out of your mind? Then Gaia and Chronos will know exactly where we . . ." The rest of Amber's thought trails as the cabin door creaks open.

Chill stares down into the ink-black water, his hands shaking as he reaches for the buckles of his life jacket. He drags down the zipper and climbs onto the gunnel, his knuckles white around the rail. The others exchange anxious glances, but I know this precipice he's standing on. It has nothing to do with conquering the cold. It's about shedding fear. It's about proving to himself that he isn't afraid of dying anymore.

He shrugs off his life jacket and drops it over the side. With quick, shallow breaths, he watches it drift farther from the boat, and with a strangled cry, he plunges in. We all rush to the railing, the boat leaning precariously as we struggle to make out his shape in the dark. Julio leaps onto the gunnel. I grab his life jacket before he jumps.

I point to a shadowy figure in the water. Chill's orange vest bobs between the moonlit waves like a raft. One arm holds it tightly to his chest. His other hand holds his glasses in place as he kicks steadily toward shore.

"Let him go. He'll be okay," I tell the others. To Julio, I whisper, "Stay close. Just in case."

Julio jumps in, swearing when his body breaks the frigid surface. Three more splashes, as Poppy, Fleur, and Marie follow. Woody unhooks the stern line from the lifeboat and jumps in after them, towing our supplies behind him.

Amber and I are the only ones left. "Are you ready?" I ask her.

Her eyes are bright and alert as they follow the group's progress. Then past it to dry land. "Definitely."

I switch off the bilge pumps and reach inside, summoning frost to my hands until the hull splinters and cracks, leaving gaps so the sea can trickle in and claim it. It's the first time I've used my magic since we fled the Observatory, and it feels like I'm running a marathon without a warm-up. When the hull begins to flood, I fall back against the deck, too exhausted to move.

Amber hauls me to the gunnel, checking the buckles on my life vest before pitching us both over the side. She grabs my hand, pulling me behind her through the murky water. Hers are every bit as warm as I remember them, but somehow not unbearable. Only once we're swimming side by side does she let go.

25

DOWNWIND

FLEUR

Chill stands alone at the water's edge, his dripping life jacket limp in his arms, staring out at the darkness he just waded through. The rest of us crumple on the sand, listening to the waves breaking as the ocean swallows our boat whole.

The wind bites through my wet clothes, but I don't care. There's solid ground beneath me. I reach out with my mind, letting it stretch into the rustling blades of the beach grass that crests the dunes.

Jack collapses beside me. He rolls onto his back, chest heaving and arms splayed, the seawater on his skin forming a layer of frost. I reach across the sand and slip my hand into his. His eyes are closed, his face ghostly pale in the moonlight, as if he spent all that remained of his energy sinking our last tie to Chronos's world. I pull away, afraid of drawing any more of his strength from him, but his hand closes fast around mine.

"Don't," he whispers. "You're warm. It feels good." His thumb traces slow sandy circles over my skin. For the first time since I woke up, I'm not the one taking, drawing, draining. I hold him as his breathing slows and he drifts toward sleep. He's peaceful, blanketed by a wind that makes my own teeth chatter, and I wonder if this is what it will always be like for us. If I'll always feel out of my element yet completely alive when I'm with him.

Slinky wriggles out of the lifeboat, his tail bristled against the dark. He pauses on the sand, ears pricked as a growl builds deep in his chest. Careful not to rouse Jack, I push up on my elbow to see what's got him ruffled. I follow the cat's line of sight to the parking lot behind the dunes.

"We're not alone," I say in a low voice.

A crow's perched on top of a lamppost. Its black wings spread as it launches into the sky with a shrill *caw*. Slinky sprints after it, kicking up sand as Marie scrambles to catch him.

Julio shoots to his knees. Amber's already up, scenting the air. I smell nothing but salt and seaweed. "We need to move," she says.

A ripple of panic rolls through me. The beach is low ground. We've got an ocean at our backs, and the onshore breeze is strong enough to carry our scents far inland. She's right. We're not safe here.

Julio hauls the backpacks and supplies from the lifeboat and tosses them onto the beach. I shake Jack awake. His eyes flutter open.

"What's wrong?" His backpack lands beside him, scattering sand. Chill pulls Poppy to her feet.

"Crow," I tell him.

Julio slashes the air from the lifeboat, compressing it into a tight ball and disposing of it in a trash barrel at the base of the dunes. He jogs back to grab the last of the bags. "There's a bathhouse in the parking lot on the other side of the dunes. We can change into dry clothes and get out of the wind there."

We pull our backpacks on over our salt-crusted sweatshirts and sling duffels over our arms. Amber flashes the "all clear" sign from the top of the dune. Behind her, Marie clutches the anxious cat to her chest as we climb the beach toward them.

The parking lot glows ahead of us. Jack slows beside me, our wet shoes dragging through the sand. His eyes search the shadows under the bathhouse stilts, then sharpen on the peaked roof where a crow alights to watch us.

"Go," Jack tells Chill, nodding sharply toward the bathhouse. "I don't know how much time we have."

"Not long." Julio's eyes flash. "You smell that?" Jack's nostrils flare. A smoky, charred odor sours the wind. Amber swears. I'm the last one to place it. "An Autumn," Julio says. "The crows must have spotted us hours ago."

Amber drops her backpack. She flexes her fingers as she scans the line of trees across the parking lot. "I guess we're about to meet my replacement."

Jack jogs after our Handlers, his feet stealth silent on the bathhouse ramp. It's well after midnight. The public utilities are closed, locked until sunrise. He kneels beside the door, a penlight clenched between his front teeth as he picks the lock for them. I let out a held breath as our Handlers disappear inside.

"You should go, too," Julio tells me. "Dry off. Warm up." I can read all the things he's not saying in the subtle lift of his nose and the way he averts his eyes. I've never battled an Autumn. He thinks I can't hunt it like Jack or fight it like Amber. Screw that.

I drop my pack and pull the knife from my pocket. "I'm staying."

Amber paces, searching the trees for movement. Julio watches the beach, his nose tipped to smell whoever's coming. But I *feel* them. The press of incoming feet against the earth is a soft push against my consciousness. The brush of arms scraping aside tree limbs is like fingernails dragging over my skin, and I suppress a shudder.

The bathhouse door creaks open.

Marie, Chill, Poppy, and Woody file out in dry clothes.

The ramp is long. High and narrow and brightly lit, it's a perfect target. Breath held, I watch our Handlers descend it. The wind shifts as they near the bottom, blowing Poppy's hair, carrying the lemon scent of her detangler, the tang of her fear, the salt that clings to her sweater. And with it, the sound of a blade hissing through the dark.

JACK

Silver sings through the air.

"Get down!" Amber shouts. Woody cries out and drops. Poppy, Chill, and Marie duck, huddled around him, the press of their hands stifling the sudden, sharp smell of blood.

The Autumn emerges from the trees, a red light glowing by his ear. He's tall, his tight buzz cut and his faded green fatigues only becoming clear once he's within reach of the streetlight. I can't make out his features, but something about his catlike gait feels familiar.

Amber roars as she hurls a scorching ball of fire at him. The Autumn sucks in a sharp breath as it skims past his cheek.

He wipes the singed flesh with the back of his hand. Then, in a single fluid motion, he fires back. The wind carries his flame hard and fast. Amber clutches her arm where it rips through her sleeve. I spring, but Julio holds me back. He shakes his head, his eyes glued to her. "He's peak. If he gets ahold of you, you're done. She can handle this." He's not worried. Not yet. Julio knows what she's capable of better than I do.

Our Handlers crouch, shielding Woody as another ball of fire soars past Amber and smashes into the rail above their heads. Fire licks up the wood, crackling as it climbs the spindles.

"I've got this." Hands uplifted, Julio pivots toward the ocean, summoning water from the surf. I take an unconscious step back as it twists through the air, shielding my eyes from the spitting mist as it gathers into a funnel and spins over the dunes. Julio closes his fist and the funnel breaks, raining seawater over the parking lot. The wood hisses as the fire sputters out.

The Autumn shakes the water from his eyes. Nostrils flared, he looks past Amber to Julio. Then to me and Fleur.

"You're outnumbered, Hunter." A memory clicks into place when Amber says his name. He's the Autumn Amber was sparring with when I snuck into their gym. She defeated him easily, no weapons or fire. And yet, if he's intimidated by our numbers, he gives nothing away.

"Looks like it." Hunter's combat knife glints under the streetlamp as he unsheathes it. Amber's attention is torn between its jagged teeth and Woody's shriek of pain as Poppy jerks a piece of silver from his thigh. Hunter smirks as he and Amber circle each other.

"He's armed," Julio says tightly. "I'm not liking the odds." Fleur hands him her knife and he starts across the parking lot.

"Wait," Fleur stiffens. "Do you smell that? It smells like . . ."

Julio's steps falter as he smells it, too. "Summer."

We all turn toward the beach as a figure crests the dunes. The boy's breathing hard, his hair slick with mist or sweat. He stops short, nearly tripping at the sight of us, the sharp scent of hot rain on asphalt close enough to choke me.

Fleur's hand brushes mine, instinct pressing her closer to my side. The Summer expels a deep, violent cough and wavers on his feet. He backs up slowly, his wide eyes leaping from me to Julio, then to the parking lot where Amber and Hunter are grappling. Suddenly, his focus sharpens. Like a magnet, it snaps to Fleur.

I slide in front of her, tucking her behind me.

"Back off," I warn him. The Summer stares past me, taking a bold step toward her.

"Cyrus!" Julio wedges himself between us and shoves Cyrus back by the chest. "This isn't your territory. The state line's twenty miles that way, man." Julio points south with a hard finger. "You should get lost before anyone realizes you're here."

"No, she's mine!" he says, pointing at Fleur. "Gaia told me to come north. She said you were in the wind. If you're not going to do your job, then move over and give someone else a shot."

My grip tightens on Fleur.

"Something's not right," I say, just loud enough for her to hear me. It makes sense that Amber's replacement would be waiting for us. But why would Gaia send another Summer here so close to the end of his season?

There's the sound of a hard punch landing. Julio turns at Amber's startled cry. Seizing the opportunity, Cyrus charges at Fleur. Frost crackles over my skin as I brace myself to stop him. At the last second, Julio recovers, tackling him from the side. The Summers go down in a tangle of limbs on the pavement. I stumble back, reaching behind me for Fleur, but there's only empty air.

I call her name, but she's already halfway across the parking lot, a blurring streak of pumping legs and pink hair. She's fast. Faster than I've ever seen her, even during her peak. She sprints for the woods. Two figures leap out of the trees, both trying and failing to grab her as she sails past them. I race after her, chasing the floating red lights of their transmitters in the dark.

Two silver scythe patches catch the streetlight as they hurtle after her.

My heart hammers wildly as the Guards tear through the trees, close on her heels. One eye tracking Fleur, I crash into the slower Guard's back. We hit the ground, and the impact knocks me breathless. She rolls out from under me, her hands white-hot, impossible to hold on to. Her knee slams into my gut. While I'm sucking wind, she grabs my hair and slams my head against the ground. Her furious face swirls in and out of focus. I taste blood. All around me is the sound of knuckles on skin. Of Julio's muffled cussing and Amber's sharp attacks.

"Now!" the Guard shouts. Her fingers are raw fire around my throat.

I shut my eyes against the sudden glow radiating through her skin, so bright it's almost blinding. For a second, I'm paralyzed by it, disoriented and confused. I'm not dead—not even close. And neither is the Guard. So why's she disappearing?

Stars ring the edges of my vision as her grip on my throat tightens and her light grows brighter. I grope wildly for the red light of her transmitter, catching her and pushing her back by the face. Pale pinpricks of light glow in my hand where it touches her. Fear seizes me and I push back harder, until her skin blisters with frostbite. "I've got him! Do it now!" she yells.

I twist and kick out hard, scrambling free of her hands just as her magic flares. Eyes watering, I shield my face from the brilliant flash as her matter condenses into a dense ball of light.

I duck as her magic soars over my head and disappears into the nearest ley line. Staggering to my feet, I stare after it, trying to make sense of what the hell just happened.

I've got him! Do it now! That was the order she shouted through her transmitter while her hands were around my throat.

I rub the burns on my palms, my ragged breath slowing as I remember Fleur's lilies—the ones I found tucked inside my hand when I awoke from stasis. The ones she sent home with me through the ley lines.

My body stills as the answer slams into me. Organic material—living, cell-based, biological material—can be carried through the ley lines. Back to the Observatory.

The Guard wasn't trying to strangle me. She was trying to *take* me. One touch is all it would take for Chronos's Guards to ruin everything.

Heart pounding, I run after Fleur.

The forest is a landscape of shadows, the blood dripping into my eyes making it harder to see. I follow her scent, tripping over fallen limbs and roots until I spot her silhouette in a gap between two oak trees.

Her attacker is at least a head taller. Lean and wiry. The red light of his transmitter is the only bright spot in the darkness. Fleur shifts uneasily, and I push myself faster as two more red lights flicker in the trees.

Three. There are three of them.

"You can't run from this." The Guard lunges at Fleur, drawing back abruptly when she raises her hands. With a frustrated growl, he conjures a spark.

"No!" I shout.

He turns, flame poised, eyes narrowed toward the sound of my voice. Suddenly, all three Guards are rushing to intercept me. Fleur roars, and the trees come alive. Roots erupt, tripping the two Guards closing in. Fleur ensnares their legs, dragging them violently over the ground. She grasps at the air, then jerks her fists. The branches bend to her will, driving like spears into the earth, impaling both Guards with a horrible wet sound.

I stumble back, nearly tripping over myself as their magic hisses past me toward the ley lines.

The third Guard skids to a halt, his flame wavering uncertainly on his palm. Fleur's face is a grim mask of concentration, her hair alive with static. He cries out as the trees lash around his wrists and suffocate his flame. Roots tear from the ground, snagging his ankles. Teeth clenched, Fleur jerks her fists abruptly apart. I avert my eyes as a spray of warm blood taints the air.

The Guard's screams stop.

I drop to my knees. His remains flare into a ball of concentrated light. It burns a trail through the forest, searching for a ley line home.

I straighten up slowly, sickened by the sensation of blood on my face. But it's not the Guard's. It's my own. The forest swims as Fleur rushes toward me.

"Don't try to get up," she says, dropping to her knees.

"I'm fine." I shrink back as she tries to take my face in her hands. I

225

can feel the heat of her blush even in the dark, as if she's embarrassed by what she's done. But she's not the one who should feel ashamed. Fleur just killed three Guards in the span of a minute. She's not even at peak. And she did it alone. "I'm sorry. I don't know what happened," I say, the shame sharp on my tongue. I'm supposed to be the stronger of us. It's cold here. Almost my season. I should be taking care of Fleur. I should have been strong enough to protect her.

"The Guard touched you. That's all," she says, as if a Guard's touch should explain everything. The bleeding knot at the back of my skull tingles where her fingers rub it. The pain fades and my dizziness begins to clear. "You'll feel better in a few hours," she says, searching me for injuries. But it's her willingness to make excuses for me that hurts worst of all.

"No, it wasn't that." I take her wrist. Make her look at me. "Guards are neutrally charged. That's why we couldn't feel them or smell them coming. A touch wouldn't have killed me, or even drained me. If she'd wanted to kill me, she would have used a weapon."

Fleur's eyes narrow in the dark. "So you got beat up by a girl. It's not such a big deal—"

"That's not it, Fleur! That Guard grabbed me just before she jumped through the ley lines. I think she was trying to take me home."

Fleur's mouth goes slack. She sinks back on her heels, the flash of the lilies reflected in her eyes along with all the fearful thoughts she's not voicing.

Fleur never had to touch her opponent—the earth is her weapon. Amber can conjure fire using the energy in the air all around her. And Julio can drown a man where he stands just by manipulating the moisture in the air. But me? Wind is an imprecise shield, and ice is a breakable weapon. I'll be easier to catch than the others. Easier to kill.

"You'll have to be careful," she says, a deep crease pulling at her brows.

A shout echoes from the beach, and a bright light soars across the sky. Fleur and I haul each other to our feet and run, the streetlights guiding us back through the trees toward the parking lot. We duck as we clear the woods, squatting at the edge of the pavement to count heads. Poppy's white-blond crown is a beacon under the bathhouse ramp. Three other shadows huddle beside her. Fleur's wound tight as a drum as she scans the dunes for Julio. I follow her gaze, but I don't see Julio or Cyrus anywhere.

A pile of toppled trash barrels stirs. Amber clambers out of it. Her face is bruised, her lip bloody. Hunter paces the parking lot, waiting for her. The light we saw from the woods must have been Cyrus. But where the hell is Julio?

"We should help her." I push myself up, but Fleur tugs me back down again. She points to a shadow under the bathhouse. It glides like a ghost between the stilts and crouches out of sight.

"Give it up, Amber." Hunter spits blood, adjusting his grip on his knife. "Come out of there, and I'll make it quick."

Amber sways on her feet, her face darkened with blood so thick I can smell it from here. Hunter looks down at his watch in a show of impatience. While his head's down, the ghost under the bathhouse strikes. Julio launches from the shadows, slamming Hunter onto his back. Hunter's combat knife skids over the pavement. They roll, one on top of the other, until Hunter has Julio pinned by the throat.

Fleur leaps to her feet, but Amber's already in motion. She swoops, scraping Hunter's knife off the ground. Julio thrashes. His eyes are wide with panic as he swats at Hunter, striking out blindly between choked breaths. Something skitters to the ground, a red light bouncing off the pavement as Amber draws the knife across Hunter's throat.

Hunter sags. Julio coughs, starved for air. He rolls out from under Hunter's body as it crumples. The breeze carries the unmistakable smell of death.

Amber backs away from the swelling pool of Hunter's blood. Away from the red light flashing in the middle of it.

The combat knife hits the ground. Her hands tremble.

Fleur and I approach slowly. Breaths held, we watch as Hunter's remains rise like sparks from a campfire. The wind tosses them over the bathhouse, over the beach and the woods, everywhere and nowhere, a shower of dying fireworks, guttering in the night.

Julio scrambles away from Hunter's transmitter, his breath wheezing through his injured throat.

"What just happened?" Amber's voice is thin, close to breaking as a tremor takes hold of her. She wraps her rms around herself and chokes out a sob.

Julio opens his mouth, but no words come.

We killed him. We sent a Season into the wind. We were supposed to disappear. To quietly fall off the grid. But now . . . now we'll be lucky if they ever stop searching for us.

"It was my fault," Julio croaks. "He had me by the throat. I couldn't breathe. I just—"

Marie snatches up Hunter's transmitter. She switches it off, shutting down its signal to the Observatory. She rounds on all of us as she closes it in her fist. "We protected ourselves. Do you hear me?" Her voice shakes, but her face is a mask of fierce determination as she stares every one of us down. "They attacked us and we defended ourselves. We're alive. All of us. And I refuse to let a single one of you regret that!" She jams her trembling fist into her pocket. "Now, quit blubbering and let's get out of here before any more of them show up."

Fleur throws herself at Julio, wrapping him in a bone-crushing hug, whispering reassurances in his ear. Poppy and Chill approach slowly, hefting Woody between them. Amber and I rush to help.

We ease Woody to the ground. Poppy rifles through her backpack for a sewing needle and thread. Chill cuts a hole in Woody's pants and Marie preps his leg for stitches.

Amber and I back out of their way. She must feel me watching her. Her eyes brush mine, holding on for a painfully short moment before darting away. I can't tell if it's her broken nose or grief that brings the tears to them. She wipes her nose on her sleeve as she stoops to retrieve Hunter's combat knife, her hands shaking as she cleans dirt from the blade. She starts to tuck it into her belt, then stops. Instead, she turns the hilt toward Woody.

"Take it," she says. He turns his head away, swiping tears from his eyes. "You took a knife in the leg. You've earned it." She presses it into his hand and sinks to the blacktop a few feet away, frowning at the charred hole in her sleeve. The skin underneath is blistered and raw. Blood trickles over her lip, and she winces as she runs her tongue over her teeth.

"I saw those Guards chase you into the woods," she says to Fleur, cringing as she tests the cartilage in her nose. "How many were there?"

Fleur's eyes flick to mine and I look away, unable to bear the weight of her stare. She clears her throat. "Only two," she says. "Jack and I took care of them. No big deal."

Amber raises an eyebrow, clearly suspicious of Fleur's lie. But before she can say a word, Julio kneels in front of her. "Here, let me fix it," he says gently. He grimaces as he inspects her nose. "Sorry, this is going to hurt." He places his hands gently on her face. Their eyes hold. With a quick snap, he sets the break. Her watering eyes squeeze shut and she lets out a yelp.

Julio peels off his sweatshirt, balling it up to stanch the flow of blood from her nose, but she grabs him instead, bringing his hands to her face and holding him there. She leans into him with an exhausted, shuddering sigh as her bruises fade and the bleeding slows.

Fleur slides her hand into mine.

After a long moment, Amber's eyes snap open.

A pink flush shines through the gore on her cheeks when she finds us all staring. She brushes Julio's hands away, prodding the bridge of her nose as she stands. "I'm going to get cleaned up. Somebody steal us a car."

"I'll go," Julio offers, a little unsteady on his feet.

"Don't get arrested," she warns him.

"Me?" he laughs. "Never."

"September 1989?" Their eyes catch. Her cheeks burn. "Just be careful," she says. "I might need you later on." She starts up the ramp to the bathhouse. Julio watches her go.

"I'll go with you." Fleur gives my hand a quick squeeze and jogs after him. I want to pull her back. Keep her here. Hunter's death is far

230

too fresh in my mind. There are no more ley lines for us. No transmitters or stasis chambers. I brought her here to keep her safe. To keep her alive. But when those Guards came for us, I couldn't do a damn thing to protect her.

Chill clears his throat behind me, and I tear my eyes from Fleur.

"Woody okay?" I ask him.

"Yeah." He strips off his glasses and rubs his eyes. "I think so."

"How about you?" Chill's shivering. Or just shaken. Fear and cold look the same sometimes, and the deepest breaks can be the hardest to see.

"You were right." Chill squints down at the frames in his hands. "It's different back at school. Just red dots on a screen. I thought I'd know what to do if I ever got in a real fight, but I froze."

I rest a hand on his shoulder. "No one expects you to be a hero."

"But that's the thing. All this time, I expected you to be." He looks up at me, no plastic frames. No lenses, real or imagined, between us. The truth stings. I'm feeling pretty far from heroic right now. All I wanted was to disappear quietly and find a place where we could all be safe. I thought I could be the one to keep us that way.

I force myself to smile. Squeeze his shoulder to remind him his padding is gone. "You did it. You conquered your fear. Seems pretty heroic to me."

"You think so?" He shakes his head, squinting at Poppy across the parking lot as she draws a stitch through Woody's leg. "She's kind of amazing, you know. When things went south, she knew exactly what to do. She's not afraid of anything."

"Everyone's afraid of something." I think back to her face on the boat, when she wasn't sure Chill was coming. How she was first to the rail when he took off his life jacket and jumped in. "She was afraid of losing you."

He casts another surreptitious glance her way, smiling to himself as he slips his empty frames back on, his eyes a little glassy, a little unfocused without the lenses. Without the magic. "I think I understand, now, why you wanted to leave."

He's light on his feet as he runs back to help the others, without the life jacket that's been weighing him down for so long. Maybe it's the heavy plastic frames obscuring his vision, or the gradual deterioration of it out here in the real world. Or maybe it's because he's only got eyes for Poppy. They're hopeful and bright, as if he's seeing the world and all its possibilities clearly for the first time. Maybe that's why he doesn't notice the crow still watching us from the trees.

26

THE LIVES WE BURIED

FLEUR

I follow Julio along a sandy path into a housing development. He hunches into his sweatshirt, hands shoved into the pockets of his wet jeans. He glances at me over his shoulder as I pluck pine needles from my sweater. "The poor bastards," he says, shaking his head. "You didn't even get your hands dirty."

"What's that supposed to mean?"

"You tore all four of those Guards limb from limb, didn't you?" he asks when I finally catch up to him.

"I never said there were four."

He rolls his eyes at me. "Guards always work in teams of four. You of all people should know."

I rub my arms against a chill, rmembering that dead-end alley where Doug's team cornered me. How helpless I felt, surrounded by Guards, trapped in a building, three flights off the ground. I was lucky this time, close to the woods. I shudder to think what might have happened if we'd been ambushed on the beach or trapped in the bathhouse when they caught up to us. "Jack was there. He helped."

"Like you needed it," he mutters, jamming his fists deeper into his pockets to mask a shiver. "I almost feel sorry for them. That shit hurts."

Blood rushes to my cheeks. That fight between us was years ago. Why bring it up now? "That was an accident. And I only maimed you."

"Some accident." Julio arches up on his toes to peek over a lattice-crowned fence gate before popping it open. "It took me years to live that down."

"Whatever." I sidestep a stack of lounge chairs and a kidney-shaped pool covered in green plastic for the season. "I was scared. You were trying to drown me. I did what anyone would do. It's not *my* fault you underestimated your opponent."

He pitches his voice low. "Pipe down, killer. You'll wake the whole neighborhood."

"If the Battle of the Bathhouse didn't wake them, I doubt we will. Besides, you said no one would be here."

He peers into the back windows of a darkened clapboard cottage.

"You want to talk about it?" I ask.

He tests the lock on the window. "Not especially."

"Julio." Something in the way I say his name makes him stop, even if he won't look at me. "It wasn't your fault."

Julio rubs his eyes, turning to rest his weight against the window-sill. He stares down at his hands as if they belong to someone else. "I grabbed his transmitter."

"It was an accident."

"Was it?" Dark bands of cloud drift over the pink and gray

horizon. The wind's as conflicted as we are, the air thick with the threat of rain.

"Marie's right. You did what you had to do to stay alive. And Amber did what she had to do to save you."

"Wouldn't be the first time." His defeated sigh smells like salt water. Like fatigue and frustration. I open my mouth to ask him what he means when he reaches up into a crevice in the deck above his head and a set of keys falls into his hand.

"You know these people?" I ask.

He unlocks the door, cracking it just enough to sniff the air inside before dragging me through it with him. He guides me by the sleeve past a rack full of surfboards, a sofa, and a big-screen TV without turning on a light. "Just people I hang out with sometimes."

I follow him up a flight of stairs to a kitchen. He helps himself to the pantry, grabbing canned soups and beans, boxes of cereal, and bags of chips. He tosses ramen noodles and packs of instant oatmeal on the counter. Then he reaches under the sink for a garbage bag and shoves the food in. When he's done, he takes the roll of paper towels beside the sink and tosses that in, too.

He avoids the fridge. The surface is covered in magnets and photos. I stand in front of it, struggling to make out the faces in the pale dawn light filtering through the window over the sink.

"This is you." I pluck a photo out from under a magnet. Julio's bronze and shirtless in a pair of turquoise board shorts, his arms wrapped around a group of surfers, all of them squinting against the sun. Their boards are scattered around them in the sand, the bathhouse we just set on fire forming the backdrop behind them. I don't know why the photo shocks me. Maybe because I can't picture us having any life other than the one we've been stuck in. Can't picture us making connections or having relationships in any permanent, meaningful way. I'm surprised by the pang of jealousy I feel. "Are these your friends?"

"I guess," he says with a dismissive shrug. "I met them a few summers ago. We surf together. I party with them sometimes." He disappears down the hall, into one of the bedrooms. Drawers open and close. A closet door slides open, hangers screeching as he pulls clothes from the racks with an efficiency that suggests he's been through them before.

I find Julio in another photo, cheek to cheek with a dark-haired girl who looks a few years younger than we are. She's in almost every picture. Posing in bathing suits with her friends. Holding a soccer ball and a pair of cleats, flanked by her proud parents. Wearing Christmas sweaters, making goofy faces with a boy who looks so much like her, he could only be an older brother—one of Julio's surfer friends from the other photo. If I didn't know better, I might assume they were all family . . . Julio's family.

"Here, these'll probably fit you." Julio hands me a stack of the girl's clothing, his expression pained as he digs mechanically under the cabinet for another bag.

"Are they . . . ?" I don't know how to ask without prying too deeply. And yet, I don't know how I couldn't have asked before. "Do you want to stay? Here, I mean. With them?"

Julio stops, the bag half open. He looks down at the clothes. At the food. At this place.

"Stay where? With who? These people who hardly know me?

And do what?" There's a quiver of emotion in his voice I've never heard before, a frustration that suggests this isn't the first time he's asked himself this. "Watch them all get older? Wait for them to wonder why I don't? Wait for them to get sick of all the lies and disappearing acts, while I just move on to a new family in a new town every time the one I'm with starts looking at me funny? Or do I just come out and tell them the truth? That the guy who crashed in their basement last summer—the one who partied with their son and taught their daughter to surf—died thirty-seven years ago trying to save the girl he *accidentally* killed with his board? While I'm at it, why don't I tell them I stalk and murder my best friend every spring? Or that I just executed some guy in a parking lot at the end of their street?" He shoves the last of the clothes into the bag. Reaches into another cabinet and grabs a set of hidden car keys. "This family's no different from the other ones. They're all better off without me." He takes the food under his arm and tosses the bag of clothes to me. "Let's go."

I follow him back downstairs, mouth parted with a million unasked questions about everything he just shared with me. Julio never talked much about his life before he was turned, never bragged about the circumstances surrounding his first death, like some Seasons tend to do. Up until tonight, Julio was so indomitably confident in my mind, so slick and secure, it seemed like nothing could touch him. And now I wish I had paid more attention to the things he never spoke about—to the wounds under the shiny armor he wore to protect the fragile parts of himself.

He opens a side door to the garage and climbs into the driver's seat of a sleek black Ford Expedition with a roof rack and tinted windows. I scramble into the passenger side as he starts the car. He sets the thermo-stats to high, cupping his hands in front of the vents for a moment as he lets the engine warm.

His eyes close, leather creaking as he leans back in his seat.

"It was an accident," I murmur. "That's all. It wasn't your fault. None of it." Not the girl he hit with his board. Not Marie's jump from the bridge. Not my slip below the red line. Not Hunter. Not any of it. "You're a good person, Julio. You don't have to prove it."

He sits up with a heavy sigh and puts the SUV in gear. "Great. If I get arrested in the next thirty minutes, you can explain all that to the cops." He eases out of the driveway. With a sharp click of a button on the visor, he shuts the garage door.

Julio turns down the next street and creeps to a stop beside the curb. He kills the headlights and checks the mirrors.

"Stay here," he says, grabbing a screwdriver from a tool case under the front seat. He gets out, looking both ways before stripping the license plates from the SUV. Hood pulled low, he crosses the street, kneeling before a car-shaped lump under a sun-bleached tarp and swapping out the plates. The entire process takes under a minute, and he climbs back in without a word.

"What were you arrested for, breaking and entering or burglary?" I ask, remembering Amber's warning to him just before she disappeared into the bathhouse.

His lip twitches as he pulls back his hood and maneuvers the SUV back onto the road. "Which time?"

"How many times have there been?"

The clouds part as Julio cracks a grin. "I lost count in 1995."

I laugh, comforted by the return of the carefree Summer I know.

Hungry to know more about him and wishing I'd asked more questions before. I don't feel like a very good friend. Certainly not a best friend. "Then tell me about 1989, with Amber."

"Should have known you were going to ask me that," he says through a sigh. He waits, probably hoping I'll lose interest. When I don't, he switches on the radio. I reach over and turn it off. He squints against the hazy rising sun.

"She's wrong about the year," he confesses. "It was 1990, the second year she came to kill me. She'd gotten me good that first time in eighty-nine." A nostalgic smile touches the creases around his eyes. "I saw her coming down the beach, with that fiery hair and that pout and that confident way she walks, and I don't know . . . I just stood there. All I could do was stare." He gives a slow shake of his head and sighs. "Next thing I knew, she was sticking a knife in my gut. Or in my heart. Maybe both. Hell, I don't remember." He gnaws at his lip. Drums the steering wheel. "I woke up in my stasis chamber three months later, and I couldn't stop thinking about her. I spent the next six months planning all the ways I was going to kick her ass and reclaim my honor. Instead, when the time came, I got shit-faced drunk and arrested, and as I was lying in my cell without my transmitter, with a fever and the shakes, the one thought that bugged me the most was that I might never see her again. Later that night, Amber came for me. And like a lovestruck, inebriated idiot, I walked myself right up to the bars of my cell and asked her to kiss me." I watch the light leave his eyes. Watch the smile on his mouth fade into a tight, thin line. "The next year, they docked our rankings and stuck us both in Reconditioning. I spent hours getting the shit knocked out of me by four of Chronos's Guards while they pumped smoke and the smell of dead leaves into the room."

"Did it work?"

"Yes. No. Maybe." He frowns, his knuckles white where they grip the steering wheel. "We never kissed each other again, but I never stopped thinking about it, either."

I lean back in the heated leather seat, the adrenaline of the morning slowly beginning to recede. It's nice, being able to talk like this, without feeling guarded. Without a clock ticking. He's shared more with me in the last thirty minutes than in all the years we've known each other.

Maybe Jack's right and we're not supposed to hunt each other. Maybe we're just supposed to *find* each other. To make a space for each other and give each other room to be strong. To hold on to each other when we're not, protect each other, and ride out the occasional storm.

Julio winds through the neighborhood, taking the long way back to South Atlantic Avenue. He navigates the streets here with an ease, making me curious about the 75 percent of his life I've never seen: the parties and surf competitions he mentions in passing, his relationship with Marie, his life at the Observatory . . . who he is the other nine months of the year. I wonder if this sudden need I feel to know him better is because we don't have to be enemies anymore, or if I'm hoping it will erase the worst of the 25 percent we've been.

He parks in front of the bathhouse and leaves the engine running. Our friends look up with weary, dirt-smeared faces, their clothes still wet and stained with gore. The beach behind them is bathed in the rosy light of a blood-red sunrise, peaceful in the daylight, as if the worst should already be over.

27

SAFE HOUSE

FLEUR

The drive to Jack's safe house is quiet, except for the occasional cough and sniffle from the back seat. Jack's driving; he's the only one aside from Chill who knows exactly where we're going.

I drop my feet from the dash, growing drowsier the more comfortable I try to make myself. Jack glances over as I peel off my sweater and aim the AC vent toward my face. No one objected when Jack set the thermostat as low as it would go. Instead, they took the sleeping bags from their packs and spread them across each other, and within minutes, they were all asleep.

One of us should stay up and keep Jack company. One of us should keep an eye out for crows, but the cold air only manages to leech my energy. I blink out the window, my eyelids growing heavier as the trees blur by. When the sun rose this morning, revealing the first turning autumn leaves I've seen in decades, I felt a rush of nostalgia, flashes of memories of plastic Halloween buckets overflowing with candy and my mother's good linens around the table at Thanksgiving, of hayrides and candy apples stuck in my teeth. But the farther west we drive, the lower the temperature falls. The piles of browning leaves along the side of the road remind me of Hunter, and the guilt sucks every ounce of warmth from my bones.

Jack hasn't said a word since we started driving. I wonder if he's battling memories of his own.

"You should rest." His voice is husky, his bloodshot eyes focused on the hypnotic white lines flashing by on the road. He points ahead of us, where a mountain range forms distant hazy peaks on the horizon. "It's not far. We'll be there in a few hours."

I turn in my seat, toward the familiar sound of Poppy's soft snores. She coughs, curled into her sleeping bag on the floorboard. Chill stirs in the seat behind her, his glasses low on his nose. Marie's mouth hangs open beside him, her head pressed against the window, with Slinky fast asleep in her lap. Woody's crammed in the rear bench seat between Amber and Julio. His skin looks sallow in his sleep, feverishly pale, but his bleeding has stopped, and for now, that's all we can do. We can't risk stopping at a hospital or a clinic. Cameras are mounted in every store and gas station. For all we know, they're on every highway marker and exit sign, too. We're eight teenagers in a stolen SUV full of camping gear and bloody clothes, midmorning on a school day. The last thing we want is to draw any more attention to ourselves.

I keep my eyes peeled for Gaia's spies and speed traps on the side of the road. But the farther west we travel, the more it begins to wind. My head lolls with the motion of the car, and I close my eyes.

Just for a second.

Tires crunch slowly over gravel. I blink, blinded by the orange glow against the inside of my eyelids and jostled by ruts in the road. Trees rise up on all sides of us, the setting sun glittering between their naked branches as we round a bend.

I sit up in my seat, my neck stiff and my bladder ready to burst. "How long was I out?"

"It's almost five. You slept through a pit stop three hours ago." Jack offers me a road-weary smile. Even so, he looks less tired than before. Refreshed, even. There's an eager shine in his eyes as he dips his head to survey the rise of the next peak.

We wind higher up the mountain, creeping around hairpin turns. The others begin to stir, roused by the sway of the car. One by one, they rub their eyes, taking in our surroundings as we turn down a narrow dirt road camouflaged by a blanket of fallen leaves. Jack pulls to a stop in front of a low wooden cabin, its unremarkable shape and weather-worn sides almost entirely hidden by the surrounding trees.

"We're home," he says quietly, to nobody. To all of us. He opens his door and slides down from his seat, taking it in from a distance. The sagging porch and leaning roof, the stacked stone chimney and a mound of moss-covered firewood, the splintered remains of an old wooden shed. He walks slowly through windblown piles of dead leaves, pausing to tap his knuckles against a rusted well pump.

The rest of us file out of the car. Slinky's gray head pops out of Marie's jacket, his nose tipped curiously and his whiskers quivering. Poppy and Chill help Woody out of the SUV. They stand slack-jawed beside it, their wide eyes moving from the rustling branches to the clear blue sky to the pockets of blaze-orange and ley line–yellow and bloodred leaves, then down to the miles upon miles of green in the valley. A tear slides down Poppy's cheek. She brushes it away with a nervous giggle that eases some of the guilt I've been carrying.

Julio blows warm air into his hands as he makes a beeline for a small wooden outhouse behind the cabin. Amber ties her sweatshirt around her waist and pops open the rear hatch, a smile on her lips as Woody limps past the cabin to get a better view.

She dumps the duffels and backpacks beside my feet, her smile fading as she watches Jack climb the warped steps to the front porch. The wooden planks creak. When he swings open the porch door, the dry-rotted screening blows loose in the breeze. I expect him to pull a pick from his pocket. Instead, he shakes out a set of keys. The door sticks, and he gently shoulders it open, releasing months, or even years, of mustiness I can smell from here.

Amber wrinkles her nose. "This is it? This is Jack's idea of a safe house?" I hate to admit I'm thinking the same thing. The place looks frail enough to crumble under the first blanket of snow. I pull on my sweatshirt, hugging myself against the biting cold, which doesn't seem to bother anyone but Julio and me.

"No power or phone lines," I point out, trying to be optimistic for Jack's sake. "We're off the grid. No one can track us."

She points to the moon-shaped cutout in the door of the outhouse as Julio swings it open. "No running water or indoor plumbing, either." Heaving a sigh, she tromps through the leaves to take her turn.

"How are you feeling?" Julio asks, huddling close.

"Tired," I say with a shiver. "You?"

He nods. Even though he's slept all day, his eyes are ringed deep purple and his lips are a little blue. He hefts an armful of duffels and carries them inside. I grab as many as I can carry and follow.

The front room of the cabin is little more than dusty floorboards, a table, and a single chair. A potbellied stove and a few cabinets function as a makeshift kitchen. The cast-iron door of the stove groans open. Jack kneels in front of it and loads it with wood. He strikes a match and sets a few pieces of kindling burning, staring into the crackling flames, his thoughts lost in the swirl of smoke.

Julio pokes his head into the next room. There's no door on the hinge, just an opening in the wall. He drops the bags on the floor, stirring a cloud of dust. Two cots line the back wall, where splinters of daylight penetrate the gaps in the timber. Above the cots, the rungs of a roughhewn ladder disappear into a loft. Julio climbs up and inspects the handful of faded bed rolls left behind by whoever was here before.

"This place is a shithole," he says, jumping down from the ladder. He claps dust from his hands and returns to inspect the kitchen. A mouse scurries out when he opens a cabinet door. Marie makes a disgusted sound from the doorway as Slinky leaps from her chest in pursuit.

Chill wanders in behind her. The reflection of the fire, or maybe a memory, flickers against his dark eyes when he sees Jack kneeling by the stove.

Someone's stomach growls loudly—maybe mine. Loud enough to get Chill's attention.

"I'll start dinner." He digs into the bags of food we stole, stacking cans of soup on the counter. Dust billows from a cast-iron pot he fishes from a cobwebbed cabinet. He lugs it outside, mumbling something about the well.

Jack shuts the stove and gets stiffly to his feet. His jeans sag on his hips, crusted with dried seawater. Even his hair hangs low over his eyes, heavy with the weight of the day's journey. His dark bangs have grown long over the last few weeks, making it hard to read his thoughts.

Woody hobbles in, leaning on Amber's shoulder. She deposits him in the lone chair and props his leg on the rickety table. Hands on her hips, she takes in the room.

"Seriously, Jack?" She drops her backpack to the floor and swears softly. Jack slips out of the cabin without a word. Through the walls, I hear the shed door slam, then the repetitive loud chop of an ax.

I start for the door, bumping into Chill as he returns from the well. He blocks my way, the dripping pot swinging from his hand. "Give him a while, Fleur," he says gently. "It's been a long time since we've been here." He passes me the pot with a melancholy smile. Reluctantly, I take it and let him steer me back inside.

The cabin grows dim as night falls. A weary hush falls over us, broken only by the relentless crack of the ax outside. Chill lights a lantern. Its mantle hisses, filling the air with the sharp scent of kerosene as it casts a warm orange glow over the room. When the silence threatens to swallow us all, Julio unzips his guitar case. He draws the instrument into his lap, softly tuning the strings as the fire snaps and pops. Chill sets a pot of stew on the stove, and we all settle on the dusty floor around it, drawing our sleeping bags close as the wind pokes cold fingers through the holes in the cabin's timbers.

Julio picks a few notes. They're vaguely familiar, the beginning of a folk song from the 1960s, one we've all heard before but I can't remember the words to. Poppy offers up a few lyrics in a nasal, hoarse voice, the measures broken by staccato fits of coughing. Woody finishes the next measure for her, humming around the words he doesn't know. Amber closes her eyes. Her lips move to the music, and when Julio breaks into the next refrain, she sings every word by heart. They both hold the final note until it fades from the room.

Chill ladles the thin stew into some chipped mugs he found in a cabinet. We pass them around the circle. Julio sets down his guitar, taking his mug greedily in both hands, not bothering to blow the steam from the surface before shoveling it down. While the rest of us wait for our stew to cool, Poppy regales us with the story of how she and Chill performed first aid on Woody's stab wound during the fight, and how Slinky chased a crow deep into the woods. Marie fills me in on the parts of the battle Jack and I missed, namely Julio's clash with Cyrus. When the conversation turns to Amber's fight with Hunter, Julio stares into his mug, as if his appetite's lost somewhere at the bottom of it. He sets it down without finishing his meal.

Amber clears her throat. "What about you?" she asks me, deftly steering the conversation away from Hunter. "What happened after those Guards chased you into the woods?" Marie makes a disgusted face, as if she's already surmised the answer. Chill shudders. Woody's the only one leaning forward. He and Amber have never battled a Spring before. They're curious, in the same morbid way I was fascinated by the firefight between Amber and Hunter at the bathhouse.

I shake off the memory of the Guard's wet scream when I sent him home.

"No big deal," I say sheepishly.

Julio raises an eyebrow, purposefully twanging a string.

With a dramatic sniffle, Marie carries her mug and sleeping bag to an empty corner of the room. She blows her nose into a piece of paper towel.

"What's the matter?" Julio teases. "Allergic to your cat?"

"It's *seasonal* allergies. I was stuck in a car all day with the princess of pollen and the reigning queen of ragweed." She juts her snotty nose toward me and Amber as she jabs a spoon into her mug. "I'm allergic to both of you."

"Don't have to ask me to keep my distance," Amber mutters into her stew.

Julio snorts, making Poppy and Woody crack up, and soon the laughter spreads through the room.

The air in the cabin is thick and close, but different than it was on the boat. Warmer. More relaxed. I wish Jack were here to see it. I listen for the crack of his ax, but it's finally fallen silent.

"I'll tell Jack the stew's ready." I climb out from the warmth of my sleeping bag and brush the dust from my jeans. They're all still laughing as the screen door shuts behind me.

28
WINTER'S KISS

JACK

I bury my ax in a stump beside a mountain of cut wood. The valley below is blanketed in moonlight, the sky dusted with stars. This view holds a million memories—school and skiing and campfires in the summer, afternoons fishing with my grandfather, and the first time I met Chill—but the memory that darkens all the rest is last night's battle at Croatan Beach.

I rub the fresh blisters on my hands, relishing the sting. My muscles burn, swollen from exertion after months of disuse. The punishing pain and fatigue feel good, like I actually earned them. Which is more than I could say for myself last night, when I needed to be strong. Or at the very least, competent.

I snatch my T-shirt from where it hangs over the waist of my jeans and shake the wood chips from it. It scratches as I mop the frost from my face and the sheen of ice from my arms. As I drag it over my head, I catch Fleur's scent and stiffen.

"There's stew inside," she says, a shiver in her voice. "Are you coming in?"

I watch the shadows of clouds drift over the valley as they pass under the moon. From the cabin comes the smell of broth and the faint notes of Julio's guitar.

I'm not ready to go inside yet. Not ready to face them.

Fleur's boots shuffle in the leaves, her scent fading as she walks back toward the cabin, but I'm not ready for her to go yet, either.

"I'm sorry." The words hurt coming out. I owe her an apology, for last night and for this place, but I don't know where to start. I picked this safe house for her. The woods—every root and branch and vine—are a weapon in her hands, but none of it's any good if I can't protect myself. Our survival depends on both of us now, and I was useless last night.

Leaves crunch behind me. The smell of her is killing me. She's all blossoms and new beginnings, all sweetness and hope.

"Sorry for what?" she asks.

"I couldn't protect myself against those Guards. How the hell am I going to keep you safe?"

"I never asked you to," she says sharply.

"What about Julio and Amber? What about the others?" I remind her. "They're all here because of me. Because all I could think about was you and that red line, and I was selfish."

"You were *selfless*!" I feel her static. Smell her standing right behind me, and I round on her.

"No, I was stupid! I was so fucking sure I could do this. That I could get us out of there!"

"You did!"

"By the skin of our teeth! And now what?" Every fear and doubt feels like it's cresting to the surface. I don't want to be the reason for that flash of sadness in her eyes. But I can't stop. "We're stuck in this *shithole* cabin with barely enough food to last the week! Poppy and Marie are sick. Woody'll be lucky if he doesn't develop an infection. We can't stay here forever. Chronos must have had Guards posted all up and down the coast, waiting for us. We killed a Season last night, Fleur! They're not going to let us just walk away from that. It's only a matter of time before . . ." I wince.

"Before what?"

I grab my jacket off the ground, my throat closing around the one thing I don't have the balls to say. "You saw what happened to Hunter. That could have been any one of us." I can't even look at her. I told her that we could go anywhere. That we could write our own ending. We crossed an entire fucking ocean and Chronos still managed to find us.

Pity you have to die.

I shrug into my jacket, kicking up leaves as I head up the mountain, deeper into the woods.

"Jack," she calls after me. "Jack, stop!"

My foot snags on a root. The ground rushes up to meet me, and I catch myself just before I fall facefirst into the dirt. I kick out to free myself, but the root's tight around my ankle. With a hard jerk, it flips me over.

"Don't you dare turn your back on me when I'm talking to you." Fleur's hair is a wild tangle of pink static and her hands are shaking. She comes close enough for me to see the anger blooming in her eyes, to smell the ozone crackle of her temper, beautiful and terrifying. I inch back on my elbows as she hovers over me. "Every single one of us is here because we wanted to be. Except maybe Marie. Whatever. She and her damn cat are both free to make their own choices from here. But the rest of us signed on for this, Jack! We chose it, for better or worse. And in case it's escaped your attention, we made it. We're alive. We're together. *Because* of you. Not in spite of you." The forest falls silent, as if she commanded it to. A flurry of voices—laughter and a playful riff of Julio's guitar—carry from the warm glow inside the cabin down the hill. "When you're done feeling sorry for yourself, come inside and eat. The only one of us with any regrets tonight is you."

Fleur stomps down the hill toward the cabin and slams the door, leaving me exactly where I thought I wanted to be—alone in the cold.

I shake my foot loose, but the root that tripped me is already gone, buried in the ground.

Regrets. Fleur thinks I regret getting her out of that place. But the only thing I regret is not being more careful. The only thing I wish I could take back was my own overconfidence when I told them we could all survive this. That there was hope for us all.

I trek uphill around clusters of rock, navigating by memory in the dark, until I reach an elevation high enough to clear my head. Lantern light flickers in the cabin's window below. The chimney puffs out clouds of poplar smoke, and through the thin walls, I can hear them laughing.

Maybe Fleur's right. None of us expected it to be easy. We're alive. Off the grid. We're together. Maybe that's enough.

I sink down on a boulder. It felt so touch and go between us on the boat, hostile and new, all of us distrustful, confined to close quarters with nowhere to go. But here . . . I look out over the endless blue ridges, as far west as my eyes can see in the dark. If we come apart here, we're lost.

I don't know how long I've been sitting when I finally push myself to my feet. The light's gone dim in the cabin, and I wander back down the hill, surprised when I creep up the porch steps and find Fleur lying outside the door. Her sleeping bag's drawn up around her ears. Her teeth chatter from the cold. Inside, I can just make out five shadowy sleeping bags spread around the belly of the stove, and Amber huddled by the draft in the opposite wall.

The sight of Chill bundled inside a thermal bag brings on a pang of loss. His body temperature's already risen, adjusted to a mortal's normal. I shouldn't be surprised; I saw it coming. The way he's squinted at the maps more each day. How he demurred when I asked him if he wanted to drive to the cabin this morning.

I kneel beside Fleur and lay a palm on her cheek. Her eyes open, confused at first until they find mine. She slides out of her sleeping bag and I give her my sweatshirt. She drags it over her own, making her body seem more solid and her hair frizzy, rousing a memory of last night's battle that only makes her seem more beautiful.

"I don't regret this," I whisper. "Not any of it."

Then I take her hand and lead her into the woods.

FLEUR

The air smells like Jack—like the crisp, cold hush that falls just before it snows. I hunch into his sweatshirt as he takes my hand and guides me down the ridge under a starlit canopy of pine. The longer we hold hands, the warmer and more awake I feel, and the stronger my legs become.

He pauses on a moon-drenched slope. Leaning close, he points out a nearby peak, its surface raked with trails.

"That's where I died the first time," he says. He drags his finger to the right, gesturing to an imposing roofline breaking through the trees near the slopes. "Second floor, third window from the left. That was home," he says, guiding me down.

"You lived there?"

"Almost four years. Boarding school for troubled boys." At my quizzical look, he says, "My dad split when I was thirteen. My parents fought all the time. My dad was never around and my mom was depressed. I started getting into all kinds of trouble, one suspension after another, but by that point, she was already dating someone new and couldn't be bothered to care. That fall, when my older brother went off to college, she got engaged and dumped me here." Jack shrugs like it's no big deal, but the furrows in his brow say otherwise. "That was the last time I was home."

I stop walking, making him stop, too. "You never went back?"

Without letting go of my hand, he bends to pick up a smooth piece of rock that's flaked away from an outcropping. He pitches it sideways into a ravine, as if he's skipping stones on a lake. "She promised every winter break she'd come get me and bring me home for Christmas. But she never came. There was always some excuse. She remarried a year later. Changed our last name from Sommers to Sullivan. I was mad. It felt like she chose him over me." My heart hurts for him. He says it with a shrug of his shoulders, like it's no big deal. But he was dumped here. Abandoned by the one woman who could have healed him. "I hated this place," he says with a slow shake of his head. "I tried like hell to get kicked out so she'd have to come get me. I even got arrested once."

"You? For what?" I ask as he starts walking again, leading me along the base of the ridge.

Jack's smile is rakish as he counts off on his fingers. "Underage drinking, destruction of property, resisting arrest—"

I can't help it. I laugh.

"What?" he asks with feigned indignation, pulling me in close to avoid a rock in our path until our shoulders brush. "What's so funny?"

"Nothing, I just have a hard time picturing you as the dangerous rebel." I think of every time I've searched for his name on the screens at the Observatory. How it's always been top of the ranks, the A student Chronos had pegged for his Guard. And yet here he is, breaking every one of Gaia's rules. "So what happened?"

"I used my one phone call to call my mom."

"And?"

"And she didn't pick up." He winces as he gazes off into the distance, as if part of him is still waiting for her.

"I'm sorry."

"Don't be. It was a long time ago," he says. But in the set of his jaw, I see a hint of that forsaken boy still raging inside him.

We reach the bottom of the ridge and Jack pauses within view of a moonlit pond. He chews his lip as he considers it. "Do you trust me?" he asks with a gleam in his eye.

He tugs me by the sleeve. I pull against him as he drags me closer to the pond. "I'm *not* swimming in any more cold water."

He laughs. "I promise I won't make you swim."

I latch onto a root with my mind, determined not to let him dunk me.

Jack steps to the water's edge. He doesn't stop.

"Jack, what are you—?"

His running shoe comes down on the water just as the pond freezes beneath it. The frost spreads to his other foot until he's standing on a platform of ice. "Come on," he says. "It's safe. I promise." I utter a protest as he takes my hand, walking backward with a cocky smile. Suddenly, I'm standing on the ice with him. My feet skim over the surface, and a laugh bubbles up inside me.

"I haven't skated since I was little." My voice is thin as I grip his hand for balance. I take an uncertain step and my feet slide out from under me.

"Easy there." Jack pulls me to him before I fall, until our bodies are pressed together, my hands on his shoulders, our faces close, our fogged breath mingling.

Close enough to kiss.

My breath catches. Jack pulls back slowly, letting my hands fall into his, his thoughts unreadable as he leads me farther out onto the pond. He steers me in slow circles across the ice.

"This is where I met Chill," he says once I'm steady on my feet, our elbows locked together.

"Where? On the pond?"

"No, about fifteen feet under it. It was winter break of my senior year. I broke out of the dorm with some booze and a few people I thought were friends. We cut through the woods after the resort closed and they'd turned off the lights on the slopes. I ended up with a snapped spine under a couple feet of snow. No one came looking for me. Except Gaia. She told me my survival would depend on my next choice—that I should choose carefully. Next thing I remember, I was wandering the hills barefoot. All I knew was that I was supposed to pick someone to watch over me and protect me, to look out for me—only I had no idea what I was supposed to be looking for." Jack turns to me then with a broken smile. "There'd never been one single person in my life who'd come looking for me if I disappeared. Not one person I could count on to make sure I made it home."

"And then you found Chill?"

Jack nods. He points to a distant corner of the pond. "A few days later, I was sitting in those trees just outside campus, wondering what would happen if I showed my face there three hours after my own memorial service. And I saw this gangly kid wearing a collared shirt and a clip-on tie. Figured he must have come from my funeral. I was surprised, I guess. I didn't know much about Chill other than his name—or at least what his name was back then—we didn't hang around in the same circles. But there he was, getting pushed around at the side of the pond by a couple of guys I knew a little too well from school. They grabbed Chill's glasses and tossed them out onto the pond. Chill walked out to get them, but the ice was thin. When he fell through, they ran."

"To get help?" I ask, trying to keep one foot in front of the other as Jack sails effortlessly over the ice.

"No. They just ran. By the time I got to him, Chill had been under for five minutes."

Suddenly, Chill's fear of the water makes sense. "You were his life jacket."

"I guess." Jack shrugs. "I dragged him out. Started CPR. It shouldn't have worked, but when I breathed into him, he woke up. No frostbite. No brain damage. He's been my Handler ever since." Jack skates us back to the edge of the pond, holding me steady as I step onto the brittle reeds.

"So you turned him yourself?" I remember the day Poppy and I died. She pulled herself off her oxygen tank while Gaia was in the room, demanding to come with us as she wheezed to death. I don't remember saving her. Gaia did that.

"What can I say? I'm pretty powerful." Jack polishes his knuckles on his T-shirt. The thin fabric clings to his chest, the muscles underneath still tight after chopping all that firewood. My cheeks warm when I remember how they glistened with frost as he tugged the shirt over his bare skin.

I shove him playfully, if only to humble him, but he's right. I've never seen him like this, on the cusp of his season. He's radiant. Aglow with magic. Unfazed by the cold and growing stronger with every second he uses it.

"Oh, you laugh?" he says, backing away and balling his hand at his side. A glittering white ball materializes out of nowhere. He winds his arm back and pitches it at me, and the snowball knocks me breathless, not from the force, but because I can't remember the last time I've seen one. "Not so tough now, are you? I've waited years to do that!" Another snowball's already forming in his hand. He howls with laughter as it erupts against my shoulder, scattering flakes in my face.

"Two can play that!" I reach out, sliding my mind into a root in the shallow mud of the bank. I yank it with a thought, tripping him as he runs backward away from me. He falls supine in the wet grass and I leap on him, pinning his hands beside his head, my knees planted on both sides of his waist. His laughter dies. His cheeks are flushed with color, his eyes clear and bright, the pale gray of his irises contrasting starkly against his dark lashes as they lower, his gaze trailing over the flakes of snow in my hair. Then down to my lips.

Jack's eyes close. His breath grows thick with frost. It shimmers as it forms a fine layer over his cheeks. His fingers grow suddenly colder in mine, thrumming with magic.

A white fleck drifts past the corner of my eye and I turn to catch it. Then another. My breath hitches as more begin to fall.

Snow.

Not the muddy slush that lingers in the gutters in March. Downy, fat flakes fall from the sky like feathers. They swirl in the air, alighting on the grass, forming a perfect circle around us. It's beautiful and magical, like we're lying in a snow globe. Jack smiles as they land on his cheeks and the tip of his nose. My throat thickens with memories— snow angels and sledding, presents and cocoa on Christmas morning, and long snow days off from school. This is a gift. The most amazing gift anyone's ever given me.

"It feels like I've waited my whole life to show you this," he whispers. His fingers curl around mine, steady and strong. I don't want to let go. Don't want to move from this place. Our noses brush, the breaths between us cold and sweet and eager. Winter jasmine. Thin ice. Lips parted.

"We shouldn't risk it," he whispers, his pulse quickening against my wrist. "If we're not balanced—"

"We're balanced." I can feel it in the hum of our skin. In how strong I feel when I'm with him.

"What if I'm wrong?"

I close my eyes. "What if you're right?"

I trace his mouth with my lips. Jack tips his face toward mine, and we meet in the middle, soft and careful at first. Then deep and careless and hungry as his tongue skates over mine. The longer we kiss, the warmer I feel. My knuckles ache where they hold him. I'm terrified to let go. That I'll open my eyes and this shining, sparkling moment will be gone.

"Who's out there?"

Our heads snap up. Lights flick on in the windows of the boarding school. I push myself up, ready to run, but Jack tugs me back down against his chest, pressing a finger to his lips.

"This is the headmaster. I know there's someone out there. You know the rules."

Jack's face breaks into a wide grin. He cups the back of my head, his fingers tangled in my hair as he steals another kiss that nearly sets me on fire.

A flashlight beam breaks through the trees.

"If there are students out of bed after hours, the punishment will be severe. Present yourselves immediately!"

Jack fights down laughter as he pulls me to my feet. He leads me from the school, leaving our circle of snow to melt behind us. We're running uphill through the dark, hand in hand, back to the safe house. But I'm certain that if he asked me to, I could fly.

29
TEETH FOR BATTLE

Fleur and I are still high on the rush of the kiss, of nearly being caught, still laughing as we climb the trail back to the cabin, giddy with fatigue.

The softening sky to the east hints at the hour. I feel like I could sleep for a week. Could be happy crammed in this shithole cabin forever, as long as Fleur's beside me.

"I'll be back in a minute. I need to . . . you know." She hooks a thumb at the outhouse behind the cabin as she peels away from me. I watch her go, and even though she must be freezing, there's a bounce in her step I've never seen before. The sweet scent she's kicking off smells like an entire garden in bloom.

A thin wisp of smoke winds up from the chimney. Inside, it must be getting cold. I head for the woodpile and grab a few logs for the fire.

Then nearly drop them, my smile crumbling.

A piece of paper's stuck in the chopping block, pinned in place by the blade of the ax. A cell phone rests beside it.

I set down the wood, glancing back through the trees to make sure Fleur's safely inside the outhouse before I tear the paper free.

Ten digits. A phone number. The handwriting is Lyon's. The same loopy old-fashioned letters. The same feathering ink of a fountain pen.

This was supposed to be a safe house. How did he find us? No one was supposed to know we were here.

The outhouse door creaks open. I stuff the cell phone and paper into my pocket before Fleur is near enough to see. She comes to me with that same bounce in her step, that same smell of hope, and that lightness in her eyes is crushing me. She takes the front of my T-shirt in her hands and rises up on her toes to kiss me. Her lips part, and I feel a little of my strength fade, my magic slipping from me as it feeds her.

I plant a guilt-ridden kiss on her forehead. "You're freezing," I tell her, rubbing her arms, though I'm probably only making things worse. "You should go inside and warm up. Get some sleep."

"Are you sure?" She hugs herself against the wind.

"I'll be in soon."

She picks up the two logs at my feet and carries them inside. Doesn't notice the scrap of torn paper still lodged under the ax's blade. Once she's gone, I search the shadows, the trees, the ridges above me for any sign that someone else might be here. I scent the air, but all I smell is woodsmoke and Fleur.

I climb the hill a safe distance from the cabin, high enough to catch a cell signal.

The line connects but remains ominously silent. Seconds tick by. I know Lyon's listening.

"What do you want?" I ask cautiously.

"Jack." Lyon breathes my name as if he's relieved to hear my voice. I wish the feeling were mutual. "Are you all right? Is Fleur with you?"

"We're fine," I bite out. "Where are you?"

"Not far," he says. But not near, either. Any hint of his scent was long gone when Fleur and I got back from the pond.

"How did you know where to find us?"

"The crows. They've been watching the coast, waiting for you to surface. I'm only sorry Chronos's Guard found you first." I lift my eyes to the moonlit branches around the cabin. I haven't seen a crow since we left Croatan Beach. I search the shadows in the woods for one of Gaia's smazes, but the darkness is too deep.

I grit my teeth, remembering the Summer who mysteriously showed up on the beach. Cyrus, already dying at the end of his season, had insisted Gaia was the one who'd sent him there. "How do you know it wasn't Gaia who told the Guards where to find us?"

"You can trust her, Jack."

"If you trust her so damn much, why'd you kill her bee?"

The line falls silent, his voice tinged with remorse when he finally speaks. "The burden of that choice doesn't fall on Gaia."

I sink down onto a boulder and rub my eyes. I'm tired. Too tired for this conversation. "I'm sorry. I didn't mean to sound ungrateful."

"You have no reason to be sorry. It's a fair question," he says. "It was the only way I could be sure you'd make it out of the Observatory. I don't expect you to understand. Not yet."

"I think I do." I bury my head in my hands. Lyon's never betrayed me before. Even still, I know I should hang up. It's too risky, communicating with him this way when he's so close to Gaia. It's hard to know where his loyalties lie. When I close my eyes, all I see is the light of the bee, dying under the sole of his shoe. But I don't have anyone else to turn to. "Amber's replacement found us at Croatan Beach. He didn't go back through the ley lines."

The phone goes quiet again, and I worry I've crossed a line. That I've confessed something unforgivable. "Did you take him?" Lyon asks.

The question guts me. Did I take him? Am I responsible? Was I the one to steal his life? Or does it only feel like I did because this whole damn trip was my idea?

"No." I press the heel of my hand into my eye, but the explosion of color against the inside of my eyelid reminds me of Hunter's magic falling from the sky. "Amber did. It was an accident."

"In the heat of battle, these things are inevitable," he says gently. "Your friends did what they had to do to survive."

"Does Chronos know where we are?"

"Not yet, but one of his teams is close. Douglas Lausks is leading them." I utter a curse. "They've narrowed your location to a radius of a few miles. They're awaiting reinforcements."

A few miles. I shoot to my feet. We have hours at most. The smoke from the chimney trails like bread crumbs over the valley. Fleur will be asleep soon with the rest of them, crashed out and vulnerable, same as we were when we washed up on the beach. "I have to go."

"No, Jack. It isn't wise to run. They'll only come after you." Lyon's instructions tumble out fast, as if he's afraid I'll hang up before I hear what he has to say. "Stay where you are and let them find you. Their distrust of each other is their weakness. They are an army only in number;

they will not fight like one. Once they're defeated, you'll have a clear path of escape."

"An army? We were nearly crushed by a single team of Guards and two Seasons last night. How many more could there be?"

"Their numbers are of little importance. The longer you remain together, the more powerful you'll become. They will not let you go quietly, Jack. Win over those who will listen. Take strength from others where you can."

"What about you? If you care so much, why the hell aren't you here?"

"I'm doing everything in my power to help you." I kick at the boulder, remembering every conversation I ever had with my mother when I called her to bail me out of that goddamn school. "My presence would only make you more vulnerable. I've no teeth for battle."

I drag my hand through my hair as I search the valley, wondering where the Guards are now and how long until they get here. "What if I can't protect them?"

Run? Fight? Are these my only choices? What if Chronos was right and every decision I make only leads us closer to the same shitty end?

"You wouldn't be a man if you weren't afraid, Jack." He says it in the same soft voice he used that day in the Control Room, after I watched Chronos foretell my death. "You are not alone. You have Fleur and the others. Hold on to each other. I've done everything I can. I believe in you, Jack."

The line goes dead before I can ask him why.

30

DISTANCE BETWEEN US

<u>FLEUR</u>

My toes are numb, my lips still tingling when I leave Jack by the wood-pile and come inside. The cabin smells like burned stew and the tang of unwashed bodies. The last serving of stew Jack never came in to eat has cooked down to a thick inedible paste at the bottom of the pot. I open the iron door to the stove as quietly as I can so I won't wake the others. Poppy stirs when I drop the first log on the coals. There's a wheeze in her cough that wasn't there last night when she went to bed. She sits up and sniffles.

"You're back," she says quietly.

"How'd you know I was gone?" I whisper.

From her sleeping bag in the corner, Marie grumbles, "Because Julio was up worrying about you two half the night. The rest of us didn't care enough to stay awake to witness your walk of shame." She rolls over, turning her back to us, but I'm sure she's listening.

"Ignore her," Poppy says, holding her sleeping bag open for me. I slide in with her, drawing it up as high as it will go. Her skin's clammy. It smells like salt, as if the six weeks we spent at sea are still lingering in her pores.

"Your feet are freezing!" she says, letting me warm them against her. I can't hold back my grin, thinking back to the pond, the snow, Jack's kiss . . . Poppy studies me sideways. "Winter looks good on you."

I rest my head on her shoulder, and hers falls against mine. "I'm sorry I kept you up. I didn't mean to make you worry."

"It wasn't that. I knew you'd be fine. It was Woody," she whispers. "He woke up sick in the night. Chill gave him some aspirin and he fell back to sleep about an hour ago, but his leg . . . it doesn't look good." Woody's long hair is tangled with sweat. I can smell it from across the room, and under it, the faint putrid odor of infection through his bandages.

Poppy coughs hard into her hand. The others begin to stir. A pale ray of sun seeps through the grime on the windowpane, revealing a feverish flush on her cheeks. She buries her next cough in the sleeping bag.

"You don't look good, either." I stroke her hair back, resting my palm on her forehead. She's warm. Too warm.

"It's nothing," she says dismissively. "I'm fine."

Chill sits up and scratches his chest, scowling at the room like he can't quite remember how he got here. He rises stiffly, grimacing into the burned pot on the stove.

The door flies open, a cold wind rushing in behind Jack.

"Nice of you to join us," Chill mutters.

Jack ignores him. I wait for our eyes to catch. For some awkward, secret acknowledgment of the night we spent together. But he walks straight to the back room.

I climb free of Poppy's sleeping bag and follow him, watching as he stuffs Chill's backpack with loose clothing and supplies. He gathers Slinky's food and Marie's toiletry bag and zips them into her backpack, stacking them beside Poppy's and Woody's bags beside the door. "Jack, what's going on?"

He brushes past me and grabs the car keys off the table.

Amber sits up and rubs her eyes. She glares at Jack like she might start hurling fire.

Julio burrows deeper into his sleeping bag and drags it up over his head. "If you all don't shut up and let me sleep, I'm going to kill every last one of you."

Jack opens the front door, letting in another blast of frigid air as he tosses all their bags onto the porch. The others look at me slack-jawed, as if I know what the hell is going on. I follow him outside, pulling the door closed behind me.

"Jack!" I brace myself against the damp cold seeping through my socks, seeping through everything, as Jack unlocks the car and starts piling the bags inside. "Jack, what's wrong?"

"They're leaving after breakfast," he says without looking at me.

"Who?"

"Poppy and Chill. Woody and Marie. They're taking the car. They need to go." He slams the rear hatch and I stand in his way.

"You can't be serious."

"They can't stay here."

I wrap my arms around myself. "What are you saying? Where is this even coming from? We can't split up!"

"Don't tell me you can't smell it. Woody's infection is spreading. If it goes septic, he'll die. Marie and Poppy are sick, too."

"So . . . we'll find a pharmacy or a doctor," I sputter. "We'll get antibiotics for Woody. Marie and Poppy are probably just coming down with colds. They just need rest."

"We can't rest!" He takes me by the shoulders. All traces of last night—of the cool, confident boy who walked on water and made snow fall from the sky—are gone. "Don't you see? They're at risk, every minute they spend with us. No one's looking for them. They're looking for *us*. They can smell us, Fleur. They can track us. Hunt us. And as long as Poppy and Chill are here with us, they're in danger. If they die on this mountain, it will be our fault."

He lets go, as if only now realizing how much he's hurting me.

"Die? Why would they die? What happened? What aren't you telling me?"

He rubs his eyes. It's been far too long since he's slept. He's just tired. He's not making any sense. "Chronos's Guards know we're here," he says. "They're coming."

"We've been here less than a day. No one hunts that fast." There's no way they could have found us so quickly. Unless we drew attention to ourselves. Unless we led them here. "Was it our fault? Was it the snow? Did someone see us at the school?"

"No." His face crumples. "No, Fleur. Nothing like that." He draws me to him, his breath shuddering against my hair. "I don't know how they found us."

"Who?" We both turn at the sound of Julio's voice. He and Amber stand side by side at the bottom of the porch steps. "Who found us?"

Jack takes my hand, keeping me close. "Doug Lausks's team." My stomach falls away. "Lyon says they've tracked us here. He's not sure how."

"What the hell do you mean, '*Lyon says*'? How does Lyon know where we are? You said no one knew where we were going." Julio looks from Jack to me as if I've betrayed him somehow.

"That's not important." Jack's frustration sounds earnest, and I wonder if he was lying about the snow. If it really was our own foolishness that drew the Guards here. "They've only got a rough idea where we are. But it won't take them long to find us."

"How soon?" Amber asks.

"A few hours, if we're lucky." Chill's and Poppy's faces appear in the window. Marie's shadow darkens the front door. Jack lowers his voice. "Lyon thinks we should stay and fight—the four of us. We already have the high ground. And we'll have a clean escape route once they're gone."

A hot wind whips over the ridge, blowing my hair over my eyes. I scrape it away, unsettled by the dark clouds gathering overhead. "I thought you said this place was safe," Julio growls.

"It is. We can fortify it. Together, we can defend it."

"And if we won't?" It sounds as if Julio's drawing a line in the sand. As if taking sides and walking away is even an option.

Jack's expression hardens. He tosses the car keys to Julio and Julio catches them against his chest. "Take the car after breakfast. Get clear of the mountain. Leave the Handlers at the first medical clinic you find; then you and Amber split off on your own. Just be sure to break away from Chill and Poppy before anyone tracks you." A strangled sound escapes my throat. They can't leave. We can't split up.

"What about Fleur?" Julio asks, his knuckles white around the car keys.

"Fleur can make her own choices." Jack lets go of my hand. He yanks the ax from the tree stump and climbs the hill into the woods.

Something splinters inside me. Cracks as he disappears.

"You can come with us," Julio says. "We'll take care of you." Amber doesn't object. So they would keep me charged. Heal me when I need it. But who will stay and fight with Jack? Who'll protect him? Who will save the Winter who risked his life for mine?

"I'm staying," I tell Amber and Julio. Then I climb the steps to the cabin to make breakfast and say goodbye.

There's no need for announcements. The windows of the cabin are thin. Marie steps out of my way to let me inside.

"We're leaving, aren't we?" Woody asks. He's awake, sitting up in the rickety chair in the kitchen, his foot elevated on a small wooden stool.

Poppy's watching me, her clear blue eyes revealing far too many of her thoughts as I grab an empty mug and spoon out flakes of instant coffee. "After breakfast. There's a town not far from here. I saw the lights last night, down in the valley. You should be able to find a doctor and get that infection treated."

"And then?" Chill asks, ripping open a box of cereal and setting it down hard on the table.

"Then you keep driving." Julio tosses the keys to Chill. His tone leaves no room for argument. Amber stands behind him in the cabin door, discreetly wiping her eyes on her sleeve. "You put distance between us and stay off the grid as long as you can. They won't be able to follow you." He stares at the floor. Doesn't look at his Handler as her mouth falls open.

Tears prick my eyes. I want to hug him. To throw my arms around both of them for staying, but it would feel selfish, knowing what this choice has already cost them.

"So that's it?" Marie snaps at him. She drops Slinky and tucks a cigarette behind her ear. "You're just going to abandon me to *them*?" She gestures to Woody with a look of disgust. "Chronos's goons are on their way, and you assume *he's* going to take care of us? He's a draft dodger, for chrissake!"

"I was a conscientious objector," Woody says. "There *is* a difference, you know."

"I don't care what he is," Marie barks at Julio, as if Woody's not even in the room. "Just because your girlfriend gave him a knife doesn't make him any less of a pussy!"

"And just because you're wearing someone else's dog tags doesn't make you a goddamn hero." Julio grabs the chain around her neck and holds the tags up to her face. "It's not your name printed on them. That honor doesn't belong to you. So quit acting like you're the only one making sacrifices here." He lets them fall against her chest.

"Screw you!"

"No, screw you!" I jump as Julio snatches the cigarette from behind her ear and tosses it to the floor. "I should have listened to Gaia on that bridge when she told me some people don't want to be saved. You've made that perfectly clear since the day we met. Well, guess what? I'm not feeling guilty anymore. Like it or not, you're alive, same as the rest of us. You don't want to go with them? Fine. Then walk. But I don't owe you anything!"

None of us speak. In all the years I've known Julio, I've never seen him lose his temper. Not like this. The sunlight through the windows dims. Dead leaves rustle in the rising wind outside, bare limbs scratching the walls of the cabin as it shifts with Julio's mood.

Marie's lip trembles. She scoops up her cat and storms out, slamming the door behind her.

Amber starts after her.

"Let her go." Julio glances at the thickening clouds through the window. He takes a slow breath, forcing the tension from his shoulders, as if he knows a storm will only draw attention we don't need right now. "There's only one way off the mountain. They can pick her up at the bottom of the road. By then, she'll have cooled down."

"And if she doesn't want to come with us?" Chill asks.

"It's her choice. I'm done making decisions for her." Julio retreats to the back room. Amber and I exchange a look, both of us probably thinking the same thing. The wind has calmed, but the sky's still dense and gray around the cabin. This is harder on Julio than he's letting on.

Amber stands behind Woody's chair. He leans his head back against her, everything they need to say to each other passing between them through the silence, as if they've known all along it was coming. As if they've already said their goodbyes. The same way Poppy and I did in our hospital room all those years ago, making peace with the inevitable.

Poppy stands alone by the window. I wrap my arms around her and stare at our reflection in the glass.

"It'll be okay," I tell her through a lump in my throat. She's frail, fragile here, and any lingering uncertainty I have about letting her leave melts away the longer I hold her. Jack's right. She's not safe with us.

None of them are. "You and Woody can find a doctor and get well. Then you can go anywhere. All the places Jack promised."

"I thought we'd have more time," she says, swiping a tear from her cheek.

"I did, too."

When she turns to hug me, I feel the rattle in her lungs, the weakness in her embrace, and I know this is the right thing to do. I brush her hair back from her face, trying my best to smile.

"We'll see each other soon," I whisper. Because I believe it. Because I have to, or I might not let her go.

The light through the window wavers and I blink back hot tears. On the other side of it, Jack descends the hill. Chill meets him at the edge of the woods. Says something. Then shoves him hard. Jack takes it, as if he deserves it somehow. He lets Chill push him again. Lets him pound on his chest. Then Jack grabs him by the shirt and pulls him into his arms, tight enough that Chill can't push him away or hurt him anymore. He holds him until Chill's shoulders begin to shake and Jack's eyes are red with tears. Until they've said their goodbyes, and the only thing left to do is let go.

31

THE LION'S DEN

JACK

We watch the cabin in shifts—me and Fleur, then Amber and Julio—alert for sudden movement through the trees. The air's been thick with tension since our Handlers left, our foul moods mirrored in the grayness of the sky, our anxiety in the restlessness of the wind. Every tree branch swaying is a false alarm, every rustling leaf a distraction. No matter how high up the ridge I climb, I can't see a hint of whatever Doug's got planned for us.

Fleur's pink hair is a small bright spot on the ridge below me. She patrols the perimeter around the cabin, stooping to set trip lines made from a spool of fishing line she found in my grandfather's shed. Her hands graze the tree trunks, as if their roots are all networked and she's somehow tapping in, the same way she touched my face this morning and could sense something was wrong. She hasn't looked at me the same way since. And I wonder if she blames me the way Julio does. If she suspects that I'm somehow responsible for the fact that this place is no longer safe for us.

Regardless of what Julio thinks, I never shared any of this with Lyon. Never told him any of our plans, even though it was obvious he knew all along what I was up to. Even so, I can't make myself believe Lyon would sell us out. He's risked too much just to help us get here. I only wish I understood why.

The wind howls over the ridge, the prevailing gusts from the southeast uncomfortably warm at my back, probably because Julio's still pissed at me. Inside the cabin, he's securing boards over the window, his hammer smacking nails into the walls hard enough to knock them down. I pick up my ax and get back to work, chopping down long trunks and stripping them of their branches, piling them one on top of another in a precarious stack at the crest of the hill before securing them with a trip wire.

After, I head to the overlook just below the cabin. Fleur sits perched on a boulder, watching the clouds, a stack of stones the size of her fist piled beside her. I consider making a joke about how they're too small to do any real damage, but I know better.

"I'm sorry," I tell her. Our shift is over. I should at least get that off my chest before we go inside and try to sleep.

"Don't be. Sending them away was the right thing to do." She turns the empty spool of fishing line in her hands. The sight of it makes me ache for my grandfather, for his reassuring presence. I hate that there's no one left to watch my back.

"Still," I say, raking my hair from my eyes, "it doesn't make it easier."

The hammering stops. A gust of wind lifts Fleur's hair as Amber and Julio's argument escalates inside.

"They've been bickering all afternoon," she says, swiping at her eyes.

"About what?"

"Everything. Nothing."

She listens to them with a pained expression. Her hair sticks in the corner of her lip and I want to reach for it, brush it away, and kiss her like we did last night. To hold her and keep everything from falling apart.

The door to the cabin flies open, smacking into the wall as Amber storms out. Julio follows her onto the porch, gripping his hammer, staring at her back as she goes.

The wind shifts abruptly with Amber's temper, carrying a hint of something that wasn't there a moment ago. I stand up, struggling to place it.

"What's wrong?" Fleur asks.

"Someone's coming." Something doesn't feel right. Doesn't smell right. We shouldn't be able to smell the Guards at all.

I take off for the cabin.

"What did he see?" Julio asks Fleur as I dash inside. I grab the fire poker from the bucket beside the wood stove and fish a knife from a kitchen drawer.

Amber meets me at the foot of the porch steps. "What's going on?"

I consider giving my ax to Fleur, but every tree in these woods is a weapon she can use to defend herself. It's the reason I picked this place. This is her safe house. Not mine. I toss the fire poker to Julio and hand Amber the knife.

"Shouldn't Fleur have a weapon?" she asks, reluctant to take it.

"I'm fine," Fleur insists.

"The mountain is her weapon," I tell her. Amber's never fought a Spring. She wouldn't know. Part of me thinks maybe Lyon had a point. We have an advantage our opponents won't. We've been fighting each other so long, we'll anticipate each other's moves before we make them. "We stay together in pairs. Back to back is the only way we'll beat them. And whatever you do, don't let the Guards touch you."

Amber takes a step back, tasting the air. "Not just Guards," she says, adjusting her grip on the knife. "There's a Summer. Coming from the south."

Julio shakes his head, angling closer to her. "Southwest."

"And a Winter from the north," Fleur says.

I'm picking up at least two Autumns. One from the northwest, and another just south of it. Julio and I lock eyes as he senses them, too. Four Seasons, closing in fast. But where are the Guards?

We form a circle, back to back, waiting.

The wind shifts, gusting over the ridge, scattering dead leaves.

A flock of black birds caws and takes flight just beyond the outhouse. Another cloud of them shrieks, peppering the sky behind the cabin.

A branch sways near the overlook, pulled by Fleur's trip line. She raises a fist, prepared to spring the trap. I reach for her and she stills.

Win over those who will listen. Take strength from others where you can.

"We don't want to fight you!" I call out.

A girl's voice echoes from the woods. "If you didn't want to fight anyone, you wouldn't have put that Autumn in the wind!"

"That was an accident." My own voice bounces back to me as I search for her. "He was trying to kill us. We couldn't let that happen.

We won't let it happen now." The wind whispers through the trees, concealing her movements. "I'll explain everything. Join us if you want to. Or just walk away. We won't stop you." A flash of color catches my attention. She peeks out from behind a trunk, then ducks back behind it, but the blue streak in her hair gives her away.

"Névé?" She doesn't answer. Névé Onding's a Winter, an old friend of Noelle's, a fact that I'm trying not to think too hard about, since she was never very fond of me. "What are you doing here?" Her region ends at the border of West Virginia, nearly a hundred miles from here.

"Chronos opened the boundaries. He put a bounty on your head. Two hundred and fifty points and a Relocation to the Season who brings you down."

A bounty? Are these the reinforcements Doug's team was waiting for—Seasons lured by the promise of a reward? Névé pokes her nose out. Her nostrils flare at the Summer I smell creeping up the slope behind us and the Autumns closing in. Even if she's tempted to come out and talk to me, there's no way she'll make herself vulnerable now. Lyon was right. They're all out for themselves.

The trip line rustles. Fleur jerks a tight fist. Two trees on the ridge snap back, releasing an avalanche of timber. Somewhere downhill, the Summer shrieks.

In seconds, the two Autumns are on us, barreling straight for Amber and Julio, scattering our group. Amber strikes out from our circle, swinging her knife in a wide arc and forcing them backward. Her blade strikes the first, tearing through his shirt. She kicks the other back when he gets too close. He darts a hostile glance at Julio.

Amber uses the distraction to swipe the blade across his face. With an enraged shout, the Autumn charges her.

I grab Fleur's hand, pulling her behind a boulder as the second Autumn hurls a ball of fire at Julio's feet. The dead leaves catch like dry tinder, igniting a blaze around him. Julio jumps back, shielding his face.

Fleur snares his attacker, pinning him to the ground with a root while I run for the well.

"Julio!" I shout through the flames. He turns toward my voice, flinching back from the heat. I wrench the lever and water gushes from the tap. Julio summons it. It swirls from the spigot, exploding like a geyser and raining down over the flames.

He shakes the water from his face and scoops up his hammer, stalking through the smoke toward the Autumn Fleur trapped. The Autumn struggles against the root. Desperate to pull himself free, he digs his nails into the plant's flesh—*Fleur's* flesh.

"Fleur?" I spin to the boulder, but she's gone. Panic grips me when there's no answer. "Fleur!"

"Up here!" I find her halfway up an oak, holding fast to its trunk. A battered Summer climbs after her, his shoes and fingernails scraping the bark, opening long scratches down her arms. "Jack! Behind you!"

I turn as Névé rushes toward me. Angry welts circle her wrists where Fleur must have tried to hold her back. I brace for the impact as she closes the distance. A spray of dirt erupts from the ground between us, and a root drags her kicking and screaming into the brush.

In the tree, Fleur grunts. Scratches bleed through the legs of her jeans. Her foot slides within reach of the Summer's hand, and I swing the ax before he can touch her. He's already glowing when his body hits the ground.

Fleur slides down the trunk. Her foot catches the nearest sturdy branch, her eyes glassy and faraway, as if her mind's still engaged in a battle with Névé. Névé struggles somewhere in the underbrush, trapped in Fleur's roots. I don't know how much longer Fleur can hold her off. Or how many other Seasons she might still be fighting in her mind.

I drop my ax and reach for her. She's shaking, her jaw clenched in concentration and her forehead beaded with blood and sweat. A victorious shout echoes from the cabin and a ball of light rushes over our heads. A second flash follows, and Fleur sags into me.

"You okay?" I press my lips to her hair, my fingers finding the warm skin at the nape of her neck.

She nods, letting me hold her weight. The Summer's gone. Névé's still tangled in the underbrush, and by the looks of it, the two Autumns are on their way home. But we're not out of the woods yet.

"Come on." I take her hand and pull her gently behind me, jogging back toward the cabin to check on the others, keeping my eyes peeled for Doug's team.

As we get close, I spot the red crown of Amber's hair. Her chest heaves as she wipes the sweat from her temples. Her jaw's purple and swollen, but she smiles through the pain when she sees Fleur and me coming.

She tosses her knife to the ground, her face falling as she looks behind us. "Where's Julio?"

Fleur's hand tightens around mine. "We thought he was with you," I say. We were supposed to work in pairs. I told them to stay together.

A cry echoes off the ridge.

Fleur rips out of my grasp and takes off running, with Amber and me tearing at her heels. She rounds the cabin and skids to a stop. Julio's on his knees beside the well. Blood trickles between his lips and blooms through his torn shirt. He slumps, his eyes rolling back in his head as he falls facedown into a runnel of water.

A third Autumn—one none of us sensed—holds the fire poker in his hand. Amber roars. Fleur flies toward him like an arrow, and the Autumn bolts.

"Stay with Julio!" I shout to Amber as our strides converge. "Don't let him go!"

Suddenly, she cries out and goes down. I turn to see her crawling, dragging Névé behind her. Before I can get there to stop her, Névé grabs Amber's knife from the ground and drives it into Amber's leg.

Amber screams, kicking out hard with her other foot. Névé's head snaps back and her body goes limp. Her transmitter light flickers, disappearing in the fallen leaves a few feet away. Amber must have kicked it loose. I drop to my knees, scattering leaves as I search for it, but it's gone dark. The signal's dead.

I rush to Amber's side, watching out of the corner of my eye for Fleur. Amber shrieks as I jerk the blade free. I push up the leg of her jeans, the wound bleeding through my fingers as I apply steady pressure, my grip slipping as she fights me to get to Julio. She barks at me to let her go. But she's no good to him like this. She's too weak. If she touches him now, we'll only lose them both.

"Hold still! Let me help you!" She slumps, tears streaming down her face. This is my fault. I should have made Julio take the keys and go. I believed Lyon when he said we should stay and fight them, but we should have run while we had the chance. Doug's team hasn't even shown up yet and we're already crushed.

I search for Fleur over my shoulder. She's close, hunched protectively over Julio's body. She growls as the Autumn hurls a flame at her. I call her name as she goes down, but she grits her teeth and pushes herself back up again. Static crackles in the air. Her furious gaze locks on a high branch. A vine comes alive, snaking down above the Autumn's head and coiling around his neck. With a quick snap of her wrist, he's yanked off his feet. Amber and I shield our eyes from the flash.

When we open them, the branch swings empty.

Fleur collapses. I call out her name, torn between staying with Amber and rushing to her side. Fleur lifts her head. Her fingertips creep over the ground toward Julio as pinpricks of light begin to penetrate his skin.

"I've got you!" she rasps, catching his hand. Her eyes roll back in her head, their fingers still touching.

Blood roars in my ears. "Fleur, no!" They're both too weak. They'll burn each other out.

I drop Amber's leg and scramble to my feet, tripping facedown on Névé's lifeless body. Her vacant eyes stare up at me, her blue lips exhaling a thin thread of light.

Take strength from others where you can.

Lyon's words hurl themselves against the walls of my mind.

. . . When we wanted more land, more power, more strength, we took it.

They're going to die.

Fleur, Julio, Amber . . . all of them. They're going to die at the safe

283

house *I* chose for them. Because I'm not strong enough to save them. All three of them will be in the wind, just like Névé. Just like Hunter. And it's all my fault.

Did you take him?

Dying magic swirls from Névé's lips. Winter magic, powerful and familiar. It calls to something inside me. A cold voice inside my head whispers, *Take it, Jack.*

I lean over her, flashes of the night I first met Chill coming back to me in a rush. Flashes of Gaia drawing the Spring girl's magic into her lungs after her Termination.

Take strength from others where you can.

I position my mouth over Névé's. It's clammy and slack.

Fighting back my revulsion, I inhale deeply, drawing her magic inside me. I feel it spread, crystallizing down my throat, burning my lungs, the cold filling me until I can't hold any more.

I reel to my feet, gasping for air. My arms are coated in ice. My breath billows white. With every lungful I draw, I smell smoke and death.

Autumn.

My heart beats faster with the need to *conquer* it, as instinct drives every other thought from my mind.

"Jack?" Amber's throat bobs. Her face pales as I kneel at her side. "Jack, what are you doing?" I pluck the knife from the ground, desperate to expel the magic I've binged on, to release the pressure—a charge. The need, relentless and demanding, builds like an avalanche in my blood.

Amber's eyes swim with tears as she pushes away from me, screaming with pain when her injured leg refuses to move. "Jack, listen to me!"

Névé's magic beats against the walls of my chest, fighting to get out. I press the knife to Amber's throat. "Julio and Fleur need us. They're dying, Jack." She closes her eyes, swallowing against the blade.

"Jack?"

I freeze, my head tipped toward the faint whisper behind me.

"Jack, where are you?" A ragged breath expels like a smaze from my lungs. I inhale the scent of lilies. Feel the ghost of their petals in my hand.

Fleur.

I drop the knife and lurch toward the sound of her voice. Dying magic shimmers on her breath.

I draw her into my lap and take her face in my hands, letting her absorb the burden of this power I can't hold. I press my lips to her forehead, pushing all my strength into her, until I'm dizzy and I can't sit up anymore. Julio coughs and sputters, still connected by the tips of his fingers. I fight to stay conscious as Amber drags herself toward him. She rests her head in the crook of his neck, her arm draped across his chest, as she collapses against him.

My eyes flutter closed, and through the current that runs through us, I feel four hearts beating.

32

AND SO WE REMAINED

❧

FLEUR

I wake as the sun breaches the ridge. At first, I think I must be dreaming when Julio, Amber, and Jack all begin to stir beside me. We're alive. All of us. But how? How is it possible that Doug's team didn't find us and kill us during the night? The only explanation is that they didn't come at all. Did they assume the bounty-hungry Seasons would be enough? Or did Lyon find some way to slow them down?

I glance over at the mud-streaked faces of my friends, grateful for small miracles. The earth is cold and damp beneath us, a film of fog rising over the wet ground beside the well. Amber and Julio limp wordlessly to the cabin to change their bloodied clothes. Jack and I survey the aftermath outside, his thoughts unreadable as he gathers our scattered weapons. His gaze repeatedly darts to the woods, searching for the Guards.

I jump when the screen door bounces shut. Julio comes out, scratching the healing hole in his chest. Amber hobbles behind him, carrying the last of our bags.

With hardly a word, we hike down the mountain, avoiding the only road in. At the bottom of the slope, Jack picks up a scent. We follow him to an abandoned Chevy sedan with Tennessee plates hidden under a pile of branches. The car's unlocked, and I turn from the rush of stale air inside as Jack swings open the door. The upholstery smells strongly of the Autumn I killed. Jack flips down the visors and rummages under the seats, searching for the keys and finding them under a floor mat. I don't want to take anything that belonged to the Autumn. Don't want to spend the next few hours sitting inside his car, remembering what he did to Julio, or how he looked swinging from the tree, but we don't have any other choice.

We dig the car out of its camouflage and push it onto the gravel road. Jack takes the first shift driving. Julio and Amber are still recovering from their injuries, and they're soon curled into each other, asleep in the back seat, a tangle of healing bruises and scars.

No one's said anything about the lingering film of frost that's been clouding Jack's eyes since we woke this morning. It's chilling, an icy veil that masks his thoughts and renders the temperature inside the car almost unbearable. I reach for him, but his hand slides away before I can touch him.

My eyes prick with tears as the mile markers roll by. I watch the colorless sky for crows, wondering where our Handlers are now. If Woody got his leg treated. If Poppy's recovering from her cold.

Jack sticks to the rural roads along the foothills, avoiding patrolled rest areas and highways with cameras. By the time we cross the state line into Tennessee, the frost has begun to fade from his eyes. Gaia's spies are nowhere in sight over the small towns we pass through, and the more distance we put between us and the cabin, the more at ease he seems to feel.

Somewhere north of Knoxville, he laces his fingers through mine, his thumb stroking my knuckles like a worry stone. Ahead of us, the purple hazy peaks of the Smokies promise a safe place to rest for the night.

At dusk, we pull off onto a pitted gravel road. The car's suspension squeaks as we wind up the mountain, the gravel eventually giving way to a rutted path through the weeds. When we're deep in the woods, Jack kills the engine.

It's near dark. The first early stars twinkle against a lilac sky through the branches around us. Julio stirs and rubs his eyes. He unbuttons the front of his shirt, examining the angry, oozing hole where the fire poker impaled him.

Amber wipes the sleep marks from her cheek.

"Why are we stopping?" she grumbles, peeling up the leg of her jeans. A long wet scab cuts up the back of her left calf like a jagged red vine. It's hardly improved from this morning, all of us too weak to be much good to each other. Our cuts and punctures seem to be healing slowly from the inside out; I only wish this were true of all our wounds.

Jack's eyelids are heavy, his face drawn. Still, he leaves the keys hanging in the ignition as if he's second-guessing his decision to stop for the night.

"Jack's tired." I reach over and pluck the keys from the car, tucking them into my pocket before he can object. "He needs to rest. We all do."

I pop the trunk, grabbing our packs as Julio and Amber ease out of the car. Amber limps in a slow circle, favoring her sore leg. Julio winces as he rubs the chill from his arms. Jack tips his nose to the wind. He draws a breath of cold mountain air, then disappears through the brush in search of a place to make camp. I get to work hiding the car, using what little magic I can muster to stretch ivy and brambles over the roof. The effort makes me woozy.

"Where are we, anyway?" Julio asks.

"Cherokee National Forest," I answer. "About an hour outside Knoxville, I think."

"Over here!" Jack calls. We scoop up our packs, following his scent to a grassy clearing where he's already busy cracking branches and twigs, stacking them inside a ring of stones. Julio and I unpack two of the pup tents Boreas stowed with our camping supplies on the boat. It's full dark by the time we've assembled them and organized our makeshift camp.

Amber hovers a few feet away, watching as Jack pulls a flint from his pocket. "Let me do it," she says impatiently.

"I've got it." He strikes the flint over and over, failing to catch a spark. "You're still healing."

"I'm fine." Julio and I both glance up at the sharp edge in her tone. She's been guarded around Jack since we woke up this morning. There's a frostiness between them that wasn't there before.

Jack continues beating up the flint. "You shouldn't waste your energy."

"I said I'm fine!" A white-hot flame ignites in her hand. Jack goes rigid, wary as it grows.

I tap a root with my mind, prepared to stop her if I have to. Julio gives me a warning look, clearly as confused as I am.

Amber circles the stones, waiting until Jack slowly backs away before tossing her flame into the ring. The kindling is dry. It catches almost immediately, popping and throwing sparks.

"You haven't told them, have you?" Amber lowers herself to the ground in front of the crackling fire as it smokes, stretching her injured leg in front of her.

"Told us what?" Julio asks, casting suspicious looks between them.

"About Jack's little experiment at the cabin."

A cold wind gusts over the fire. It flares as Jack jabs a finger toward Julio. "That experiment saved his life!"

"And it almost took mine! Don't spoon-feed me some bullshit line about teamwork and trust, and how we need each other to survive. Yesterday, you proved the only person you need is you."

"That's not true!"

"You held a knife to my throat!"

"I wasn't myself!"

"And if you hadn't come to your senses, the rest of us would have been nothing more than disposable batteries to you!"

Jack's eyes glaze white through the billowing smoke.

"Does someone want to tell me what the hell happened last night?" Julio's tone is murderous.

Lightning flashes in the distance, and I step between Julio and Jack as the wind picks up a humid undertone. "Everyone calm down before you draw attention we don't need. Whatever happened, we all survived. That's all that matters now."

"Is it?" Amber asks.

Jack turns from the fire. Amber watches him, glaring at his back as if she'd like to put a knife into it.

"Did you know anything about this?" Julio asks me.

I shake my head, massaging the faint pink welts on my arms as I struggle to recall what happened after Julio was stabbed. All I remember was being knocked off my feet by a ball of fire, the rage and desperation I felt. I remember the Autumn boy swinging from the tree, flailing and tearing at my vine. And the feel of Julio's bloody, cooling fingers. I remember Jack dropping beside me, staring down at me through clouded eyes as if he wasn't entirely sure who I was.

Or who *he* was . . .

"What happened?" I hear myself ask.

He bows his head. When he finally answers, his voice is choked with emotion. "You were dying, and there wasn't anything I could do to help you. I couldn't . . ." He turns to me. Clenches his teeth to keep the words from trembling. "I couldn't lose you. Névé couldn't be saved. She was almost gone. Her magic was already leaving her. And something Lyon said gave me an idea."

"You never did tell us how Lyon knew where we were." Julio practically spits the professor's name. "Or how you knew those Seasons were coming."

Jack turns to Julio, his tone teetering toward defiant. "He left me a note at the cabin—a number and a cell phone. I don't know how he found us. We probably picked up a smaze when we left Croatan Beach, but it hardly seemed like the time to argue about it."

"So you called him instead of telling us something was up," Julio says with a disgusted look. "Weren't you the guy who said we all had to ditch our phones so we couldn't be tracked? For all we know, that cell phone pinged a tower and led those Seasons right to us."

"There's a bounty on our heads! They would have found us anyway. And if Lyon hadn't warned us they were coming, we'd probably all be dead."

"So you're taking advice from the man who crushed a Season under his shoe?"

Jack's eyes swirl white in the firelight. "When I told him about Hunter, he asked me if I '*took*' him." Julio shrinks back at the mention of Hunter's name. "I thought Lyon was speaking figuratively, but when Névé was dying and her magic was leaving her, it occurred me to that maybe he wasn't. It made sense. It's how Gaia reclaims her magic when we're Terminated, the same way she transfers it to something else—the crows and the bees, the flies and the smazes. I thought if I took Névé's magic before it was gone, I'd be strong enough to save the rest of you."

Jack's face pleads with me, as if he's waiting for me to yell or take sides or pass judgment. But I don't know what to think. Or what to feel. Guilt, because I wasn't strong enough to hold Névé safe under my roots? Shame, that Jack stole a dying soul to save us? Revulsion, that he could even comprehend doing something like this, or horror, because I'm thankful that he did?

"Névé's transmitter was dead," he says, desperate to explain himself. "Her neck was broken. There was nothing any of us could have done to bring her back."

Amber tears at bits of grass and tosses them into the fire. "Her magic changed you," she says without looking at Jack. "I looked in your eyes when you held that knife to my throat, and you weren't you. How do we know we can trust you?" She jerks her chin toward the tents. There are only two of them. This entire journey has been based on trust. Trust we've all blindly given and fought for, because we need each other to survive. I think back to that moment at the cabin, when Julio and Amber stood side by side against Jack and I was forced to choose between them.

They stayed because I did. Because I believed in him. And now he's looking at me from the edge of our camp, asking me if I still do.

"I didn't know what taking her magic would do to me." Jack's voice breaks. "It was too much magic. Too much power. I didn't know how much of myself I would lose in the moment or how much of Névé's death I'd carry with me, and for that I'm sorry," he says to Amber. To me. To all of us. "But don't ask me if I regret it. Because I'd do it again, a million times over, rather than lose a single one of you."

When none of us speak, he stalks away through the brush, beyond the light of the fire. My heart leaps, ready to rush after him.

"Jack!" Amber calls out.

His footsteps fall silent.

"Do you still want to kill me?" she asks.

I feel him, breath held, still close.

"No more than usual," he says quietly.

Some of the tension leaves Amber's shoulders. She reaches into her backpack and tosses a can of beans into the darkness. It smacks into his palm. "Then stop being a snowflake and come eat."

"So that's it?" Julio asks, rising to his feet. "He holds a knife to your throat and you're just going to forgive him?"

Amber shrugs, but there's a lingering leeriness in the way she looks at Jack as he nears. "It wasn't the first time."

The flames snap, fueled by a torrent of hot wind. "But this time was different," Julio says. "You could have died. Forever. For real."

"You could have died, too!" Her throat's thick. Her fiery gaze drops to the puncture in his chest. "If I had been in Jack's position, I would have done the same for you."

Julio's mouth opens. The wind shifts, uncertain as it settles. Slowly, he sits back down, closer to Amber than he was before.

Jack returns to the fire, hovering just beyond the reach of its heat. We're quiet, all of us probably thinking the same thing as we divide up cans of vegetables and beans, wondering how this revelation changes us. All this time, we thought we had to balance our power to preserve our strength, to share it equally. But maybe we're no more than animals. If we get hungry enough, desperate enough, the strongest of us will take what they need to survive.

Julio makes a face, jabbing his spoon into his uneaten can of beans and shoving it away from him. "Couldn't you have stopped at a Burger King or something?"

"Fast-food restaurants have security cameras." Jack fights with the lid of his own can, giving up with a curse when the aluminum tab breaks off. "If we lie low, we can still get to Arizona in one piece."

"Says the soul sucker who held a knife to Amber's throat."

They glare at each other over the fire. It snaps, scattering sparks.

Someone's stomach growls.

There's so much wrong with us. So much I can't fix. I can't bring our Handlers back, or Hunter's life, or the magic we stole from Névé to save ourselves. I can't change our mistakes, or take back the things we've said to one another in moments of weakness. But maybe I can bring comfort to the deep wounds we're all feeling. Maybe tonight, my strength can heal us.

"Give me a minute," I say, brushing the dirt from my legs and slipping silently into the night.

I think about following her. It's long past dark, and the longer Fleur's gone, the more anxious I feel. I pace the perimeter of our camp, watching the fire from a distance, listening for the sound of movement in the brush, wondering where she went and what she must be thinking of me right now. Worrying that maybe tonight, she's the one with regrets.

When I catch the first sweet whiff of lilies, I'm overcome with relief. Fleur picks her way toward camp, a limp rabbit dangling in one hand and a pheasant swaying in the other. Julio wrinkles his nose. Doesn't notice her forced smile or the wet, red rims of her eyes.

"Roots make good snares." She holds out her kill, ignoring his grimace.

Amber side-eyes him. "You said you were hungry." She takes the proffered animals and gets to work field dressing the rabbit while Fleur plucks the bird.

I select a few branches to sharpen into skewers. But when I reach to borrow Fleur's knife, Julio snatches it without a word. He sits close to the fire, watching me as he whittles the tips of the sticks into points.

As night falls, I still feel it, the lingering shadow of distrust, even as the smell of sizzling meat seems to distract their minds from everything else.

The heat of the fire is as good an excuse as any to keep my distance. I hover outside the ring of muted light it casts, watching them from the shadows. Amber, Julio, and Fleur lean close to it, their doubts soothed by its warmth and the smell of the meal it promises, if not entirely forgotten. Julio strums a few songs to pass the time while our dinner cooks. He and Amber argue over who sang them first, whose version was a cover, and what year the original came out. A nostalgic smile settles on her lips as she sings all the lyrics by heart.

When the meat's blackened and sizzling, Julio strips it off his skewer before it has a chance to cool. He passes a steaming chunk of pheasant to Amber.

"That's hot!" She blows frantically into her cupped hand, gingerly testing a piece before popping the rest into her mouth.

Julio raises an eyebrow, watching her catch the juice with her tongue as it runs down her fingers. "I thought you like to play with fire."

"Should I assume you like cold showers?"

"I might need one if you keep licking your fingers like that."

She throws him a look, but their eyes hold a second too long and her cheeks flush red in the firelight. She eats the rest of her meal in silence. When she's done, she darts a shy glance at Julio and pushes herself to her feet.

"I'm pretty worn out." She clears her throat, wiping her hands on her jeans. "My leg's still sore. And we've got a long day ahead of us tomorrow. I was thinking . . . it might be a good idea if we . . . you know . . . recharge for a while."

"I can come with you." Fleur starts to get up, but Amber's gaze slides to Julio.

Julio stops chewing. Amber's face floods with color. "On second thought, forget I said anything."

Julio drops his pheasant wing into the fire. He launches to his feet as Amber limps toward one of the tents. "Actually, I'm feeling pretty rough, too," he says. Amber pauses, tucking a loose lock of hair behind her ear as she glances at him over her shoulder. "I could join you. In your tent. If you want me to. Strictly for medicinal purposes."

I can't hold back a snort. Julio flips me off behind his back.

Amber shrugs. "I mean . . . I guess that'd be okay. As long as it's okay with Fleur." She hooks her thumbs in her pockets, then folds her arms over her chest, waiting. Fleur's eyes flick to mine over the fire. An uncomfortable silence draws out between us.

So this is it. No one wants to share a tent with the soul-sucking vampire.

I pitch my skewer into the fire, my appetite gone. "It's okay," I say with a tight smile, sparing both of us the embarrassment. "Fleur can take the other tent. I'll sleep out here."

Fleur's eyes drop to her skewer, and for a second I wonder if I misread her.

"You're sure?" Amber asks.

"We're sure," Fleur and I say at the same time.

"Good night, then." Amber ducks into the tent, and Julio follows. Zippers whine and the canvas sides sway as they struggle out of their shoes and jackets in the confined space.

"Your hands are freezing!" Julio hisses.

"This only works if we're touching! Do you have a better suggestion?" Amber snaps.

"Actually—"

"Don't answer that."

"I'm just saying, this would work a lot better if you get *inside* the sleeping bag."

"It's hot in here."

"I'm not opposed to the idea of taking off our clothes."

"Keep talking if you want to die."

Even muffled through the tent, their argument is impossible not to overhear. Fleur rolls her eyes, fighting back a grin. But then the tent falls silent. Awkward silent. The kind of silent I feel guilty listening to. Fleur looks uncomfortable, too. Too far away to make conversation, too alone with me not to. I think about moving closer, but that would just make things weird.

"It's been a long day. You should go catch some z's." I get up and stoke the last of the embers. Then I grab my sleeping bag and spread it a comfortable distance from the fire.

Fleur rises. She looks at me over her shoulder with a sadness I can't place as she slips inside her tent.

I open my sleeping bag and lie back on top of it, staring up through the canopy at a sky thick with stars. They glitter like snowflakes, and all I can think about is the way Fleur looked at me two nights ago by the pond, with the snow falling around her face. How she trusted me with a kiss. I wonder what she sees when she looks at me now.

I still feel it inside me, a tiny piece of Névé's soul slithering like a smaze, the guilt lurking like a cold, dark cloud in the recesses of my mind. I don't know who I am anymore.

A twig cracks. I open my eyes. Fleur's standing over me with her sleeping bag under her arm. She unrolls it and lies down on her back beside me, lacing her warm fingers with mine. We lie for a long time staring up at the stars, until all the things I want to say build like a dam in my throat.

"Back at school, Professor Lyon made me read a story about a lion who fell in love with a girl." I squeeze my eyes shut, struggling to get the words out. I tell her everything I remember: the manipulative father, the helpless girl, and the lovestruck lion who gave up his teeth because the girl's father convinced the lion that he was too strong and the girl was too fragile—that he might accidentally hurt her. That part hadn't seemed important at the time, but suddenly I can't stop thinking about it.

"Are you afraid of me?" A weight settles on my chest as I brace for her answer.

"No. I know why you did what you did. You did it to keep us together. Because you were scared we wouldn't make it. I would have done the same. But if we're going to be together, it should be because we want to be, not because we're afraid we're falling apart." She turns her face to mine. Suddenly, I'm not sure we're talking about the four of us anymore.

"I would never hurt you," I whisper.

"I know."

I swallow the yearning that rears up in me as she turns back to watch the stars. Her breath shudders. I ache to kiss her. To lose myself in the heat of her skin and her breath, but everything I want right now feels desperate and needful. Like I have to fix something, or regain control of what's slipping through my fingers. To feel something other than the pain and fear and guilt I'm feeling now.

I lay my head back. Resist the urge to tell her I love her. That the one thing that terrifies me more than anything else in this world is losing her, because that need feels desperate, too.

Instead, I hold fast to her hand. Let her ground me as I shelter her from the darkness and the cold. This. This is what we're running to. This is what we're fighting for. For now, for tonight, forever, this is enough.

33

COLD AWAKENING

FLEUR

Jack's voice is rough, hoarse from woodsmoke and the cold mountain air. "How'd you sleep?" he asks as I emerge from the tent. Neither of us fell asleep easily, both of us too keenly aware of the nearness of the other's body, the wire-tight tension between us impossible to ignore. When we finally drifted off, Jack tossed and turned, his sleep fitful with nightmares, making him impossible to hold on to. Eventually, I retreated into the tent and slept the rest of the night alone.

"Okay," I lie. "You?"

"Terrible."

"Me too," I confess with a weak smile. His sleeping bag's already rolled up.

Julio and Amber tumble through their tent flap, leaning on each other as they slip their shoes on.

"Morning," Julio says, radiating sunlight as he shrugs into his jacket.

Jack responds with a resentful grunt.

Amber's smile is a little sheepish, her hair and clothes perfectly disheveled. She's the embodiment of fire, wild red waves framing glowing cheeks, her cider-brown eyes bright and alive. The smile I return feels disingenuous.

I try and fail to smooth the snarls in my hair. "I should find a place to wash up."

Julio points into the woods. "I smell fresh water about a hundred yards off. It runs to the east. Probably a creek."

"I'll go with you," Amber offers, grabbing her toiletry bag. "Fleur and I will go that way." She points vaguely in the direction Julio indicated. "You boys can catch the creek over there," she says, pointing a little farther east.

Julio's laugh is brusque. "Dudes don't go to the bathroom in groups. Jack and I can take turns." Julio walks the opposite way, disappearing behind a tree to relieve himself. Jack takes his backpack and wanders east alone.

Amber and I follow Julio's directions to the creek. The forest thickens around us, dense with the scent of conifers and ferns. We hear the murmur of the water before we see it. The fresh, cool scent of moss creeps from the edges of a bubbling stream, and we follow it to a shallow pool. The rocks are like ice against my knees as I kneel beside it to brush my teeth.

Amber strips down to her underwear. The pale pink scar on her leg is hardly noticeable this morning, and the cold doesn't seem to faze her as she wades in thigh-deep. She splashes water under her arms and over her face. I test the water with a bare foot. My toes begin to sting and I quickly pull it out again.

"Aren't you coming in?" she asks, her eyes lathered in soap. She rinses it off and looks surprised to see me still standing at the water's edge. My teeth chatter. I give a noncommital shake of my head, mostly to clear the light-headed wooliness brought on by the cold.

"I don't know if I can."

She wades toward me, her arm outstretched. "You can hold on to me. It won't be that bad."

I think back to the night I skated with Jack on the frozen pond. When we kissed on the ground in the snow. And last night, even after the fire burned out. The cold didn't bother me as long as we were touching. With a shudder, I peel off my clothes and let Amber lead me into the creek, yelping when the water climbs above my knees. I wash quickly with one hand, the other locked tightly around Amber's. The rush of her power is almost dizzying.

"Julio's a total baby about the cold, too. He made me hold his hand all night." Amber rolls her eyes, but she's not fooling anyone. She's practically radiating magic after their night together. "It's a good thing he didn't share a tent with Jack. He might have frozen to death."

I throw water over my neck, both of us wavering on the uneven stones as I pull her off balance.

"You didn't stay with him last night, did you?" she asks.

I fight off a shiver. "How'd you know?"

"Because Jack looks terrible and you're sucking up all my power."

"Sorry," I say, not sorry enough to let go of her hand.

"Are you and Jack okay?" she asks. "Is it because of what I said yesterday? About what happened at the cabin?"

"No," I rush to say. "It was nothing like that. We're fine." I think. "His head was just in a weird place last night. And things between us felt a little . . . intense." My cheeks warm at the memory. How his pulse raced where our hands touched. How my breaths were so shallow as every inch of me listened to the taut silence between us, aching to close the gap. But he was so raw last night. So vulnerable and uncertain. It wouldn't have felt right. "We all did and said things that felt wrong yesterday. I guess I didn't think Jack and I needed one more regret."

I bend forward to dunk my hair, but something about Amber's stillness makes me lift my head. I brush the soap from my eyes. Her brow's furrowed, and her full lips are turned down at the edges. "Would you? Regret sleeping with him?" she asks.

I'd be lying if I said I'd never thought about it. Truth? I've thought about it almost constantly since that kiss at the pond. If we hadn't been caught by the headmaster, if Lyon hadn't called, then maybe we would have then.

"No, I don't think so."

"Then why didn't you?"

"Nerves, I guess." I hadn't realized how it would feel to just come out and say it. "That's probably stupid. I mean, there is no perfect first time, right? No perfect moment or perfect place. If you know you're with the right person and it's what you both want, then—"

"Wait, you mean your first time, like . . . ever?" Amber looks surprised.

"Why?" I ask. "How many times have you . . . ?" She raises an eyebrow. I can't tell if she's waiting for me to finish or daring me to.

"Enough to know that *last* times can come with their own set of regrets, too." She looks away and I wonder if she's thinking of Julio. If she's scared of letting herself get too close to him, or if she's afraid because she already has. "Do you love him?" she asks.

It feels strange to confide something so intimate to her when I haven't even confessed it to Jack. "I do."

"Do you trust him?"

"With my life."

"What about your heart?" she asks, as if this is the only answer that matters. As if this one piece of me weighs more heavily than all the others.

"I trust him with everything."

She nods, and a knot of self-doubt loosens inside me. "Then don't sweat all that other stuff. You'll know when you're ready."

I give her hand a playful squeeze. "So will you and Julio." Her jaw drops and her face breaks into a wide smile. She uses her free hand to splash me with a spray of cold water, and we erupt into a fit of shrieks and giggles. The more time I spend with her, the more I see why Julio's so crazy about her. "I'm glad he has you," I say when our laughter quiets.

Her face sobers. Deep worry lines cut into her brow. She looks down at the water. "I'm glad he has you, too."

She waits for me, lost in her thoughts as I wash my hair. When I'm finished, we stumble over the rocky bottom back to the creek's edge and drag fresh clothes over our chilled, wet skin. A *pop* echoes through the forest as I tug on my jeans.

Amber and I freeze. The wind carries an acrid bite.

"Gunshot," she whispers.

We rush to pull on our shoes and take off running.

Leaping fallen logs, we hurtle through the dense undergrowth toward the coppery smell of blood. Out of the corner of my eye, I catch the white flash of Julio's sneakers sprinting from our campsite. Fear seizes me when I don't see Jack behind him.

Amber's faster, stronger than the rest of us. She tears into a clearing and pulls up short in the middle of it. Wind stirs the high grass. The smells of blood and winter are everywhere.

My eyes snap to the far edge of the clearing. To a boy holding a rifle loosely in his hand. Not a Season. He reeks like panic and sweat—human smells, mortal smells. His eyes widen at the sight of us and he takes off running. Amber charges after him.

Rage and instinct kick in. I reach for him with my mind. The ground in front of him surges and shudders. A root breaks free, spraying him with dirt and knocking the rifle from his hand. Another lashes around his ankle and jerks him viciously to the ground.

Amber snatches up the rifle. The next second, she's on top of him. She raises the barrel. Aims it at his head.

"Where is he?" Her voice shakes.

"It was an accident!" the boy cries. "I thought he was a deer. I didn't mean to kill him. I swear."

My heart stutters. Amber stumbles away from him. Her stricken eyes find mine and suddenly I can't breathe. The world swims as I call Jack's name. Amber's shouts fade into the background. I'm only distantly aware of the pull of the boy's limbs against my roots, of the blunt smack of the rifle stock against flesh as I follow Jack's scent to a depression in the weeds.

My breath catches. Jack's on his back, his eyes closed and skin pale, a small hole darkening his shirt. A red stain's spreading between his chest and his shoulder. I sink to my knees beside him.

"Jack." I brush back his hair. Pat the side of his face with shaking hands. "Jack, wake up!"

His eyes flutter open. Struggle to focus on me. Panic grips me when they drift closed again.

I spin at the sound of the rifle being cocked. "If he's dead, I'll kill you!" Amber screams. "I'll burn you! I'll—"

"He's over here!" I shout.

Julio speaks to Amber in a low voice, wrapping his arms around her and prying the gun from her hands. I keep a firm hold on the root, pinning the boy down by his ankle as Amber and Julio sprint toward me. Julio shoves the rifle into my arms. He kneels in front of Jack, pulling aside Jack's collar with a muttered curse. Jack's head rolls as Julio and Amber hoist him up, his body hanging limp between them.

"Get him to the car," I say with a forced calm. "I'll be right behind you."

"What are you going to do with the kid?" I know exactly what Julio's thinking. There is no easy cleanup here. No ley lines or magic. No ash in the wind. He's human. Messy.

"I'll figure it out. Just go!" Julio and Amber bow under Jack's weight as they carry him back toward camp.

I stalk through the high grass and find the hunter where Amber left him, tangled in my roots. His unkempt bangs hang low over his eyes and the oversize jacket he's wearing hides a coltish build. His nose and mouth are bloodied, his jaw swollen. He's groaning, in too much pain to focus on me.

I stand over him, the rifle cold in my hand.

Julio was right. He's just a kid.

And no matter how badly I want to look him in the face and see Hunter or Névé staring back at me, this is different. He wasn't trying to kill Jack. He's not a threat to us anymore.

Unless he survives and reports what he saw.

My finger trembles on the trigger. One call to authorities could reveal our location to Chronos. But taking a life to cover our tracks and ease our escape feels like crossing a line—a line I could never come back from.

I reach into the pocket of the boy's jacket and find his phone. He recoils, his breath hitching on a sob as I smash it under the rifle's butt and toss its guts as far into the trees as I can throw them. As I run back to camp with his rifle in my hand, all I can hope is that I've made the right choice.

34

THE CALM

JACK

I wake sometime after dark, cramped in the back seat of the sedan. Julio's got the driver's seat pushed back as far as it'll go, reclined about fifteen degrees into the tiny bubble of space he's left me. I'm propped sideways in my seat, my back against the door and my head against the window, my legs stretched across the length of the bench seat. Fleur lies between them, her body flush with mine, her cheek warm against my chest. The buttons of a strange shirt—one of Julio's madras ones—are unfastened to my waist, the collar spread wide, revealing a bloody square of gauze.

I try to shift without waking her, peeling back the edges of the tape to find a puckered pink scar.

"Hey, the Iceman's awake," Julio says, catching my awkward stretch in the rearview mirror.

Amber turns in her seat. "It's about time."

My throat's sore. My tongue feels like sandpaper. "What happened?"

"You got shot."

"I gathered that much. What did I miss?" Last thing I remember is a searing pain as Julio and Amber jogged on either side of me. Then Julio saying, "This is going to hurt," right before he stuck his finger through the bleeding hole in my shoulder.

"We had to haul ass out of Tennessee," Julio says. "Been driving all day."

"Where are we?"

"A couple of hours west of Little Rock."

I do the math in my head against the time on the dashboard clock. The speedometer's tickling eighty, the radio's tuned to a local news station, and there's a bag of empty granola bar and jerky wrappers on the floorboards beside me.

"What aren't you telling me?" I ask quietly, so I won't wake Fleur.

Julio lowers the volume on the radio. "The kid who shot you was human. Fleur left him alive."

"So?"

"So the last thing we need is to end up on a wanted poster if he made it down that mountain and his parents decide to squeal to the cops."

"*He* was the one who pulled the trigger."

"But we're the ones who look guilty. That scar on your shoulder's not exactly Exhibit A in our defense. It just makes you look like a punk with a rap sheet, and blows a big fucking hole in our story." I rub the smooth dip in the skin. Julio's right. It looks like it happened months ago, not hours ago. No one would ever believe us. "And then there's the small problem that Amber beat the crap out of him, and Fleur tied him up and took his gun."

"And she didn't use her hands to do it," Amber adds.

So there's the rub. Not only does it look like the kid was mugged by four teenagers, but he saw Fleur's magic in action. If he does make it down that mountain, we'll be lucky not to end up in the headlines of some crappy sensational grocery-store tabloid.

"The good news is we made it out of the state." Julio changes lanes to pass a slow-moving car. "And we haven't heard any news reports about it yet. Either the kid was eaten by a bear or he was smart enough to keep his mouth shut."

"Any signs of Chronos's goons?" I ask.

"None so far. But we've only made two pit stops since we broke camp this morning. Unless Lyon knows exactly where we're headed, it won't be easy for Chronos to find us." His eyes find mine in the rearview mirror.

"Thanks," I tell him. "For getting us this far. I owe you one."

"One? You owe me a lot more than that. Fleur made me spend three hours in the back seat with you, holding your frigid-ass hand."

I try not to picture Julio back here with me. It's bad enough that I woke up wearing his shirt. I grimace at the smell of it, shea butter and some tropical-breeze deodorant. "Why couldn't Amber do it?" I ask, though I can't exactly blame her for not wanting to touch me after the knife incident at the cabin.

"I offered," she says, batting her lashes. "But Julio wouldn't let me."

Julio's knuckles are tight on the wheel and he sinks deeper in his seat.

"How incredibly selfless of him," I mutter.

"As far as I'm concerned, you all owe me." He wrenches the wheel, kicking up dust as the tires hit the highway's shoulder. Our headlights close in on a handful of cars in a gravel parking lot. A neon light flickers in the window of the low wooden building behind it.

"Why are we stopping?" I ask.

"Because I'm hungry and my ass is asleep. And after three hours suffering in the back seat with you, I could really use a drink. If you don't like it, you can fight me."

He swings the sedan into a parking spot, bringing us to an abrupt halt that sets my shoulder throbbing and jolts Fleur awake. He jerks the keys from the ignition and gets out before any of us can argue, shoving them deep into the front pocket of his jeans as he saunters to the bar.

Amber's jaw drops. She chokes out a nervous laugh, pushes open her door, and follows him. Warm woody light and the bittersweet smell of whiskey and cheap beer pour out of the bar as Julio holds open the door for her. The car falls dim and silent as they disappear inside.

"Where are we?" Fleur asks, pushing herself up. Her hair's tousled from sleep, the pink tangles catching the headlights of the cars rushing past us on the highway.

"Don't know, exactly." Her lips are pouty and full, her hands hot on my chest, easing the pain in my shoulder. "Looks like we're stuck here."

The engine ticks as it cools. I take her cheek in my hand, rub away a spot of my blood that's dried there. I can't stop thinking about last night. How badly I wanted to kiss her by the fire. I run my fingers through her hair and draw her toward me. The seat creaks as she leans into me, her mouth soft, her fingers grazing my ribs, making my skin tighten with goose bumps as our kiss deepens. My hands move down her back, my nails digging into the seams around the pockets of her jeans.

"Jack," she whispers. The breathless sound of my name on her lips slays me. "Jack, I really have to pee."

I feel her smile. Feel my own spread wide across my face. She reaches

311

down and starts buttoning up Julio's shirt, and I'm pretty sure this is the most painful way she's ever killed me. I thunk my head back against the window, willing my heart to slow and my body to chill before I have to stand up and go inside.

A fist bangs the window behind me, and we both jump out of our skins.

"Hurry up, Sommers. You owe me. That means you're buying."

Fleur and I nearly spill out of the car as Julio yanks open the door. He looks down at Fleur, sprawled on top of me, with his mouth agape. Fleur turns a shade of red I've never seen her wear before. She climbs over me, awakening the pain in my shoulder, calls Julio a name that gives me a newfound admiration for her, and strides off into the bar.

I feel every bit of my fifty years as I extricate my stiff limbs from the back seat. Julio offers me a hand, a hint of liquor already on his breath. My shoulder groans when he pulls me upright, and I adjust his shirt to cover the bloodstained bandage underneath.

I pause beside the car, trying to figure out how to say what needs to be said. "Thanks."

"For what?"

"For coming back for me." He didn't have to. He and Amber could have taken Fleur and the car and hauled ass off that mountain, never once looking back. When the shot rang out and I went down, I wasn't afraid of the pain. I was terrified of the possibility no one would come. That they would leave me to die there alone.

He shrugs off my gratitude like a jacket that doesn't fit. "Whatever. You did the same for me, right?"

A chill wind slices through the parking lot. He turns and heads for the bar, his hands jammed into the pockets of his jeans and his shoulders hunched. I start to follow him. Out of the corner of my eye, I see soemthing move—a shadow in the dark. I turn to catch it, but the parking lot is empty. All I smell are diesel fumes and dust.

Julio holds open the door. "You coming?"

"Yeah," I say, dismissing the wisp of doubt in the back of my mind that it's colder here than it should be. "I'm coming."

I follow Julio inside, into the dim light and the clink of glasses. There's no bouncer. Nobody carding at the door. The lone bartender barely acknowledges us. A handful of old men sit around the bar, staring down at their drinks or up at the evening news on the muted TV behind it with weathered, tired faces. The place is warm, musty, and drowsy, the air sweet with hops. Maybe Julio's right, and I'm worrying for nothing.

I follow him to a lone pool table in the back where Fleur and Amber have already racked the balls, ready to play. He downs a quick shot of bourbon from their table. Chases it with a swig of beer.

"Keys." Fleur waits as Julio fishes the car keys from his pocket.

"Doubles?" He drops them into her hand. She tosses them to me. Guess I owe everybody. I just became the designated driver.

"Not this time," Amber says, lining up her break. She slams the cue, scattering balls and sinking two. We watch her run the table for her next three shots while Julio finishes his beer. Fleur chalks a stick, ready for a turn.

I drag Julio with me to the bar. "I'm starving. Let's find something to eat." The bartender takes his time with the patrons he knows by name. He scrutinizes us as he pours everyone else's beers from the tap, probably trying to guess our ages. I help myself to a peeling laminated menu from a stack tucked under a napkin holder.

"Do you want a club sandwich or a burger?" I ask.

Julio's distracted. He leans on his elbows, watching Amber and Fleur play. When the bartender finally comes around, I order four burgers and two plates of fries, a soda for me and a beer for Julio. The bartender makes me pay for the food up front, only sliding me our drinks after I lay cash, along with an overly generous tip, on the bar. Julio reaches for the beer, watching Amber sink another shot.

The soda's warm and a little flat. I reach for Julio's glass, checking to make sure no one's looking as I wrap my chilled fingers around it. I hand it back to him with a layer of frost. He raises an eyebrow and clinks his glass against mine.

"So it worked," he says between sips. "You and Fleur kissed, right?" It takes me a second to figure out what he's getting at. "Guess no one shorted out."

I look at him sideways. He looks back expectantly.

I had assumed he and Amber tested the kissing theory in their tent last night. That the heavy silence on the other side of the thin canvas was more than just the awkward kind, when you stay up half the night wondering if the other person's sleeping, wishing you had the guts to make the first move.

"Still here." I gesture to myself—to my bandages, bedhead, and his ugly-ass shirt—all indisputable proof of my existence. "We'll be in Arizona in two days. Maybe it's time you make a move."

Julio's quiet, the sun-kissed skin around his eyes pinched as he watches Amber play. A waitress walks by, less than subtle in the way she checks him out, but when he doesn't seem to notice, she moves on to a table of road-tripping frat boys who just came in.

I don't believe for one second that Julio's never been with a girl before. There've been too many rumors floated around the Observatory about how many Summer girls have been caught walking home from his dorm room after hours. No way he's a virgin. Amber, either, for that matter. She died in '69, in the days of free love and Woodstock. It was only a few winters ago that I caught her half dressed before dawn, sneaking out of some university coed's bedroom.

He shakes his head. "I don't know, Jack. We're so different."

"Or maybe you're just scared you'll screw it up?"

Julio finally looks at me. For a second I worry he'll crack his glass over my head. He slumps back against the bar with a heavy sigh. "The last time I kissed her, she disappeared."

"So did you," I remind him. Julio may have been the one to dematerialize on that jail cell surveillance video, but Amber was the one left behind. And that hurts, too. "Maybe she's scared."

"Of what?"

"Same things you are." Same things we all are. Of being left. Of not being enough. Of being alone.

The waitress pushes open the swinging door to the kitchen. My stomach rumbles at the smell of our burgers sizzling on the other side. Julio watches Amber with the same kind of hunger as the girls rack up the balls for another game, their laughter and sidelong glances occasionally drifting our way.

Two of the frat boys head for a dusty jukebox in the corner. They laugh as they read the selection of song titles, then abandon the machine without choosing any. The other two saunter to the pool table, stacking quarters on the rail to reserve the next game. I can smell the cigarette smoke and weed on them from here. By the wrinkle in Fleur's nose, I'm guessing she can, too. One of the boys cues up some music on his phone. The old men at the bar turn, searching for the source of the persistent, loud beat streaming through the phone's speakers.

"Look at these assholes," Julio mutters as one of them sidles up to Fleur, insisting on a game of doubles. He checks out her near-empty bottle and calls for another round, but I grab the waitress's attention first.

The guys look annoyed when she delivers two drinks to Amber and Fleur. She sets them down on a couple of napkins and hitches her thumb over her shoulder, pointing us out. Amber and Fleur tip their bottles to us with angelic smiles. "Pretty sure they can take care of themselves," I assure him.

They let the boys break. The taller one throws himself into it. The loud *crack* barely moves the balls, and when the girls start to run the table, the boys quickly switch their tactics. The loud one comes up close behind Amber—too close. He bumps her stick as she takes her shot, and she stiffens as her ball bounces off the rail.

An alarm goes off in my head when Julio pushes off the bar. Breath held, I wait for the temperature in the room to rise, but neither Amber nor Julio reacts. She watches Julio out of the corner of her eye as he moves toward the darkened jukebox.

"Don't bother, sweetheart," the waitress calls out to him. "That thing's so old, the wires are all corroded. It hasn't fired up in years."

"Jack, want to give me a hand with this?" Julio slides the machine away from the wall. I chew on a smile as I ease off my bar stool.

"This isn't exactly keeping a low profile, you know."

I kneel beside him behind the jukebox. He blows the dust off the end of the loose plug and holds it out to me.

"Desperate times," he says with a hopeful lift of his brow. "All we have to do is get it started, right?"

A quick tap of our knuckles jolts just enough power into the machine. It comes to life in cherry reds and muted yellow lights, and Julio discretely plugs it in before anyone sees. The lights flicker, resisting the weak current from the outlet on the wall before finally giving in. We push the jukebox back into place. The old men at the bar watch as Julio wipes the dust from the glass and thumbs a few quarters in. A record swishes into place, the needle dropping into its track with a velvety scratch that makes Amber's eyes close for a moment, her head tipped.

"Unchained Melody" begins to play, the soulful notes drowning out the chatter of conversation and the clatter of balls. The club music from the boy's phone dissolves away with them. Fleur hangs on her pool cue with a dreamy smile, watching as Julio leads Amber to the middle of the floor and draws her close, gently swaying her.

"Hey." The waitress taps me on the shoulder. I turn on my stool, expecting our food to be ready, but she pushes a slip of paper across the bar. "Are you Jack?" That same cold sensation I felt in the parking lot slithers under my skin. I never gave her my name. "Some man asked you to call him. Says it's important. You can use the pay phone out back."

I turn over the receipt. A phone number's written on it.

I check to make sure Fleur's okay before carrying the number past the restrooms and slipping out the rear door. The lot out back is surrounded by shadowy fields of culled corn. I stare into the darkness, the hair on my neck rising the longer nothing moves. Tearing my gaze from the field, I reach for the pay phone. It's about as old as the jukebox inside, rusted and grimy, faded by the sun. I shove in a couple of quarters, surprised when I actually get a dial tone.

Lyon answers on the first ring. "Jack, I'm glad you got my message."

"That makes one of us." I rub the ache in my shoulder as I scan the field. "Tell Gaia to call off her damn smazes. I know they're out here."

"Gaia and I are only concerned for your safety. We've been following your progress since you left the cabin."

"If you were so concerned about our safety, maybe you could have sent your almighty girlfriend to help us out."

"You know she can't do that, Jack. The Guard is too powerful. And with Chronos at the helm of the Observatory, there's far too much risk. If he suspects Gaia of being disloyal, he could turn them all loose upon her—Seasons and Guards alike. She can't leave. Not yet. Not until you've garnered enough sympathy for your cause."

"Cause?" Ice crackles over the receiver. "There is no cause! We're just trying to survive! Chronos put a bounty on our heads. He's opened up the borders to make it easier for them to hunt us. You seriously think anyone will sympathize with us now?"

"All he's managed to do is show them the hypocrisy of his own laws. The Seasons have always been told the borders between regions are unbreachable. That there is no reward in pushing boundaries. In more ways than one, you've proven him wrong." The edge in his voice softens. "You did well at the cabin."

"We all nearly died!"

"And yet," he says, "here you are."

I grind the heels of my palms into my eyes and lean against the pay phone. "I killed another Season. Névé Onding." It hurts to say her name. I have no right to hold even that small piece of her inside me, and the weight of what I took from her feels heavier with every hour I carry it around. "I took her magic. The last thing I deserve is anyone's sympathy."

His voice falls soft. "You did what you felt you must. Of this, I have no doubt. As far as anyone at the Observatory is aware, Névé died in battle. There was no footage to prove otherwise. The brief clips the other Seasons have seen will win over their minds and hearts. At Croatan Beach, you proved you will kill to protect one another. At the cabin, you presented them with the choice to walk away, join you, or die. That's one more choice than Chronos has ever given them. You've shown them their assumptions are wrong, Jack. You've proven that alliances are possible. That hearts are penetrable. That rules can be challenged. You've given them much to think about. Now you must show them how powerful you've become."

My fist smacks the wall. "No! We're not showing anyone anything. There's been no sign of Chronos's Guard since we lost them at Croatan Beach, and that's how it'd better stay. Tonight, we rest. Then we run." There's no way I'm telling him where. We'll be in Arizona in two days as long as no one finds us. If Chronos follows the dummy routes we planted in my memories, he'll be looking for us in Wyoming, Seattle, or the Dakotas. We'll make a quick stop to see Amber's mother and get out of Phoenix before anyone knows we're in town.

"The mortal boy you left in the woods survived," Lyon says, slicing through my thoughts. "His parents have filed a report with the police. He told them you're in possession of a firearm, and he's provided physical descriptions of each of you. By tonight, every law enforcement agency will be alerted to you. If you're sighted, every Season in the central states will be upon you by morning."

I swear under my breath, ready to smash the receiver against the machine. This is exactly what Julio was afraid would happen. All he wanted was one night. All I wanted was to get us to Arizona in one piece. To get Fleur someplace safe. For Chronos and Gaia and everyone else to just forget about us.

"This battle is not yet lost," Lyon says, his voice low. There's a rumble in it, like thunder in the distance. "In the midst of chaos, there is also opportunity. A perfect storm lies ahead. You can let it destroy you, or you can take control of it. How the story ends is up to you."

The line goes quiet.

"Professor? Professor!" An operator's recorded message tells me our call is over.

I slam down the receiver. Head in my hands, I sink down the wall. Another slow song plays softly through the wooden slats. I listen to the snap of pool balls. To the low laughter of the frat boys inside. I can't go in yet. My arms are glazed over with ice and Fleur will know something's wrong the second she looks at me. I don't have the heart to break the news to them, and no one but Lyon knows exactly where we are. Not yet. All we have to do is lie low, keep moving, and ditch Gaia's spies.

Hands jammed in my pockets, I walk around the building to the front of the bar. When I'm sure I'm alone, I pop the sedan's trunk.

The kid's rifle is draped over Julio's guitar bag. My shoulder aches at the sight of it. I look around for a sewer hole or a culvert, somewhere safe to dump it, when I see something move across the parking lot.

I scoop up the rifle.

Finger on the trigger, I swing the barrel, chasing a fast-moving shadow as it ducks behind a row of trash barrels.

"Who's there?" I call out. I scent the air, taking a slow step toward the foul-smelling cans.

A wisp of gray mist slithers between them. Probably the same damn smaze that's always chasing me around the Observatory, eager to rat me out. My shoulders slump and I let the rifle tip sag.

"Go! Get out of here!" I bark at it. Maybe I should feel relieved to see it. Relieved that Lyon was probably the one to send it. That he's been watching our backs all along. But as the smaze's smokelike tendrils peer around the can, something else about my conversation with Lyon wraps darkly around my mind.

You did well at the cabin.

It was more than a reflection or an observation. More than a show of sympathy or support. It felt like we passed some kind of a test. He warned us they were coming. He knew when they would arrive, told us how to prepare . . .

Now you must show them how powerful you've become.

The curious gray mist creeps closer. Was it Lyon? Was he the one who's been leaking our location to Chronos? Has he been using us all along?

The Guard is too powerful. And with Chronos at the helm of the Observatory, there's far too much risk. . . . She can't leave. Not yet. Not until you've garnered enough sympathy for your cause. . . .

I've no teeth for battle. That's what he told me, right before he convinced me to stay at the cabin and fight.

The truth knots itself inside my chest. Lyon's been *using* me. Using all of us.

My thoughts run red when I think back to the bee he crushed under his shoe the day we escaped from the Observatory. The way he looked at

321

me as he snuffed out the bee's soul. He wasn't trying to keep our secrets from Chronos. It was a show, a demonstration—a vivid reminder of the fate awaiting Fleur, just to keep me from having second thoughts.

It was the only way I could be sure you'd make it out of the Observatory.

Just like with the Termination in Gaia's office. Gaia *knew* Chronos would punish those girls, and Lyon made damn sure I was there in time to see it. To frighten me. To keep me focused on a goal I'd thought was my own. He'd told me to forget Alaska, to follow my heart and change the ending. But it's *his* ending he wants me to change. Not mine.

I cock the rifle and swear.

All this time, I thought Lyon understood me. That he wanted to help me. All that talk about choices. About how I was the only one who could see into my heart. It was all bullshit. All this time, he had me convinced the ending I was fighting for was my own.

I track the smaze, wondering whose soul is stuck inside it. Remembering the way it followed Lyon around the Observatory like an obedient dog. Wondering if it's the restless spirit of the last poor sucker Lyon duped into fighting his war.

I rest my finger on the trigger just to satisfy my own rage. But it's stupid. Pointless. All I see is the bee's light going out and Hunter's magic dissolving. All I feel inside me is the weight of Névé's soul.

I let out a breath. Let the tip of the rifle drop. It's just a goddamn dark cloud anyway. I slump against the wall of the bar. Through the windows behind me, I hear glass shatter, and someone screams.

35

A KISS AND ALL WAS SAID

FLEUR

Julio and Amber are the only ones dancing, but to see them—the way they look at each other—you'd think they were the only two people in the room. Julio whispers into her ear, their cheeks touching. When she tips her head back and laughs, he glows brighter than the sun.

Maybe that's the secret to breaking down barriers: to dance so close it's impossible to tell who's leading. To stand near enough to speak softly. To hold each other's hands so you can't throw stones.

The song ends. The sound of glasses being stacked behind the bar and raucous laughter from the frat boys' table breaks the spell, and Amber reluctantly unwinds herself from Julio's arms. Their fingers brush, almost letting go as the record changes. But as "When a Man Loves a Woman" begins to play, she chews on her grin and settles back into his arms. They sway, turning in slow circles as he mouths the lyrics against her ear. Even the waitress rests her chin on her hand to watch them.

"Where's your boyfriend?" The tall boy we played pool with slides his arm around my shoulder.

"He's around." I shrug out from under him, ignoring his slurred mutters as he withdraws back to his friends.

I look for Jack, but his stool is still empty. He's been gone too long. Long enough to make me anxious as the frat boys' table grows rowdier. They bark at the waitress for another round, and a quiet tension builds as they watch Julio and Amber with more than a passing interest.

One of them snatches a beer off the waitress's tray. He carries it onto the dance floor and spills the entire bottle down Julio's back. The air in the room crackles, hot and close, as Julio turns slowly around.

The boy smugly surveys Julio's shirt. "Sorry about that."

"I bet you are." Julio's eyes dart to Jack's empty stool. Then to me. I give a tight shake of my head.

"You should go home and clean that up. We'll keep an eye on the girls for you."

A fire lights in Amber's eyes. She stalks to the pool table and palms a cue. I pour the last of my beer into the potted plant beside me and turn the bottle around, holding it by the neck. "I don't think they need a babysitter," Julio says. "I'm thinking they're good."

The boy leers at us. "I bet they are."

"Too bad you'll never find out," Amber says over the music. The old men at the bar chuckle into their beers. The guy's face reddens when his friends start laughing, too.

"Are you even old enough to be in a bar?" He calls out to the waitress, "Hey, did you check their IDs?"

"Your mom called, kids," one of his friends shouts from their table.

"She says you're late for curfew." Their group explodes with laughter and I want to string every single one of them from a tree.

"Look, I get it," Julio says. "Two very capable ladies schooled you in a game of pool. But just because your ego's bruised—"

The guy shoves Julio, pushing him back a step. Julio throws Amber a warning look when she shifts her grip on the cue.

He raises his hands. "I don't want to fight with you."

The guy shoves Julio again, knocking him into a chair and drawing the bartender's attention. The waitress reaches for the phone.

Julio lowers his voice. "Look, we don't want any troub—"

The sucker punch catches him under the ribs.

Amber swings the cue into the backs of the boy's knees. It's at his throat before they hit the floor. Chairs topple as one of his friends makes a run for Julio. The tall one grabs me from behind. I dig my heel into his shin and throw my hips backward, using his own momentum to toss him over my shoulder, where he lands supine on the floor.

I smash my bottle, the shatter echoing as I bring it under his chin.

The bar stills, deadly quiet except for the soft whir of the record. A cold draft blows through the room. When I look up, Jack's standing in the open door, the rifle poised to fire.

"We're leaving," he says, sighting down the barrel at the only guy left standing of the frat boys' group. Jack's arms shimmer with frost. His eyes cloud over with the same icy look he wore the morning we left the cabin. Without lifting them from his target, he says, "We'll take our food to go."

The waitress lets go of the phone. Her hands shake as she puts the burgers and fries in a bag and sets it on the bar.

"I apologize for the disruption." Jack jerks his head toward the door. I set down the broken bottle. Amber throws down her cue and follows me, glass crackling under our shoes. Julio shoves his attacker back by his collar, taking the bag of food on his way out the door. Jack backs out behind us, instructing everyone in the bar to count to a thousand before they move.

"Get in the car," he says when we're all outside. He throws open the trunk. I nudge past Amber and Julio and run to the front passenger door.

Amber's still standing frozen on the top step, a wild uncertainty in her eyes. "Julio, wait."

We all pause. I scent the air. Jack tightens his grip on the rifle, darting glances into the shadows around us.

"What?" Julio looks up at her, worry pulling on his brow as she shuts her eyes tight and swears quietly. He climbs up a step until they're eye to eye. "What is it? What's wrong—?"

She grabs him by the front of his shirt and kisses him. Julio's body goes rigid with shock as her arms slide around his neck and their kiss deepens. I cover my mouth, trying and failing to stifle a grin.

"Are we seriously doing this now?" Jack snaps, when neither one of them comes up for air.

Julio's eyes close as she melts into him. He tosses the bag of burgers on the hood of the car and wraps his arms around her, lifting her off the step. Her legs curl around his waist as sirens wail in the distance.

"Can we please get in the fucking car?" Jack throws the rifle into the trunk and slams it closed. I grab the bag of food off the hood and jump into the front passenger's seat. Julio eases Amber to the ground, their lips close, their chests heaving.

"We're okay?" she asks, as if she's not entirely sure.

"We're okay," he says, a little breathless.

He takes her hand and they scramble into the back seat. Jack pauses, one leg still out of the car, his eyes narrowed against the darkness.

"What is it, Jack? What's going on?" I ask, feeling the night and his anger and the heat and the sirens and the faces in the window of the bar pressing in around us.

Jack gets into the car and puts the keys in the ignition. "They're coming for us," he says, peeling out of the parking lot.

"Who?" I ask him.

"Everyone."

36

CHAOS AND OPPORTUNITY

JACK

I slam down the accelerator, kicking up gravel as the tires squeal onto the highway. Without taking my eyes from the road, I reach into the glove box for Woody's map and hand it to Fleur.

"Look for someplace safe to pull over and get rid of the gun. A bridge or a ravine. Somewhere we won't be seen." We're close to the Arkansas River. There must be a bridge or an overpass somewhere.

"Maybe we should hold on to it. What if we need it?" Amber asks.

"Getting arrested for possession of a stolen gun will only slow us down." We've got bigger things to run from.

"Relax." Julio leans around my headrest. His breath reeks of Amber and booze, and his knee's jabbing the back of my seat. "We can outrun the cops. If we drive through the night, we'll be in Texas by morning."

"It's not the cops I'm worried about."

"I didn't smell anything." Julio's drunk and reckless, still riding the adrenaline of the fight and the high of that kiss. He doesn't know what's coming for us.

"Jack?" Fleur reaches for me. "What's wrong?"

I move my hand before she can take it. It's too hot in here. Too close. I need to think.

I crack the window. Julio slumps back in his seat, away from the cold air rushing in. Fleur presses me in spite of it.

"Jack, what's going on? What did you see back there?"

I clench my teeth to keep from biting her head off. "A smaze. In the parking lot."

"Are you sure?" Amber asks, a hint of worry underlying her skepticism. For all we know, the damn thing could be in here with us. Smazes aren't like the other creatures Gaia employs as spies. They can pass under doors and through cracks in windows. They can hide in the chassis of a moving car. Amber's spent most of her life watching shadows for smazes. Like a bad omen, their arrival means her time is nearly up. She's as attuned to them as any Winter would be, maybe more so. "I didn't see anything."

"No?" I ask sharply. "Guess it's hard to smell the enemy when your tongue's down someone's throat."

"It's one smaze," Julio says. "There's no a reason to freak out. We don't even know that it was looking for us."

"Of course it was looking for us!" I shout. "Same as the crow at Croatan Beach. Why else would it be here?" Fleur reaches for my arm and I shake her off. I can't breathe. My blood pressure's rising with every inch Amber encroaches between the front seats. "Would someone open another fucking window, please?"

"You talked to him again," Fleur says. It's not a question, so I don't answer. "You had the same meltdown after you talked Lyon at the cabin. What did he say?"

A flurry of dry snow flashes white in the headlights. It drifts over the road, pushed by a chaotic northern wind. "The kid who shot me filed a police report. He gave them our descriptions. It's only a matter of time before Chronos knows we were at that bar. It won't be hard to track us. We'll probably be into it thick by morning."

I should calm down. I *need* to calm down. A storm will only make it easier for Chronos to find us. Fleur lowers her window, letting in a frigid cross breeze that must make her miserable. I drink it in, focusing on the lines of the highway to clear my head. Amber's hunched back in her seat under Julio's arm, watching me in the rearview mirror with the same distrustful look she wore last night by the fire.

"I'm sorry," I tell them, dragging my fingers through the frost in my hair. "I just want to get rid of the gun and find a place to think."

Fleur studies the map. "The highway crosses a creek in a few miles. There's a turnoff to an old railroad bridge up ahead. We can stop there."

By the time we reach the exit, the flurry's over. I park the sedan under a cluster of trees at the end of a gravel road. Ahead of us, the swollen creek rushes over the concrete footings under the bridge.

Julio walks ahead, making sure we're alone. Amber keeps her distance, still wary of me.

I sit on the edge of the open trunk. Fleur corners me against it. She wraps her arms around my waist and lowers her voice so the others won't hear.

"What aren't you telling us?" It feels wrong to look her in the eyes after all the things I haven't said. She takes me gently by the chin. Turns my face up to hers. "You can tell me."

I draw her into me and press my lips into the crown of her head, breathing the scent of her deep into my lungs, suppressing instincts that feel like they belong to someone else. I don't know who I am anymore. Not if Lyon isn't who I thought he was.

"It's Lyon. What if Julio was right? What if we can't trust him?"

"But Lyon was the one who made sure we got out of the Observatory."

"Exactly. What if he's been engineering this whole thing all along? The battles, the escape routes, our decision to go . . ." My throat thickens at the possibility that Lyon's plan goes back even further. To the very beginning. To the day I first told him my name. The year before I first met Fleur.

She pulls back, studying my face. "What are you saying?"

I slide my hands down her arms and lace our fingers together. "It all makes sense now, how we fit." Each stage of our journey has been turning over in my mind since we left the bar, the pieces coming together in ways that feel too perfect to be chance. "Amber was a runaway. And Julio had a reputation for bucking authority. Anyone who saw that video of their kiss could see they had a spark. Then I came along, a miserable kid who'd died trying to break out of a place like the Observatory. And then you . . ." I touch her cheek. Fleur's beautiful and strong, gentle and smart. I'd have been a fool not to fall for her, and Gaia knew it. She dumped Fleur right into my lap, assigning both of us to the same region where we grew up, in defiance of her own rules, throwing all four of us together in some crazy experiment, hoping the chemistry between us was right. That we'd bond rather than break under the pressure.

Suddenly, Chronos's criticism of Gaia's leadership feels like a prism held to a light.

Your choices of late have been questionable, he told her.

Were Fleur and I one of them?

The possibility that none of this is real or mine, no matter how badly I want it to be, hurts to swallow. "What if we weren't the ones who chose this?"

She backs out of my arms, her face stricken. "Are you saying all this because you don't trust Lyon, or because you don't trust yourself?" Her eyes are determined and clear. She reaches around me for the rifle and slings it over her shoulder. "I chose this," she says defiantly. "I still choose this. Whatever regrets we have, whatever mistakes we made before, whatever our reasons, they don't matter now." She gives me one last look before she carries the rifle to the creek and pitches it in, letting the churning brown water carry it away. She wipes her hands of it, calls Julio and Amber back to the car, and spreads the map over the hood.

"We still have time to come up with a plan," she says, giving me no room to second-guess myself. "Regardless of his motives, Lyon wouldn't have warned us they were coming if he didn't want us to survive. What else did he say, Jack? Think."

"I don't know. Nothing specific. He disconnected before I could ask him anything else." I scrub the shadow of stubble on my face as I study the map, overwhelmed by all the possible routes, all the likely pitfalls and traps.

. . . every Season in the central states will be upon you by morning.

"We have to assume we'll be grossly outnumbered." This is the only thing I'm certain of. "Chronos won't make the mistake of leveling the playing field. We've come too far for that."

"So what's our plan of attack?" Julio asks.

I rake my bangs roughly from my eyes, as if some hidden answer might suddenly reveal itself. But if there's a solution on the map, I'm not seeing it. "We'll never survive if it comes down to a fight. There has to be another way."

This won't be like Croatan Beach, when we had the sea at our backs. Not like the cabin, where we held the high ground. We're in the middle of the plains, between multiple territories. They'll come at us from every direction. With a hopeless shake of my head, I stare at the expanse of open highway on the map. I'd give anything for a transmitter line to Chill right now. Strategy has always been our Handlers' role. They're the ones who see the big picture, the cool-headed voices in our ears when we're pinned down. I look to Amber. "What would Woody do?"

She shakes her head, her eyes sharp and her face sober as she twists her long hair into a tight ponytail. "I don't know. Probably suggest a distraction. A barricade, maybe. Evasive maneuvers will only get us so far. At some point, we'll have to engage them."

But engage who? There's a maelstrom of potential enemies. Crows and smazes. Lyon and Gaia. Seasons and police. Chronos and his Guard. It's hard to imagine a clear path without knowing exactly what's coming for us. We're not organized or prepared enough to engage an army, which is exactly what Chronos will be counting on.

Even as I push it away, Lyon's advice comes unbidden.

In the midst of chaos, there is also opportunity.

Chaos.

My skin prickles as an idea begins to take root in my mind.

Chaos was the key to escaping before. And if it worked before, it can work again.

"We don't have to engage them to go *through* them." Saying it out loud, it feels right. We were outnumbered, cornered at the elevators when we ran from the Observatory. Every imaginable obstacle hit the fan until shit was raining down all around us.

I think back to the solutions our Handlers came up with: the rain from the sprinklers, the howl of the alarms, the wind that slammed doors between us and our enemies, the electricity we generated to escape in the dark . . .

A perfect storm lies ahead . . . you can take control of it.

I look at Fleur. At Julio and Amber. And in them—in *us*—I see possibilities I haven't let myself see before. Together, we *are* the storm.

PART

THREE

37

BUT FIRE, BUT THUNDER

FLEUR

The interstate stretches on like a steel-gray ribbon through western Oklahoma. A rose-gold sun breaches the horizon at our backs. The rest area is near empty at this hour. Just a few truckers asleep in their rigs. We sit in the car, sucking down weak coffees and donuts from the vending machine inside, but the sugar doesn't do much to settle my nerves.

I flip through the local radio stations, searching for a weather report. Instead, I find the news.

"Police responded to an emergency call from a bar in Altus, Arkansas, at approximately ten thirty last night, where patrons reported they were held at gunpoint by teenagers matching the descriptions of four suspects wanted in the assault and battery of a minor two days ago in Tennessee. The two young men and two young women are considered armed and dangerous, and were last seen driving a late-model Chevy Impala westbound on Route 64, heading toward Fort Smith. . . ."

Jack turns it off.

Julio's knee bobs anxiously against the back of my seat. "Are you sure this is going to work?"

"No." Jack rubs his eyes. He's been driving most of the night so the rest of us could sleep, but we were all too keyed up. My stomach's sour. My eyelids burn, and my brain feels hazy, as if I've just awoken from stasis.

We get out and toss our cups into a trash can, rousing a flurry of black flies. A bee buzzes past us, doubles back, and hovers close until Julio bats it away. Every caw of every bird has us holding our breath. It's only a matter of time until they find us.

We're all jumpy as we watch the sky above the highway for signs. The sedan's parked along the curb, our exit unobstructed, the tank topped off with fuel.

In theory, Jack's plan should work.

He paces beside the car. He's second-guessing himself, I know it. I can read the burning question on his mind in every line etched in his brow.

What if I'm wrong?

Up until now, the only thing he doubted was his logic. Now, thanks to Lyon, he's questioning everything—his instincts, his motivations, his choices. He stops pacing when I take his hand. I draw him close and kiss him, a single lingering touch of our lips, reminding him why I'm here. "This is *our* plan. We control it. It'll work," I tell him. "I know it."

He catches my face as I pull away. When he bends to return the kiss, it's slow and strong, vulnerable and deep, his eyes closed and his soul bared to me.

"I love you," he whispers, leaving me breathless and reeling, struggling to form coherent thoughts.

Julio pushes off the trunk of the car. He points to a patch of dark sky in the distance. "Are you all seeing this?"

I shake off the buzzing in my head and force myself to focus.

Amber inhales deeply, her nose tipped to the wind. "Winters coming from the northwest."

Jack's eyes fog over, distant, as he says, "I'm getting Autumns from the south."

We all squint, struggling to make out anything in the early-morning light, but it's all farmland on either side of the highway as far as the eye can see. "They must be coming on foot," Julio says, watching the fields.

"Not all of them." I point at the still-dark stretch of road in front of us. A tight procession of headlights appears on the horizon, two lanes wide and several cars deep. Jack was right. This is worse than the beach. Worse than the cabin. This is every Season, in every territory in the region, closing in on us at once.

Jack tosses me the keys. Amber and I get in and I start the engine. Julio and Jack stand shoulder to shoulder in front of the car.

"Ready?" Jack asks him.

"As I'll ever be."

They turn back to back. Julio faces south, his upturned face catching the light of the rising sun and his fists clenched at his sides. A warm breeze builds. It crests over the fields, balmy and hot, whipping my hair through the open window of the car. I scrape it from my eyes as a swarm of black birds rises from the southernmost field and launches into the sky. Three figures stand in the middle of the sowed acres of dirt, shielding their faces from the dust devils swirling up from the ground.

"Three on foot to the south, less than a mile out!" I shout.

Jack faces north, a mirror of Julio. The warm southerly wind flows over him, hardening when it makes contact with his skin, cloaking him in a layer of frost.

"Uh-oh." Amber points into the field to our right.

"Jack!" He turns to me, his eyes clouded white and his lashes laced in ice. "Three more coming in!" Jack lifts his face to the sky. Clouds gather, ominous and black, as a rolling thunderhead builds over the field. A burgeoning line of rain falls like a shadow below it and the incoming Seasons hunch against the sudden downpour.

Cold misty wind begins to beat against the side of the car. Amber rolls up her window. "How long is it supposed to take? Why hasn't it formed yet?"

"I don't know." I tap an impatient beat on the steering wheel.

The Seasons in the fields press in on both sides, leaning into the wind. The headlights ahead draw closer.

Amber gnaws her thumbnail. "This could all go really, really wrong."

"It won't," I tell her. It can't. It's too late to come up with anything else. This storm is our only hope.

Julio's muscles strain. His skin shines with mist and sweat. Icicles coat Jack's hair, his ears, his clothes . . .

"Nothing's happening," Amber says, her voice rising.

I grip the wheel. The headlights in the distance are close enough to count now.

Julio's jaw tenses. Lightning flashes like a strobe. The thunderhead begins to swirl counterclockwise and the wind roars. The Seasons in the fields pause, watching the storm grow. They shield their heads as it bears down on them, pushing them back.

Lightning cracks. The sky opens above us, drenching Julio and

Jack with torrents of rain. Wind rocks the car. I turn on the wipers, scattering pebbles of ice that bounce off the hood.

"Ready?" Jack shouts.

Hail pelts Julio's face and he blinks it away. "Now!"

Arms raised, they turn west, shoulder to shoulder. They clasp hands, straining to stay upright under the barrage of ice and wind as their storms converge over the highway in front of us. Slowly, they draw their hands down, their joined magic pulling a twisting funnel from the sky. The oncoming traffic brakes, skidding to a stop as the tip of the tornado reaches the ground. Drivers turn, crossing the median, changing direction to avoid it. The rest flee their cars and scramble to the ditches along the shoulder as the base of the funnel stretches across the highway. Wide enough to shield us from the army on the other side.

Julio shouts something to Jack, but the words are sucked away by the howling wind.

Through the flapping wipers, I watch as they release each other's hands, and in a single coordinated movement, they push. Palms out and shoulders forward, they nudge their perfect storm along the road. My breath catches. It's beautiful and violent and terrifying, throwing cars and uprooting trees. Powerful enough to blind our enemies—to blow power lines, disrupt frequencies, and tear asphalt from the roads.

The Seasons in the fields keep their distance, shielding their eyes from flying debris, unable or unwilling to turn their backs on the funnel cloud and the four of us. We'll have to be careful. Have to maintain control of it. If we can keep it on a steady course, we can force our enemies from the road without hurting anyone.

Our phalanx in motion, Jack and Julio stumble to the car. They fall into the back seat and slam the doors, drenched and shaking.

"Go," Jack pants. "Chase it as close as you can. We'll keep it on course."

Jack holds my shoulder, his frigid hands finding the warmth of my skin. Julio leans close to Amber, her right hand clutching his over the back of her seat. I put the car in drive, and Amber and I lock hands over the gearshift, creating the same powerful loop that saved us back at the cabin. The air in the car sizzles with static. I push the pedal to the floor, rubber screaming from the tires as we peel out onto the road.

The tornado sways in serpentine patterns, ravaging the edges of the fields, throwing billboards and sucking speed limit signs from the ground. I match its speed, keeping back a cautious distance.

"Can you see anything?" Julio uses his shoulder to wipe water from his eyes.

"I can't see in front of it," Amber says. "It's too big."

The funnel is huge. A monster. There's no way our enemies can get close. And the police will be far too preoccupied with the aftermath to worry about anything else. The power Jack and Julio are pulling leaves me lightheaded as they fight to maintain control of the storm.

They slump, heads resting on the backs of our seats. I dart a quick glance in the rearview mirror to make sure they're okay, surprised by the flash of headlights behind us. Two sets, slicing through the strange dusty gray light, coming up fast.

"Jack?"

Jack's head snaps up. He catches my eyes in the mirror. He and Julio turn in their seats and the funnel turns with them, veering far off the road. It doubles back violently as I swerve, and Jack and Julio recapture their focus.

A pickup truck closes the gap. It rams me from behind as a sports car pulls alongside me. A chill creeps over me as I recognize the driver. "It's Doug Lausks." I press the pedal harder, but it's already touching the floor.

Jack's fingers dig into my shoulder as the sports car inches closer. We lurch as the pickup rams us again. Jack turns over his shoulder. "Denver Whittaker."

Julio swears as Doug rams us again. "Their whole team must be out there. We've got to lose them, Fleur."

No one wants that more than I do. I jerk the sedan left, forcing the sports car onto the shoulder. Doug's car kicks up dust, nearly running off the road. Straddling the lane line, I gun the engine and pull ahead of them, careful to keep my distance from the funnel. It's all I can do to maintain control of the car so Julio and Jack can keep control of the storm.

A shot rings out. I swerve, and we all duck our heads.

Denver holds a gun out the window of his truck. There's a sharp *ping* as a bullet lodges in the sedan's trunk. He takes another sloppy shot between leaps at my bumper.

"I've had enough of this bullshit." Amber drops Julio's hand and rolls down her window.

"What are you doing?" Julio sounds panicked as she drags her upper body out of the car. The funnel wavers as Julio reaches for her, shouting at her to get back inside. I grab onto her foot, one eye on the road as I anchor her in place. Another shot rings out from Denver's truck and we all scream her name. I grip the wheel tight, terrified of losing control at this speed and throwing her through the window. Amber summons a ball of fire. She winds it back, pitching it hard into Denver's front grill.

The engine erupts in flames. We all let out a breath as Denver slams on his brakes, his truck veering violently off the road. In my mirror, I read the curse on Doug's lips, the flash of panic in his eyes as he watches Denver's truck flip in his rearview mirror. Doug hesitates, the distance widening between our bumpers, his eyes darting back and forth between us and his mirror as Denver climbs from the wreckage.

Doug lays into his accelerator.

Amber spins another flame, stretching it between her fingers until it's the size of a cannonball. Doug rams us from behind. The car lurches and the fire tumbles uselessly to the ground. Jack lunges for Amber as I lose my grip and she slips from the edge of the car. With a cry, Julio thrusts his hand out the window, catching her by the front of her jeans before she falls.

The tornado zigzags, chipping away wide swaths of the highway. A piece of debris smacks Doug's windshield, splintering the glass and pushing him back.

Amber regains her balance. Ignoring Julio's pleas to come inside, she cups another spark, stretching it into a hot white fireball as she waits for Doug to get close. Just before he slams into our bumper, she hurls it at the crack in his windshield. The fractured glass shatters. The sports car falls back, the interior lit with flames and billowing black smoke. Doug's door flies open. He leaps from the car, tumbling into a ditch alongside the road.

We pull Amber into the car as the flames shrink behind us.

I steady us on the road. Julio and Jack steady the storm. Amber lays her head back and breathes, steadying her heart. And this time, when we reach for each other's hands, it feels like we're sharing more than energy. More than magic or strength or power. It feels like we're sharing a promise.

38

CLAWS AND TEETH

JACK

We make it to the outskirts of Phoenix just before midnight. I pay cash for two adjacent rooms in the smallest, crappiest motel I can find and park the sedan around back. We sit in the darkened car, too exhausted to move. Too scared to ask what happens in the morning. For months, Arizona has been the destination, the milestone none of us were entirely sure we would reach alive. Now we're here, together. But for how long? Where do we all go next?

I clear the dust from my throat. "Tomorrow, when we wake, we'll take Amber to see her mom. After that, Fleur and I will head north to the Canyon." No one speaks.

I hand Amber a key to one of the rooms. We all get out of the car. This time, we break into pairs without any awkward preambles. Julio holds their door open, but Amber pauses outside. Her eyes are glassy as she turns to me and says, "Thanks, Jack. For bringing me home."

She places a cool peck on my cheek. The weight of it lingers as she and Julio disappear into their room.

Fleur unlocks our door and dumps her backpack beside the bed. The peeling wallpaper and threadbare carpet are sour with the odor of bodies and tobacco. Yellowing stains creep over the ceiling tiles, the sink, and the bedspread. The lighting in the room is harsh, and the haggard face staring back at me in the cracked mirror above the sink across the room feels almost unrecognizable.

Home. I'm not even sure where that is for me anymore.

The cabin? My old boarding school? My grandfather's headstone? My mother's? All Amber's wanted is to make it here, to Arizona. All Julio's talked about is going to the coast. But my destination isn't wrapped up in a city or the place where I came from. All I've wanted is to leave everything behind and disappear with Fleur. To keep her alive. I hadn't stopped to think about who we'd become. Or where we'd go.

She disappears into the bathroom. On the other side of the door, the shower sputters to life and the hooks screech over the curtain rod. I turn on the faucet in the rust-stained sink and let the water run cold. Standing in front of the mirror, I unbutton Julio's shirt, surprised to find the gauze bandage still taped to my shoulder. The adhesive clings stubbornly around the faded, puckered scar. That night by the campfire feels like it happened years ago, not days ago. We've all changed so much since.

I splash handfuls of water over my face, wishing it would wash away all my doubts about tomorrow. The four of us together were unstoppable, the perfect storm. But what happens if we're not together anymore?

The bathroom door opens with a soft *click*. The steam billowing from it is thick with the scent of lilies and Fleur's shampoo. I freeze at the sight of her, cold water dripping down my face as I reach mindlessly for the tap.

Fleur's cheeks are flushed from the heat. Beads of water trail from the wet ends of her hair, over the rise and fall of the towel cinched tightly around her chest. The sight of her knocks me breathless and I force myself to look away.

"I can wait outside." My voice is strained as I turn for the door.

She reaches for me. "Wait." The air between us feels charged, like we could electrify the room. "Is that . . . ?" She holds her towel in place. Tucks her wet hair behind her ear. "Is that what you want?"

I shut my eyes. Lick the water from my lips, trying to find the right words to answer that. She smells like wildflowers in moonlight, like forests of night blooms, and if I look at her again, I'm done. Game over.

"No," I whisper through a thin breath. "That's not what I want."

I shiver at her tentative touch, at the heat of her skin as she takes my hand and draws me to her.

"Why won't you look at me?" She rests her hand in the open collar of my shirt and tenderly traces my scar. I shiver. My nails dig into my palms.

A desperate laugh crawls up my throat. How do I tell her that this crappy motel room suddenly feels sacred? That no matter how many times I've fantasized about this moment, how many times I've wished for it, suddenly I don't feel worthy or ready? I'm terrified I'll screw this up.

"Because you're beautiful and warm and you smell so . . ." I swallow hard as she places a fragile kiss on my neck, her breath a soft caress against the ache in my throat. "God, you smell amazing. And if you keep touching me like this, I don't think I can trust myself to do the right thing."

"*I* trust you." Her palm skims down my chest, and the ache spreads everywhere. I sink my teeth into my lip as her hand slips lower, and I take it before she does something we both might regret.

"You were right," I say, my pulse racing. "Back in Tennessee, you said we should be together for the right reasons. Not because we're afraid."

"I'm not afraid," she whispers. Suddenly, she stops. "Are you?"

My voice breaks. "Yes."

"Why?" She sounds so surprised. "Have you never . . . ?"

"No," I blurt. "I mean, I have. I just . . . I think we should be sure." And I'm not sure of anything anymore. I've dreamed about this moment for years. But my dreams haven't only been mine, my instincts haven't only been mine. I'm not even sure my choices are my own. What if they're not hers, either? What if—

"Open your eyes, Jack."

My breath shudders out of me. When I open my eyes, she rests her forehead against mine, and her softly spoken words silence everything else. "This is what I want." She presses a delicate kiss to my lips. Then another. Bolder. The same reassuring kiss she gave me before we started the storm early this morning. And this time, I give in.

My arms slide around her waist. Her mouth is warm, and the soft brush of her tongue sets my blood on fire. She backs me slowly against the wall. My nails dig into the thin towel around her hips as she slips her hands inside my shirt and pushes it over my shoulders.

My hand stills over the knot in her towel.

Her hand closes gently over mine, tugging it free. The towel falls down her hips to the floor. There's a quiver in her breath and her eyes are wide on mine.

"We're okay?" I ask, searching them.

"We're okay," she says, a little breathless.

I let her lead, careful and slow as I sink down with her onto the bed. I keep my eyes open, pushing everyone and everything else from my mind, because I don't want to be anywhere else. Don't want to share this moment with anyone but her. For the first time, in all my lives, I finally feel like I'm home.

39

THE LION'S HEART

JACK

A phone rings and I lurch awake.

The motel room is dimly lit, hazy sunlight filtering around the heavy curtains. Fleur stirs, burrowing deeper under the blankets and curling into my side when the phone rings again, shrill and insistent. It must be Amber. She's probably anxious to get going. But Fleur's breath is warm in the space between my shoulders, her soft legs tangled around mine, and I don't want to leave. The phone rings a third time. I slip out of her arms with a muttered curse, groping for the receiver.

I rub my eyes. "Hello?"

"Jack."

Lyon.

I sit up, the tousled sheets pooling around me. Fleur snuggles closer in her sleep. I grip the phone and swing my legs off the side of the bed. We were careful. We were so careful. How did he know we were here?

"What do you want?" I ask quietly.

"I know you're resting. I won't keep you long."

"Who else knows we're here?"

"No one, I hope." He sounds sincere, if not convinced. "Chronos's Guard has been greatly diminished. Only a handful of them remain in the region. Most of the others were sent back through the ley lines during your storm."

"How many people were hurt?" We didn't put on the news. Didn't listen to the damage reports on the radio as we left the scene of the storm, all of us remembering Marie's speech at Croatan Beach when Hunter died and she ordered us not to feel guilty about it. We did what we had to do to survive, same as before, but that doesn't mean we didn't wreck ourselves the whole way here thinking about it.

Lyon's answer feels filtered, carefully watered-down. "Sometimes collateral damage is inevitable."

I push the images of the tornado from my mind. We never intended to kill anyone when we started down this road. I'm not sure I can say the same about Lyon. "Where are you?"

"Not as close as I would like to be. I've lost contact with Gaia. I'm concerned she may have fled the Observatory. If so, you may not hear from me again." I should be relieved. Grateful, even. But I can't shake the feeling that I'm being abandoned. "Jack," he says solemnly, "when all seems lost, when you and Fleur have traveled this road as far as you can alone, remember: You already possess all you need to survive this journey. Yours is the heart of a lion, and in it I've seen immeasurable courage."

"How long?" I ask through gritted teeth. "How long have you been seeing inside my heart?"

Lyon's silence tells me everything I need to know. I'm not sure which stings worse—that single truth, that he's been manipulating me from the beginning, or that every affection he showed me was based on a lie. "Since the first time I found you," he confesses, "hiding in the catacombs under the Winter wing, searching for a way out."

I grip the receiver. "Hiding and running don't exactly reek of courage."

"It's natural to feel afraid, Jack. Fear of death doesn't make you any less of a man. If anything, it makes you more of one."

"And Fleur? Did you choose her, too?"

"It's not that simple."

"Try me."

He doesn't answer right away, as if he's searching for a way to explain. "The magic Springs possess is unique—it requires empathy to place oneself inside the limbs of another living thing, to feel its pain and its strength enough to move it. To bend it. The balance of power and empathy is extraordinarily difficult to master. In this regard, Gaia always knew Fleur's magic was exceptionally strong, and because she would hesitate to wield that power at the expense of another, Chronos would have few opportunities to see it. He did not recognize the power she held in check before, and he will not be looking for it now.

"Fleur did not fall below the red line because she was weak, Jack. Fleur does not fear death the way most Seasons do. She does not fear her own pain as much as she fears the suffering of those she *loves*.

"Gaia chose *Fleur* because she knew Fleur would choose *you*, Jack. That when the time came, Fleur would use every ounce of her strength to fight for you. That she would protect you above all others. And I chose *you* because you reminded me so much of myself. And because being with you made me feel closer to the person I wished I could be."

"A Winter?"

"A father."

My throat constricts painfully. I shut my eyes, hating myself for the ways those words make me feel. I hate that even as he's destroying everything I thought I knew about myself, he still knows exactly what I want to hear. And more than any of it, I hate myself for not wanting him to go.

"So what now? You've been pulling our strings all along and now you're just going to disappear? What are we supposed to do?"

"Finish what you've started."

"We didn't start this!" I hiss into the phone.

"Maybe not, but *you* have the power to bring about its end. Chronos is afraid of you."

"Afraid?" I almost laugh. Chronos's piercing blue eye and the swing of his scythe are still emblazoned in my memory. He wasn't afraid when he whispered my fate in my ear. Fleur stirs and I lower my voice. "He saw me *die*. He watched his own Guard kill me."

"But at what cost? What else did he see in that vision beyond the small piece he revealed to you?"

All I remember is Kai Sampson's face as she drew back her bowstring and bloody water rushing over my head. My death was all I registered in those tightly cropped images. It was enough. I have no burning desire to face Kai Sampson in real life.

"No thanks. This is your battle. Not mine."

"It's not me he fears. He is only now beginning to realize the threat you pose to him. That's why he sends his Guard, while he hides in the Observatory behind monitors and screens. That's why he'll only look upon you through the eye of his staff. Because he's afraid, Jack. Only when he's certain of his own future will he muster the courage to face you."

Fleur sleeps peacefully beside me, the pale yellow bedspread pulled snugly to her chest. I fight back the memory of Chronos's scythe cutting through the Spring girl he Terminated, the color of the blood as it spread through her shirt. We can't let him find us. I don't care how strong Fleur is. I can't let her face him. Not for Lyon. Not for anyone.

"You have inspired them, Jack. The Seasons and their Handlers have been watching you. They saw your storm. Whispers of rebellion are breaching the walls of the Crux."

"Rebellion?" I think back to the Seasons we saw walking in the fields on the sides of the highway in Oklahoma . . . they watched us summon the storm. I press the heel of my hand into my forehead, imagining the rumors that must be circulating back on campus. No less than six Seasons saw us touch and generate that tornado, proof of everything we're capable of. And now the entire Observatory is probably convinced I'm starting some kind of war.

"Soon, Chronos will be forced to leave the Observatory, either to hunt for you himself and snuff out the spark you've ignited or to flee the insurrection we've begun."

"'We'?" He lumps us together as if we're somehow on the same side, as if any of this was my doing, or even my choice. "All *we* wanted was to run. To disappear."

"When has hiding helped you evade death before?" I bury my head, remembering every death I suffered at Fleur's hand. How futile it all seemed. That's why we left, to break the cycle. Yet here we are again, finding death on the road we took to avoid it, just like Lyon said.

"So Chronos was right? No matter what I do, I'm going to die?"

Lyon's quiet for too long. A chill passes over me when he says, "Sacrificing for others takes courage, Jack. Sometimes, that means imagining a different ending for them, if not for yourself." Fleur shifts toward me in her sleep, warm against my back. Her arms come around my waist, holding me to her. "When you grow tired of running, go to that place you hold in your heart. The strength you need will find you."

Lyon disconnects. The silence on the other end of the line leaves me feeling strangely untethered.

Numb, I rest the phone in the cradle and ease back under the sheets, staring at the ceiling.

Fear makes me more of a man, he said. But I don't feel like one. I'm scared of what waits for us outside this room. Outside this bed. I'm terrified I'll follow my heart and it will get cut down right in front of me. I curl around Fleur and bury my face in her hair, praying Lyon's right. That there is another ending, if not for me, then for her. And that somehow, the strength to face it will find me.

40

HOWEVER MEASURED OR FAR

FLEUR

Visiting hours at the nursing home start at noon. Jack follows Amber's directions to the facility where her mother lives, one hand on the wheel and one resting in my lap. No music plays. There's no bickering or small talk. We're each shrouded in our own thoughts. Mine are torn, some still tangled in memories of last night—the way it felt to wake up beside Jack and know that everything has changed. The rest of my thoughts hover closely around Amber.

She spends most of the drive staring out the window, loosely holding Julio's hand across the back seat. No other part of them touches. As if she's reluctant to get too close. She doesn't look at any of us. Not at Julio. Not at Jack in the mirror. Not at me when I turn in my seat with an encouraging smile that probably doesn't mask the worry beneath it.

We park down the street from the senior center, away from the security camera by the vestibule doors and the ones high on the lampposts in the parking lot.

"You okay?" I ask her when she doesn't get out.

There's a quiver in her voice. "I don't recognize any of it. Not any of the streets, the stores, the houses . . . I'm not even sure where we are. It's all different," she says, fixated on the swiftly moving clouds reflected in the tinted windows of the brick building beside us. "My mother's ninety-two years old. Ninety-two," she says, her brow creasing as if the number is somehow unfathomable. "What if . . . ?" She shakes her head. "I was going to say, what if she doesn't remember me, but what if she does? How do I explain . . . ?" She swallows hard, like she's fighting back tears. I've never seen Amber so fragile before. So unsure of herself. Jack and I were both assigned to territories in the same regions where we died. We faced our own painful homecomings years ago. We've watched our childhood friends age and our families move away, the homes of our youth bought and sold. Whole cities have grown up around landmarks we've mourned. The losses came gradually, year after year. I can't imagine what Amber must be feeling right now, as she prepares to face it all at once.

Her breath hitches on a sigh. "How do I tell her I've been alive all this time? That I've known where she was all these years, and I never came to say goodbye?"

Goodbye.

The word sucks the oxygen from the car, and I wonder if the others are having as hard a time breathing as I am. Suddenly, all the little things Amber hasn't entirely come out and said are shouting in my head all at once—the silent, stoic way she parted with Woody, as if she'd made peace with their parting a long time ago. The way she refused to take the car keys and leave with Julio at the cabin. Her reluctance to sit close to him now.

Last times can come with their own set of regrets, she told me that morning in the creek. *I'm glad he has you. . . .*

This moment has been Amber's destination all along. This is as far as she ever committed to go. So who's Amber preparing herself to say goodbye to? Her mother, or all of us?

She slings on her backpack and reaches for the door.

"If I'm not back in an hour, go on without me." She gets out without looking back.

Julio leaps out of the car, catching her on the sidewalk.

"So this is it?" he asks, his face flushed with anger as he blocks Amber's path. "If you're not here in an hour, we're just supposed to leave?"

She stares at his feet. "I'm just saying you shouldn't wait for me. You'll be fine with Jack and Fleur."

Jack squeezes my hand tight, as if he knows how close I am to launching myself out of the car.

Julio reels as if he's been punched. "What does that even mean?"

"I abandoned my mother once. I can't leave her again. Not if she needs me."

She steps around him, but he takes her by the arm.

"Don't run from this!" The wind stirs, hot and urgent. He pitches his voice low, but there's no way to avoid hearing it. "Don't run from *us*. Please. I'll go with you. I swear, I won't get in the way."

"I have to do this alone."

"Then tell me you're coming back." He searches her face for some reassurance. "What about last night? Didn't last night mean anything to you?"

358

She looks at him, into his eyes for the first time since we all woke up this morning, and a tear slides down her cheek. A lump hardens in my throat when she says, "I have to go." She backs away from him, giving him one last look before she draws her arms around herself and goes on alone.

Julio gets back in the car and slams the door. He slumps in the corner of the back seat and glares off into the distance for the next thirty minutes, not really here, lost somewhere inside his own head. I've never seen him like this. Deep worry lines cut into his face, and under them, I see the old man hiding inside him. The one who cares. The one confronting the possibility of dying alone. And every minute that goes by and Amber's not here, my heart breaks for him. For all of us.

"She'll come," I assure him. "We'll wait as long as we have to."

Julio rubs his eyes and watches the place where she disappeared down the sidewalk thirty-two minutes ago, as if by the sheer will of his longing, he can somehow bring her back.

Jack taps the steering wheel, studying the faces of pedestrians and the cars passing on the other side of the road, his head tipping to check the snap of the flag in the parking lot for shifts in the wind. I rest my head against the window, watching the filmy desert clouds move across the sky. It hardly seems real. A plane ticket to the Grand Canyon more than twenty years ago was the closest I've ever come to the desert before now. It was supposed to be my wish, my dream trip, the milestone marking the end of my life, and somehow it feels all right and all wrong that we're here, staring off into a chasm of our own dark thoughts. And just like that, I don't want to see the Grand Canyon anymore.

Gray clouds begin to gather like tumbleweeds. They roll over the sun, casting a shadow over the car. I close my eyes and take a slow deep breath, determined to rein in my mood. Jack cracks his window as Julio shifts anxiously in the back seat. The air prickles with a feeling I can't place, and I open my eyes, suddenly uneasy.

Jack rolls his window all the way down. A cool wind claws through it, thick with dust and heavy with the scent of creosote. A raindrop splatters on the windshield. Then another. The dashboard thermometer begins to fall.

"Do you see that?" Jack asks, stiffening.

Julio swears under his breath and reaches for the door handle.

I don't trust the reckless look in his eyes. "What are you doing?"

"Amber's in there alone. I'm not leaving her." The sky blackens overhead. Thunder rumbles in the distance. I throw open my door and run after him. Behind me, Jack's door slams and I hear the fast fall of his shoes on the pavement.

Julio rushes through the vestibule door. He stops dead in the center of the lobby. A gust of hot air rushes in with him, rustling papers on the receptionist's desk and throwing them end over end across the marble floor.

Julio hardly breathes as he follows the drifting papers into an empty sitting room. A broken lightbulb crackles under his foot. He weaves slowly between the overturned chairs and the shattered lamps, his shoes soft on thick rugs littered with scattered magazines and toppled brochures. The TV on the wall flashes images of tornado damage in Oklahoma and Texas.

Amber's scent is everywhere. And by the looks of the room, she wasn't alone.

Julio shakes me off, pacing like a caged tiger when I try to reassure him that we'll find her. He storms back into the lobby just as the receptionist returns. She clutches her chest, nearly dropping her phone when Julio flings open the door to a stairwell and sniffs around inside.

"I'm so sorry. In all the commotion, I didn't realize anyone had come in," she says. "What can I do for you?"

Julio ignores her, nudging his way past a man with a walker to sniff inside the open elevator doors. "She's not here," he growls. "She never even made it upstairs."

"We're looking for someone," I explain to the receptionist. "She came in about thirty minutes ago. Red hair. About my age."

"Oh, the poor dear," the woman says, pointing to the next room. "She's waiting in the . . ." Her face pales as she takes in the mess. "Oh, my. I've no idea where she went. She was just here a moment ago. By the sounds of it, she'd traveled a very long way to get here. I felt terrible, having to break the news."

Jack approaches her desk. "What news?"

"Her grandmother passed," the woman says delicately. "Less than a month ago."

Jack's eyes catch mine. We were on the boat. On our way here. Amber had no way of knowing.

"Your friend . . . she didn't take the news well," the woman says with another pained glance at the sitting room. "I was calling a nurse to come check on her, but it seems she's already gone."

"Was anyone else with her?" I ask.

"No," the woman says, fidgeting with her necklace. "As far as I could tell she was alone." The dark sky, the quick-passing storm, the ransacked room. It's possible Amber was just grieving. She could have caused all that on her own. If so, maybe she's still somewhere close. "Although I did notice a few young people loitering out front. Were they friends of yours?"

Julio stops pacing, his attention laser-focused on the receptionist.

"Do you remember what they looked like?" he asks.

She thinks for a moment. "There were two young men. One of the boys—the blond one—was handsome, if a bit intimidating. He and his friend were a little banged up. I thought maybe they were football players, as big as they are. And they were wearing patches on their jacket sleeves, like a uniform or something. There was a girl with them, with short dark hair."

"Doug," Jack mutters.

"And Denver and Lixue." I remember their three shadowy silhouettes herding me toward the building in the alley, while the fourth Guard on their team waited inside. "Noelle must have been around back."

Julio looks like he might be sick. Amber firebombed their cars and ran them off the road. I don't want to think about all the ways they'll make her suffer for it if they've caught her.

"Did you see where they went?" I ask.

"No." She looks back at the mess in the sitting room. "It was so strange. She was crying on the sofa in the lounge. I couldn't get her to say a word. I held her hand, but she was so cold, I thought she might be in shock. So I went to the office to call a nurse, and the next moment, you were here. I never even heard what was happening in the next room. It must have happened so fast. She must have been very distraught. If she had left through the lobby, I'm sure I would have seen her. She must have left through the courtyard out back."

"Thank you," I manage to say. "I'm sorry for any damage she caused."

I turn away, my mind churning over all the possible scenarios. Was she attacked here, while the receptionist was gone? Or did she wreck this room all on her own and simply walk away—from us and her own grief—before Doug and the others realized she was gone? If so, where would she go? I turn back to the receptionist. "Excuse me. Could you tell me where our friend's grandmother was buried?"

The receptionist wrings her hands. "There was no burial. Your friend's grandmother didn't name any next of kin in her living will. She requested her ashes be scattered by one of the nurses here. We had no idea she had a granddaughter, or we would have waited."

I reach for Jack's hand. Amber's mother is in the wind. Nothing left to memorialize. No place to anchor Amber's grief. She's just . . . gone.

"We have to find her." Julio's practically burning out of his skin.

"Come on," Jack whispers, steering us from the receptionist desk. "Maybe we'll pick up a scent." We follow Jack through the lounge. He pulls up short in front of the TV. Julio and I nearly trip over him as he turns toward the news ticker.

TEEN SUSPECTS IN TN ASSAULT HOLD UP BAR IN AR.
SUSPECTS LAST SPOTTED IN OK HEADING WEST ON I-40,
CONSIDERED ARMED AND DANGEROUS.

A newscaster's face fills one side of the split screen. My throat goes dry as I recognize the face on the other. Jack rushes to the TV and raises the volume.

"We have with us Dr. Michael Chronos, head of psychiatry at the private youth rehabilitation center from which he says these four teen suspects escaped just days ago. Doctor, tell us what you know about these young people." The newscaster taps his note cards on the desk and stares grimly into the camera.

Chronos's eye twinkles, the same deep shade of blue as his suit jacket and his matching patch, the thick cake of TV makeup concealing the worst of his scars. His cufflinks, two gleaming silver scythes, catch the light as he adjusts his sleeves for the camera, a clear message intended for us. He smiles through his beard, looking every bit the respectable doctor he's claiming to be. "I've known these children a long time, as long as they've been under my care. And while I believe this may have started as a game . . . a joyride, if you will . . . their misadventure seems to have spiraled out of their control. If they aren't returned to our care, more lives may very well be in danger."

"If any of our viewers have seen these young people, we encourage you to call the tip line on the bottom of the screen." A number flashes across the ticker, one Chronos will no doubt be closely monitoring. "Doctor, you told our producers you have a message for the four of them, in case they're out there watching?"

Chronos gazes deeply into the camera. "Jack. We've all made mistakes, son." He taps his eye patch with a self-effacing smile that could almost be genuine. "I'm no exception. I know how it feels, to be afraid, to make impulsive choices you can't take back. But if you don't put an end to what you've set in motion, someone's going to get hurt. Maybe one of your friends. Maybe all of them." He pauses long enough for us to recognize the threat behind the plea. To see the promise of violence under the feigned sadness of his smile. "You've made some dangerous choices, and the ice you're treading is thin. But you already know that, don't you, son?" Jack's eyes glaze white and his fists clench. "The only way to set your future back on course is to face the consequences of your actions and turn yourselves in."

A chill creeps over the room. Jack looks angry enough to trash the place all over again as he storms to the reception area. "Jack, what are you doing?"

"Excuse me," Jack asks the woman. "May I borrow your cell phone?"

She hesitates. Her eyes flick anxiously toward the television as she hands it over to him.

JACK

"Jack, don't." Fleur takes my arm before I can dial. "He'll know exactly where we are."

"His Guards were here. He already knows." I carry the phone a safe distance down the hall and punch in the tip line number. When the police operator answers, I demand to speak with Dr. Michael Chronos. The operator stalls, asking a series of questions I don't bother answering. Suddenly, the line goes silent. It begins to ring. Then clicks over as if it's been forwarded and picked up again.

"Mr. Sommers." The connection is crystal clear. As clear as the eye of his staff. He's rerouted the call, plucked it right off the police line, and dropped it onto the Observatory's secure network. "I assume you received my message."

"I have no fight with you. Whatever happened between you and Daniel Lyon's got nothing to do with us. Why can't you just let us go?"

Julio and Fleur lean close, struggling to hear.

Chronos sighs. "I can't do that, Jack. What kind of precedent would that set? Especially after that impressive display in Oklahoma yesterday. You've forced me to make an example of you. If I let your behavior go unpunished, the Observatory will be spawning lovestruck tornadoes everywhere."

"Where is she?" Julio hisses. "Ask him where his goons took Amber?"

I muffle the microphone too late. Chronos has gone quiet, listening. I can picture him on the other end of the line, sifting through my memories, contemplating the odds of our next move.

"What do you want?" I ask him.

"I would like you and your friends to surrender to my Guards for immediate Termination."

"That's not going to happen."

"Then I suppose we'll just have to see this through to the bitter end. You already know what that looks like." I grit my teeth, remembering the images Chronos was so eager to show me. "Kai Sampson has already been dispatched to find you. It's only a matter of time, Jack." The details of my death stir in the dark corners of my mind, where I've kept them hidden—Kai Sampson's piercing dark eyes, the ice cracking under me . . . But if Kai's going to kill me, she'll have to catch me first. Doug got lucky. We took a risk coming here, stopping anywhere with ties to our old lives. I won't let that happen again.

As if reading my thoughts, Chronos says, "It's too late to change the outcome, Jack. The decision that set your destiny in motion has already been made, as has mine. We've both made choices," he says, the gravel in his voice betraying some sadness. Or regret. "And I will not let mine be in vain."

"You're talking about Ananke." The line goes quiet. Lyon said Chronos killed her because he couldn't bear the idea that the future he saw in her eyes was inevitable. Because he was desperate to change it.

"I loved her, as much as you love your Fleur. And I assure you, while your commitment to saving her may seem heroic, it is flawed. In the end, those sworn to protect both of you will succumb to the burden of that oath. Your choice to place the life of that girl over your own will cost more than either of you were willing to part with when you began this journey. Your Handlers will die, as will you, Jack. Leaving your beloved Fleur alone on the battlefield to grieve for you."

"You're lying," I bite out, angling away from Julio and Fleur so they won't hear. Our Handlers are long gone. Chronos has no idea what he's talking about.

"I've seen it, Jack," he says with feigned sympathy. "But I don't need to show you your future to prove myself. Deep in your gut, you already know it's true. Otherwise, you wouldn't have insisted they leave you." I feel the blood drain from my face. "But that's of no consequence. One of them is already ill; her days are numbered. As for the other . . ." Chronos clucks his tongue. "I was surprised such a timid young man would choose to die defending you."

I disconnect, unwilling to listen anymore. I cross the lobby and set the phone down on the desk. The receptionist watches, clutching her necklace as we retreat back through the visitors' lounge.

Chronos is wrong. Chill and Poppy will be fine. Our Handlers are long gone. He's wrong about the ending.

I throw open the door to the courtyard, Julio and Fleur following close behind.

"What did he say?" Fleur asks, the second the door shuts behind us.

"He wants us to surrender." There's no point in telling her any more. It'll only upset her. We've got enough to worry about right now.

Julio spins me around. "Did he say anything about Amber?"

I shake my head. The air outside smells like creosote and hot concrete after the rain. Every trace of Amber has been washed clean away. Julio throws a fist against the brick wall, hard enough to bring tears to his eyes. Fleur wraps her hands around his bleeding knuckles, holding them fast even when he tries to pull away.

Through the window, the receptionist casts wary glances at us. She picks up the front desk phone, tucking the receiver against her shoulder as she dials. The TV screen on the wall projects an image of the bar in Arkansas, along with four artist sketches and descriptions of each of us.

"We have to go," I tell them. "The sooner we get off the grounds, away from here, the better off we'll be."

Fleur holds tightly to Julio, her voice low and soothing. "Let's go back to the car," she says. "Maybe Amber's there."

I lead them around the far wing of the building toward the street where we parked, but the sidewalk is empty. Amber's nowhere I can see or smell. We can't stay here any longer. Not while Chronos's Guards are so close.

"Now what?" Julio paces beside the car. "Where would they go? Where would they take her?"

I meet Fleur's eyes. Someone has to say it.

"What?" Julio asks, holding a thin leash on his rage. "Whatever you're thinking, spit it out, Sommers!"

"They won't take her anywhere," I say, hating myself for the stricken look on Fleur's face. "They won't risk losing us again. Their orders are to Terminate us. He won't be satisfied until we're in the wind."

Julio backs away, shaking his head. His voice breaks when he finds it. "No. She's here. I know she's still here."

A swirl of hot wind tosses loose trash over the street. Fleur reaches for him, but he won't let her touch him. I can feel her panic taking root as she watches Julio back farther away from the car.

The keys bite into my palm. "She's gone, Julio. It's not safe. We can't stay here."

Heat lightning flickers in the distance. Reflects in the tears in his eyes. He pounds his chest with his fist. "I would feel it if she were gone. I would know it!"

Fleur's eyes widen on something behind me. I look over my shoulder as a police car eases to a stop at a red light at the end of the block. "Come with us," she pleads with Julio. "We'll figure something out, but Jack's right. We have to go now."

Julio just keeps backing away, until he's standing in the center of the four-lane road, his fingers laced behind his head, eyes closed and face to the sky like he's praying. The traffic light turns green. Blue lights flash as the police car accelerates toward us.

"Get in the car, Fleur." My door is already open, one foot inside, the other cemented to the sidewalk. Fleur runs to the passenger side, gets in, and slams the door. "Julio, come on!" I holler.

The patrol car siren whoops twice. Julio spins, shocked out of his trance to see its lights accelerating toward him.

"Go!" Julio shouts. "Take Fleur and get out of here!"

The police car squeals to a stop in front of him and the officer throws open his door. Julio takes off running down the middle of the road. The cop and I lock eyes across the median. He talks into the radio on his vest, then gets back in his car, speeding after Julio with his sirens wailing.

I get in, watching Julio in the rearview mirror as I fumble with the keys and start the sedan. Another police cruiser appears in my rearview mirror. The midday sun is scorching hot, but that only makes Julio strong here. He opens up in a full-on sprint, arms and legs pumping hard as the two police cars close in on him from opposite directions. Julio races past a fire hydrant and it ruptures behind him, sending geysers of water into the air and flooding the street. The cops swerve to avoid the blast. One crashes over the median. The other chases after Julio.

Another siren wails close. With a muttered curse, I peel away from the curb. There's nothing we can do for Julio. This is what he wanted, for me to leave and protect Fleur. She cries out like part of her is dying, turning in her seat when he disappears from view. As I speed away, putting distance between us and Phoenix, she watches the sky behind us for signs of them. For the flash of lightning in the desert, or the sparkle of a lost soul.

41

LIGHT IN THE CANYON

<u>JACK</u>

Fleur and I make it to the South Rim of the Grand Canyon by late afternoon. Coming here was Fleur's wish once. Fulfilling it has been mine. But now, sitting in the middle of a crowded parking lot, watching tourists file into their cars with their maps and souvenirs through the heat waves rising off the sedan's hood, neither one of us gets out of the car. A month ago, I daydreamed about being here with her, the two of us framed by the sunrise over the canyon. About what it would feel like to kiss her with our feet dangling over the abyss. Now it just feels as if we're falling toward something we're not strong enough to climb out of. Like we're being pushed.

"I don't know about this," I tell her. There's an itch under my skin, a need to keep moving. To keep running. To get Fleur to the mountains under a high, dense canopy of trees where we'll both be stronger. But maybe that's just where Lyon wants me to go. Maybe that's exactly what Chronos expects of me.

I rub my eyes, blotting out the visions of my death. At the very least, I know I won't die here. It's too damn hot, no thin ice to fall through.

"It's just the desert getting to you. You'll feel better once the sun's down." Fleur takes my hand. Her warmth and strength take the edge off, make the heat and thirst and nerves almost tolerable. But what happens to her if this journey ends the way Chronos insists it will—if I die at the end of this road, and Fleur's left with no one?

"Amber and Julio will come. I know it," she says.

"The Grand Canyon's huge." There's too much ground to cover. The longer we stay in Arizona, the easier it will be for Chronos's Guards to find us. There are too many crowds. Too many people who've probably seen our faces on the news.

"There's only one state road in and out. Julio and Amber knew we'd planned to come here next. If they're still . . ." She shuts her eyes. Doesn't let herself speak the word *alive* out loud. "If they're still in Arizona, they'll find us."

But so might everyone else.

"One night," I remind her. This was the promise I made to her when we left Julio behind. I take her face in my hand, stroking the tracks of the silent tears she cried all the way from Phoenix. We'll give them one night to make it to the Canyon. Then I'm taking her someplace safe.

We leave the car where Amber and Julio will be sure to spot it, in the middle of a sprawling parking lot near a visitor center and a cluster of shops. Fleur draws the hood of her sweatshirt low to cover her hair. I tuck her close to my side as we veer away from the crowds, cutting through the trees on foot toward one of the waypoints along Hermit Road. The desert sun beats down on me. My legs are sluggish, my feet heavy. The trees here are short—scrubby and spare—and don't offer any relief. Fleur awakens around them. She moves through the growths of pine and fir and cottonwood, touching the woody branches of juniper and mesquite as we pass, leaving a trail for Julio and Amber to follow, assuming they're alive.

My mind twists with worry as I watch her trail her scent over the landscape, imagining all the other Seasons and Guards who could track her this same way.

I peel off my shirt and tuck it into the waistband of my jeans. The temperature's gradually falling, the evening breeze over the canyon cooling the sweat on my skin. In a few hours, night will fall over the desert, and I worry how Fleur will handle the cold, if my strength will be enough to see her through until morning, or if we'll both be too tired to be much good to each other.

We emerge from a copse of scrawny trees onto the winding road that traces the rim. Fleur draws in an awed breath. The wide red mouth of the Canyon stretches for miles. Clouds unwind themselves over crevices and gorges, the setting sun spilling watery orange light over the endless peaks. A breeze catches Fleur's hair, plucking at a memory. . . . The sun rising behind her on a mountain in early spring. Me, turning off my transmitter to be alone with her, only to wake up two months later and discover she did the same. That she held me and kept me from blowing away.

If the vision I saw in the staff is true—if every choice I've made means I drown in blood and ice for her—then Chronos is right. There is only one way this will end. Because I will never regret it. I just hope he's lying about the rest of it.

I wrap my arms around her. Maybe just to keep her close, to keep her safe while her toes tease the cliff's edge. I press my cheek to the warmth of her temple, inhaling the sweet smell of her skin and the softness of her hair as the sun shrinks down to a hot gold flash against the horizon. When the colors have all but melted from the sky, I guide her down a steep decline in the rock face, hidden from the road.

"Where will we go if they don't come? If they don't find us?" She shivers against my chest, our bodies cradled on a crag overlooking the cliff. It's the first time her faith in this place has wavered.

"Somewhere warm." I wrap my sweatshirt around her, tucking her into me as the temperature begins to fall. My mind wanders to a poster on the wall of Lyon's classroom, a landscape of trees and flowers where spring lives forever. "Somewhere you'll be safe."

"What about you?" She leans back against me, her body nestled between my legs so that every inch of us touches.

"What about me?" I don't know how to tell her that there is no safe place for me. No way to hide from what's coming for me.

"Do you remember that night on the construction site last year," she asks, "when you first told me you wanted to run away? I asked you what you wanted from all this, and you never had a chance to answer me."

I think back to that day on the mountain when she held on to me. Then to the note she left for me with Poppy—how she signed it *yours*. I think about the Guards she shredded to protect me, the night she kissed me by the pond, and last night in the hotel. I think about all those times she trusted me, believed in me, *chose* me. All along, Lyon knew. He knew that was the one thing I truly wanted more than anything else. And yet it's something I could never ask her for. Even now, after all we've been through, I won't.

Instead, I turn her face to mine, tip her head back, and kiss her, a featherlight brush of my lips.

"I love you," she says.

My heart stops, clenched around those words. She snuggles deeper into me, her warm breath puffing out in thin clouds as she falls asleep in my arms.

"I choose you," I whisper against her hair. I'll choose her, again and again, over everything else.

I stay up for a while, keeping watch, listening to the wind rustle in the quaking aspen. Watching the moon rise. I lean my head back against the rock face and close my eyes, ignoring the hard stone digging into my back, lulled by the sound of night insects, the scratch of crickets and chirping cicadas. A low buzz rises up from the canyon, rousing me from the edges of sleep. Not the soft howl of the wind or the hushed rush of the river below us. This hum feels out of place.

Like bees.

I ease out from under Fleur and crawl to a ledge, listening as the intensity of the hum builds. With a brilliant flash, a green light rises over the canyon wall. I scramble back from the drone as it rises, then falls, hovering inches in front of me.

Shielding Fleur, I crane my neck, searching the cliffs above us for the person controlling the remote. White light floods the edge, and I put my arm up to cut the glare. The drone zips closer, its searchlight swinging back and forth across us. I kick out wildly, my foot slicing the air. I kick out again, strike the edge of the drone, and send it flying.

"Fleur! Wake up!" It hums louder as it swoops down for another pass. Fleur stirs. She sits up fast, shielding her eyes when the searchlight cuts across her. "Run! Get to the trees!" I boost her to the ledge. She struggles for a fingerhold, showering me with dust. The drone buzzes close behind us as she scales the remaining feet to the road. I'm right behind her when she reaches back and drags me over the edge. Hand in hand, we run, dodging the light as we duck into the trees. They're thin and sparse, no canopy to shield us.

"Where are they coming from? Who's controlling it?" She pants, peering around a trunk.

"I don't know."

The drone hums above us, dousing us with light. Heavy footsteps close in, flashlights cutting in and out of the trees.

A voice calls out. "There! I see them!"

I reach for Fleur's hand, ready to run, but there's no time. They're too close. She plants herself in front of me, directly in the path of their lights. Her hair rises in a halo of static and the ground shudders.

She jerks her fist. The trees rustle and something heavy smacks the ground.

Someone swears Gaia's name.

A voice cries out as the drone loses control and crashes in the brush. A cat yowls. Fleur jerks her fist again. I call out her name, too late to stop her as she drives the point of the branch into the ground.

FLEUR

Woody blinks up at me, his horrified expression framed by a tangle of long hair.

He looks down at his chest, then lower, at the space just below his groin where my branch pierced the dirt. His head drops back against the ground and he exhales a tremulous sigh.

"What are you doing here?" I fall to my knees and throw my arms around him, squeezing every last ounce of breath from his lungs.

"Narrowly avoiding death, apparently," he says, working his ankles free of the creeping juniper. Marie holds Slinky a few yards off. I rush toward her, then stop myself as she backs away. We settle for an awkward wave.

Jack helps Woody to his feet. "How the hell did you find us?"

"Are you kidding?" Slinky leaps from Marie's arms, startled by her coarse laugh. "That tornado was ridiculous. It made national news."

"So did your police sketches," Woody says. "When they said you were spotted in Phoenix, we figured you might be on your way here."

I search the gaps in the trees behind them, my delirious smile withering.

"Where's Poppy?"

"And Chill?" Jack asks, still breathing hard.

Woody and Marie look past us toward the canyon, their faces falling when they realize we're alone. Woody turns away, favoring his injured leg as he recovers Chill's drone. He dusts it with his shirt, picking absently at a broken propeller.

"Chill's bringing Poppy. They'll be here soon," he says with a tight smile.

Something feels off. Why won't either of them look at me? "What's wrong?"

Marie flicks the wheel of her lighter over and over in her pocket. The look she exchanges with Woody nearly stops my heart.

"It's Poppy. She's really tired," Woody says. "She's . . . not doing so well."

Jack stiffens. "What do you mean?"

"We were right . . . about what we thought might happen," Woody says hesitantly. "Chill doesn't see so well anymore. And Marie's allergies have come back." He glances up at me, an apology glittering in his eyes. I reach for Jack.

"Poppy," I whisper. Cystic fibrosis isn't a virus or an infection. It's an aggressive, progressive disease that's rooted in her genes. I should have known it would come back. In retrospect, all the early signs seem so clear—her fatigue on the boat, the cough I thought was the start of a cold, the salty tang that clung stubbornly to her skin . . . I foolishly chalked it up to the sea air lingering in her hair and on her clothes.

This is why she didn't want to leave the Observatory. This is why she wanted me to stay and fight.

We all turn toward the sound of shuffling feet. Chill's got one of Poppy's arms slung over his shoulder, bearing her weight as they hobble toward us.

I run for her, scooping her into a hug. How can it be that we've been apart for less than a week? She's a bird, her bones light as feathers, and I'm terrified I'll break her. I bite my lip, trying not to cry, because I have already broken her just by bringing her here.

"I'm so sorry," I whisper. "I never would have agreed to go."

"I know," Poppy says, brushing a tear from my cheek.

Jack takes Chill in a bone-crushing hug. Chill hangs lopsided in his arms, holding fast to Poppy's hand. Jack releases him slowly, his gaze lingering on their laced fingers with a curious expression as Chill strokes Poppy tenderly with his thumb. I raise an eyebrow at her through my tears. Her face lights up with a goofy grin, and a choked giggle escapes me. All those late-night arguments they had through video cameras where neither one would be the first to hang up, all those stupid excuses he made for calling our room . . . How did I never notice before?

"Amber?" Woody murmurs. "Did she see her mom?"

My smile slides away. I'm too close to breaking. I can't be the one to say it.

Jack clears his throat, the words reluctant to come out. "We were too late. Her mother passed a month ago."

Woody's lips part. His Adam's apple bobs. "Where is she?"

"We don't know," Jack says gently. "Chronos's Guards were close. She never made it back to our meeting point."

The rasping wheel of Marie's lighter goes silent. She narrows her eyes at us. "Is Julio with her?"

"The cops were after us. Julio took off on foot to buy us time, and we got split up. We were hoping . . ." Jack looks back at the canyon, wearing that same unsettled expression he wore when we left the nursing home in Phoenix.

Woody sinks down onto a boulder, cradling the drone in his lap, as if his legs won't hold him up anymore. Suddenly, I'm grateful just to know where Poppy is. Grateful for whatever small amount of time I might have left with her.

"We were hoping they'd find us here," Jack says. "We planned to wait for them until morning."

"And then what?" Marie asks bitterly. "Julio takes the heat so you two can escape, and you're just going to leave him out there alone?" She mutters a string of expletives. "*If* Julio and Amber are alive, they sure as hell aren't coming here."

Woody looks up, his long, limp hair falling back from his eyes. "I hate to say it, but she's right. Amber never intended to leave Phoenix. Her only goal was to see her mother and say goodbye."

My devastation yields to anger. He's saying all the same things Jack's been saying, but that doesn't make them right. They didn't see the way Julio and Amber looked at each other. Or the way they danced. The way they kissed. "No," I say with an emphatic shake of my head. "That may have been her plan in the beginning, but you weren't with us the last few days. You didn't see them together!"

"Amber made her choice a long time ago," Woody says.

"But that wasn't Julio's! He *begged* Amber to come back. He didn't *want* to be alone." My eyes well at the memory, my throat burning with guilt. Yes, Julio was devastated. And yes, he made the choice to run rather than get in our car. But he made that choice so we could get away. So Jack and I could be safe. "Marie's right. If he's still out there, we owe it to him to find him."

"How?" Woody asks. "He could be anywhere by now."

"We can check the police station back in Phoenix," Chill suggests. "See if he's in custody."

Marie rolls her eyes, dragging a cigarette from behind her ear. "Give Julio a little credit, will you?"

"Marie's right," Jack says. "We listened to the radio for hours. The manhunt was still going on when we left town."

Woody tucks the drone under his arm and rises to his feet. "Then *we'll* have to hunt him."

"How do you suggest we do that?" Chill asks. "You just said the person most qualified for the job is in the wind."

A heavy silence falls, broken only by the hum of insects. Up until this moment, none of us has actually come out and said it. The words are gutting, the certainty of Amber's death suddenly palpable and real.

Woody clears his throat. "We follow the weather patterns. Same as before."

"That only worked because Poppy knew where Jack and Fleur were heading," Chill says. "The California coast is huge. If a weird pressure system develops, it could take hours, or even days, to get to it. We might as well throw darts at a map if we don't know exactly where he's going."

Marie scrapes the wheel of her lighter as she steps closer to our group, not quite inside it and not quite apart when she says, "I do."

42

THOSE WHO WILL LISTEN

❧⟡☙

<u>JACK</u>

Fleur leads the way to the sedan, doubling back over the scent trail she left for Julio and Amber. Woody limps along behind her, carrying the broken drone. I follow behind Poppy and Chill, my thoughts heavy as I watch them. Chronos said, in the end, Fleur will be left alone. Julio and Amber are already gone. And he was right about Poppy. What if he was right about Chill, too?

Marie lags behind all of us, the cherry of her cigarette glowing red in the dark and tainting the air with smoke. I check over my shoulder, making sure she stays close, as Slinky picks his way curiously through the brush.

The parking lot ahead is dimly lit, and I spot the SUV we stole back in Virginia parked close to our sedan. Fleur steps up her pace once we're in sight of the cars. She's anxious, distracted, clearly eager to get on the road. I run to catch up, holding her back before she gets too far ahead of us.

I have that same nagging feeling I had at the bar, as if we're not alone. Or we're being watched.

"Get down!" Marie shouts. We duck at a sharp pop. Glass rains over the parking lot as a ball of ice takes out the bulb in the nearest light post. Fleur and I reposition, sheltering our Handlers behind us.

All but one.

Marie's cigarette glows on the ground. Her hands are up in supplication, and a blade glints at her throat. The Guard is shrouded in darkness, her dark curls blowing like shadows over the patch on her shoulder.

Fleur edges closer.

"Stay back!" the Guard calls out.

Marie sucks in a sharp breath, and Fleur goes still.

I know that voice. The air prickles around Fleur as she recognizes it, too.

"Noelle?" I look past her, making sure she's alone. There's no sign of Doug or the rest of her team anywhere. "What are you doing here?"

"You're all under orders for Termination."

Fleur's hand fists at her side and I reach to still it. If Noelle had any intention of using that knife, she would have done it already.

"I want to talk to Jack. Alone," she says.

"Zero chance of that happening," Fleur growls. The air crackles with the swell of her magic. A low vibration takes hold of the parking lot, dirt and stones popping off the surface as it builds. Noelle stumbles back, dragging Marie with her. We all reach to steady ourselves as the pavement begins to splinter and a narrow crack forms, carving a clear line between Noelle and the rest of our group.

I touch Fleur's shoulder. She recoils, shaking me off with a shudder. We all turn to gape at her as the tremor stills.

"How did you do that?" Noelle asks, wide-eyed and breathless, her knife pointed at the gap in the pavement.

I don't know. By the awed looks on our Handlers' faces, neither do they. Lyon's words echo in my mind. *The longer you remain together, the more powerful you'll become.* Lyon was right. There's no way Chronos will let us walk away from this.

"I should have done it a year ago." Fleur seethes. "I should have taken that entire building down and buried you and your team with it." Every word simmers with rage, her disdain too raw to be anything but personal.

Doug was quick to take all the credit for Reconditioning Fleur. But Noelle was there. At the very least, she stood by and watched. That day I ran into her in the Crux, I assumed she felt guilty about the Termination she'd observed, or the bruises Doug gave me, or the fact that she was the one who had reported me and Fleur. It never occurred to me that she might have slipped her card key into my hand because she felt guilty about something worse.

Noelle reaches for her ear as Fleur takes a step closer, but there's nothing there. No flicker of red, no flashing light. Just the glowing stub of Marie's dying cigarette on the ground between us.

"She's not wearing a transmitter," I say, just loud enough for Fleur to hear me. "If she's here to kill us, why risk removing her tracker?" Unless she has something to say. Something she doesn't want anyone else to hear.

Noelle backs away, her grip on Marie tentative, as if she's thinking about running.

"Who else knows you're here?" I ask her.

"No one. Just me."

"If no one knows, how did you find us?"

"I followed them." Noelle jerks her chin toward our Handlers. "I've been following them since they left DC." She reaches deep into the front pocket of Marie's army jacket and tosses something across the gap between us. I snatch it out of the air by reflex, not registering what it is at first.

Hunter's transmitter. The one Julio knocked from his ear during that first battle at Croatan Beach. Marie picked it up, turned it off, and put it in her pocket. We were all so tired, so shell-shocked after Hunter died, I didn't bother to make sure she'd gotten rid of it. She's so fiercely protective of Julio, I foolishly assumed she would destroy it before we ever left the beach.

My skin hardens with frost. Marie cowers behind her veil of dark bangs. A cold wind whips across the canyon and blows them from her eyes. "We only turned it on for a few hours," she confesses. "Until we were a safe distance from the cabin. We thought you'd stand a better chance if we drew them away."

We? Chill lifts his chin. Woody meets my eyes without a shred of remorse.

That's why Doug's team never made it to the cabin. Because our Handlers drew them away. If they hadn't, we never would have survived that attack.

Marie swallows against the knife at her throat. "If we'd thought we'd be followed here, we never would have come. When we saw the tornado on the news, we figured every Guard in the country would be on their way to Oklahoma to find you. We had no idea she was tailing us. We thought we were clear."

I close my fist around Hunter's transmitter. It should be so easy to destroy the damn thing and disappear. Same as we did with the bee back in the Observatory. I should crush it under my foot, kill Noelle, and keep running. That's what we should have done with that human boy in Tennessee.

A shadowy thought twists inside me. I study Noelle's silhouette, then Fleur's. Through the static of a video feed, they could easily be mistaken in the dark. All I need is one video—one transmission of a girl's magic dispersing into a windy night sky. That's all it would take to fake Fleur's death and get rid of the one person who knows where we are.

"No one else knows you're here?" I ask, thumbing the transmitter.

She shakes her head. "I saw the tornado on TV. The one Doug and Denver were chasing. Doug said it was you, but I wanted to see for myself, to know if the rumors were true." I feel her eyes searching for mine. "Doug is determined to bring you down. He told Chronos your group was split up in Phoenix. That you and the Spring are the only ones left."

"Are we?" I ask.

"I don't know," Noelle says. "I can't be sure. I wasn't there."

Marie's eyes close. Even if Julio managed to evade the police in Phoenix, he won't survive long out there alone. Poppy rests a hand on Woody's shoulder. He swipes at his eyes.

"Chronos is coming for you, Jack. He left London this morning."

I tamp down a flutter of panic. Lyon said Chronos would only face me once he was certain of his future. Or mine. I block out the memory of Kai Sampson's face. Of falling through the ice. I block out the sound of Chronos's voice in my head, telling me Chill and Poppy are going to die. If Noelle's telling the truth, then we have a day, maybe only hours, until he reaches Arizona.

"And you? Are you coming for us, too?"

Her voice rises. It shakes as if she might cry. "I never signed on for this! Never wanted to be on a death squad, Terminating my friends."

"Are we still? Friends?" I don't know why I ask. It would be easier not to know. It's easier to hurt someone when you don't stop to ask them how they feel, or what they want. Easier to stop someone's heart if you never bother to care about what's beating inside it.

"I don't know anymore. Everything's crazy back at school since Gaia and Professor Lyon left campus to find you. Every Season you've killed and sent back . . . they're all missing."

"Good for them." And for us. The more Seasons who manage to escape, the harder Chronos will have to work to find them. Maybe Chronos will finally get tired of chasing us down.

She shakes her head, her face anguished. "You don't get it, Jack. Those Seasons didn't run away. They *disappeared*. They dropped off the ley lines without a trace. All the surveillance footage from their transmitters has been wiped from the Control Room servers. Their Handlers are missing, too."

I reel. The weight of all those lives—lives I'm somehow responsible for—nearly knocks me off my feet. The Seasons who watched us from the fields in Oklahoma, the ones who attacked us at the cabin, and Cyrus, the Summer who tried to kill Fleur at Croatan Beach . . . Chronos must be killing them. Plucking them off the ley lines before the rumors have a chance to spread.

"Seasons are rioting on campus," Noelle says. "The whole place is on lockdown. Professor Lyon said you've started a rebellion."

You have inspired them.

The ground feels like it's being pulled out from under me. Whether

I want to admit it or not, this is as much my doing as it is Lyon's. "What if he's right?" I ask in a strangled voice. "What if I did start a rebellion? Whose side are you on?"

A tear catches the moonlight as it slides down her cheek. "Does it matter? If Chronos finds out I let you go, I'll be the next one disappearing off the lines."

"Is that what you plan to do? Let us go without a fight?" If she lets us go, she might buy herself some time, and maybe a return ticket to the Observatory if she can convince them she never found us. But if they find out she left us alive, she might as well be in the wind.

"I don't suppose you'd take a Guard with you?" Noelle asks hopelessly.

Fleur stiffens. Marie's eyes find mine across the gap. I feel the added weight of Chill's and Woody's beside me.

Noelle nods, her brows pulling low as the reality of her fate sinks in.

"That manhunt in Phoenix is all over the news. Every Season in the region will be in sniffing distance soon. Go." She pushes Marie toward us. "I'll hold Doug off as long as I can, but it won't take him long to find you." Head bowed, she turns away.

Hunter's transmitter is cold in my hand. Lyon's the last person I should be taking advice from, but I can't make myself ignore it.

Win over those who will listen. Take strength from others where you can.

Which choice is right? Which choice is *mine*? Do I trust Noelle to walk away? Could I bear the responsibility of one more life?

Fleur rests her hand on my shoulder as if she knows the crushing weight it's carrying. She nods, a single shallow dip of her head.

"Noelle!" She turns, and I toss the transmitter across the gap. "I need time. A day, maybe two, to look for our friends." Fleur's eyes snap to mine. "Tell Doug about the transmitter. Tell him you've been secretly tracking our Handlers, that we've all reunited, and we're headed north. Take the transmitter as far into Utah or Wyoming as you can. Broadcast a clear signal for him to follow. Let Doug think he's chasing us. Then ditch the transmitter before his team catches up to you." I gnaw my lip, hoping like hell I'm not making a mistake. "Get rid of yours, too. Keep an eye on the weather reports in Southern California tomorrow. If you find us before we leave the state, you can come with us."

Noelle nods, slowly backing away as if she's afraid I'll change my mind. She tucks Hunter's transmitter into her pocket, then disappears like a smaze into the night.

43

TO WEATHER THE STORM

FLEUR

Jack and I make it to San Diego just after sunrise, an hour ahead of schedule, to the rapid slap of the windshield wipers and a driving rain that bounces like bullets off the hood. I can hardly see the road, and I'm forced to slow down as high waters threaten to lift my wheels from the freeway. I lost sight of the SUV in my rearview mirror miles ago. We split up to keep our Handlers safe, in case we run into any police or Guards, but now, with angry thunderheads churning in the sky, splitting up feels like a mistake.

We follow Marie's directions, exiting at La Jolla. Traffic lights flash yellow at every intersection, and cars sit abandoned along the side of the road.

I turn up the radio, maneuvering the sedan around fallen limbs and debris.

"*. . . Sustained gusts up to forty miles per hour . . . rain falling at a rate* *of a half inch per hour . . . power outages reported . . . trees down and road closures throughout the area . . ."*

I follow signs for the cove, parking as close to the beach as I can manage. Once we're out of the car, I smell Julio everywhere—in the salt spray and the rain that lashes our faces, in the ozone as lightning streaks across the sky. The surf is wild, the viewing area empty of tourists. A few surfers in wet suits run past us for shelter, carrying their boards under their arms.

Jack and I battle the wind until we reach the tip of the rocky overlook. A high tide sweeps over the cove, throwing froth over the rail. Below it, the swollen surf has reduced the beach to a narrow strip of sand.

According to Marie, this is the same stretch of surf where Julio died. His little sister had been showing off, desperate for his attention, when he accidentally collided with her board. He drowned trying to save her. A few weeks after Julio died, they pulled her off life support. The trauma of that day—the shame he's kept buried, the details he's kept carefully guarded from me—seems to roil, trapped in the seething water of the cove.

A lone haunting figure stands knee-deep in the middle of it.

Rain pours down Julio's face. The breaking waves crash around him, booming off the high stone bluff at his back. I call his name, but it's lost in the howling wind. Julio stumbles deeper into the surf. I run toward the winding concrete stairs leading down to the beach, but Jack holds me back.

"You can't go to him," he shouts over the downpour. "It's too dangerous. The wind's too strong. He doesn't know we're here."

"We have to do something! We can't just stand here—" A curtain of rain streaks sideways across the rail, stealing my breath, pushing me back. Lightning cracks close, striking a palm tree and shaking the overlook. Jack and I duck as it echoes off the bluff.

The swaying palm groans above us. We rush down the steps to escape the burning fronds as they fall, scattering sparks over our heads. Halfway down the bluff, Jack stops short. He squints down the narrow strip of beach, pointing to the far side of the cove where a figure's bent against the wind. She lurches and sways. I can't be sure if it's the wind working against her, or if she's on the brink of collapse. I swipe water from my eyes. Catch a flash of red hair whipping in the wind.

"Amber!" With a death grip on Jack's hand, I drag him behind me into the churning water at the base of the stairs. The tide pulls hard at our feet, threatening to drag us under. Holding fast to each other, we move steadily into the cove.

Amber stumbles as the water crests over her hips. She cries out as Julio wades deeper, but the wind devours every scent and sound.

Waves crash over Julio's head. Jack and I shout his name, but the storm's too loud. Too strong. It feels like we're moving in slow motion.

The next cresting wave knocks Amber off her feet. She disappears under the surge. We're not close enough. There's no way we'll reach her without being swept away.

Jack's eyes frost over. He lets go of my hand, nudging me back toward the bluff as his breath coalesces into a thick white fog and the temperature of the wind plummets. Sleet pelts the cove, ricocheting off Julio's shoulders.

Julio stiffens. He turns, his eyes narrowed at the change in the air just as Amber's head breaks the surface. He takes a shocked step toward her, but she slides under again. Julio dives, disappearing under the waves, the surf pushing him faster toward her. For a moment, I lose them in the endless gray. I clasp a hand to my mouth, gasping with relief when they both surge from the water. She grabs hold of him, choking on seawater, her arms a vise around his neck as he carries her into the shallows.

Jack and I collapse against the bluff. The wind begins to calm. The rain slows to a steady patter against the sand.

Amber and Julio stand waist-deep in the water.

Bruises dot her cheeks. Lacerations cover her arms. She lifts her hands to his face, her knuckles blistered and raw, as if she battled the world to get to him. They kiss tenderly at first, between whispers. Then deeply, their hands tangled in each other's hair, as her bruises heal and his storm begins to fade.

For a brief and shining moment, I'm not afraid of Chronos. Not afraid of Doug or the police or anything else the world might try to hurl at us. We're here, the four of us, together and alive, and the clouds above us part, making way for a sliver of sunlight.

44

OF FATE, KINGS, AND DESPERATE MEN

JACK

The waves call off their assault and the tide recedes, leaving Julio and Amber in a hazy patch of sunlight in water up to their knees, their drenched clothes pasted to their skin. I head for the stairs to give them some privacy, but Fleur won't budge. She holds me captive at her side, unwilling to let them out of her sight.

Julio holds Amber's face, looking at her between kisses as if he can't quite believe she's real. "How are you still alive? I thought the Guards found you."

She shakes her head. "I saw them coming and escaped out the back doors. They were too close. I didn't want to risk drawing them straight to you. So I led them on a wild goose chase to the other side of town. By the time I managed to find my way back, you were gone."

He brushes back her wet hair with a look of awe. "How did you know where to find me?"

"Woody told me about this place, a long time ago," she says. Julio looks away, his eyes wounded as they skate over the cove. "I figured you might come back here. That maybe you had things you needed to say." She touches his cheek, turning him gently toward her. "Crazy, huh? How the people we hurt—the ones we *love* the most—can be the hardest to face."

He pulls her against his chest. "I'm sorry you didn't have the chance to say goodbye to your mom."

Her eyes shine with tears. "That wasn't the goodbye I regretted most."

Fleur rests her head on my shoulder as Julio leans in for another kiss. "I told you we would find them," she whispers.

"Get a room!"

Our attention snaps to the top of the bluff. Julio and Amber break into wide smiles when they spot Chill and Poppy waving from the ledge above us. Amber squeals, erupting in fresh tears when Woody appears beside them.

Marie juts her chin at Julio. She flicks the ash from her cigarette and blows a ribbon of smoke out through her nose. "You owe me ten dollars."

He squints up at her with a crooked grin. "What for?"

"The bet we made in eighty-nine. I told you if you kept bottling everything up, you were eventually gonna pop. And *that*," she says, leveling her cigarette at the cove, "was the most ridiculous tantrum ever."

"Just making it easy for you to find me."

"Me and everyone else."

Woody hobbles down the stairs, clutching the rail, his long hair bouncing behind him. Chill guides Poppy down after him, one slow step at a time, pointing out a sea lion and the cormorants and pelicans and gulls that have begun to appear on the rocky shoreline. When they finally reach us, the sun's so bright, it stings my cheeks. It's hard to believe it's only been a week since we were last all together. Despite what Chronos said, we're all here, all alive, because of the choices we made. Because we were willing to take risks for each other. Maybe Lyon was right. Maybe we can change the ending.

"Where'd you crazy kids disappear off to?" Amber asks them.

Chill counts off on his fingers. "We did the whole Smithsonian, Air and Space, the International Spy Museum, all the monuments—"

"Whoa, whoa, whoa." Julio flashes the time-out sign. "What happened to lying low and staying off the grid?"

Poppy flashes me a conspiratorial smile. "We took a few lessons from Jack. Hiding out in DC isn't as hard as you'd think."

I grin down at Fleur. "That depends on who's looking for you."

Her laugh is contagious. Between the subway system, the crowds, and all the tight security, our Handlers must have run Doug's team ragged for days.

"I even found my brother." We all fall silent at Woody's quiet confession.

Fleur's laughter dies. Julio, Fleur, and I exchange grave looks. Taking Amber to see her elderly mother was one thing. But none of us needs a boundary map to understand why reentering the lives of your friends and family after being presumed dead for fifty years is a terrible idea.

Woody withdraws a notebook from his backpack. Tucked carefully inside is a sheet of tracing paper shaded in pencil lead. He passes Amber the rubbing of a soldier's name.

She wipes a tear from her eye before passing it back. "It's beautiful, Woody. I'm glad you found him."

Marie appears at the foot of the stairs, the telltale rattle of her dog tags muffled behind Slinky's fur. She and Woody exchange a smile that seems to bridge the distance between them. "We went to Arlington National Cemetery, too," Woody says. "To visit Marie's dad."

Julio takes Marie in a bear hug, whispering something that sounds like an apology as he musses her hair.

"You're such an idiot," she says, swiping her eyes. "I was afraid you were dead."

Fear . . . the word parks itself at the front of my mind, the effect compounded by the sharp sudden sense that something's wrong. Fleur's hand becomes tense in mine. Julio's and Amber's smiles fall, their bodies shifting, as if unconsciously, closer to their Handlers. I lift my gaze to the top of the bluff, but the offshore breeze does me no good here. We're low. Trapped. Vulnerable.

"We should go." I lead Fleur and the others to the steps.

Only we're not alone.

Noelle stands on the overlook at the top of the stairs, her dark curls blowing around her face. She's not wearing her jacket. There's no patch. No transmitter light in her ear.

A hot wind whips over the cove, and a spark crackles to life behind me. I hold up a hand, sensing the threat of Julio's magic in the sudden roar of the surf.

I told Noelle exactly where to look for us. I shouldn't be surprised that she's here, but that doesn't mean I trust her. "Are you alone?"

Two Winters appear at her side: Gabriel and Yukio. It's far too early for either of them to be outside the Observatory. What the hell are they doing here?

Amber's fire swells with a hiss, and breakers build behind the overlook. Julio slams one over the rail, startling them all. Six more shadows creep over the edge of the bluff. We're surrounded.

Fleur clenches her fist. The ground shudders. A crack forms in the concrete stairway, zigzagging up the treads and risers until it reaches Noelle's feet. Our Handlers jump back as the cliff face rattles, shale and dust raining down over the bluff. A Season above us yelps, losing her footing as the ledge crumbles under her. Another reaches to catch her, hoisting her back to solid ground. They back away from the edge, looking to Noelle for direction.

I can't believe I was so stupid. I should never have trusted her. "Did you bring Doug and Denver, too?" I call up to her.

"No!" She looks stung. "You told me to go north. I lured Doug and the others to Utah, and that's exactly where I left them."

"Then who the hell are *they*?" I gesture to the bluff.

"They want to come, too," she says. "All of us . . ." Noelle looks to each of them, as if giving them one last chance to bow out. "We want to go with you."

Last time I saw Gabriel and Yukio, they were hurling snowballs, waving me over to their table in the mess hall. Now they look scared, exhausted. Noelle must have pulled some strings to get them out, but this climate isn't doing them any favors.

"They're not wearing transmitters," Marie says in a low voice. "I don't think this is a setup. I think she's telling the truth."

Amber's fire gutters. "I recognize some of the Autumns," she says. "Two of them were in the fields watching us when we made the tornado. They must have survived the storm."

Julio squints up at the ledge. "I count three Summers on that bluff. If they wanted us dead, they would have drowned us by now."

"No." I rake my hands through my hair, kicking at the sand. "I am not starting a homeless shelter for lost Seasons. I'm not taking responsibility for that."

"You wanted a rebellion!" Noelle shouts, tears welling in her eyes. "I brought you an army. What more do you want?"

Fleur takes me aside. "Maybe we should think about it," she says. "There's strength in numbers. We can't keep running, Jack. At some point, we're going to have to fight." At my weary sigh, she turns to Noelle. "Stand back. We're coming up."

Noelle and the other Seasons keep their distance as we climb the stairs to the overlook. Gabriel and Yukio give me uncertain smiles as I brush past them. The coast is littered with fallen branches, the roads and parking lots awash in mud, devoid of cars except the ones abandoned during the storm. Amber, Julio, Fleur, and I huddle close around our Handlers. The other Seasons break into clusters, Winters with Winters, Summers and Autumns standing apart, and a lone Spring standing off on her own, all of them a cautious distance from us. Like all the other Seasons who've hunted us since we left the Observatory, they must have used Chronos's bounty as an excuse to leave their assigned territories while they were released for their hunts. Now they're defectors. I don't see a single transmitter light among them, and I can't help wondering about their Handlers—what will happen to them when Chronos returns to the Observatory and discovers what their Seasons have done. As I look around at their expectant faces, their misplaced faith in me feels staggering.

"We'll need to move fast," Noelle says, approaching our group. "Chronos is on his way to Utah to rendezvous with Doug. When they realize you're not there, they'll come after us. He's only dispatched five teams. He won't risk sending any more and leaving the Observatory unstaffed. We're outnumbered, but not by much. So what's the plan?"

"Plan?" I choke out a laugh. "What plan? There is no plan." My only plan was to run. To hide. I never intended to lead an army. Never intended to take responsibility for the lives of these Seasons or their Handlers back at the Observatory. I never intended to fight. The thought of facing off against Chronos and twenty of his Guards sends a shudder of fear straight through me.

Fear . . . There's that word again. It wedges itself stubbornly in my mind, dislodging a memory.

Fear of death doesn't make you any less of a man, Lyon said. *If anything, it makes you more of one.*

"Fear of death . . . That's the answer." It's only when the others turn with quizzical looks that I realize I've said it out loud. "Lyon was right. Chronos is *afraid*. That's why he didn't come after us himself, not until he believed we were divided and vulnerable. Because he was terrified of the same thing we are." I think back to the Termination Chill, Noelle, and I witnessed, how Chronos insisted on having his personal Guard in the room. Noelle wasn't at his side to satisfy Chronos's vanity. She was there because Chronos was too smart to risk being in a roomful of Seasons alone.

And Gaia was *afraid*, terrified, when Chronos held his scythe to her throat. *If you will not maintain order in my house, then you will find yourself replaced as easily as your pets.*

"They can be killed," I whisper, certain I'm right.

"Is that even possible?" Julio asks.

Noelle's eyes light. "Chronos killed Ananke. It must be possible."

"You can't kill *time*." Amber looks between us like we're crazy. "What would happen to the world? To the universe?"

Poppy steps forward, resting her weight on Chill's arm. "Chronos *isn't* time. He's the embodiment of it. The same as you all aren't really seasons and Gaia's not really the earth. You only wield its magic. You're vessels."

And vessels can be replaced.

. . . few of us use our given names here.

"His name was Michael," I say in a low voice, my mind spinning back to my conversation with Lyon in his office. The other Seasons dart wary glances at one another, as if maybe I'm losing my mind. "He was someone else once, just like we were. Chronos isn't a name; it's a title. And titles can be handed down. If we're replaceable, then it stands to reason Chronos and Gaia are, too." I think about the paintings in the corridor to the Control Room. How in every image, Chronos was depicted slightly differently. The image of one horrible painting comes crashing to my mind, the Titan Cronos devouring his son's heart because he feared his children would one day overthrow him. How many Chronoses have there been throughout time? How many Gaias?

"How do we do it?" There's a rabid hunger in Julio's eyes. "How do we kill him?"

I look to our Handlers. Analyzing vulnerabilities, ferreting out weaknesses . . . these are *their* strengths. But this isn't an enemy any of us have battled before.

"Gaia's magic comes from the earth," Poppy says. "It's why she built the Observatory underground. As long as she's touching it, she can control it. Chronos's magic must come from something, too. Something he touches."

"His staff," Noelle says. "I've never seen him without it."

Suddenly, it's as if the crystal itself is right here in front of me, light streaming through every facet of Lyon's plan. "That must be what Lyon's after. If Lyon possessed the Staff of Time, he could assume the throne." He'd live forever and recover his teeth. This must be the ending he envisioned all along, the happy ending to his story with Gaia. "If Lyon made the rules, he could eliminate the systems Michael put in place."

Hope shines in Fleur's eyes. "We could all be together. Stay together. Poppy, too."

Chill draws himself up, his focus sharpening. "Lyon's been using us long enough. It's about time we get something out of this."

"Using us for what?" Marie flicks the wheel of her lighter as she thinks. "If Gaia's so powerful and Lyon's so smart, what did they need us for?" She frowns at the ground, like she hasn't figured it out. But Marie, of all people, should know.

"We're a diversion," I answer. "Just like you and Hunter's transmitter. You wore it to draw away Chronos's Guards so we could escape the cabin without being noticed." All this time, we were a beacon, a flashy distraction in the eye of the staff to keep Chronos from looking too deeply into Lyon's own mind—a mind Chronos no longer considered dangerous once he'd plucked out Lyon's teeth. "Lyon used us to draw out Chronos's Guard and thin the herd. He knew Chronos would eventually be forced to leave the Observatory and come after us himself, making him vulnerable to attack."

"He's staging an ambush," Woody says, thinking aloud. "And we're the bait."

"Georgia Avenue. The Red Line Station," Fleur whispers. The others look perplexed, but I know exactly what she's remembering—our last hunt. I'd drawn Fleur into the city, rather than the mountains, making her weakness my strength. I'd left bread crumbs—the lilies and the notes and the maps—forcing her to stop and think so she wouldn't follow too closely, giving me time to stay one step ahead of her. I led her underground to a subway, disabling communication and limiting her escape routes. When we finally came face-to-face, I was careful to place a barrier between us. "It was the perfect setup," she says. There's a scheming twinkle in her eye. "We've been hunted so long, we almost forgot what it feels like to be the hunters. "We leave him a clear trail to follow, but enough mess to slow him down. Then we position ourselves off the grid, claim the high ground, and wait. We play to our strengths, pick off his Guards, and hope Lyon and Gaia get there in time."

"How will they know where to find us?" Julio asks.

"He knows." My throat closes around the words. Lyon knows where we're going. He's known all along. I recall every cryptic piece of advice the man's ever offered me—every word of encouragement, every thoughtful nudge . . .

. . . *when you and Fleur have traveled this road as far as you can alone . . . go to that place you hold in your heart. The strength you need will find you.*

But he meant *he* would find us. He and Gaia. All this time, I should have known my choice of destination was never entirely my own. It was a seed he'd planted deep within me, long ago—a thoughtfully placed picture on his office wall. All those years I'd stared at that poster, day-dreaming about Fleur. All I needed was a reason to save her and a shove out the door. He knew exactly where I'd end up.

Fear not, young lion . . . you hold eternal spring in your heart.

Cuernavaca. The City of Eternal Spring.

I look around me, at my friends. At our Handlers. At this ragtag army that's fallen into my lap. They're all watching me, waiting for me to come up with a plan. To make the right choice.

"We'll need a map of Mexico," I tell them. "We're going someplace warm."

We unload our packs from the sedan. Anything we can't carry on our backs goes into the trash cans beside the public bathhouse. Noelle and the other eight Seasons wait for us, forming a caravan of three more cars down the street.

Julio unzips his guitar bag, his fingers barring the strings to keep them silent as he pulls the instrument from its case. A vagrant sits bare-foot on the ground under the shelter of the bathhouse. He watches us through the threads of his dirty wet hair with the piercing eyes of a crow.

Julio sets his guitar in the man's lap, wrapping the strap around the man's shoulder. The old man stares down at the strings as if he's not quite sure what to do with it. I fight the urge to pluck it out of his hands. To tell Julio we'll all take turns carrying it. It's hard to watch him walk away from the one thing he refused to part with when he started this journey, a thing that brought us peace on our hardest days, when it was easier to speak through song lyrics than to struggle to find the right words of our own. But looking at Julio now, his hand in Amber's and Marie close by his side, I decide maybe the guitar wasn't the one thing he really needed after all.

I toss the car keys to Chill. He nearly drops them, catching them clumsily against his body. He squints at them for a moment before placing them in Woody's hand.

"It's okay. Woody can drive." Chill takes off his glasses, wrapping his fingers around the holes where the lenses should be. He taps the glasses against his palm, and with a reassuring nod to himself, he dumps them in the trash along with all the other unnecessary things we're ready to leave behind. "Let's get out of here. I want to see as much of Mexico as I can before Chronos comes to kick our asses." He helps Poppy into the back seat of the SUV and climbs in behind her.

I bite my lip as I watch them, hoping I'm not making a mistake. Our survival depends on so many choices—choices we can only make in the moment, from our hearts—in order for this plan to work. As I look out over the Pacific, every doubt and second thought glares back at me. We could steal a boat. Keep running. But it would feel too much like going back to the beginning. And we've already come so far.

The other three cars fall in behind our SUV, waiting for me.

"You ready?" Woody asks, spinning the keys on his finger. Hunter's combat knife hangs from the belt loop of his jeans.

I shake my head at the improbability of it all. We're waging war against Father Time. It's hard to imagine any ending to this story that isn't a tragedy. We're probably all going to die. Maybe, if I'm lucky, just me.

"Yeah," I say. "I'm ready."

45

BORDER CROSSING

FLEUR

Our caravan reaches the border crossing at Tecate by midmorning. The eight members of our original group lead in the SUV, followed closely by Noelle's group of nine. They've segregated themselves into vehicles by season, with the exception of the lone Spring, who reluctantly agreed to ride in the back seat of the Autumns' car.

Jack watches them in the passenger-side mirror, the furrow in his brow teetering between worry and distrust. He's been quiet since we left the coast. Every few miles, I reach over his headrest and touch him—a reassuring hand on the cool nape of his neck—letting him borrow whatever strength he needs from me. Getting across the border won't be easy. Four of us are wanted in three US states. The other four don't have passports, or any other legal form of identification, for that matter. And now we have nine more to worry about.

Woody eases the SUV into a parking space. Jack watches people shuffle in and out of the immigration offices, carrying passports and customs declaration papers. Armed border guards patrol the vehicle inspection lanes with telescoping mirrors and drug-sniffing dogs.

Julio gets out of the car with Amber in tow, her bright hair tucked into a baseball cap and dark dollar-store sunglasses obscuring her eyes. He pauses to ask a border guard for directions to the bathrooms, sliding effortlessly into Spanish while Amber's attention drifts to the junction boxes powering the building's computers and phones.

"Everyone ready?" Jack's eyes slide to Noelle's group in the mirror. They're already out of their cars, clustered in the parking lot, waiting for our signal. We strap on our backpacks and huddle close to the doors.

Julio thanks the guard for his help. He follows Amber behind the building toward a row of portable toilets, glancing back at us with a barely perceptible nod.

Jack and I get out of the SUV. He slips his hands in mine and seductively backs me against the door until we're eye to eye. The handful of random travelers in the parking lot obligingly look away. But I can't tear my eyes from them.

"Ready?" he asks, his forehead pressed to mine.

"There are too many people. What if I can't control it? What if I'm not strong enough?"

"*We're* strong enough." The kiss he steals doesn't feel staged. Doesn't feel like it's for anyone but me.

I nod. Then I close my eyes and let my mind reach through the pavement. I feel it snake into the ground, through rhizomes and roots, into a capillary network of cells. Then deeper, into the earth itself. My body trembles with the effort. Jack braces me against the hot metal of the door as I shove my mind into a narrow fault line and push.

The ground responds with a series of low tremors. Concrete dust sheds from the arched overhang of the immigration building. Bits of debris pepper the ground. Sweat trails down my neck as I stretch my mind, widening the rift. The SUV begins to sway as the asphalt shakes.

I hear the sharp intake of breaths. Hear the scramble of feet as people retreat into their cars. I feel the pavement crack and splinter, every movement of the quake echoing in the fibers of my own body. A fissure splits the sidewalk. The jagged line creeps past the immigration building through the entry ports, then under the electronic gates.

"That's it," Jack says low in my ear as the crack turns, stretching across the highway. "Just a little more." The windows of the immigration building rattle. Shouts ring out.

There's a hiss and pop as Amber and Julio blow the electrical transformers. The wind carries the scent of smoke. Boots pound the pavement, border guards calling out orders as they rush toward the fire.

Jack's voice grows urgent. "More, Fleur."

I keep pushing. Grit my teeth as the earth stretches and tears. Jack catches me as I slide down the side of the car.

"Now!" he shouts.

Suddenly, I'm on my feet, one arm slung around him. Noelle and the others, all of us running, not away from the chaos, but toward it. Border patrol officers disappear into the building, shouting *"¡Terremoto!"* and calling for *bomberos* into their radios. We duck under the collapsing archway, dodging cracks in the ground.

Amber and Julio shout from the other side of the gates, waving us on. A sinkhole opens behind them, the ground devouring itself in increasingly large bites. I grope for the falling pieces with my mind, desperate to put them back, but it feels like I'm grasping for an animal that's slipped its leash.

"We're good, Fleur!" Julio shouts when we catch up to him. "You can turn it off now!"

"I can't! I can't hold it!" The ground shudders all on its own, splitting the road ahead of us.

"Not good!" Julio swerves to avoid the growing crack. We all back away as it moves past us over the highway, eating pavement and belching dust, severing us from our escape route.

"We have to cross now, before it's too wide to jump! Go!" Jack shouts.

Julio and Amber sprint toward it. They launch themselves into the air and land hard on the other side. Noelle leaps next, turning back to extend a hand to Yukio and Gabriel as they jump. The other Seasons are quick to follow.

Julio and Amber shout at our Handlers to hurry. Behind us, electrical wires hiss and spark and another archway collapses. Sirens wail from both sides of the border.

The fissure is jagged, as deep as I saw it in my mind. Marie and Woody take a running leap, the weight of their backpacks propelling them to their knees on the other side. Chill holds Poppy around her waist, close to the edge. It's already too late, the fissure's too wide. There's no way they'll make it across together.

The other Seasons watch as Marie and Woody stretch their hands over the gap, calling for Chill and Poppy to throw their packs. Chill slides them off and hurls them across as Amber and Julio lean over the crack.

"We'll catch you," they shout. "Hurry, Poppy!"

"Don't worry," Chill says. "I won't let go."

They jump. My breath catches on a silent scream when Poppy's feet land short, one hand still clinging to Chill's, one grabbing blindly for Julio's outstretched fingers as she slides down the wall of the fissure. Noelle reaches down, catching her under her arms. Her eyes find mine across the rift as she hauls Poppy to her feet.

"We go together, on three." Jack takes my hand and counts us down. Our feet push off the precipice and we jump, propelled across the gap by a blast behind us as the immigration building's windows blow out and the structure is engulfed by fire. Amber and Julio drag us off the ground, running toward a hole in a chain-link fence. No one notices as our group slips among the cars parked inside it.

Crouching low, Julio assesses the lot, guiding us to a Winnebago that looks older than all of us. I squat against the side of it, willing the earth to settle as Jack picks the locks. We all file in. Julio climbs into the driver's seat and reaches under the dash. He strips a few wires, pinching them together in one hand. Then he reaches across the console with a crooked grin at Jack.

Jack chokes out a laugh. He slaps a palm into Julio's outstretched hand. With a spark and a sputter, the van's engine turns over, and the border disappears in a cloud of smoke behind us.

46

DUST TO DUST

<u>JACK</u>

The Sonoran Desert is brutal in the daylight. The Winnebago's window tinting is a weak shield against the sun's daggers, and the AC only manages to blow more hot, dry air through the vents. The hazy peaks on the horizon feel like a mirage, slipping farther into the distance the longer we drive. I lick my parched lips at the sight of them. Would give anything to stick my bare feet in a cold mountain stream or lie naked for one minute in a bed of snow. But these aren't the mountains I'm used to. They're jagged and bare as bone, cutting up through flat, fiery landscapes dotted with yellow grass and thorny scrub.

Julio drives the first leg of the trip. Mostly because he's more awake than the rest of us. The climate favors him, makes him nod his head and hum along to the *ranchera* music on the radio. I lay mine back and try to rest, but I'm kept awake, unable to ignore the familiar disquieting cough that's started somewhere in the back of the camper. I turn in my seat.

Gabriel and Yukio slump beside each other on the floor, hugging their knees. Their skin's flushed, their eyes glassy, wary as they watch the Autumns huddled on the far side of the cab. According to the map we picked up at a gas station south of Tecate, we have at least thirty hours of driving ahead of us, a third of it through Sonora.

"Oh, for Chronos's sake," Amber grumbles, holding the back of a chair for balance as she surveys the lot of them. "You," she says, pointing to the row of Summers taking up the length of the couch. One of them yelps as she grabs him by the elbow. "Don't be such a baby. It doesn't hurt." She shoves him into the tight gap between Gabriel and Yukio. Their eyes widen as their skin brushes.

I turn back to the road, drifting in and out of a hazy sleep as the coughs quiet. Every few hours the terrain changes and the air smells different, pungent oils of parched vegetation and dust giving way to the smoke of carne asada vendors in passing towns, then to sage as night falls.

"Smell that?" Julio asks just after dusk, one arm draped out the RV's open window. The sky's swirled with lavender and gray, our headlights catching the dark flash of bats swooping over the highway. A mile marker puts us about an hour north of Hermosillo. I take a deep breath. Catch a hint of something sweet.

"What is it?"

"Cactus flowers," he says, frowning at the road ahead of us. "I haven't smelled saguaro flowers since I was a kid."

"So?"

"They don't bloom this time of year." Julio turns off the radio, plunging the RV into silence.

The perfume grows stronger, the cab filling with the scent of pollen and the chorus of insects along the side of the road. Our headlights drill a tunnel through the dark. At the end of their reach, a shadow cuts across the highway.

Julio slams on the brakes. Our tires squeal, kicking up smoke as we skid to a stop. Jolted awake, the Seasons in the back of the RV scramble forward to see over the front seats.

Fifty feet in front of us, a van's parked sideways across the road.

"They're Summers," Fleur says, peering over my shoulder. "Maybe Julio should try talking to them first."

Two figures throw open the van doors and get out. They stand in the path of our headlights, brandishing weapons. Transmitter lights blink behind their ears.

"Okay, maybe no talking," Fleur says.

"There are only two of them." Julio cracks open a water bottle and takes a swig as he sizes them up. He wipes his mouth with the back of his hand and caps the bottle. "Amber and I can take them. You all stay here."

"Yeah, right," I mutter as I follow Fleur out of the RV after them.

The roadside is barren. The vegetation, sparse. I have that same exposed feeling I had back in Arizona. The asphalt's scorching, the rising heat waves carrying all my strength with them. I stay close to the hood so I'll have something to grab if I fall over.

Julio stands between the RV and the van, his water bottle dangling from his fingers. *"¿Qué onda?"*

"I speak English, asshole." The driver squints against our headlights. He's fidgety, nervous. All cables and wires, as if Gaia caught him in a growth spurt, with a sinewy attitude to match. His friend carries more weight, broad in the shoulders but soft in the middle, with doughy cheeks.

"Fine. In English, then," Julio says, with a baiting degree of sarcasm. "How about you get the fuck out of our way. You're hogging the road."

The back door of the van slides open and four more Summers get out, all six of them in peak. They carry weapons—pipes, chains, and knives. Julio tenses as the driver tests his blade against the pad of his thumb. "Chronos is offering an automatic relocation for the Season who brings you down. And that's exactly what I plan to do. I'm going home." The word *home* comes out on a quiver, and I feel a stab of pity for the kid.

"Where's home?" I ask him.

His nostrils flare as he drags his eyes from Julio. I can't tell if he's pissed off or fighting back tears. "Houston," he says with a disdainful curl of his lip.

I reach for the RV's hood, fighting a wave of dizziness that's only made worse by the engine's heat. "You don't need to kill us for that. You can just go. We won't stop you."

He shakes his head like I'm crazy. "And spend the rest of my short life running from Chronos? No thanks. It'd be easier just to kill you."

He advances toward Julio, then falters midstride. His friends' eyes widen behind him. I turn to see the rest of our group spilling out of the RV, a circle of Seasons and Handlers fanning out around us—all thirteen of them. Gabriel's got his arms around a Summer boy. Another holds Yukio up. They acknowledge me with nods as they position themselves behind me.

For a split second I'm numb, transported in time, paralyzed on that same mountain pass I died on thirty years ago. Only this time, I'm not alone.

The driver of the van backs up a step, turning his knife over and over in his hand, his eyes assessing our group—our weak Winters, our vulnerable Handlers, our obvious lack of weapons.

Without warning, he lunges. Amber throws her fireball but misses, hurling it past him across the highway. With a deafening explosion, it slams into their van. I drop to my knees, shielding my face from the searing heat as a plume of black smoke spews from the hood. Windswept flames lick across the pavement. I shake my head to clear the soot from my eyes. All around me is shouting, the scuffle of feet. Coughing and fighting. I choke into my sleeve. Can't see anything through the glare of smoke against the headlights. I set off through the haze, calling Fleur's name.

A fist swings through the dusky air. It smacks into my jaw with a dizzying force. I draw back, dodging the next two hits, my ears peeled for the sound of Fleur's voice. All I hear are the smack of fists hitting flesh and the clatter of chains. A red light cuts through the smoke as a Summer charges me. I drop low, using his own momentum to throw him over my shoulder, sending him tumbling behind me.

I follow the sounds of fighting. The wind shifts, the smoke thinning with it. Through it, I spot a flash of red hair. Amber feints, dodging the driver's knife. Over the roar of the fire, I hear Woody shout her name.

"Woody, no!" He dashes into the thick of the fight. With a feral yell, he swings his combat knife down. Amber's attacker falls. His magic flares, condensing into a blinding ball and surging toward a ley line.

The fighting stops as we all shield our eyes from the glare. From the image it illuminates.

Woody's mouth parts.

He drops to his knees at Amber's side. Her lip trembles as he collapses against her. Stunned, we all gape at the knife in Woody's back.

The wind dies, the air suddenly too thin to breathe. The car fire crackles and hisses. It's the only sound as Amber brushes the hair back from Woody's eyes. All the light in them disappears.

The Summer boy who stabbed him watches expectantly, as if he's waiting for some glimmer of magic to take Woody home. But Woody doesn't fade. Doesn't float away neatly into the night. The Summers who attacked us fall back, staring openmouthed at his sagging body as Noelle's group surrounds them.

Tears stream down Amber's smoke-blackened cheeks as she eases Woody to the ground. My mouth goes dry, angry tears pushing to the surface as she kisses his forehead and closes his eyes.

"He's not magic," the Summer boy says, his soft cheeks slack with surprise. He backs away slowly, as if only just realizing what he's done. "He's not one of us."

"He *is* one of us!" Julio snatches the boy by the collar and slams him to the ground. Amber scrapes up Woody's combat knife and holds it against the Summer's throat. Her other hand claws savagely at his ear, at his transmitter.

"Amber, no!" My vision clears as I realize what she's trying to do. Another pile of ashes won't replace the life she's lost. We've left too many behind us already. The kid's shadow will haunt her as much as all the others. Even Woody's. "This won't bring him back. Woody wouldn't want this."

Fire rages against the tears in her eyes. The knife clatters to the pavement. Julio gathers her to him as she falls, whispering into her hair as she curls in on herself and sobs.

Fleur steps into my embrace, her body cold with shock. Chill and Poppy hold each other, their tears steady and silent. Marie sits alone at

Woody's side. I barely register the five flashes of light that soar off into the desert as our enemies are quietly dispatched by Noelle and the others. They circle around us, their faces pained in the firelight, Summers beside Autumns, Winters beside the Spring, shielding us as we try to find the words to say goodbye.

Chill, Julio, and I carry Woody's body behind a rocky desert hillside far off the road. Marie walks with Poppy. Fleur guides Amber, her arm draped protectively around her shoulders. The other Seasons watch from a distance as Fleur erects a pyre. Using her magic to summon the roots of the surrounding brush to the surface, she weaves them into a bed strong enough to hold Woody's thin frame. Stone-faced and broken, Amber conjures a spark. The fire catches too quickly. Burns too brightly. Hurts too deeply. Huddled together as the desert grows cold, we stand vigil over his body through the night.

When the sun rises, the fire is out, his ashes gone, taken by the wind.

47

WHEN ALL SEEMS LOST

FLEUR

I awaken, I don't know how many hours later. My forehead smacks the window as the Winnebago bounces around sharp curves and hairpin switchbacks, eventually turning off onto a pitted dirt road.

"We'll hike in. Set up camp," Jack tells Julio. The other Seasons stir, lifting their heads from each other's shoulders as they rouse from sleep.

I stretch stiffly, struggling to make out anything through the dust and grime on the windows. "Where are we?"

"We're here," Jack says, as if that answers anything. Or maybe everything.

Julio parks the Winnebago beside a copse of trees. The other Seasons throw open the door of the RV, anxious to set foot on stationary ground. There's no exhaust on the air. No drone of traffic anywhere close. I climb down after them, breathing in a cool breeze dense with the scent of cedar and fern. We seem to be in some kind of park. Pine-capped mountains rise up around an emerald valley dotted with picnic areas and trail signs. Jack stares at the gleaming lake in its center, one foot still perched inside the RV.

"It's beautiful," I murmur, brushing the air as I walk, feeling the power of this place. The soil pulses and the air hums. Every snaking root, every dewy fiddlehead, every mat of lichens and floating algae speaks to me. I haven't felt this alive since our kiss at the mountain pond. Haven't felt this strong since my last spring.

Jack climbs down from the cab and shuts the door. "It suits you," he says, but the words feel tinged with worry.

"Where are we? I thought we were going to Mexico City." I've lost all sense of place and time. This could easily be Appalachia, late March, back at Jack's mountain, if it weren't for the thinness of the air. I'm almost dizzy with it.

"We're not far. About an hour south of it," Jack says.

Julio shrugs into a jacket, pale and a little peaked. "It's hard to breathe."

"It's the elevation," Jack says. "We're at 9,500 feet. The effects will pass in a few hours."

I dart an anxious glance at Poppy, listening to her labored breaths. Her face is pale, her lips faintly blue. Jack rests a hand on her shoulder. He juts his chin toward a high ridge above the lake. "Think you can make it?" There's a playful challenge in his eyes, but under it I sense his unease. When she nods, Jack hauls our gear from the storage compartments under the RV. He pauses over Woody's backpack, wincing as he unzips it to divide the contents among us—waterproof matches, batteries, a first-aid kit, and a few canned goods—taking only what we can use. He hands me Poppy's pack without meeting my eyes. "We should get moving. Make camp before dark."

Jack starts hiking, his shoulders weighed down with gear, casting brief sideways glances at the lake as we walk. I feel the rest of our group fall in behind us, their steps heavy against the earth as we wind through the valley, then up a steep footpath into the woods. Curious, I explore the flora as we hike, slipping my mind into the curling ferns and oaks, pausing over the strange exotic flowers and fungi I've never seen. A rabbit darts into the underbrush. I look to the limbs of the trees, desperate for signs of a crow, or even a smaze—for any sign of Gaia. Bees hover close to the flowers, but none look like the ones that inhabited the walls of the Observatory. By now, Chronos and his Guards must have heard about the quake at the border. They'll have seen reports of our confrontation with the Summers in the desert. It's only a matter of days, or even hours, before Chronos finds us, but how long until Lyon gets here?

Jack seeks out the high ground, dropping his pack on the mountain face overlooking the lake. The densely wooded ledge offers a distant but clear view of the road. A handful of taillights gleam red as the last of the cars abandon the park before sunset.

Filthy and exhausted, we throw off our gear in piles beside Jack's, bending over our knees to catch our breath. Chill's last to crest the hill, carrying Poppy on his back. Her skin's a sickly shade of gray as he eases her down onto a log to rest.

I stand close as Jack pulls Noelle and Julio aside. "Our group will take the eastern slope. We'll be able to see Chronos coming from here. Noelle's team can cover the southern slope tonight. They'll be safer there." He checks his watch. Signals for Marie to join them. He juts his chin at Noelle's sagging, ragtag group. "They'll need practice working together, fighting in pairs. There's a clearing just over the ridge—a good place to set up camp. We've got a few hours before dark. Might as well make the most of it."

Noelle and Julio gather the new Seasons and lead them off through the woods. Marie brings up the rear, laying into them like a drill sergeant when Gabriel and Yukio lag behind and start whining about the heat.

Jack's shoulders are heavy as he watches them go. When they're gone, he slips his ax through a belt loop on his jeans and wanders off in search of firewood. Amber and I get to work assembling the tents.

"There aren't enough for everyone. We'll take shifts. Sleep in pairs," she says.

Chill unpacks the rest of our supplies, shaking his head as he counts our last remaining cans of food.

"There isn't enough. We've got nine extra mouths to feed."

I hoist the last tent pole into place as Amber secures the stakes. Wiping my hands, I survey the woods around us. "I saw some rabbits and quail on the hike in. I'll grab us a little extra to eat."

I set off in the direction I saw the rabbit run earlier. After a few minutes, the trees thin, and through them I see Noelle's camp. The grunts and sounds of grappling grow louder as I near it. In the clearing, Julio and Marie have broken the new Seasons into opposing pairs, pushing them through some kind of hand-to-hand sparring exercise that forces them to touch while teaching them to work together. The wind over the mountain shifts erratically, the air thick with the threat of rain as they practice. Jack stands at the far edge of the clearing, watching. Thunder rumbles, but he doesn't seem concerned. There's no point in concealing our presence here.

"Get your hands off me!" Julio turns in time to see Gabriel shove his partner. The Autumn—Aidan, they call him—shoves him back. He sparks a flame.

"Knock it off, both of you!" Julio manages to draw a little moisture from the air, but it's not enough to quench the fire as their argument escalates. Noelle grabs Gabriel. He shoves an elbow into her ribs, shouting and swearing. Julio jumps between them as Aidan's flame grows.

Jack storms into the clearing, and before anyone gets hurt, I tap a root. It erupts in a spray of dirt, grabbing Aidan by the wrist and choking his flame. It jerks him to his knees in a single fluid movement.

Every eye in the clearing finds me. Gabriel stops fighting.

Jack gives me a slight nod. I loosen my hold on the Autumn, and Jack offers him a hand, pulling him to his feet. "If you can't figure out how to work together, you won't survive what's coming."

"I didn't come here to die for some Crispy," Gabriel says, glaring at Aidan.

"Well, I didn't come here just to save a damn Snowflake!"

"Why the hell did you come, then?" Jack snaps, silencing both of them. "To be free? To go home? If you're only in this for yourselves, what's the fucking point?"

"Easy for you to say." Gabriel jerks free of Noelle to point at me. "You're only willing to die for the Spring because you want to get in her pants!"

My face flames. I tighten my grip on the root, ready to take Gabriel down by the tongue. Jack grabs Gabriel by the collar with a look of disgust. "You're wrong," he says through clenched teeth. "I would die for all of them."

The clearing falls silent. Jack lets Gabriel go. His fingers lightly graze my arm, a single reassuring touch, as he leaves the clearing to find wood for our fire. Julio's eyes trail Jack as he goes.

Marie claps her hands, drawing everyone's attention. "You heard the man. Let's try it again," she orders the group, failing to hide the catch of emotion in her voice. "This time, I want to see you work together. Watch each other's backs. Keep each other strong. We survive if we stay focused on what matters."

48

THIN ICE

<u>FLEUR</u>

I miss Julio's guitar, the way it filled the gaps and settled our nerves. I miss our voices, warm and discordant, our laughter crackling like sparks off a campfire. Tonight, there is no music. We eat in the same heavy silence that's clung to our group since Woody died.

I stand watch over our camp as the sun sets, eyes peeled for headlights on the road. It's the only route into or out of this place, according to the torn section of a map Marie studies next to me.

"They'll come from the northeast," she says, holding it up to catch the waning light. "The wind's in their favor, but we've had more time to become familiar with the terrain. We should position Julio as close to the lake as possible. Jack's strongest at the higher elevations. We'll need you out front, tight to the trees. You're our strongest asset here. This place is practically a shrine to you." I can't tell if she's being acerbic or if she's just being Marie.

"What do you mean?"

She gestures to the missing headers of the map. To the carefully torn edges that barely hint at where we are. "I don't need the entire map to know why Jack picked this place. The elevation, the climate, those cool little smiling salamanders in the lake? We're near Cuernavaca. The City of Eternal Spring."

Somewhere warm. . . . Somewhere you'll be safe.

I rise slowly to my feet, a little dizzy.

Cuernavaca.

One of a handful of places in this world where I could live, with or without anyone, off the grid. Forever. Alone.

I pick up Marie's map and study it. The location of the lakes. The patterns of the roads. There's nothing on this paper that either confirms or denies Marie's assumption. Just the heartsick feeling that she's right. That I should have seen this all along.

"Keep watch for me." I drop the map and take off running through the trees, listening for the stroke of an ax.

I find Jack in a darkening grove of pine, high on the north face just above our camp. The wind carries my scent straight to him, but his rhythm doesn't falter. "Did you tear that map to hide our destination from Chronos or to keep it from me?" I shout over the crack of the ax. His jaw hardens at my accusation, and he tosses another cut log onto an already mountainous pile. "Why this place? Why Cuernavaca?"

He swings his ax down hard, scattering kindling. "High ground. Good cover. Perfect temperature," he says, setting another log upright on the stump. Frost shimmers on his shoulders, a cold sweat trickling down his arms as he drives the ax down. "You'll have everything you need here."

"What's that supposed to mean?"

He tosses his ax to the ground without looking at me. "It means no matter what happens to me, you'll be safe."

"So you're just assuming you're going to die? Isn't that a little defeatist? Where is this even coming from?"

"I'm not *assuming* anything. But if I don't make it, then at least you'll survive." He scoops his shirt off a fallen log and mops his face with it before jerking it over his head. Then he loads his arms with split wood and turns back toward camp.

I fight the urge to trip him as I follow him through the maze of trees. "Is that all I am to you? Some damsel in distress? A rescue mission?"

Jack doesn't slow his pace. A cool wind whips over the mountain, and I'm filled with a sense of dread.

"If you're planning to do something reckless and heroic, then you need to stop right now." He ducks under a low-hanging branch, pretending not to hear me. I reach my mind out in front of him, weaving branches into a barricade, blocking his path. "I don't need you to save me, Jack! I'm a lot stronger than you think!"

"But I'm not!" He drops the wood at his feet. Cold curls in and out on his breath as he rounds on me. There's a fear in his eyes I haven't seen since the last time I hunted him, the same shade of desperation they always took on in the moment before I killed him. "Back at the Observatory, before we even planned to escape, Chronos saw my future in his staff. I died, Fleur! In every possible outcome. Chronos said it himself: There's only one way this ends. For *me*. But maybe not for the rest of you."

I take a step away from him, determined not to see the future he's describing. But the truth of it is written in the agony on his face. "No," I say firmly. "You'll be fine. We'll all be fine. Lyon and Gaia will come."

426

"And what if they don't?"

"That's the old Jack talking. The one who died on that ski slope. The one who got left behind by his mother at school."

"Exactly!" He steps closer, forcing me to meet his eyes. "Whose future do you think Chronos saw in that staff? Whose choices do you think he's watching? I'm the bait, Fleur. In order for an ambush to work, Chronos has to believe he already knows the outcome. I have to make the same choices now I would have made then. Chronos knew I would give up my teeth the day I fell in love with you, that I would be willing to die for you. And that hasn't changed." He reaches for me. "That will *never* change."

I shove him back. Why is he so willing to just give up? "I don't want you to die for me! I want you to fight for me! For us!"

He takes my face in his hands with a fierce intensity. "I will never stop fighting for us, Fleur. But it's not my teeth that give me strength. It's you." His jaw softens, his eyes overcome by a sadness deep enough to ruin me. His thumb brushes my cheek tenderly, as if it's the last time and he's committing it to memory. "I get it now, what Lyon's been trying to show me since the beginning. All along, there was only ever one person in the story who had the power to change the outcome. It was never the lion or the girl's father. It was the *girl*. She only had to choose. To fight for what she wanted. You're the one who has to be strong. Because your choice will determine the ending. For both of us." He's looking at me, *through* me, as if he's trying to make me understand. But I don't want to. I don't want to think about a world where Jack doesn't exist.

I close my eyes and pull him to me. I don't want to talk about the end. I don't want to hear any more about Jack's willingness to die or Chronos's stupid visions. I don't want to talk about how I'm strong, how I can survive alone. I back him into a tree, press every part of my body to his, determined to give *him* strength. Determined to remind him why we started down this road. Determined to make him fight for *us*, not just for me.

Jack kisses me deeply, his mouth rough and cold and hungry. His teeth catch my lips. His fingers dig into my sides, holding me close, his body thrumming with electricity. I kiss him back until I'm dizzy. Until my pulse races and neither of us can breathe. Chest heaving, he rests his forehead against mine.

"Stay with me," I whisper, taking him with me to the ground, where I feel strong, where we feel safe, where I feel the steadiness of our hearts beating.

JACK

I wake to the smell of burning poplar and wet leaves.

"Wake up." Amber prods me. "It's your turn to take watch."

I blink against the dark. A root's digging into my back, and there's a shoe in my side. My arm's asleep where Fleur shivers, curled in the crook of it. I ease out from under her, careful not to wake her.

Amber unrolls a sleeping bag and drapes half of it over Fleur. She doesn't ask any questions about why we never made it back to camp or what happened to Fleur's shoes. Doesn't make any wisecracks as I search the ground for my shirt and shake the pine needles from it before sliding it inside out over my head.

I pause, giving Fleur one last look before heading back to camp. Her pink hair's splayed in a tangle of feral waves around her, her brow creased even in her sleep. There's something fierce about her, a grim determination that wasn't there yesterday.

"Don't worry. I'll stay with her," Amber says quietly. She's hardly spoken since Woody died. Some of the fire in her eyes has gone out. It's as if part of her own soul crumbled and blew away with him.

"Are you going to be all right?"

She thinks for a moment. Stares up at the stars through a break in the canopy above us. "Woody and I said our goodbyes a long time ago. This is exactly how he would have wanted to go. Standing up for what he believed in. Protecting the people he loved."

It hurts, thinking about him. "It was brave, what he did."

"He was always brave," Amber says. "It takes more courage to love than to fight."

"Did Woody teach you that?"

"No," she says. "You did."

I don't know what to say. None of this ever felt like courage. It felt like fear, the mind-numbing terror of knowing exactly what I stood to lose. How much it would hurt. All the ways it would kill me. Seeing Fleur curled around the empty space where I lay with her, I can't imagine a world without her. It's the only kind of death I could never come back from.

"Better get to your post, soldier," Amber says, tossing my shoes at me. She leans back against a fallen log and closes her eyes, a wry grin tugging at her lips. "You've been courageous enough for one night. You can be brave again in the morning."

I pick my way downhill by moonlight. The wind carries the charred smell of the burned-out campfire, and I navigate more by scent than by sight, circling wide around the zippered tents to avoid startling the others awake.

"You're an idiot, you know."

I nearly jump out of my skin, breaking out in a layer of frost before I recognize the voice.

"Poppy? What are you doing out here?" She sits on a boulder watching the reflection of the moon on the lake. I ease down beside her, close enough to hear her strained breaths.

"Can't sleep," she says in a thin, hoarse voice. "I guess I shouldn't be surprised. Fleur never slept well on the nights before Julio found her. It's as if something inside us always knows."

"When something's coming?"

"When we're dying." She says it so matter-of-factly, this flat, unvarnished truth. Not even a sigh to suggest she has the slightest wish to dwell on it.

I look away when our eyes meet. "You're not going to die," I tell her.

She shakes her head. "Any fool could see why you picked this place. It's going to kill her, you know. Whatever it is you have planned."

"No plan." I purse my lips. Just a crystal-clear picture in my mind of how things might go down. I've been too busy praying that Lyon and Gaia get here in time. And that if they don't, when the time comes, Fleur will fight. That she'll make the choice I hope she will.

That they all will.

"What do you think she's going to do when you and I are gone?" Poppy asks, the words broken by crackling labored gasps. "You think she's going to live on that hill alone? You think she'll be happy as Julio and Amber's third wheel after she loses you?"

Up until this moment, I've tried not to imagine what happens after the ashes settle if the dominoes don't fall like I hope they will. "Chill will take care of her."

"No, Jacob Matthew Sommers. You will." Poppy rises to her feet and jabs her finger in my breastbone, her sunken eyes suddenly wide-awake and ferocious. "You will stand with her or you will die with her, but if you break her heart, so help me Gaia, I will haunt you from both my graves!" She pauses for a rasping breath that leaves her pale and shaken. "I granted Fleur a dying wish when we left the Observatory. Now I'm asking one of you. Don't let her die alone, Jack."

With weak fingers, she pats my shoulder. Slowly, she makes her way back to her tent, and I stand in the dark, rubbing the ache she's left in my chest.

49

OUR BEST MEN WITH THEE

JACK

At some point, every Season knows it's time to fade. This is why the snow melts and the seas grow cold. It's why the leaves turn and the blooms wither. Because after a while, we're not strong enough to hold on anymore.

Eventually, we all let go. But that doesn't mean we go quietly.

Lyon and Gaia will come; I believe that. Maybe others will, too. But the truth is, sometimes help doesn't come in time, and we have to find the strength to face what lies ahead on our own. We have to trust in our own choices. This was mine.

I watch the lake as if the answer's hidden somewhere in it, wishing I could look under that rippled surface and know exactly what's about to unfold. All I know for certain is where we've been, what we've learned about each other, and how many miles we've managed to come.

All I know is that I trust them. If Chronos is right and I fall through the ice, I won't be left alone.

The valley succumbs to fog. As the new day looms below the horizon, the milky-white film rolling over the lake feels like an omen. The insects have gone silent; the night creatures foraging in the brush are still.

The wind shifts.

I shoot to my feet and ease back from the ledge, deeper under the trees. Behind me, a tent zipper slowly whines open and Julio slides through the narrow flap. Quiet as a cat, he's at my side, blade unsheathed.

How many? he mouths.

I shake my head slowly. I can't be sure. He slips off toward the southern slope to warn Noelle's team.

I catch a scent behind us. The crackle of twigs and the flash of a knife as Fleur and Amber creep down the hillside toward us. Thunder echoes in the distance.

"Could you see them from the top?" I ask, barely above a whisper.

Fleur and Amber shake their heads.

I slink to the edge of the trees. The sky to the northeast is smudged with billowing clouds, obscuring the sunrise. A stiff breeze nudges the fog over the valley, exposing the landscape underneath. Lyon and Gaia are nowhere in sight. Eight members of Chronos's Guard are spread around the opposite shore of the lake. Four more are positioned near the only road in. The other eight must be somewhere behind us, probably already creeping up the south slope.

"Jack Sommers!" A treeful of parakeets awakens, shrieking from their branches. A startled crow swoops over our heads and disappears across the valley. "I order you and your accomplices to surrender to me!"

Chronos.

I lean my head back against a tree trunk, weighing my options as the air grows heavy with the threat of rain.

The tent flaps barely move as Chill, Poppy, and Marie poke their heads out.

"If I do, what happens to the others?" I shout.

"Your friends will be escorted to the Observatory to face Termination before an audience of their peers, to repair what you have broken."

Julio reappears, nodding to let me know Noelle's team is in position.

"And if we choose to fight?"

Amber's, Fleur's, and Julio's answers are written in their stances, on the points of their knives. I search Chill's face. He looks naked, vulnerable without his glasses. Yet his eyes are steadfast on mine, even through the dark. Poppy gives me an approving nod. Marie, who's been clutching Slinky against her chest, lets him down. She chooses a sturdy log from the woodpile and brandishes it like a weapon.

"Then you and your friends will perish here."

Slinky darts off with a hiss as lightning strikes close.

There's a muffled cry from Noelle's camp on the south slope. Two golden flares soar high above the trees, catch the wind, and slowly gutter out. Fleur and I exchange an anxious glance. We've lost two from Noelle's group already, and the battle hasn't even started yet.

Fleur maneuvers closer to the ledge. "They're too far," she whispers. "I can't disarm them from here. I'm going down."

"No," I say. "We stay together. We let them come to us. Noelle's team will thin them out. We'll pick off the rest here."

"They're coming. I can feel them." Fleur presses her fingers to her temples, her eyes closed in concentration. She jerks her fist twice, in close succession. Two more screams echo from the south slope. This time, the two flares gather into tight, bright balls of light and soar through the forest toward a ley line. "Two Guards down," she says. "But the rest are too close to Noelle's team. I can't tell which are the Guards and which are ours anymore."

The wind whistles through the trees, rattling branches. Grunts and shouts grow louder, the roar of fireballs and the clash of knives building to a crescendo as the Guards cut through Noelle's camp. Flare after flare lights up the south slope and dies out, each light closer and closer to our position. Julio and Amber look to the sky, tensing as they keep count. A cold dread seizes me when Noelle calls out, ordering what's left of her team to fall back.

"Something's burning." Amber turns to Fleur as the wind shifts, blowing gray smoke toward us.

Fleur winces and shakes out her hands. "They've set fire to the south slope."

I swear under my breath. "They're going to try to smoke us out."

"Leave it to me." Julio closes his eyes. There's a sharp fall in air pressure as the barometer plunges. Raindrops spatter the forest floor, and within moments, the sky rips open. The fire hisses under the barrage of rain, and the smoke billows around us. I shift the wind with the brush of a thought, and a cold mist falls over the camp.

"I feel them. They're here. Five of them. Just over that ridge." Fleur points between the trees as the smog clears. Julio, Amber, Fleur, and I fan into a line as five transmitter lights blink around us, evenly spaced, slowly converging through the hazy gray light. Amber wields Woody's combat knife. Fleur and Julio wield knives we took from the Summers on the highway, and Chill kneels like a sprinter in the opening of his tent. Poppy withdraws a length of rope from her pocket, silently passing one end to Marie in the next tent.

The Guards can't smell our Handlers. Won't know they're out-numbered.

Chill and I lock eyes as the Guards come into view. I rest a hand at my side where our Handlers can see it, counting down the seconds with my fingers, measuring the Guards' strides. Taking stock of the enemy's strengths.

Five red lights.

Four Guards advancing—one in the trees.

Three . . .

I lose count, my heart missing a beat when Kai Sampson slides out from behind a trunk, an arrow nocked in her bow. The moment's too familiar in my mind. Her utter stillness. Her piercing gaze. This is how the vision of my death begins.

I force my focus back to Chill, trying not to wonder how he'll die or if he'll suffer.

Two . . . two Guards advance past the tents, one closing in on me, the other on Fleur. I lock eyes with my Handler—my best friend—one last time.

I give the signal.

Poppy and Marie pull the rope, tripping the first Guard. She falls hard on her face, and Marie bludgeons the girl with her log. Chill grabs a cast-iron pot off the fire pit and swings it mercilessly into the second Guard's skull. Two blinding balls of magic race past me, down into the valley.

I blink against the bright impressions they leave in my eyelids. But they're not spots I'm seeing. They're lights. Small and distant, forming dotted lines across the dark landscape.

Headlights . . . dozens of them, a few miles down the road.

Lyon. It has to be.

A fireball crashes into a tree beside me, the wet sparks hissing under the fall of rain. I turn as the Guard behind me winds his arm back to throw another. Amber surges between us, taunting him as she heads into the forest. He chases after her, close on her tail. Julio takes down the last Guard, wrestling him to the ground and showering him with punches a few yards away.

Leaving Kai and her bow.

The tip of her arrow shifts toward Fleur's back. Fleur's attention is turned toward the valley, her mind already engaged in battle with the next team of Guards ascending the ridge toward us. Kai takes aim. Releases the arrow. I blow a gust of wind across the gap, sending the empty tents hurtling toward her and throwing her arrow off course.

Kai turns. Finds me. There's a spark of recognition in her eyes as she nocks another arrow. I run from the campsite, drawing her fire away from Fleur.

The first arrow whistles past my head as I duck. The bow releases again. I stagger as a white-hot pain rips through my thigh. I fall hard onto my knees, groping behind me for the shaft. The arrow's slick with rain and blood, and my leg screams when I try to pull it out.

Kai draws another arrow from her quiver.

Teeth clenched, I break the shaft close to the skin. Then I push myself to my feet and run.

I have to get to Chronos. Have to get to the lake. Have to keep his Guards distracted until Lyon and Gaia get here.

An arrow rushes past my ear. The next finds its mark, jolting my body. Two more slice through me, hot pokers in my back. I stumble, blinking back stars as I slide down an embankment. Roots scrape my skin and grab at my clothes.

An arrow whistles close. I crawl to the next slope, letting gravity pull me over. Branches crack as I tumble past them in a shower of mud and loose stones.

I land facedown in the dirt, unable to move for the pain, listening to the crunch of Kai's feet getting closer and closer in the brush.

No. This is not where I end. Not here. Not yet.

On shaking arms, I push myself up, struggling to breathe, resisting the urge to look behind me as another arrow impales the ground by my feet. As I stumble to the bottom of the hill, Kai swears and I stop running.

She's out.

She tosses her bow to the ground. I turn and plant my feet, gripping the broken shaft close to my side. She bares her teeth as she hurtles toward me. I thrust out with the broken point just as her body slams into mine. She sucks in a sharp breath. Her blood's warm on my hands, her tiny frame too heavy to hold as she falls limp against me and slides to the ground. I turn my face from the bright flare when her magic soars home.

Fleur calls my name, her shouts distant and muted. The stars at the edge of my vision close in, and I drop to my knees, then down on all fours.

"Impressive, Jack!" Chronos calls out. His cold voice cuts through the fog. "You would have been a worthy Guard, were it not for your ill-informed choices."

The arrows sting like bees as I force myself to rise and limp to the lake's edge. Chronos stands on the far side of it, the pointed foot of his staff digging into the soft soil where the water laps. Lightning forks over the valley, its flash captured in the eye of the scythe. The lake is all that stands between us.

Behind me, I hear the others descending the hill, searching for me. And Fleur, frantically calling my name.

Chronos bellows, "Come down from there and face me, Jack!"

We both know how this ends.

I don't have to look far beyond him to know Lyon and Gaia won't make it in time. It's all happening exactly the way it did in his staff. And because of that, he'll never see the true ending coming. The one Fleur controls. The one she decides. The only one I have faith in.

I stumble to the water's edge. Summoning all the cold left in me, I step out onto its surface, struggling to stay upright.

I am the bait. The distraction. The chaos. The one who'll clear the path for the others. They will fight him and fight like hell for each other. Chronos will underestimate all of them, because he can't imagine any other way this could end. Because he has only chosen to see as far as my death. He can't fathom the power of the bonds we all share—the risks and sacrifices and choices we would make for each other; he's only ever looked out for himself.

The lake freezes under me, the ice spreading like a mirror beneath my feet. No past. No future. Just my bleeding reflection staring back at me.

"I'm here!" Chronos turns toward the sound of my voice, a smile stretching over his face when his blue eye finds me. *That's right. Look right here, old man. Here I am, alone and dying on the ice, exactly as you saw*

439

me. Doug and Denver flank him, their faces bruised, their jackets black with burns from their last run-in with us.

"Come forward, Jack." Chronos beckons with his scythe.

I push the cold out in front of me, forming a bridge of ice between us. It ends at his feet. "You first."

Even from here, I can see the twitching scars on his cheek, the same involuntary spasm he failed to control when he first recognized me in his staff, as if whatever he'd seen in that vision had deeply unsettled him. "Have you forgotten? This is the part where you die, Mr. Sommers."

But at what cost? What else did he see in that vision beyond the small piece he revealed to you?

"Then come get me!" I shout. "I'm done running from you."

A tremble takes hold of my body. The ice under me blooms red with blood. I don't know how much longer I can hold the freeze.

"Jack!" Fleur's cry pierces me.

I shut out the pain. Swallow my fear. My fear that no one will come. That Gaia and Lyon will abandon us. That the headlights I saw on the horizon weren't real. I have to trust. Have to believe they will not leave us to die here, alone.

I limp farther onto the lake, trailing blood, my island thinning. "What are you afraid of? You said it yourself—we both know how this ends." *Do it. Send your dogs out here to fetch me. I'll take them all down with me.*

Chronos grinds his teeth behind his beard. He signals to Doug. "Bring him to me."

Doug charges onto the lake like a hound unleashed, the ice hardening under him as he skates toward me. A pack of Guards runs after him, tight on his heels. I hold Doug's furious gaze as I drop to my knees. The world sways, the dogs swimming in and out of focus, their howls muffled under the crack of the ice and the roar of bloody water rushing in my ears.

50

HOW THIS ENDS

<u>FLEUR</u>

"No!" The ice cracks under Jack's knees. I cry out as it breaks clean, plunging him in. The lake bubbles red where he disappears.

Doug skids to a stop at the edge of the ice, searching the dark water for him.

"Fleur, wait!" Poppy shouts after me, insisting there are too many of them.

But I don't care how many there are. I will shred them all.

I round the shoreline on a wave of hot wind. Chill calls Jack's name. He charges into the water, breaking through the cracks in the surface. Julio kicks off his shoes and dives in after him.

The lake steams as the ice melts in Julio's wake. The Guards pace the shrinking edges of the island, their heads down as they search for Jack. Out of the corner of my eye, I see a hand snake up through the hazy water and grab a Guard by the ankle. He shrieks and disappears beneath it, leaving a silent ripple in his wake. The others exchange wary glances. A second Guard cries out as Julio drags her down with a soft splash. The water glows, their lights erupting from the surface as Julio takes them one by one. I don't stop to count them as I rush at the remaining Guards.

They fan out in front of me, forming a wall in front of Chronos. Denver grins back at me from the center of their formation. I remember his face, the shape of his fists, his sneer framed in the rearview mirror of the Chevy and the sound of his gun firing. My roots burst from the soil and snag him by the feet. I drag him toward me across the wet grass, his shirt riding up, his fingers digging into the soil. A slithering vine coils around his transmitter. He twists, groping frantically for it, but I yank it out of his reach. His eyes go wide with terror as my roots deliver him to me. I bury my knife in his gut, and with a vicious twist, I jerk it free.

Denver's magic drifts aimlessly into the sky.

I stand up fast, expecting the next Guard to be on me. But something's stolen their attention. White lights flicker through the trees. Car doors slam. Through the soles of my feet, I feel the steady pounding of boots on the soil, bodies brushing past limbs and branches.

Lyon and Gaia. They came. They're here.

The wind shifts, stirring the surface of the lake. The Guards fall back, forming a perimeter around Chronos. Weapons ready, they peer into the trees.

There's a soft splash behind them as Doug crawls to shore. His eyes lift to the wispy stream of guttering light overhead, then follow it to its source. I back away as he lurches from the lake and scrambles toward

Denver's body, trying and failing to gather it in his arms as it flakes to ash. With a keening wail, he watches the last of Denver's light drift skyward and die. I blink back tears and blot out the sound, unable to process anyone else's grief. Doug falls silent, his chest heaving as he looks down at the wet ashes stuck to his hands. Then, with a sharp jerk of his head, his fury finds me.

I scramble back as twin flames roar from his palms, building in intensity as he surges toward me. He hurls flame after flame. I shield my face as they hiss past me, unable to find a root in the single heartbeat between assaults. Doug plows into me, snapping my head against the ground, his transmitter light blinking above me. I grope blindly through the pain, sliding my mind into a root. Doug's hands are ice and rage and fire. His mind reaches savagely for mine, pushing my root back with the force of his own dark thoughts. I kick and thrash beneath him, my mind scrabbling for traction, for a weapon.

An arm reaches around his neck, grabbing him from behind. A flurry of dark curls falls over his shoulder and Doug's eyes go wide with shock.

"I'm sorry," Noelle whispers as his grip goes suddenly limp.

A tear slides down his cheek, his face a mask of betrayal and pain as he collapses against me, his transmitter blinking in his ear. I drag myself out from under him. Noelle's on her knees, her knife in his back. She stares at his blood on her hands as his magic flares and soars away.

The sky peels open, unleashing hot rain and filling the valley with fog. Feet sprint from the road, surrounding the lake and the hills. Shouts echo from the woods, the smack of fists and the clatter of steel. The smell of blood and Seasons is everywhere, balls of light whooshing through the trees as bodies and magic are swept home through the ley lines.

Noelle wipes her eyes. She points at the lake. "There!" Julio and Chill break the churning surface, struggling to hold Jack's weight between them. "Go!" she says. "Go to him!"

I tear my eyes from Jack to thank her. There's a flash of silver behind her. "Noelle!"

Chronos's scythe catches her around her waist. Her mouth falls open as he jerks it free. The frost fades from her eyes. Her light drifts into the sky, and I back away, unable to breathe, as her body crumbles in the wind.

Chronos wipes the blade with a look of disgust. A muscle in his cheek twitches as he stalks to the water's edge. The last of his Guards stand sentry beside him as Julio and Chill drag Jack's body ashore.

The sight of him stops my heart. Three arrows protrude from his back, the first pinpricks of light already shimmering through his skin. I crawl toward him, but Chronos swings his scythe into my path, anchoring the blade in the ground in front of me. "His death has been written in the eye all along. There's nothing you can do to change it now."

No. No, no, no, no!

Julio works fast. He snaps the arrows close to the skin. Jack's head rolls, water spilling from his mouth as Julio lays him on his back and starts compressions. Jack's face is ghost white. Amber and Marie skid to a stop beside them, taking up defensive positions around them as Chill feels for a pulse and puffs rescue breaths into Jack's mouth.

"Fleur?" Julio's voice breaks on my name as he leans on his hands, pushing them into Jack's rib cage. Jack's glowing, the light fighting to leave him as Julio and Chill double their efforts. I call out his name, and Chronos jerks his staff in warning.

"Don't you dare let him go!" I shout to Julio over the scythe.

"I've indulged this nonsense long enough." Chronos sweeps up his staff, and I scramble in front of him, blocking his path as I summon a root. It slithers like a viper toward his ankle. Just before I strike, Chronos swings his scythe, slicing deep into the root.

My ankle gives out. The sharp sting rings through my leg. Warm blood spills into my shoe as he presses toward me. I call another root. It lunges for his back. Chronos swings the scythe behind him. I feel the bite of the blade and yank my mind free before the scythe slashes clean through it. I draw my bleeding arm to my chest.

"Dammit, Jack! Breathe!" Julio shouts. Chill pinches Jack's nose, puffing air into his lungs. But Jack's magic glows brighter through his skin with every compression.

"Leave him!" Chronos bellows.

I tumble sideways, pain shooting through my chest as Chronos knocks me out of the way with his staff to get to them. With a savage yell, Amber hurls herself onto Chronos's back and locks her arms around his throat. As if she's nothing more than a pest, he reaches back with his scythe and brushes it across her shoulders. She screams and falls away from him, cradling her injured arm.

"I said leave him!" Chronos's cheek twitches violently. Julio counts out compressions between Chill's breaths. In a rage, Chronos drives the handle of his staff through Chill's shoulder like a spear. A distant cry echoes across the valley as Poppy calls out for him.

A sob takes hold of me. Jack, Chill, Poppy . . . how many more of my friends will Chronos take? I can't fight him. He's too strong.

He shakes Chill's blood from the handle. Then shakes his head. "It's a shame your lives have come to such a tragic end."

A tragic end. I once told Jack there was no hope for people like us. That stories like ours were called tragedies for a reason. I hate that I was right.

Of course there was hope! They just had a shitty plan. . . . They should have gone down fighting!

I lift my head.

Jack always had a plan. He knew this might happen, that he might not make it. And he told me to be strong. To fight. That's the only thing Jack ever asked of me. To choose what I want. To fight for it.

And I want to live.

I pick myself up off the ground.

Chronos may have taken Jack from me, but I'm still here. I am the girl. The girl in the fable. And *I* have the power to choose how this ends.

I dig my mind into the soil, deep into the dirt, into the dozens of twisted roots from the line of cedars at Chronos's back. With a snap of my wrist, I impale his Guards, their screams lost in a crack of thunder. I snare Chronos by his arms and ankles. By his elbows and wrists and throat. I haul him down, pinning him like an insect to the ground.

A vine snakes around his staff and I jerk it away from him, into my hands. The long, slender handle is heavy as a lance, balanced like a sword. The razor-sharp tip's already dipped in blood—blood he never should have taken. I stand over him, aiming the point at his throat.

"Give it to me, girl." Chronos fights against the roots. I shake with the effort of holding him down. Through the earth, I feel movement. Two sets of feet approaching, running. I don't look up or let down my guard as Gaia and Lyon run breathless into the clearing. Rage and relief battle inside me. Rage because they weren't here soon enough. Relief that they came at all.

Professor Lyon slows as he approaches, taking us all in. His gaze falls on the staff with an unmistakable hunger. The ground trembles when he reaches for it, and when I growl, Lyon takes a wary step back from me.

"Give him the staff, child," Gaia commands me in a quiet voice.

"Not until you fix them!" I choke back the burning knot in my throat. This staff is all I have to barter with.

The professor's gaze drifts to my injured arm. Then behind me. To Marie's desperate attempts to stanch Chill's bleeding. To Julio and Amber, struggling to keep air in Jack's lungs, fighting to keep his heart beating.

"Do it!" I shout at Lyon. We did our part, followed his plan, started his rebellion, got him this far. . . . What is he waiting for? "Do it, or I'll kill Chronos myself!"

Lyon takes another step toward me, close enough for me to see the terror in his eyes. "You don't want to do that."

This is what he fears. That I'll kill Chronos. That the power will be mine.

Lyon must see the thought flit fast across my mind. "His power would destroy you. You cannot be both a Season and Time. One draws its magic from chaos, the other from order. They are diametrically opposed. It would tear you to pieces." The rest of his thought is written all over his face. This is *his* goal, *his* rebellion. And no matter how much Jack and I have sacrificed, this is not a prize Lyon is willing to give me.

"If it's no good to me, I'll shove the staff so far underground, I'll liquefy the damned thing." I dig my mind into the soil, feel it tear like flesh. A chasm opens, and the ground between us crumbles inward.

"I know you're angry," Lyon says in a low, measured voice. "But think about the power you wield. If you destroy the staff, you destroy all of us. Without time, the world would fall into chaos. There would be no cycles. No balance. There must be natural order for the world to survive. Gaia and I can bring that balance back. That's all we want to do."

But he's wrong. There is no balance. Not for us. Not without Jack.

"I can help them. But not without the staff." Lyon looks between me and the deadly point of the long handle with deep concern. "The choice is yours," he says gently.

Cautiously, Lyon reaches across the gap.

Behind me, Julio grunts with exhaustion. Marie's low curses are laden with panic. All I can think about is what Jack said, about how my choices are the only ones that can change the outcome. Is this what I'm supposed to choose? Is this what he meant?

"Promise me you'll help them."

Gaia rests a hand on Lyon's back. "We've waited decades for you, for the right Seasons to emerge," Lyon says, his eyes never leaving mine. "I assure you, your efforts will be rewarded."

"Fleur! I'm losing him!" Julio's shout cinches around my heart. My bloodied arm burns with the effort of restraining Chronos. A soft nudge pushes at my mind as Gaia's thoughts twine around mine and take hold of my roots, relieving me of my burden.

"Go to him," she tells me.

I thrust the staff into Lyon's hand and run to Jack's side. His skin glows, warm and gold. It feels all wrong when I touch him. A thin stream of magic shimmers between his lips. I'm afraid to kiss him, terrified of stealing his magic from him.

"Do something!" Amber shouts.

"You betray me." Chronos turns to meet Gaia's unrepentant stare. "How many years have you spent conspiring against me?"

"Not nearly as many years as you've spent taking those I love from me."

Chronos practically spits. "I protected your kingdom!"

Gaia's diamond eyes shimmer with hatred. "You put my kingdom in a cage!"

"So you take up arms with the mortal and return to his side?"

She laughs, but it's a doleful, joyless sound. "I never left his side. You took him from me." Gaia draws a glass orb from a pocket inside her coat. Chronos's eyes grow fearful when he sees the smaze thrashing inside it, twisting in its cage like an angry black cloud. She sets the orb at Lyon's feet.

"And now I take my magic back." Lyon drives the tip of the scythe down on the orb, shattering the glass and setting the smaze free. *My* magic, Lyon said, as if this smaze was his all along. As if Gaia's been keeping a piece of him in that glass orb all this time, waiting for this moment to return it. Gaia sucks in a long breath, drawing its magic deep into her lungs. She takes Lyon's face in her hands, her lips lingering close to his as a chilled, shadowy breath billows between them. His hair glazes with ice, and his eyes swirl with fog. The staff laces over with frost as he places a reverent kiss on Gaia's lips.

Chronos wrenches himself against the roots. "You are unworthy of my power. She is weak and you are a fool. You are both out of control!"

Lyon rounds on him, the chill in his eyes terrifying. "What we are is nature! We are forces that should never be tamed." He points to us. "You've made them naive and weak. But I remember who I was. I remember who *you* were, Michael, before the eye showed you a future you were too afraid to face. A future where your own children would rise up and overthrow you. Your choices have made this very outcome inevitable." Lyon shoves the frozen staff into Chronos's trapped hand. Chronos cries out, his flesh seared by the frosted metal. "Tell me. What do you see of your future now?"

Lyon grabs Chronos's chin, turning his face toward the crystal, forcing him to look. Reluctantly, Chronos gazes into the prism. A frown pulls at his cheeks.

"You've surprised me, Daniel," Chronos says through cold, cracked lips. "This was not a possibility I gave much consideration. Had I thought you to be so reckless and defiant, I would have watched your future more closely."

"You have a habit of discounting those you consider weak. I assure you, there is nothing weak about the hearts of mortal men. Or children," he adds, his eyes briefly flicking to mine. "You only saw in the eye what you wished to see."

Chronos's face pales as Lyon gently pries the staff from his hand. "And now you have come to reclaim your teeth?"

"Not my teeth," Lyon says, his eyes pinched with regret. "I've come for yours."

I recoil, shielding Jack from the blinding flash as Lyon plunges the scythe into Chronos's heart. Chronos's magic jumps from his body into the staff, passing into Lyon like a finger of lightning. Chronos's lips part around a silent scream as his body crumbles to ash. Our group huddles close around Jack and Chill as a frigid wind howls through the valley. Thunder claps. The ground shivers. We duck our heads, holding each other's shoulders, shielding Jack and Chill from debris as waterspouts rise off the lake, pulling trees up by their roots.

Suddenly, the air stills. The leaves hush and the surface of the lake settles.

When I open my eyes, Chronos's ashes are gone.

I pull myself from Jack, hopeful that maybe something has changed. But he's pale. So pale, it's as if he's empty. The last spindle of light is already puncturing his skin. I press his hand to my cheek, willing him to hold on.

"It's done." Lyon staggers, grasping the staff for balance. He sinks to his knees.

"What's wrong with him?" I shout. Lyon clutches his chest. "What's happening?" And what does that mean for Poppy, Jack, and Chill?

Gaia takes him by the shoulder as he sinks to his knees. "He cannot be both a Season and Time. No mortal man is strong enough to take the power from the staff. I gave him his Winter magic for this task, but those powers are too strong to live in harmony within him. He's made his choice."

She kneels in front of him. Taking his chin in her hand, she reclaims his smaze with a long kiss, drawing it out of him, until the light of Lyon's magic burns brightly in the back of her throat.

The hem of Gaia's coat brushes the grass as she kneels beside Jack. She rests a hand on his chest as if she's listening to his heart, and the sadness in her eyes steals my breath. Tenderly, she brushes Jack's hair back from his face.

"No," I sputter. "You have to bring him back! Send him through the ley lines. Put him in stasis. Give him Lyon's magic. Just do something! Anything! Please!"

"There's nothing I can do for him, child," Gaia says, rising to her feet. "Jack made his choice."

My mind goes numb when she bends over Chill's body. *No. No. No! There must be some mistake.* Lyon's magic pours from her lungs into Chill. And suddenly I see it, as clear as the eye of the crystal itself—the only possible outcome. The one Jack wanted. The one he *chose.*

I would die for all of them.

Jack will die so Chill can be saved. The same as he would die for any of us. Jack wouldn't take Lyon's magic even if Gaia offered it, because one of us needs it.

Chill bolts upright. He blinks at us, his Winter eyes eerily white.

He scrambles to his knees, crying out Poppy's name as if he's been drowning in dreams of her. Frost blooms on his breath. Crystallizes over his skin. Staring at the blood on his hands, he clambers away from us. A tear freezes on his cheek as he searches our faces. Without a word, he staggers off, drawn toward a small mound in the grass.

If there's anything left of my heart, it's gone, shattered, when Chill pulls Poppy's limp body into his arms. She heard Chill scream, probably saw us all struggling. She must have used her last breaths to make it down that hillside, to get to us. She'd always been terrified of dying alone.

I start to stand, to go to her, but I can't let go of Jack. I won't.

"Jack's made his choice," Gaia says again, tipping my chin up to look into my eyes. "But you've never truly made yours. Poppy has always known her mind. She knew it the moment you died in the hospital all those years ago, when she insisted on coming with you. But perhaps, not until very recently, have you truly known your own."

Chill scoops Poppy into his lap and presses a kiss to her lips. He closes his eyes, like he's making a wish.

Or a choice.

All along, there was only ever one person in the story who had the power to change the outcome. . . . Your choice will determine the ending. For both of us.

"I never made a choice," I whisper, the lines of Jack's plan coming together in my mind until I finally understand. "In the hospital, when I died, I didn't choose to save Poppy. Poppy chose to die with me. Because she didn't want to be left behind. She was afraid to die alone. That was never my choice." I told Jack as much that night we walked to the pond. "But that means I . . ." I look down at Jack. Then across the field at Poppy, guilt and obligation and love warring inside me as Chill gathers her to him. Finally, I understand what Jack knew all along. He knew the ending, right up until this very moment. Up until the part I had to figure out on my own.

That it never mattered what happened to the lion's teeth, or that the father cast the lion out. In the end, the girl could rise up against her father and bring her lion back whenever she wanted. That Jack would choose to die for us, because he trusted me to save us, to save *him*, even if it meant losing a piece of himself.

"I choose you," I whisper to him, taking his cold face in my hand. "I chose you years ago, in that bus station bathroom, the day you first asked me what it was I wanted. I've chosen you every day since. And I promise, magic or no magic, I'll hold on to you. I will not let you go."

EPILOGUE

Six Months Later

JACK

I wake up to the smell of morning blooms on the mountain and a pounding on my chest. Fleur sits astride me, which normally I'd never complain about, except for the fact that the car keys in her pocket are jabbing into my thigh.

"Wake up, Jack! It's almost eleven and we have a lot to do before we pick up Amber and Julio at the airport." She bounces, knocking the wind from my lungs and sending a shot of pain through my groin. I roll sideways, burying my head under a huge feather pillow. She yanks it away and tosses it behind her.

"I'm tired," I mutter.

"You're a sloth. I should hang you from a vine."

"I'm injured. I'm still healing." I grab another pillow from her side of the bed to shield myself. It's unnatural how alive she is at this hour.

"You're lying," she says, sliding a warm hand up my bare back over one of my scars. I mask my sleepy smile under the pillow. If I lie still, maybe she'll keep searching for my other ones. With an exasperated sigh, she tears it away from me. "You think this is funny, do you?"

I feign sleep.

Fleur goes unusually quiet. I hear the tinkle of ice in the bedside pitcher a second before I realize why.

"Gaia, Chronos, and Ananke!" I shout as a trail of ice water drenches the small of my back. I squirm wildly, ice cubes sliding between me and the mattress as Fleur collapses on top of me in a fit of hysterics. I grab her by the wrists and wrestle her onto the sheets, rolling her onto her back on the dry side of the bed. I pin her under me, holding her arms over her head as she wheezes with laughter. Her cheeks are flushed, her hair spilling over the edge of the mattress. A languid breeze blows through the open walls of the villa, playing with the pale pink ends. She's the most beautiful thing I've ever seen.

Her laughter quiets. The last few giggles slip out of her as I lean in slowly, pausing a breath away. She lifts her chin expectantly, but I keep just out of reach.

"I could totally kick your ass if I wanted to," she says as I lace our fingers together. She's right, but I don't resent her for it. She's the most powerful Spring in the western hemisphere. And I get to wake up with her every day here. In the end, the choice was mine—I got exactly what I wanted.

"You're not trying very hard," I murmur as my lips graze her collarbone.

She makes a noncommittal noise in her throat as I work my way back up, nuzzling the vulnerable spot behind her ear. This close, I can still smell her magic on her hair, though Lyon says over time, my heightened senses will fade.

"That's not fair." She sighs, looping a leg around me.

"I'm your Handler. It's my responsibility to know your weaknesses." I brush kisses over her neck, her cheek, the corners of her lips. "It's in the job description. I take my work very seriously."

I give in to her, into a slow, deep kiss, our bodies melting into the mattress. I would die a million deaths for this.

A bird shrieks through the open doors of the patio. I reach up, blindly groping for a pillow, anything I can throw, but they're all already on the floor.

"Go away," I moan into Fleur's shoulder.

The bird shrieks again. We both look up. The black crow's bobbing on a branch of the tree overlooking our bedroom, its head tipped and its beady eye focused on us.

"Okay, okay. Relax, we're coming." Fleur rolls me aside, leaving me to languish in a tangle of cold, wet sheets and my own frustration. She runs her fingers through her tousled hair and adjusts her tank top. Then she grabs the remote from a side table and clicks on the TV.

The flat screen across the room flickers to life and Chill's face fills the screen.

"Hey, handsome," Fleur greets him. I drag the sheet over myself and cover my head.

"I see your manservant's working hard."

"I can hear you, you know," I grumble through the sheet.

Fleur flops down on the edge of the bed. "How's Poppy?"

457

"I'm here!" Poppy says. Her overly chipper tone at this hour makes me want to plug my ears. "Where's Jack?"

Fleur yanks back the sheet, and I give Poppy an obligatory wave.

"When are you bringing Fleur to visit me in Alaska?" she nags me. Always with the nagging. "Chill's stasis chamber is scheduled to be installed next week, and I'm going to be bored out of my mind for the summer."

I almost forgot about that. Fleur doesn't need to worry about a change of seasons here. And Julio and Amber have each other when the weather in their region shifts. But Chill doesn't have a partner Season to balance him. When his season is up in Fairbanks, he'll have to go into estivation for the summer. At least he gets to wake up at home, with Poppy looking out for him.

I toss off the sheet and sit up in bed. Even if his timing sucks, I should still say goodbye before he goes offline.

"I promise. Fleur and I will come visit," I reassure Poppy. "As soon as the weather's warm enough." Chill's face pops back on the screen and I force myself to smile. "See you on the other side, my friend." The crow squawks at me again, reminding me I'm late for a meeting with Lyon. I give Chill a salute goodbye and pad off down the hall in my pajama pants to the office, leaving Fleur and Poppy to catch up.

I detour to the kitchen for a cup of coffee and a pastry. Birds whistle and chirp at me as I carry my breakfast onto the veranda. Leaning my elbows on the open wall, I survey the grounds from up high while I eat. The infinity pool below me ripples under a slight southwesterly wind. Built into the side of a high hill, the front of the U-shaped villa is secured by iron bars and ironwood doors, all equipped with cameras. The back is open to the flora around us, an assortment of palms and pines, flamboyants and guavas, zapote and oaks. Only an idiot would try to breach it. Still, it's my job to make sure the perimeter is secure. Change is hard. And while the Seasons are adjusting to the new rules laid out by Gaia and Lyon (or the new Chronos, as he's called now), old feuds die hard. Even though our territory is supposed to be under a protective order, I'd be a fool to take Fleur's safety for granted. Or mine.

I wipe the crumbs from my hands, leaving them for the chattering jays, and head to my office. My workspace looks a lot like Chill's old one—wall-to-wall computer monitors, speakers, and ergonomic keyboards above a sleek glass desk—but with a lot more air and sunlight. The walls above my computer are plastered with vintage posters— Black Flag, the Ramones, and *The Empire Strikes Back*. A framed photo of Fleur and me stands propped on my desk, along with worn volumes of John Donne's poetry and *Aesop's Fables*—housewarming gifts from Gaia and Lyon.

I sip my coffee, taking a few minutes to check the security footage from the night before. Then I look over the regional weather reports and skim through my email. A calendar notification pops up on my screen, reminding me of Julio's and Amber's arrival, but Fleur would never let me forget it. She's been talking about this visit for weeks, about all the sightseeing we'll do and the stories we'll share. She and Amber want to hit all the shops and museums, and Fleur made me promise we'll make a special trip to Calle Bolivar to buy Julio a new guitar.

Truth? I'm happy they're coming. I've missed them. Also truth? It's . . . weird. We've all changed since we first met, but I'm the only one who's really different. And even though I wouldn't trade our life here for the world, bringing the world into our life here has me feeling vulnerable and exposed. Onscreen, I can pretend nothing's changed. That I'm the same person I was before. I look the same on the outside. It's the inside that feels . . . weak, sometimes.

I set down my coffee and rake a hand through my bedhead before logging into the Observatory's secure chat center. Lyon . . . Chronos (I'm never going to get used to calling him that) answers on the first ring.

"You're tardy, Mr. Sommers." He raises an eyebrow, making me feel like I'm back in the fat leather chair in his office.

"These meetings are too early."

"Sorry to drag you out of bed." He gives me a wry look that says he knows exactly what I was doing. I hide a grin behind my mug of coffee.

"How are things back at the ranch?" I ask, changing the subject.

He rubs his receding hairline as if a headache is blooming behind it. "Instituting the new policies has been more challenging than I anticipated."

"Still dealing with the infighting?" I can picture what those first few months must have been like, as warring Seasons woke to find their rankings had been erased and the rules had changed.

"Some, which was to be expected. But desegregating the dormitories has been . . . eye-opening, to say the least."

I laugh out loud and then stifle it at the look on his face. I try to imagine what it would be like to keep Julio and Amber apart if they were living in the dorms. The last time we visited them at their home in Southern California, they were practically attached at the hip. Marie managed to find them a house in Montecito, in the high foothills overlooking the

Santa Barbara coast. With warm winters and cool summers, it's the perfect compromise—a home where they can survive together year-round. There's a community college nearby for Amber, and Julio gets to surf. But with Marie busy managing security for both of them, I'm pretty sure Amber and Julio just spend most of their days in bed.

"What's Gaia have to say about it?" I'm surprised London isn't burning or flooding or quaking to the ground, for all the lack of focus probably going on there right now.

Lyon sighs. "She's happy. The chaos suits her. Which brings me to the reason for my call."

"Shoot." I lean back in my chair and swing my feet up on the desk.

"Are you . . . okay, Jack?"

My smile slides away. "Yeah, sure. Why do you ask?"

"Because I know what it's like to lose your magic," he says delicately. "Letting go of that kind of power is not an easy loss to bear."

"I'm fine. It's fine," I tell him, dropping my legs back to the floor. I rub a spot of coffee from the desktop; it doesn't quite disappear. "I chose this. Remember?"

"Who are you reminding, Jack? Me, or yourself?"

Our eyes meet on the monitor, and I have the strange sense that he's seeing me through the glass eye of his staff. That he's seen the demons I'm hiding from, and he knows exactly when they'll finally catch up to me.

"I love her," I tell him. "I don't regret that."

"And I know you won't. Just remember, your magic is here for you, if you ever want it back." The camera pans away, revealing the orb on Lyon's desk. The gray smaze that swirls inside it—my smaze—is all

461

that's left of my magic. It pushes at the glass, and I force myself to look away. The magic Gaia salvaged from my dying body, and blew into that smaze in the moments after Fleur made her choice, isn't me. Not any-more. I have no magic now. I'm human, as mortal as they come, just like Holly and Boreas back at the Observatory—a fact I've tried not to spend too much time thinking about. I'm lucky, I guess, that my soul and my body are still intact at all. Had Gaia arrived any later, it could have been much worse.

There's something broken in that smaze. Gaia senses it, too. When she recovered my magic as it was slipping away, I was already so far gone, she was forced to sift through it for the bits of my soul the magic was clinging to. She let the magic have some of the darkest parts—my worst fears and regrets, the pain of my most horrible memories— because she was afraid I'd already suffered too much. My happiness—a new life with Fleur—was a gift, she said when she blew the rest of my soul back inside me and brought me back to life. And like the last gift she had given me, my desperate body reached to take it, even if it had come with a sacrifice.

I glance at the dark cloud inside the glass. I could try to become a Winter again, to reclaim my smaze, like Lyon had. Lyon offered as much when he took it with him back to the Observatory.

"Gaia and I would be here for you, if you decided to try," Lyon says, as if he's reading my thoughts. "We won't let you go through it alone."

But I've heard that before. And I bear scars from injuries I haven't entirely forgiven him for. Injuries I suffered alone.

As much as I would give to feel that cold magic race through my veins again, I'm afraid of the parts of me that live inside that smaze.

Afraid whoever it is thrashing around inside that glass is angry enough to break us. I made a promise to Fleur. To keep her safe. To honor her choices. And that's exactly what I plan to do.

"Keep it," I tell him. "I like my infinity pool, my endless spring breaks, and my powerful, immortal, and very sexy girlfriend."

Lyon laughs. "Very well."

"But Professor?" I lower my voice, guilty for even asking. "Keep it safe for me, okay?"

"Of course."

The crow shrieks from the veranda.

"Jack?" Fleur calls down the hall.

Lyon raises an eyebrow. "I believe that's your powerful, immortal girlfriend looking for you," he mocks. "Perhaps we should bring this meeting to a close. Same time next week?"

Fleur appears in the doorway, and her eyes light from within when she finds me. She leans against the doorframe, dangling our car keys from her hand. Her hair's still mussed, her skin's still flushed, and her smile erases every doubt.

"Let's make it an hour later." I switch off the monitor and reach for her, pulling everything I will ever need safely into my lap.

ACKNOWLEDGMENTS

Writing this book was an epic adventure, and just like Fleur and Jack, I could never have survived it without the support of an incredible cast of magical and heroic characters. My endless thanks to my fearless Handler, Sarah Davies, for your unwavering enthusiasm for this story and your steadfast confidence in me. As I look back upon eight years and eight books, I am astounded by how far we've come together.

I have so much gratitude in my heart for Jocelyn Davies, the first mortal to fall in love with Jack and Fleur. Thank you for acquiring my story.

Behind every great love story (and every published book) stands an army willing to fight for it. I am eternally indebted to Tara Weikum, Sarah Homer, Renée Cafiero, Jenna Stempel-Lobell, Pauline Boiteux, Shannon Cox, Sam Benson, and my entire team at HarperTeen. Thanks for bringing Jack and Fleur's story to life. And my deepest thanks to the team at Rights People, for bringing my Seasons to other parts of the globe.

The story of the lion and the girl was derived from Sir Roger L'Estrange's *Fables of Aesop* (1692), and several chapter titles from the works of Bram Stoker ("And So We Remained"), Victor Hugo ("A Kiss and All Was Said"), Frederick Douglass ("But Fire, but Thunder"), Henry David Thoreau ("However Measured or Far"), and John Donne ("Of Fate, Kings, and Desperate Men" and "Our Best Men with Thee"). Portions of his poem "The Good-Morrow" from *Songs and Sonnets* (1633) also appeared in, and provided inspiration for, various parts of the story.

Behind the scenes, books experience countless deaths and rebirths. It's a painful but necessary part of the creative cycle. I count on my critique partners to be ruthless in their handling of my stories, so that when each version is born, it's stronger than the one before it. They are my bees and my smazes, all magic and soul, and always keeping an eye out for me.

Tessa Elwood, your first revision letter made the whole story hold water, and for every supportive and insightful email after, for all the brainstorming sessions, for your keen critical eye and your fondness for all my projects, I am thankful. This story (and my craft) is so much stronger because of you.

I would never have met Fleur and Jack had it not been for the original founding members of the *Hanging Garden* short story blog (Natalie Parker, Julie Murphy, Annie Cardi, Amber Lough, Bethany Hagen, Rosamund Hodge, and E. K. Johnston), who assigned me a GIF of a pink-haired girl with butterflies on her face and challenged me to come up with her story.

Ashley Elston and Megan Miranda, where do I begin? For all the years and all the books, all the laughs and all the stories, for all the brain-storming, celebrations, and bitch sessions. You both mean the world to me. Thanks for being the best part of this crazy journey.

Christina "If You Move That Chapter Forward" Farley will forever and henceforth be known as the CP who saved my book. Thanks for your razor-sharp and insightful feedback, and for putting your finger on the perfect solution to my pacing and stakes dilemma. Megan Shepherd offered sage advice and encouragement exactly when I needed it most. Thanks for your pitch-perfect comments, and for reminding me that bruises (even magical ones) between characters take time to heal. And Chelsea Pitcher, I'm grateful for your enthusiasm for this story and all your encouraging notes. Thanks for falling in love with my characters and challenging me to know them better.

Lastly, for my family. Always for my family.

For my mother—Cuernavaca was your idea.

For my parents, for daring me to escape off the grid.

For Tony, for saying yes when I asked you to run away with me—you keep me balanced, and I'm certain I'd be in the wind without you. And for my children, for filling my world with a simple kind of magic.

Anywhere. We can go anywhere.